Mrs. Molesworth

Grandmother Dear and Two Little Waifs

Mrs. Molesworth

Grandmother Dear and Two Little Waifs

ISBN/EAN: 9783337217815

Printed in Europe, USA, Canada, Australia, Japan

Cover: Foto ©Andreas Hilbeck / pixelio.de

More available books at **www.hansebooks.com**

"GRANDMOTHER DEAR"

AND

TWO LITTLE WAIFS

BY

MRS. MOLESWORTH

AUTHOR OF "CARROTS," "CUCKOO CLOCK," "TELL ME A STORY"

ILLUSTRATED BY WALTER CRANE

New York

MACMILLAN AND CO.

AND LONDON

1893

CONTENTS.

"GRANDMOTHER DEAR."

v

CONTENTS.

TWO LITTLE WAIFS.

vii

CHAPTER VII.

CHAPTER VIII.

CHAPTER IX.

CHAPTER X.

CHAPTER XI.

CHAPTER XII.

LIST OF ILLUSTRATIONS.

"GRANDMOTHER DEAR."

LIST OF ILLUSTRATIONS.

TWO LITTLE WAIFS.

"I HOPE IT ISN'T HAUNTED." — p. 190.

Frontispiece.

"GRANDMOTHER DEAR"

A Book for Boys and Girls

BY

MRS. MOLESWORTH

AUTHOR OF "CARROTS," "CUCKOO CLOCK," "TELL ME A STORY"

ILLUSTRATED BY WALTER CRANE

New York

MACMILLAN AND CO.

AND LONDON

1893

"I HOPE IT ISN'T HAUNTED."—p. 190.

Frontispiece.

"GRANDMOTHER DEAR"

A Book for Boys and Girls

BY

MRS. MOLESWORTH

AUTHOR OF "CARROTS," "CUCKOO CLOCK," "TELL ME A STORY"

ILLUSTRATED BY WALTER CRANE

New York

MACMILLAN AND CO.

AND LONDON

1893

First Edition printed November, 1878. Reprinted December, 1878;
September and December, 1882; 1886, 1887, 1889, 1892.

TO

OUR "GRANDMOTHER DEAR"

A. J. S.

Maison du Chanoine
October 1878

"GRANDMOTHER DEAR."

CHAPTER I.

MAKING FRIENDS.

"Good onset bodes good end."
                                SPENSER.

"WELL?" said Ralph.

"Well?" said Sylvia.

"Well?" said Molly.

Then they all three stood and looked at each other. Each had his or her own opinion on the subject which was uppermost in their minds, but each was equally reluctant to express it, till that of the others had been got at. So each of the three said "Well?" to the other two, and stood waiting, as if they were playing the old game of "Who speaks first?" It got tiresome, however, after a bit, and Molly, whose patience was the most quickly exhausted, at last threw caution and dignity to the winds.

"Well," she began, but the "well" this time had quite a different tone from the last; "*well*," she repeated emphatically, "I'm the youngest, and I suppose you'll say I shouldn't give my opinion first, but I

1

just will, for all that. And my opinion is, that she's just as nice as she can be."

"And I think so too," said Sylvia. "Don't you, Ralph?"

"I?" said Ralph loftily, "you forget. *I* have seen her before."

"Yes, but not to *remember*," said Sylvia and Molly at once. "You might just as well never have seen her before as far as that goes. But isn't she nice?"

"Ye-es," said Ralph. "I don't think she's bad for a grandmother."

"'For a grandmother!'" cried Molly indignantly. "What do you mean, Ralph? What can be nicer than a nice grandmother?"

"But suppose she wasn't nice? she needn't be, you know. There are grandmothers and grandmothers," persisted Ralph.

"Of course I know *that*," said Molly. "You don't suppose I thought our grandmother was everybody's grandmother, you silly boy. What I say is she's just like a real grandmother—not like Nora Leslie's, who is always scolding Nora's mother for spoiling her children, and wears such grand, quite *young lady* dresses, and has *black* hair," with an accent of profound disgust, "not nice, beautiful, soft, silver hair, like *our* grandmother's. Now, isn't it true, Sylvia, isn't our grandmother just like a *real* one?"

Sylvia smiled. "Yes, exactly," she replied. "She would almost do for a fairy godmother, if only she had a stick with a gold knob."

"Only perhaps she'd beat us with it," said Ralph.

"Oh no, not *beat* us," cried Molly, dancing about. "It would be worse than that. If we were naughty she'd point it at us, and then we'd all three turn into toads, or frogs, or white mice. Oh, just fancy! I am so glad she hasn't got a gold-headed stick."

"Children," said a voice at the door, which made them all jump, though it was such a kind, cheery voice. "Aren't you ready for tea? I'm glad to see you are not very tired, but you must be hungry. Remember that you've travelled a good way to-day."

"Only from London, grandmother dear," said Molly; "that isn't very far."

"And the day after to-morrow you have to travel a long way farther," continued her grandmother. "You must get early to bed, and keep yourselves fresh for all that is before you. Aunty says *she* is very hungry, so you little people must be so too. Yes, dears, you may run downstairs first, and I'll come quietly after you; I am not so young as I have been, you know."

Molly looked up with some puzzle in her eyes at this.

"Not so young as you have been, grandmother dear?" she repeated.

"Of course not," said Ralph. "And you're not either, Molly. Once you were a baby in long clothes, and, barring the long clothes, I don't know but what—"

"Hush, Ralph. Don't begin teasing her," said Sylvia in a low voice, not lost, however, upon grandmother.

What *was* lost upon grandmother?

"And what were you all so busy chattering about when I interrupted you just now?" she inquired, when they were all seated round the tea-table, and thanks to the nice cold chicken and ham, and rolls and butter and tea-cakes, and all manner of good things, the children fast "losing their appetites."

Sylvia blushed and looked at Ralph; Ralph grew much interested in the grounds at the bottom of his tea-cup; only Molly, Molly the irrepressible, looked up briskly.

"Oh, nothing," she replied; "at least nothing particular."

"Dear me! how odd that you should all three have been talking at once about anything so uninteresting as nothing particular," said grandmother, in a tone which made them all laugh.

"It wasn't *exactly* about nothing particular," said Mollie: "it was about *you*, grandmother dear."

"Molly!" said Sylvia reproachfully, but Molly was not so easily to be snubbed.

"We were wishing," she continued, "that you had a gold-headed stick, and then you'd be quite *perfect.*"

It was grandmother's and aunty's turn to laugh now.

"Only," Molly went on, "Ralph said perhaps you'd beat us with it, and I said no, most likely you'd turn us into frogs or mice, you know."

"'Frogs or mice, I know,' but indeed I don't know," said grandmother; "why should I wish to turn my boy and girl children into frogs and mice?"

"If we were naughty, I meant," said Molly. "Oh, Sylvia, you explain — I always say things the wrong way."

"It was I that said you looked like a fairy godmother," said Sylvia, blushing furiously, "and that put it into Molly's head about the frogs and mice."

"But the only fairy godmother *I* remember that did these wonderful things turned mice into horses to please her goddaughter. Have you not got hold of the wrong end of the story, Molly?" said grandmother.

"The wrong end and beginning and middle too, I should say," observed Ralph.

"Yes, grandmother dear, I always do," said Molly, complacently. "I never remember stories or anything the right way, my head is so funnily made."

"When you can't find your gloves, because you didn't put them away carefully, is it the fault of the shape of the chest of drawers?" inquired grandmother quietly.

"Yes, I suppose so, — at least, no, I mean, of course it isn't," replied Molly, taking heed to her words half-way through, when she saw that they were all laughing at her.

Grandmother smiled, but said no more.

"What a wool-gathering little brain it is," she said to herself.

When she smiled, all the children agreed together afterwards, she looked more like a fairy godmother than ever. She was really a *very* pretty old lady. Never very tall, with age she had grown smaller,

though still upright as a dart; the "November roses"
in her cheeks were of their kind as sweet as the June
ones that nestled there long ago — ah! so long ago
now; and the look in her eyes had a tenderness and
depth which can only come from a life of unselfishness, of joy and much sorrow too — a life whose
lessons have been well and dutifully learnt, and of
which none has been more thoroughly taken home
than that of gentle judgment of, and much patience
with, others.

While they are all finishing their tea, would you,
my boy and girl friends, like to know who they were
— these three, Ralph, Sylvia, and Molly, whom I
want to tell you about, and whom I hope you will
love? When I was a little girl I liked to know
exactly about the children in my books, each of
whom had his or her distinct place in my affections.
I liked to know their names, their ages, all about
their homes and their relations *most* exactly, and
more than once I was laughed at for writing out a
sort of genealogical tree of some of my little fancy
friends' family connections. We need not go quite
so far as *that*, but I will explain to you about these
new little friends of yours enough for you to be able
to find out the rest for yourselves.

They had never seen their grandmother before,
never, that is to say, in the girls' case, and in Ralph's
"not to remember her." Ralph was fourteen now,
Sylvia thirteen, and Molly about a year and a half
younger. More than seven years ago their mother
had died, and since then they had been living with

their father, whose profession obliged him often to change his home, in various different places. It had been impossible for their grandmother, much as she wished it, to have had them hitherto with her, for, for several years out of the seven, her hands, and those of aunty, too, her only other daughter besides their mother, had been more than filled with other cares. Their grandfather had been ill for many years before his death, and for his sake grandmother and aunty had left the English home they loved so much, and gone to live in the south of France. And after his death, as often happens with people no longer young, and somewhat wearied, grandmother found that the old dream of returning "home," and ending her days with her children and old friends round her, had grown to be but a dream, and, what was more, had lost its charm. She had grown to love her new home, endeared now by so many associations; she had got used to the ways of the people, and felt as if English ways would be strange to her, and as aunty's only idea of happiness was to find it in hers, the mother and daughter had decided to make their home where for nearly fourteen years it had been. They had gone to England this autumn for a few weeks, finally to arrange some matters that had been left unsettled, and while there something happened which made them very glad that they had done so. Mr. Heriott, the children's father, had received an appointment in India, which would take him there for two or three years, and though grandmother and aunty were sorry to think of his going

so far away, they were—oh, I can't tell you how
delighted! when he agreed to their proposal, that
the children's home for the time should be with
them. It would be an advantage for the girls'
French, said grandmother, and would do Ralph no
harm for a year or two, and if his father's absence
lasted longer, it could easily be arranged for him to
be sent back to England to school, still spending his
holidays at Châlet. So all was settled; and grandmother, who had taken a little house at Dover for a
few weeks, stayed there quietly, while aunty jour-
neyed away up to the north of England to fetch
the children, their father being too busy with preparations for his own departure to be able conveniently
to take them to Dover himself. There were some
tears shed at parting with "papa," for the children
loved him truly, and believed in his love for them,
quiet and undemonstrative though his manner was.
There were some tears, too, shed at parting with
" nurse," who, having conscientiously spoilt them all,
was now getting past work, and was to retire to her
married daughter's; there were a good many bestowed
on the rough coat of Shag, the pony, and the still
rougher of Fusser, the Scotch terrier; but after all,
children are children, and for my part I should be
very sorry for them to be anything else, and the
delights of the change and the bustle of the journey
soon drowned all melancholy thoughts.

And so far all had gone charmingly. Aunty had
proved to be all that could be wished of aunty-kind,
and grandmother promised more than fairly.

"What *would* we have done if she had been very tall and stout, and fierce-looking, with spectacles and a hookey nose?" thought Molly, and as the thought struck her, she left off eating, and sat with wide open eyes, staring at her grandmother.

Though grandmother did not in general wear spectacles — only when reading very small print, or busied with some peculiarly fine fancy work — nothing ever seemed to escape her notice.

"Molly, my dear, what are you staring at so? Is my cap crooked?" she said. Molly started.

"Oh no, grandmother dear," she replied. "I was only thinking —" she stopped short, jumped off her seat, and in another moment was round the table with a rush, which would have been sadly trying to most grandmothers and aunties, only fortunately these special ones were not like most!

"What is the matter, dear?" grandmother was beginning to exclaim, when she was stopped by feeling two arms hugging her tightly, and a rather bread-and-buttery little mouth kissing her valorously.

"Nothing's the matter," said Molly, when she stopped her kisses, "it only just came into my head when I was looking at you, how nice you were, you dear little grandmother, and I thought I'd like to kiss you. I don't want you to have a gold-headed stick, but I do want one thing, and then you *would* be quite perfect. Oh, grandmother dear," she went on, clasping her hands in entreaty, "just tell me this, *do* you ever tell stories?"

Grandmother shook her head solemnly. "I *hope*

not, my dear child," she said, but Molly detected the fun through the solemnity. She gave a wriggle.

"Now you're laughing at me," she said. "You *know* I don't mean that kind. I mean do you ever tell real stories — not real, I don't mean, for very often the nicest aren't real, about fairies, you know — but you know the sort of stories I mean. You would look so beautiful telling stories, wouldn't she now, Sylvia?"

"And the stories would be beautiful if I told them — eh, Molly?"

"Yes, I am sure they would be. *Will* you think of some?"

"We'll see," said grandmother. "Anyway there's no time for stories at present. You have ever so much to think of with all the travelling that is before you. Wait till we get to Châlet, and then we'll see."

"I like *your* 'we'll see,'" said Molly. "Some people's 'we'll see' just means, 'I can't be troubled,' or 'don't bother.' But I think *your* 'we'll see' sounds nice, grandmother dear."

"I am glad you think so, granddaughter dear; and now, what about going to bed? It is only seven, but if you are tired?"

"But we are not a bit tired," said Molly.

"We never go to bed till half-past eight, and Ralph at nine," said Sylvia.

The word "bed" had started a new flow of ideas in Molly's brain.

"Grandmother," she said, growing all at once very grave, "that reminds me of one thing I wanted to

ask you; do the tops of the beds ever come down
now in Paris?"

"'Do the tops of the beds in Paris ever come
down?'" repeated grandmother. "My dear child,
what *do* you mean?"

"It was a story she heard," began Sylvia, in explanation.

"About somebody being suffocated in Paris by
the top of the bed coming down," continued Ralph.

"It was robbers that wanted to steal his money,"
added Molly.

Grandmother began to look less mystified. "Oh,
that old story!" she said. "But how did you hear
it? I remember it when I was a little girl; it really
happened to a friend of my grandfather's, and afterwards I came across it in a little book about dogs.
'Fidelity of dogs' was the name of it, I think. The
dog saved the traveller's life by dragging him out
of the bed."

"Yes," said aunty, "I remember that book too.
It was among your old child's books, mother. A
queer little musty brown volume, and I remember
how the story frightened me."

"There now!" said Molly triumphantly. "You
see it frightened aunty too. So I'm *not* such a baby
after all."

"Yes, you are," said Ralph. "People might be
frightened without making such a fuss. Molly declared she would rather not go to Paris at all. *That's*
what I call being babyish — it isn't the feeling
frightened that's babyish — for people might feel

frightened and still *be* brave, mightn't they, grandmother?"

"Certainly, my boy. That is what *moral* courage means."

"Oh!" said Molly, as if a new idea had dawned upon her. "I see. Then it doesn't matter if I am frightened if I don't tell any one."

"Not exactly that," said grandmother. "I would *like* you all to be strong and sensible, and to have good nerves, which it would take a good deal to startle, as well as to have what certainly is best of all, plenty of moral courage."

"And if Molly is frightened, she certainly couldn't help telling," said Sylvia, laughing. "She does *so* pinch whoever is next her."

"There was nothing about a dog in the story of the bed we heard," said Molly. "It was in a book that a boy at school lent Ralph. I wouldn't ever be frightened if I had Fusser, I don't think. I do so wish I had asked papa to let him come with us — just *in case*, you know, of the beds having anything funny about them: it would be so comfortable to have Fusser."

At this they all laughed, and aunty promised that if Molly felt dissatisfied with the appearance of her bed, she would exchange with her. And not long after, Sylvia and Molly began to look so sleepy, in spite of their protestations that the dustman's cart was nowhere near *their* door, that aunty insisted they must be mistaken, *she* had heard his warning bell ringing some minutes ago. So the two little sisters came round to say good night.

"Good night, grandmother dear," said Molly, in a voice which tried hard to be brisk as usual through the sleepiness.

Grandmother laid her hand on her shoulder and looked into her eyes. Molly had nice eyes when you looked at them closely: they were honest and candid, though of too pale a blue to show at first sight the expression they really contained. Just now too, they were blinking and winking a little. Still grandmother must have been able to read in them what she wanted, for her face looked satisfied when she withdrew her gaze.

"So I am *really* to be 'grandmother dear,' to you, my dear funny little girl?" she said.

"Of course, grandmother dear. Really, *really* I mean," said Molly, laughing at herself. "Do you see it in my eyes?"

"Yes, I think I do. You have nice honest eyes, my little girl."

Molly flushed a little with pleasure. "I thought they were rather ugly. Ralph calls them 'cats',' and 'boiled gooseberries,'" she said. "Anyway Sylvia's are much prettier. She has such nice long eyelashes."

"Sylvia's are very sweet," said grandmother, kissing her in turn, "and we won't make comparisons. Both pairs of eyes will do very well my darlings, if always

'The light within them,
Tender is and true.'

Now good night, and God bless my little granddaughters. Ralph, you'll sit up with me a little longer, won't you?"

"What nice funny things grandmother says, doesn't she, Sylvia?" said Molly, as they were undressing.

"She says nice things," said Sylvia, "I don't know about there being funny. You call everything funny, Molly."

"Except you when you're going to bed, for then you're very often rather cross," said Molly.

But as she was only *in fun*, Sylvia took it in good part, and, after kissing each other good night, both little sisters fell asleep without loss of time.

CHAPTER II.

"Oh how I wish that I had lived
In the ages that are gone!"
A Child's Wish.

It was — did I say so before? the children's first visit to Paris. They had travelled a good deal, for such small people quite "a *very* good deal," as Molly used to maintain for the benefit of their less experienced companions. They knew England, "of course." Ralph would say in his lordly, big-boy fashion, Scotland too, and Wales, and they had spent some time in Germany. But they had never been in Paris, and the excitement on finding the journey safely past and themselves really there was very considerable.

"And, Molly," said Sylvia, on their way from the railway station to the hotel where rooms had been engaged for them, "remember you've *promised* not to awake me in the middle of the night if you begin thinking about the top of the bed coming down."

"And, oh, Sylvia! I *wish* you hadn't reminded me of it just now," said Molly pathetically, for which all the satisfaction she received was a somewhat curt observation from Sylvia, that she shouldn't be so silly.

15

For Sylvia, though in reality the kindest of little elder sisters, was sometimes inclined to be "short" with poor Molly. Sylvia was clever and quick, and very "capable," remarkably ready at putting herself, as it were, in the place of another and seeing for the time being, through his or her spectacles. While Molly had not got further than opening wide her eyes, and not unfrequently her mouth too, Sylvia, practical in the way that only people of lively imagination can be so, had taken in the whole case, whatever it might be, and set her ready wits to work as to the best thing to be said or done. And Molly would wonderingly admire, and wish she could manage to "think of things" the way Sylvia did.

They loved each other dearly, these two — but to-night they were tired, and when people, not children only, but big people too, very often — are tired, it is only a very little step to being cross and snappish. And when aunty, tired too, and annoyed by the unamiable tones, turned round to beg them to "*try* to leave off squabbling; it was so thoughtless of them to disturb their grandmother," two or three big tears welled up in Molly's eyes, though it was too dark in the omnibus, which was taking them and their luggage from the station, for any one to see, and she thought to herself what a terrible disappointment it would be if, after all, this delightful, long-talked-of visit to Paris, were to turn out not delightful at all. And through Sylvia's honest little heart there darted a quick sting of pain and regret for her sharpness to Molly. How was it that she

could not manage to keep the resolutions so often
and so conscientiously made? How was it that she
could not succeed in remembering at the time, the
very moment at which she was tempted to be
snappish and supercilious, her never-*really*-forgotten
motive for peculiar gentleness and patience with her
younger sister, the promise she had made, now so
many years ago, to the mother Molly could scarcely
even remember, to be kind, *very* kind, and gentle to
the little, flaxen-haired, toddling thing, the "baby"
whom that dear mother had loved so piteously.

"Eight years ago," said Sylvia to herself. "I
was five and Molly only three and a half then.
Poor little Molly, how funny she was!"

And a hand crept in under Molly's sleeve, and a
whisper reached her ear.

"I don't mean to be cross or to tease you, Molly."

And Molly in a moment was her own queer, happy,
muddle-headed little self again.

"Dear Sylvia," she whispered in return, "of course
you don't. You never do, and if the top of the bed
did come down, I'm sure I'd pull you out first, however sleepy I was. Only of course I know it *won't*,
and it's just my silly way, but when I'm as big as
you, Sylvia, I'll get out of it, I'm sure."

"You're as big as me now, you silly girl," said
Sylvia laughingly, which was true. Molly was tall
and well-grown for her age, while Sylvia was small,
so that very often, to Molly's delight, they were
taken for twins.

"In my body, but not in my mind," rejoined

Molly, with a little sigh. "I wish the growing would go into my mind for a little, though I wouldn't like to be *much* smaller than you, Sylvia. Perhaps we shouldn't be dressed alike, then."

"Do be quiet, Molly, you are such an awful chatterbox," growled Ralph from his corner. "I was just having a nice little nap."

He was far too "grown-up" to own to the eagerness with which, as they went along, he had been furtively peeping out at the window beside him — or to join in Molly's screams of delight at the brilliance of the illumined shop windows, and the interminable perspective of gas lamps growing longer and longer behind them as they rapidly made their way.

A sudden slackening of their speed, a sharp turn, and a rattle over the stones, told of their arrival at their destination. And "Oh!" cried Molly, "I *am* so glad. Aren't you awfully hungry, Sylvia?"

And grandmother, who, to tell the truth, had been indulging in a peaceful, *real* little nap — not a sham one like Ralph's — quite woke up at this, and told Molly it was the best sign in the world to be hungry after a journey; she was delighted to find her so good a traveller.

The "dinner-tea" which, out of consideration for the children's home hours, had been ordered for them, turned out delicious. Never had they tasted such butter, such bread, such grilled chicken, and fried potatoes! And to complete Molly's satisfaction the beds proved to have no tops to them at all.

"I told you so," said Ralph majestically, when

they had made the tour of the various rooms and settled who was to have which, and though neither Sylvia nor Molly had the slightest recollection of his "telling you so," they were wise enough to say nothing.

"But the little doors in the walls are quite as bad, or worse," Ralph continued mischievously. "There's one at the head of your bed, Molly," — Molly and Sylvia were to have two little beds in the same room, standing in a sort of alcove — "which I am almost sure opens on to a secret staircase."

Molly gave a little shiver, and looked up appealingly.

"Ralph, you are not to tease her," said aunty. "Remember all your promises to your father."

Ralph looked rather snubbed.

"Let us talk of something pleasant," continued aunty, anxious to change the subject. "What shall we do to-morrow? What shall we go to see first?"

"Yes," said grandmother. "What are your pet wishes, children?"

"Notre Dame," cried Molly.

"The Louvre," said Sylvia.

"Anything you like. I don't care much for sight-seeing," said Ralph.

"That's a pity," said aunty drily. "However, as you are the only gentleman of the party, and we are all dependent on you, perhaps it is just as well that you have no special fancies of your own. So to-morrow I propose that we should go a drive in the morning, to give you a general idea of Paris, return-

ing by Notre Dame. In the afternoon I have some
calls to make, and a little shopping to do, and you
three must not forget to write to your father. Then
the next day we can go to the Louvre, as Sylvia
wished."

"Thank you, aunty," said Sylvia. "It isn't so
much for the pictures I want to go, but I do so want
to see the room where poor Henry the Fourth was
killed. I am *so* fond of Henry the Fourth."

Aunty smiled, and Ralph burst out laughing.

"What a queer idea!" he said. "If you are so
fond of him, I should think you would rather *not* see
the room where he was killed."

Sylvia grew scarlet, and Molly flew up in her
defence.

"You've no business to laugh at Sylvia, Ralph,"
she cried. "*I* understand her quite well. And she
knows a great deal more history than you do—and
about pictures, too. Of course we want to see the
pictures, too. There's that beautiful blue and orange
one of Murillo's that papa has a little copy of. *It's*
at the Louvre."

"I didn't say it wasn't," retorted Ralph. "It's
Sylvia's love of horrors I was laughing at."

"She *doesn't* love horrors," replied Molly, more
and more indignant.

"*You* needn't talk," said Ralph coolly. "Who
was it that took a box of matches in her pocket to
Holyrood Palace, and was going to strike one to
look for the blood-stains on the floor? It was the
only thing you cared to see, and yet you are such a

goose — crying out if a butterfly settles on you. I think girls are —"

"Ralph, my boy," said grandmother, seeing that by this time Molly was almost in tears; "whatever you think of girls, you make me, I am sorry to say, think that boys' love of teasing is utterly incomprehensible — and oh, *so* unmanly!"

The last touch went home.

"I was only in fun, grandmother," said Ralph with unusual meekness; "I didn't mean really to vex Molly."

So peace was restored.

To-morrow turned out fine, deliciously fine.

"Not like England," said Molly superciliously, "where it *always* rains when you want it to be fine."

They made the most of the beautiful weather, though by no means agreeing with aunty's reminder that even in Paris it did sometimes rain, and the three pairs of eager feet were pretty tired by the time bed-time came.

And oh, what a disappointment the next morning brought!

The children woke to a regular, pouring wet day, no chance of fulfilling the programme laid out, for Sylvia was subject to sore throats, and grandmother would not let her go out in the damp, and there would be no fun in going to the Louvre without her. So, as what can't be cured *must* be endured, the children had just to make the best of it and amuse themselves in the house in the hopes of sunshine again for to-morrow. These hopes were happily fulfilled.

"A lovely day," said aunty, "all the brighter for yesterday's rain."

"And we may go to the Louvre," exclaimed Sylvia eagerly.

Aunty hesitated and turned, as everybody did when they were at a loss, to grandmother.

"What do you think?" she said. She was reluctant to disappoint the children — Sylvia especially — as they had all been very good the day before, but yet — "It is Saturday, and the Louvre will be so crowded you know, mother."

"But *I* shall be with you," said Ralph.

"And *I!*" said grandmother. "Is not a little old lady like me equal to taking care of you all?"

"Will you really come too, dear grandmother?" exclaimed Sylvia and Molly in a breath. "*Oh*, how nice!"

"I should like to go," said grandmother. "It is ever so many years since I was at the Louvre."

"Do let us go then. Oh, do let us all go," said the little girls. "You know we are leaving on Tuesday, and something might come in the way again on Monday."

So it was settled.

"Remember, children," said grandmother as they were all getting out of the carriage, "remember to keep close together. You have no idea how easily some of you might get lost in the crowd."

"*Lost!*" repeated Sylvia incredulously.

"Lost!" echoed Molly.

"LOST!" shouted Ralph so loudly that some of

their fellow-sight-seers, passing beside them into the palace, turned round to see what was the matter. "How could we *possibly* get lost here?"

"Very easily," replied aunty calmly. "There is nothing, to people unaccustomed to it, so utterly bewildering as a crowd."

"Not to me," persisted Ralph. "I could thread my way in and out of the people till I found you. The *girls* might get lost, perhaps."

"Thank you," said Molly; "as it happens, Master Ralph, I think it would be much harder to lose us than you. For one thing we can speak French ever such a great deal better than you."

"And then there are two of us. If one of us was lost, grandmother and aunty could hold out the other one as a pattern, and say, 'I want a match for this,'" said Sylvia laughing, and a little eager to prevent the impending skirmish between Ralph and Molly.

"Hush, children, you really mustn't chatter so," said aunty. "Use your eyes, and let your tongues, poor things, rest for a little."

They got on very happily. Aunty managed to show the children the special picture or pictures each had most wanted to see — including the "beautiful blue and orange" one of Molly's recollection. She nearly screamed with delight when she saw "how like it was to the one in papa's study," but took in good part Ralph's cynical observation that a thing that was copied from another was generally supposed to be "like" the original.

Only Sylvia was a little disappointed when, after looking at the pictures in one of the smaller rooms — a room in no way peculiar or remarkable as differing from the others — they suddenly discovered that they were in the famous "Salle Henri II.," where Henry the Fourth was killed.

"I didn't think it would be like this," said Sylvia lugubriously. "Why do they call it 'Salle Henri II.?' It should be called after Henry the Fourth; and I don't think it should have pictures in, and be just like a common room."

"What would you have it? Hung round with black and tapers burning?" said her aunt.

"I don't know — any way I thought it would have had old tapestry," said Sylvia. "I should like it to have been kept just the way it was then."

"Poor Sylvia!" said grandmother. "But we must hurry on, children. We have not seen the 'Petite Galérie' yet — dear me, how many years it is since I was in it! — and some of the most beautiful pictures are there."

They passed on — grandmother leaning on aunty's arm — the three children close behind, through a room called the "Salle des Sept Cheminées," along a vestibule filled with cases of jewellery, leading again to one of the great staircases. Something in the vestibule attracted grandmother's attention, and she stopped for a moment. Sylvia, not interested in what the others were looking at, turned round and retraced her steps a few paces by the way they had entered the hall. A thought had struck her.

"I'd just like to run back for a moment to Henry the Fourth's room," she said to herself. "I want to notice the shape of it exactly, and how many windows there are, and then I think I can fancy to myself how it looked *then*, with the tapestry and all the old-fashioned furniture."

No sooner thought than done. In a moment she was back in the room which had so curiously fascinated her, taking accurate note of its features.

"I shall remember it now," she said to herself, after gazing round her for a minute or two. "Now I must run after grandmother and the others, or they'll be thinking I am lost."

She turned with a little laugh at the idea, and hastened out of the room, through the few groups of people standing or moving about, looking at the pictures — hastened out, expecting in another moment to see the familiar figures. The room into which she made her way was also filled with pictures, as had been the one through which she had entered the "Salle Henri II." She crossed it without misgiving: she had no idea that she had left the Salle Henri II. by the opposite door from that by which she had entered it!

Poor little Sylvia, she did not know that grandmother's warning was actually to be fulfilled. She was "lost in the Louvre!"

CHAPTER III.

" What called me back ?
A voice of happy childhood,

* * * * * *

Yet might I not bewail the vision gone,
My heart so leapt to that dear loving tone."
MRS. HEMANS, "An Hour of Romance."

SHE did not find out her mistake. She passed through the room and entered the vestibule into which it led, quite confident that she would meet the others in an instant. There were several groups standing about this vestibule as there had been in the other, but none composed of the figures she was looking for.

"They must have passed on," said Sylvia to herself; "I wish they hadn't; perhaps they never noticed I wasn't beside them."

Then for the first time a slight feeling of anxiety seized her. She hurried quickly across the ante-room where she was standing, to find herself in another "salle," which was quite unlike any of the others she had seen. Instead of oil-paintings, it was hung round with colourless engravings. Here, too, there were several people standing about, but none whom, even for an instant, Sylvia could have mistaken for her friends.

26

SYLVIA LOST IN THE LOUVRE. — pp. 26, 27.

"How quickly they must have hurried on," she thought, her heart beginning to beat faster. "I do think they might have waited a little. They must have missed me by now."

No use delaying in *this* room. Sylvia hurried on, finding herself now in that part of the palace devoted to ancient pottery and other antiquities, uninteresting to a child. The rooms through which she passed were much less crowded than those containing pictures. At a glance it was easy to distinguish that those she was in search of were *not* there. Still she tried to keep up heart.

"There is nothing here they would much care about," she said to herself. "If I could get back to the picture rooms I should be sure to find them."

At last, to her delight, after crossing a second vestibule, from which descended a great staircase which she fancied she had seen before, she entered another of the long galleries completely hung with paintings. She bounded forward joyously.

"They're sure to be here," she said.

The room was very crowded. She dared not rush through it as fast as hitherto; it was *so* crowded that she felt it would be quite possible to overlook a group of even four. More than once she fancied she caught sight of grandmother's small and aunty's taller figure, both dressed in black. Once her heart gave a great throb of delight when she fancied she distinguished through the crowd the cream-coloured felt hat and feathers of Molly, her double. But no — it was a cream-coloured felt hat, but the face below it was not

Molly's. Then at last a panic seized the poor little
girl. She fairly lost her head, and the tears blinding
her so, that had Molly and all of them been close
beside her, she could scarcely have perceived them,
she ran half frantically through the rooms. Half
frantically in reality, but scarcely so to outward
appearance. Her habit of self-control, her uncon-
querable British dislike to being seen in tears, or to
making herself conspicuous, prevented her distress
being so visible as to attract general attention. Some
few people remarked her as she passed—a forlorn
little Evangeline — her pretty face now paler, now
more flushed than its wont, as alternations of hope
and fear succeeded each other, and wondered if she
had lost her party or her way. But she had disappeared before there was time to do more than notice
her. More than once she was on the point of asking
help or advice from the cocked-hat officials at the
doors, but she was afraid. In some ways she was
very ignorant and childish for her age, notwithstanding her little womanlinesses and almost precocious
good sense, and to tell the truth, a vague misty
terror was haunting her brain — a terror which she
would hardly have confessed to Molly, not for worlds
have told to *Ralph* — that, being in France and not
in England, she might somehow be put in prison, were
the state of the case known to these same cocked-hat
gentlemen ! So, when at last one of these dignitaries,
who had been noticing her rapid progress down the
long gallery " Napoléon III., " stopped her with the
civil inquiry, " Had Mademoiselle lost her way ? was

she seeking some one?" she bit her lips tight and winked her eyes briskly not to cry, as she replied in her best French, "Oh no," she could find her way. And then, as a sudden thought struck her that possibly he had been deputed by grandmother and aunty, who *must* have missed her by now, to look for her, she glanced up at him again with the inquiry, had he, perhaps, seen a little girl like her? *just* like her?

"Une petite fille comme Mademoiselle?" replied the man smiling, but not taking in the sense of the question. "No, he had not." How could there be two little demoiselles, "tout à fait pareilles?" He shook his head, good-natured but mystified, and Sylvia, getting frightened again, thanked him and sped off anew.

The next doorway — by this time she had unconsciously in her panic and confusion begun actually to retrace her steps round the main court of the palace — brought her again into a room filled with statuary and antiquities. She was getting so tired, so out of breath, that the excitement now deserted her. She sat down on the ledge of one of the great marble vases, in a corner where her little figure was almost hidden from sight, and began to think, as quietly and composedly as she could, what she should do. The tears were slowly creeping up into her eyes again; she let two or three fall, and then resolutely drove the others back.

"What shall I do?" she thought, and joined to her own terrors there was now the certainty of the anxiety and misery the others must, by this time, be

suffering on her account. "Oh, poor little Molly,"
she said to herself. "How dreadfully she will be
crying! What shall I do?"

Two or three ideas struck her. Should she go
down one of the staircases which every now and then
she came upon, and find her way out of the palace,
and down in the street try to call a cab to take her
back to the hotel? But she had no money with her,
and no idea what a cab would cost. And she was
frightened of strange cabmen, and by no means sure
that she could intelligibly explain the address. Besides this, she could not bear to go home without
them all, feeling certain that they would not desert
the palace till they had searched every corner for her.

"If I could but be sure of any place they *must*
pass," she said to herself, with her good sense reviving; "it would be the best way to wait there till
they come."

She jumped up again. "The door out!" she
exclaimed. "They *must* pass it. Only perhaps,"
her hopes falling, "there are several doors. The best
one to wait at would be the one we came in by, if I
could but tell which it was. Let me see — yes, I
remember, as we came upstairs, aunty said 'This
is the Grand Escalier.' If I ask for the 'Grand
Escalier.'"

Her courage returned. The very next cocked-hat
she came upon, she asked to direct her to the "Grand
Escalier." He sent her straight back through a vestibule she had just left, at the other entrance to which
she found herself at the head of the great staircase.

"I am sure this is the one we came up," she thought, as she ran down, and her certainty was confirmed, when, having made her way out through the entrance hall at the foot of the staircase, she caught sight, a few yards off, of an old apple woman's stall in the courtyard.

"I remember that stall quite well," thought Sylvia, and in her delight she felt half inclined to run up to the apple woman and kiss her. "She looks nice," she said to herself, "and they must pass that way to get to the street we came along. I'll go and stand beside her."

Half timidly the little girl advanced towards the stall. She had stood there a minute or two before its owner noticed her, and turned to ask if Mademoiselle wanted an apple.

Sylvia shook her head. She had no money and did not want any apples, but might she stand there to watch for her friends, whom she had lost in the crowd. The old woman, with bright black eyes and shrivelled-up, yellow-red cheeks, not unlike one of her own apples that had been thrown aside as spoilt, turned and looked with kindly curiosity at the little girl.

"Might Mademoiselle wait there? Certainly. But she must not stand," and as she spoke she drew out a little stool, on which Sylvia was only too glad to seat herself, and feeling a little less anxious, she mustered courage to ask the old woman if every one came out at this door.

"To go where?" inquired the old woman, and when

Sylvia mentioned the name of the hotel and the street
where they were staying, " Ah, yes ! " said her in-
formant ; " Mademoiselle might be quite satisfied.   It
was quite sure Madame, her mother, would come out
by that entrance."

" Not my mother," said Sylvia.   " I have no
mother.   It is my grandmother."

" The grandmother of Mademoiselle," repeated the
old woman with increased interest.   " Ah, yes !   I
too had once a granddaughter."

" Did she die ? " said Sylvia.

" Poor angel, yes," replied the apple-seller ; "she
went to the good God, and no doubt it is better.   She
was orphan, Mademoiselle, and I was obliged to be
out all day, and she would come too.   And it is
so cold in Paris, the winter.   She got a bad bron-
chitis and she died, and her old grandmother is now
alone."

" I am so sorry," said Sylvia.   And her thoughts
went off to her own grandmother, and Molly, and all
of them, with fresh sympathy for the anxiety they
must be suffering.   She leant back on the wall
against which the old woman had placed the stool,
feeling very depressed and weary — so weary that
she did not feel able to do anything but sit still,
which no doubt from every point of view was the
best thing she could do, though but for her wearied-
ness she would have felt much inclined to rush off
again to look for them, thus decidedly decreasing
her chance of finding them.

" Mademoiselle is tired," said the old woman,

kindly. "She need not be afraid. The ladies are sure to come out here. I will watch well those who pass. A little demoiselle dressed like Mademoiselle? One could not mistake. Mademoiselle may feel satisfied."

Somehow the commonplace, kindly words did make Sylvia feel less anxious. And she was very tired. Not so much with running about the Louvre; that, in reality, had not occupied more than three quarters of an hour, but with the fright and excitement, and the excitement of a different kind too, that she had had the last few days, poor little Sylvia was really quite tired out.

She laid her head down on the edge of the table on which the apples were spread out, hardly taking in the sense of what the old woman was saying — that in half-an-hour at most Mademoiselle would find her friends, for then the doors would be closed, and every one would be obliged to leave the palace. She felt satisfied that the old woman would be on the look-out for the little party she had described to her, and she thought vaguely that she would ask grandmother to give her a sixpence or a shilling — no, not a sixpence or a shilling, — she was in France, not in England — what should she say? A franc — half a franc — how much was equal to a sixpence or a shilling? She thought it over mistily for a moment or two, and then thought no more about it — she had fallen fast asleep!

But how was this? She had fallen asleep with her head on the apple woman's stall; when she looked round her again where was she? For a minute or two she did not in the least recognise the room — then it suddenly flashed upon her she was in the Salle Henri II., the room where poor Henry the Fourth was killed! But how changed it was — the pictures were all gone, the walls were hung with the tapestry she had wished she could see there, and the room was but dimly lighted by a lamp hanging from the centre of the roof. Sylvia did not feel in any way surprised at the transformation — but she looked about her with great interest and curiosity. Suddenly a slight feeling of fear came over her, when in one corner she saw the hangings move, and from behind the tapestry a hand, a very long white hand, appear. Whose could it be? Sylvia's fear increased to terror when it suddenly struck her that this must be the night of the 14th of May, the night on which Henry of Navarre was to be killed. She gave a scream of terror, or what she fancied a scream; in reality it was the faintest of muffled sounds, like the tiny squeal of a distressed mouse, which seemed to startle the owner of the hand into quicker measures. He threw back the hangings and came towards Sylvia, addressing her distinctly. The voice was so kind that her courage returned, and she looked up at the new comer. His face was pale and somewhat worn-looking, the eyes were bright and sparkling, and benevolent in expression; his tall figure was curiously dressed in a fashion which yet did not seem quite unfamiliar to the little girl — a sort of doublet or jacket of rich crimson velvet, with lace at the collar and cuffs, short trousers fastened in at the knees, "very like Ralph's knickerbockers," said Sylvia to herself, long pointed-toed shoes, like canoes, and on the head a little cap edged with gold, half coronet, half smoking cap, it seemed to her. Where had she ever seen this old-world figure before? She gazed at him in perplexity.

"Why are you so frightened, Mademoiselle?" said the stranger, and curiously enough his voice sounded very like that of the most amiable of her cocked-hat friends.

Sylvia hesitated.

"I don't think I am frightened," she said, and though she spoke English and the stranger had addressed her in French, he seemed quite to understand her. "I am only tired, and there was something the matter. I can't remember what it was."

"I know," replied her visitor. "You can't find Molly and the others. Never mind. If you come with me I'll take you to them. I know all the ins and outs of the palace. I have lived here so long, you see."

He held out his hand, but Sylvia hesitated. "Who are you?" she said.

A curious smile flickered over the face before her.

"Don't you know?" he said. "I am surprised at that. I thought you knew me quite well."

"Are you?" said Sylvia — "yes, I am sure you must be one of the pictures in the long gallery. I remember looking at you this afternoon. How did you get down?"

"No," said the stranger, "Mademoiselle is not quite right. How could there be two 'tout à fait pareils'?" and again his voice sounded exactly like that of the cocked-hat who would not understand when she had asked him if he had seen Molly. Yet she still felt sure he was mistaken, he *must* be the picture she remembered.

"It is very queer," she said. "If you are not the picture, who are you then?"

"I pass my time," said the figure, somewhat irrelevantly, "between this room, where I was killed and the 'Salle des Caryatides,' where I was married. On the whole I prefer this room."

"Are you — can you be — Henry the Fourth?" exclaimed Sylvia. "Oh! poor Henry the Fourth, I am so afraid of them coming to kill you again. Come, let us run quick to the old apple woman, she will take care of you till we find grandmother."

She in turn held out her hand. The king took it and held it a moment in his, and a sad, very sad smile overspread his face.

"Alas!" he said, "I cannot leave the palace. I have no little granddaughter like Mademoiselle. I am alone, always alone. Farewell, my little demoiselle. Les voilà qui viennent."

The last words he seemed to speak right into her ears, so clear and loud they sounded. Sylvia started — opened her eyes — no, there was no king to be seen, only the apple woman, who had been gently shaking her awake, and who now stood pointing out to her a little group of four people hurrying towards

them, of whom the foremost, hurrying the fastest of
all, was a fair-haired little girl with a cream-coloured
felt hat and feathers, who, sobbing, threw herself
into Sylvia's arms, and hugged and hugged as if she
never would let go.

"Oh, Sylvia, oh, my darling!" she cried. "I
thought you were lost for always. Oh, I have been
so frightened — oh, we have all been so frightened.
I thought perhaps they had taken you away to one
of the places where the tops of the beds come down,
or to that other place on the river, the Morgue,
where they drown people, only I didn't say so, not
to frighten poor grandmother worse. Oh, grandmother *dear*, aren't you glad she's found?"

Sylvia was crying too by this time, and the old
apple woman was wiping her eyes with a corner of
her apron. You may be sure grandmother gave her
a present. I rather think it was of a five-franc
piece, which was very extravagant of grandmother,
wasn't it?

They had been of course hunting for Sylvia, as
people always do for anything that is lost, from a
little girl to a button-hook, *before they find it*, in
every place but the right one. I think it was grandmother's bright idea at last to make their way to the
entrance and wait there. There had been quite a
commotion among the cocked-hats who had *not* seen
Sylvia, only unfortunately they had not managed to
communicate with the cocked-hats who *had* seen
her, and they had shown the greatest zeal in trying
to "match" the little girl in the cream-coloured hat,

held out to them as a pattern by the brisk old lady
in black, who spoke such beautiful French, that they
"demanded themselves" seriously if the somewhat
eccentric behaviour of the party could be explained,
as all eccentricities should of course *always* be explained, by the fact of their being English! Aunty's
distress had been great, and she had not "kept her
head" as well as grandmother, whose energies had a
happy knack of always rising to the occasion.

"What *will* Walter think of us," said aunty
piteously, referring to the children's father, "if we
begin by losing one of them?" And she unmercifully snubbed Ralph's not unreasonable suggestion
of "detectives;" he had always heard the French
police system was so excellent.

Ralph had been as unhappy as any of them,
especially as grandmother had strenuously forbidden
his attempting to mend matters by "threading his
way in and out," and getting lost himself in the
process. And yet when they were all comfortably
at the hotel again, their troubles forgotten, and Sylvia
had time to relate her remarkable dream, he teased
her unmercifully the whole evening about her description of the personal appearance of Henry the
Fourth. He was, according to Ralph, neither tall
nor pale, and he certainly could not have had long
thin hands, nor did people — kings, that is to say, at
that date — wear lace ruffles or pointed shoes. Had
Molly not known, for a fact, that all their lesson
books were unget-at-ably packed up, she would
certainly have suspected Ralph of a sly peep at Mrs.

Markham, just on purpose "to set Sylvia down." But failing this weapon, her defence of Sylvia was, it must be confessed, somewhat illogical.

She didn't care, she declared, whether Henry the Fourth was big or little, or how he was dressed. It was very clever of Sylvia to dream such a nice dream about real history things, and Ralph couldn't dream such a dream if he tried ever so hard.

Boys are aggravating creatures, are they not?

CHAPTER IV.

THE SIX PINLESS BROOCHES.

" They have no school, no governess, and do just what they please,
No little worries vex the birds that live up in the trees."
THE DISCONTENTED STARLINGS.

NOT many days after this thrilling adventure of
Sylvia's, the little party of travellers reached their
destination, grandmother's pretty house at Châlet.
They were of course delighted to be there, everything was so bright, and fresh, and comfortable, and
grandmother herself was glad to be again settled
down at what to her now represented home. But
yet, at the bottom of their hearts, the children were
a little sorry that the travelling was over. True,
Molly declared that, though their passage across the
Channel had really been a very good one as these
dreadful experiences go, nothing would *ever* induce
her to repeat the experiment; whatever came of it,
there was no help for it, live and die in France, at
least on this side of the water, she *must*.

"I am never going to marry, you know," she
observed to Sylvia, "so for that it doesn't matter, as
of course I *couldn't* marry a Frenchman. But you
will come over to see me sometimes and bring your
children, and when I get very old, as I shall have no
one to be kind to me you see, I daresay I shall get

40

some one to let me be their concierge like the old woman in our lodge. I shall be very poor of course, but *anything* is better than crossing the sea again."

It sounded very melancholy. Sylvia's mind misgave her that perhaps she should offer to stay with Molly "for always" on this side of the Channel, but she did not feel quite sure about it. And the odd thing was that of them all Molly had most relished the travelling, and was most eager to set off again. She liked the fuss and bustle of it, she said; she liked the feeling of not being obliged to do any special thing at any special hour, for regularity and method were sore crosses to Molly.

"It is so nice," she said, "to feel when we get up in the morning that we shall be out of one bustle into another all day, and nobody to say 'You will be late for your music,' or, 'Have you finished your geography, Molly?'"

"Well," said Sylvia, "I am sure you haven't much of that kind of thing just now, Molly. We have *far* less lessons than we had at home. It is almost like holidays."

This was quite true. It had been settled between grandmother and their father that for the first two or three months the children should not have many lessons. They had been working pretty hard for a year or two with a very good, but rather strict, governess, and Sylvia, at no time exceedingly strong, had begun to look a little fagged.

"They will have plenty to use their brains upon at first," said their father. "The novelty of everything, the different manners and customs, and the complete change of life, all that will be enough to occupy and interest them, and I don't want to over-work them. Let them run wild for a little."

It sounded very reasonable, but grandmother had her doubts about it all the same. "Running wild" in her experience had never tended to making little people happier or more contented.

"They are always better and more able to enjoy play-time when they feel that they have done some work well and thoroughly," she said to aunty. "However, we must wait a little. If I am not much mistaken, the children themselves will be the first to tire of being too much at their own disposal."

For a few weeks it seemed as if Mr. Heriott had been right. The children were so interested and amused by all they saw that it really seemed as if there would not be room in their minds for anything else. Every time they went out a walk they returned, Molly especially, in raptures with some new marvel. The bullocks who drew the carts, soft-eyed, clumsy creatures, looking, she declared, so "sweet and patient;" the endless varieties of "sisters," with the wonderful diversity of caps; the chatter, and bustle, and clatter on the market-days; the queer, quaint figures that passed their gates on horse and pony back, jogging along with their butter and cheese and eggs from the mountain farms — all and everything was interesting and marvellous and entertaining to the last degree.

"I don't know how other children find time to

do lessons here," she said to Sylvia one day. "It is quite difficult to remember just practising and French, and think what lots of other lessons we did at home, and we seemed to have much more time."

"Yes," said Sylvia, "and do you know, Molly, I think I liked it better. Just now at the end of the day I never feel as if I had done anything nicely and settledly, and I think Ralph feels so too. *He* is going to school regularly next month, every day. I wish we were too."

"*I* don't," said Molly, "and it will be very horrid of you, Sylvia, if you go putting anything like that into grandmother's head. There now, she is calling us, and I am not *nearly* ready. Where *are* my gloves? Oh, I cannot find them."

"What did you do with them yesterday when you came in?" said Sylvia. "You ran down to the lodge to see the soldiers passing; don't you remember, just when you had half taken off your things?"

"Oh, yes, and I believe that I left them in my other jacket pocket. Yes, here they are. There is grandmother calling again. Do run, Sylvia, and tell her I'm just coming."

Molly was going out alone with grandmother to-day, and having known all the morning at what time she was to be ready, there was no excuse for her tardiness.

"My dear child," said grandmother, who, tired of waiting, just then made her appearance in their room, "what have you been doing? And you don't look half dressed now. See, your collar is tumbling off.

I must really tell Marcelline never to let you go out without looking you all over."

"It wasn't Marcelline's fault, grandmother dear," said Molly. "I'm so sorry. I dressed in such a hurry."

"And why in such a hurry?" asked grandmother. "This is not a day on which you have any lessons."

"No-o," began Molly; but a new thought struck grandmother. "Oh, by the by, children, where are your letters for your father? I told you I should take them to the post myself, you remember, as I wasn't sure how many stamps to put on for Cairo."

Sylvia looked at Molly, Molly looked at Sylvia. Neither dared look at grandmother. Both grew very red. At last,

"I am *so* sorry, grandmother dear."

"I am *so* sorry, dear grandmother."

"We are both *so* sorry; we *quite* forgot we were to write them this morning."

Grandmother looked at them both with a somewhat curious expression.

"You both forgot?" she said. "Have you so much to do, my dear little girls, that you haven't room in your minds to remember even this one thing?"

"No, grandmother, it isn't that. I should have remembered," said Sylvia in a low voice.

"I don't know, grandmother dear," replied Molly, briskly. "My mind does seem very full. I don't know how it is, I'm sure."

Grandmother quietly opened a drawer in a chest

"WHOSE DRAWER IS THIS?" — p. 45.

of drawers near to which she was standing. It was very neat. The different articles it contained were arranged in little heaps; there were a good many things in it — gloves, scarfs, handkerchiefs, ribbons, collars, but there seemed plenty of room for all.

" Whose drawer is this? " she asked.

" Mine," said Sylvia.

" Sylvia's," answered Molly in the same breath, but growing very red as she saw grandmother's hand and eyes turning in the direction of the neighbour drawer to the one she had opened.

" I am so sorry, grandmother dear," she exclaimed; " I wish you wouldn't look at mine to-day. I was going to put it tidy, but I hadn't time."

It was too late. Grandmother had already opened the drawer. Ah, dear! what a revelation! Gloves, handkerchiefs, scarfs, ribbons, collars; collars, ribbons, scarfs, handkerchiefs, gloves, in a sort of *potpourri* all together, or as if waiting to be beaten up into some wonderful new kind of pudding! Molly grew redder and redder.

" Dear me! " said grandmother. " This is your drawer, I suppose, Molly. How is it it is so much smaller than Sylvia's? "

" It isn't, grandmother dear," said Molly, rather surprised at the turn of the conversation. " It is just the same size exactly."

" Then how is it you have so many more things to keep in it than Sylvia? "

" I haven't, grandmother dear," said Molly. " We have just exactly the same of everything."

" And yet yours looks crowded to the last degree — far too full — and in hers there seems plenty of room for everything."

" Because, grandmother dear," said Molly, opening wide her eyes, " hers is neat and mine isn't."

" Ah," said grandmother. " See what comes of order. Suppose you try a little of it with that mind of yours, Molly, which you say seems always too full. Do you know I strongly suspect that if everything in it were very neatly arranged, you would find a very great deal of room in it; you would be surprised to find how little, not how much, it contains."

" *Would* I, grandmother dear?" said Molly, looking rather mystified. " I don't quite understand."

" Think about it a little, and then I fancy you will understand," said grandmother. " But we really must go now, or I shall be too late for what I wanted to do. There is that collar of yours loose again, Molly. A little brooch would be the proper thing to fasten it with. You have several."

Poor Molly — her unlucky star was in the ascendant this afternoon surely! She grew very red again, as she answered confusedly,

" Yes, grandmother dear."

" Well then, quick, my dear. Put on the brooch with the bit of coral in the middle, like the one that Sylvia has on now."

" Please, grandmother dear, that one's pin's broken."

"The pin's broken! Ah, well, we'll take it to have it mended then. Where is it, my dear? Give it to me."

Molly opened the unlucky drawer, and after a minute or two's fumbling extracted from its depths a little brooch which she handed to grandmother. Grandmother looked at it.

"This is not the one, Molly. This is the one aunty sent you on your last birthday, with the little turquoises round it."

Molly turned quickly.

"Oh yes. It isn't the coral one. It must be in the drawer."

Another rummage brought forth the coral one.

"But the turquoise one has no pin either!"

"No, grandmother dear. It broke last week."

"Then it too must go to be mended," said grandmother with decision. "See, here is another one that will do for to-day."

She, in turn, drew forth another brooch. A little silver one this time, in the shape of a bird flying. But as she was handing it to Molly, "Why, this one *also* has no pin!" she exclaimed.

"No, grandmother dear. I broke it the day before yesterday."

Grandmother laid the three brooches down in a row.

"How many brooches in all have you, Molly?" she said.

"Six, grandmother dear. They are just the same as Sylvia has. We have each six."

"And where are the three others?"

Molly opened a little box that stood on the top of the chest of drawers.

"They're here," she said, and so they were, poor things. A little mosaic brooch set in silver, a mother-of-pearl with steel border, and a tortoise-shell one in the shape of a crescent; these made up her possessions.

"I meant," she added naïvely, "I meant to have put them all in this box as I broke them, but I left the coral one, and the turquoise one, and the bird in the drawer by mistake."

"*As you broke them?*" repeated grandmother. "How many are broken then?"

"All," said Molly. "I mean the pins are."

It was quite true. There lay the six brooches — brooches indeed no longer — for not a pin was there to boast of among them!

"Six pinless brooches!" said grandmother drily, taking them up one after another. "Six pinless brooches — the property of one careless little girl. Little girls are changed from the days when I was young! I shall take these six brooches to be mended at once, Molly, but what I shall do with them when they are mended I cannot as yet say."

She put them all in the little box from which three of them had been taken, and with it in her hand went quietly out of the room. Molly, by this time almost in tears, remained behind for a moment to whisper to Sylvia,

"Is grandmother dreadfully angry, do you think, Sylvia? I am so frightened. I wish I wasn't going out with her."

"Then you should not have been so horribly careless. I never knew any one so careless," said Sylvia, in rather a Job's comforter tone of voice. "Of course you must tell grandmother how sorry you are, and how ashamed of yourself, and ask her to forgive you."

"Grandmother dear," said Molly, her irrepressible spirits rising again when she found herself out in the pleasant fresh air, sitting opposite grandmother in the carriage, bowling along so smoothly — grandmother having made no further allusion to the unfortunate brooches — "Grandmother dear, I am so sorry and so ashamed of myself. Will you please forgive me?"

"And what then, my dear?" said grandmother.

"I will try to be careful; indeed I will. I will tell you how it is I break them so, grandmother dear. I am always in such a hurry, and brooches *are* so provoking sometimes. They won't go in, and I give them a push, and then they just squock across in a moment."

"They just *what?*" said grandmother.

"Squock across, grandmother dear," said Molly serenely. "It's a word of my own. I have a good many words of my own like that. But I won't say them if you'd rather not. I've got a plan in my head — its just come there — of teaching myself to be more careful with brooches, so *please*, grandmother dear, do try me again when the brooches are mended. *Of course* I'll pay them out of my own money."

"Well, we'll see," said grandmother, as the

carriage stopped at the jeweller's shop where the poor brooches were to be doctored.

During the next two days there was a decided improvement in Molly. She spent a great part of them in putting her drawers and other possessions in order, and was actually discovered in a quiet corner mending a pair of gloves. She was not once late for breakfast or dinner, and, notwithstanding the want of the brooches, her collars retained their position with unusual docility. All these symptoms were not lost on grandmother, and to Molly's great satisfaction, on the evening of the third day she slipped into her hand a little box which had just been left at the door.

"The brooches, Molly," said grandmother. "They have cost just three francs. I think I may trust you with them, may I not?"

"Oh yes, grandmother dear. I'm sure you may," said Molly, radiant. "And do you know my drawers are just *beautiful*. I wish you could see them."

"Never fear, my dear. I shall be sure to take a look at them some day soon. Shall I pay them an unexpected visit — eh, Molly?"

"If you like," replied the little girl complacently. "I've quite left off being careless and untidy; it's so much nicer to be careful and neat. Good night, grandmother dear, and thank you so much for teaching me so nicely."

"Good night, granddaughter dear. But remember, my little Molly, that Rome was not built in a day."

"Of course not — how could a big town be built in a day? Grandmother dear, what funny things you do say," said Molly, opening wide her eyes.

"*The better to make you think, my dear,*" said grandmother, in a gruff voice that made Molly jump.

"Oh dear! how you do frighten me when you speak like that, grandmother dear," she said in such a piteous tone that they all burst out laughing at her.

"My poor little girl, it is a shame to tease you," said grandmother, drawing her towards her. "To speak plainly, my dear, what I want you to remember is this: Faults are not cured, any more than big towns are built, in a day."

"No, I know they are not. I'm not forgetting that. I've been making a lot of plans for making myself remember about being careful," said Molly, nodding her head sagaciously. "You'll see, grandmother dear."

And off to bed she went.

The children went out early the next morning for a long walk in the country. It was nearly luncheon time when they returned, and they were met in the hall by aunty, who told them to run upstairs and take off their things quickly, as a friend of their grandmother's had come to spend the day with her.

"And make yourselves neat, my dears," she said. "Miss Wren is a particular old lady."

Sylvia was down in the drawing-room in five minutes, hair brushed, hands washed, collar straight. She went up to Miss Wren to be introduced to her, and then sat down in a corner by the window with a book. Miss Wren was very deaf, and her deafness had the effect, as she could not in the least hear her own voice, of making her shout out her observations in a very loud tone, sometimes rather embarrassing for those to whom they were addressed, or, still worse, for those concerning whom they were made.

"Nice little girl," she remarked to grandmother, "very nice, pretty-behaved little girl. Rather like poor Mary, is she not? Not so pretty! Dear me, what a pretty girl Mary was the first winter you were here, twelve, no, let me see, fourteen years ago! Never could think what made her take a fancy to that solemn-looking husband of hers."

Grandmother laid her hand warningly on Miss Wren's arm, and glanced in Sylvia's direction, and greatly to her relief just then, there came a diversion in the shape of Molly. Grandmother happened to be asked a question at this moment by a servant who just came into the room, and had therefore turned aside for an instant as Molly came up to speak to Miss Wren. Her attention was quickly caught again, however, by the old lady's remarks, delivered as usual in a very loud voice.

"How do you do, my dear? And what is your name? Dear me, is this a new fashion? Laura," to aunty, who was writing a note at the side-table and had not noticed Molly's entrance, "Laura, my dear, I wonder your mother allows the child to wear so much jewellery. In *my* young days such a thing was never heard of."

Aunty got up from her writing at this, and grandmother turned round quickly. What could Miss
Wren be talking about? Was her sight, as well as
her hearing, failing her? Was grandmother's own
sight, hitherto quite to be depended upon, playing
her some queer trick? There stood Molly, serene as
usual, with — it took grandmother quite a little while
to count them — one, two, three, yes, *six* brooches
fastened on to the front of her dress! All the six
invalid brooches, just restored to health, that is to
say *pins*, were there in their glory. The turquoise
one in the middle, the coral and the tortoise-shell
ones at each side of it, the three others, the silver
bird, the mosaic and the mother-of-pearl arranged in
a half-moon below them, in the front of the child's
dress. They were placed with the greatest neatness
and precision; it must have cost Molly both time
and trouble to put each in the right spot.

Grandmother stared, aunty stared, Miss Wren
looked at Molly curiously.

"Odd little girl," she remarked, in what she honestly believed to be a perfectly inaudible whisper,
to grandmother. "She is not so nice as the other,
not so like poor Mary. But I wonder, my dear, I
really do wonder at your allowing her to wear so
much jewellery. In *our* young days — "

For once in her life grandmother was *almost* rude
to Miss Wren. She interrupted her reminiscences
of " our young days " by turning sharply to Molly.

"Molly," she said, "go up to your room at once
and take off that nonsense. What *is* the meaning of

it? Do you intend to make a joke of what you should be so ashamed of, your own carelessness?"

Molly stared up in blank surprise and distress.

"Grandmother dear," she said confusedly. "It was my *plan*. It was to make me careful."

Grandmother felt much annoyed, and Molly's self-defence vexed her more.

"Go up to your room," she repeated. "You have vexed me very much. Either you intend to make a joke of what I hoped would have been a lesson to you for all your life, or else, Molly, it is as if you had not all your wits. Go up to your room at once."

Molly said no more. Never before had grandmother and aunty looked at her "like that." She turned and ran out of the room and up to her own, and throwing herself down on the bed burst into tears.

"I thought it was such a good plan," she sobbed. "I wanted to please grandmother. And I do believe she thinks I meant to mock her. Oh dear! oh dear! oh dear!"

Downstairs the luncheon bell rang, and they all seated themselves at table, but no Molly appeared.

"Shall I run up and tell her to come down?" suggested Sylvia, but "no," said grandmother, "it is better not."

But grandmother's heart was sore.

"I shall be so sorry if there is anything of sulkiness or resentfulness in Molly," she said to herself. "What *could* the child have had in her head?"

CHAPTER V.

MOLLY'S PLAN.

". . Such a plague every morning with buckling shoes, gartering, and combing."   THE TWIN RIVALS.

SOON after luncheon Miss Wren took her departure. Nothing more was said about Molly before her, but on leaving she patted Sylvia approvingly on the back.

"Nice little girl," she said. "Your grandmother must bring you to see me some day. And your sister may come, too, if she leaves her brooches at home. Young people in *my* young days — "

Aunty saw that Sylvia was growing very red, and looking as if she were on the point of saying something; Molly's queer behaviour had made her nervous: it would never do for Sylvia, too, to shock Miss Wren's notion of the proprieties by bursting out with some speech in Molly's defence. So aunty interrupted the old lady by some remark about her shawl not being thick enough for the drive, which quite distracted her attention.

As soon as she had gone, grandmother sent Sylvia upstairs to look for Molly. Sylvia came back looking rather alarmed. No Molly was there. Where could she be? Grandmother began to feel a little uneasy.

"She is nowhere in the house," said Sylvia. "Marcelline says she saw her go out about half-an-hour ago. She is very fond of the little wood up the road, grandmother: shall I go and look for her there?"

Grandmother glanced round. "Ralph," she said. "Oh, I forgot, he will not be home till four;" for Ralph had begun going to school every day. "Laura," she went on, to aunty, "put on your hat and go with Sylvia to find the poor child."

Sylvia's face brightened at this. "Then you are not so vexed with Molly now, grandmother," she said. "I know it seemed like mocking you, but I am sure she didn't mean it that way."

"What did she mean, then, do you think?" said grandmother.

"I don't quite know," said Sylvia. "It was a plan of her own, but it wasn't anything naughty or rude, I am sure."

Aunty and Sylvia went off to the little wood, as the children called it — in reality a very small plantation of young trees, where any one could be easily perceived, especially now when the leaves were few and far between. No, there was no Molly there. Hurriedly, aunty and Sylvia retraced their steps.

"Let us go round by the lodge," said aunty — they had left the house by the back gate — "and see if old Marie knows anything of where she is."

As they came near to the lodge they saw old Marie coming to meet them.

"Is Mademoiselle looking for the little demoiselle?"

she said with a smile. "Yes, she is in my kitchen
— she has been there for half-an-hour. Poor little
lady, she was in trouble, and I tried to console her.
But the dear ladies have not been anxious about her?
Ah yes! But how sorry I am! I knew it not, or I
would have run up to tell Marcelline where she was."

"Never mind, Marie," said aunty. "If we had
known she was with you, we should have been quite
satisfied. Run in, Sylvia, and tell Molly to come
back to the house to speak to your grandmother."

Sylvia was starting forward, but Marie touched
her arm.

"A moment, Mademoiselle Sylvie," she said, —
Sylvia liked to be called "Mademoiselle Sylvie," it
sounded so pretty — "a moment. The little sister
has fallen asleep. She was sitting by the fire, and
she had been crying so hard, poor darling. Better
not wake her all at once."

She led the way into the cottage, and they followed her. There, as she had said, was Molly, fast
asleep, half lying, half sitting, by the rough open fire-
place, her head on a little wooden stool on which
Marie had placed a cushion, her long fair hair falling
over her face and shoulders — little sobs from time
to time interrupting her soft, regular breathing.

Sylvia's eyes filled with tears.

"Poor Molly," she whispered to aunty, "she must
have been crying so. And do you know, aunty,
when Molly does cry and gets really unhappy, it is
dreadful. She seems so careless, you know, but once
she does care, she cares more than any one I know.

And look, aunty." She pointed to a little parcel on the floor at Molly's side. A parcel very much done up with string, and an unnecessary amount of sealing-wax, and fastened to the parcel a little note addressed to " dear grandmother."

"Shall I run with it to grandmother?" said Sylvia; and aunty nodding permission, off she set. She had not far to go. Coming down the garden-path she met grandmother, anxiously looking for news of Molly.

"She's in old Marie's kitchen," said Sylvia, breathlessly, "and she's fallen fast asleep. She'd been crying so, old Marie said. And she had been writing this note for you, grandmother, and doing up this parcel."

Without speaking, grandmother broke the very splotchy-looking red seal and read the note.

"My dear, dear grandmother," it began, "Please do forgive me. I send you all my brooches. I don't *deserve* to keep them for vexing you so. Only I didn't, oh, indeed, I didn't mean to *mock* you, dear grandmother. It is that that I can't bear, that you should think so. It was a plan I had made to teach me to be careful, only I know it was silly — I am always thinking of silly things, but oh, *believe* me, I would not make a joke of your teaching me to be good. — Your own dearest   MOLLY."

"Poor little soul," said grandmother. "I wish I had not been so hasty with her. It will be a lesson

to me;" and noticing that at this Sylvia looked up
in surprise, she added, "Does it seem strange to
you, my little Sylvia, that an old woman like me
should talk of having lessons? It is true all the
same — and I hope, do you know, dear? — I hope
that up to the very last of my life I shall have lessons to learn. Or rather I should say that I shall
be able to learn them. That the lessons are there to
be learnt, always and everywhere, we can never
doubt."

"But," said Sylvia, and then she hesitated.

"But what, dear?"

"I can't quite say what I mean," said Sylvia.
"But it is something like this — I thought the difference between big people and children was that the
big people *had* learnt their lessons, and that was why
they could help us with ours. I know what kind of
lessons you mean — not *book* ones — but being kind
and good and all things like that."

"Yes," said grandmother, "but to these lessons
there is no limit. The better we have learnt the
early ones, the more clearly we see those still before
us, like climbing up mountains and seeing the peaks
still rising in front. And knowing and remembering
the difficulties we had long ago when *we* first began
climbing, we can help and advise the little ones who
in their turn are at the outset of the journey. Only
sometimes, as I did with poor Molly this morning,
we forget, we old people who have come such a long
way, how hard the first climbing is, and how easily
tired and discouraged the little tender feet get."

Grandmother gave a little sigh.

"Dear grandmother," said Sylvia, "I am sure *you* don't forget. But those people who haven't learnt when they were little, they can't teach others, grandmother, when they don't know themselves?"

"Ah, no," said grandmother. "And it is not many who have the power or the determination to learn to-day the lessons they neglected yesterday. We all feel that, Sylvia, all of us. Only in another way we may get good out of that too, by warning those who have still plenty of time for all. But let us see if Molly is awake yet."

No, she was still fast asleep. But when grandmother stooped over her and gently raised her head, which had slipped half off the stool, Molly opened her eyes, and gazed up at grandmother in bewilderment. For a moment or two she could not remember where she was; then it gradually came back to her.

"Grandmother, will you forgive me?" she said. "I wrote a note, where is it?"—she looked about for it on the floor.

"I have got it, Molly," said grandmother. "Forgive you, dear? of course I will if there is anything to forgive. But tell me now what was in your mind, Molly. What was the 'plan'?"

"I thought," said Molly, sitting up and shaking her hair out of her eyes, "I thought, grandmother dear, that it would teach me to be careful and neat and not hurried in dressing if I wore *all* my brooches every day for a good while — a month perhaps. For

you know it is very difficult to put brooches in quite
straight and neat, not to break the pins. It has
always been such a trouble to me not to stick them
in, in a hurry, any how, and that was how I broke
so many. But I'll do just as you like about them.
I'll leave off wearing them at all if you would
rather."

She looked up in grandmother's face, her own
looking so white, now that the flush of sleep had
faded from it, and her poor eyelids so swollen, that
grandmother's heart was quite touched.

" My poor little Molly," she said. " I don't think
that will be necessary. I am sure you will try to be
careful. But the next time you make a plan for
teaching yourself any good habit, talk it over with
me first, will you, dear?"

Molly threw her arms round grandmother's neck
and hugged her, and old Marie looked quite pleased
to see that all was sunshine again.

Just as they were leaving the cottage she came
forward with a basketful of lovely apples.

" They came only this morning, Madame." she said
to grandmother. " Might she send them up to the
house? The little young ladies would find them
good."

Grandmother smiled.

" Thank you, Marie," she said. " Are they *the*
apples? oh, yes, of course. I see they are. Is there
a good crop this year?"

" Ah, yes, they seem always good now. The
storms are past, it seems to me, Madame, both for

me and my tree. But a few years now and they will
be indeed all over for me. 'Tis to-morrow my fête
day, Madame; that was why they sent the apples.
They are very good to remember the old woman —
my grand-nephews — I shall to-morrow be seventy-
five, Madame."

"Seventy-five!" repeated grandmother. "Ah,
well, Marie, I am not so very far behind you, though
it seems as if I were growing younger lately — does it
not? — with my little girls and my boy beside me.
You must come up to see us to-morrow that we may
give you our good wishes. Thank you for the beautiful apples. Some day you must tell the children
the history of your apple-tree, Marie."

Marie's old face got quite red with pleasure.
"Ah, but Madame is too kind," she said. "A stupid
old woman like me to be asked to tell her little stories
— but we shall see — some day, perhaps. So that the
apples taste good, old Marie will be pleased indeed."

"What is the story of Marie's apple-tree, grandmother?" said Sylvia, as they walked back to the
house.

"She must tell you herself," said grandmother.
"She will be coming up to-morrow morning to see
us, as it is her birthday, and you must ask her about
it. Poor old Marie."

"Has she been a long time with you, grandmother
dear?" said Molly.

"Twelve or thirteen years, soon after we first
came here. She was in great trouble then, poor
thing; but she will tell you all about it. She is

getting old, you see, and old people are always fond
of talking, they say — like your poor old grandmother
— eh, Molly?"

"*Grandmother*," said Molly, flying at her and
hugging her, for by this time they were in the
drawing-room again, and Molly's spirits had quite
revived.

The apples turned out very good indeed. Even
Ralph, who, since he had been in France, had grown
so exceedingly "John Bull," that he could hardly
be persuaded to praise anything not English, con-
descended to commend them.

"No wonder they're good," said Molly, as she
handed him his second one, "they're *fairy* apples
I'm sure," and she nodded her head mysteriously.

"Fairy rubbish," said Ralph, taking a good bite
of the apple's rosy cheek.

"Well, they're something like that, anyway," persisted Molly. "Grandmother said so."

"*I* said so! My dear! I think your ears have
deceived you."

"Well, grandmother dear, I know you didn't
exactly say so, but what you said made me think
so," explained Molly.

"Not quite the same thing," said grandmother.
"You shall hear to-morrow all there is to tell — a
very simple little story. How did you get on at
school, to-day, Ralph?"

"Oh, right enough," said Ralph. "Some of the
fellows are nice enough. But some of them are
awful cads. There's one — he's about thirteen, a

year or so younger than I — his name's Prosper something or other — I actually met him out of school in the street, carrying a bundle of wood! A boy that sits next me in the class!" he added, with considerable disgust.

"Is he a poor boy?" asked Sylvia.

"No — at least not what you'd call a poor boy. None of them are that. But he got precious red, I can tell you, when he saw me — just like a cad."

"Is he a naughty boy? Does he not do his lessons well?" asked grandmother.

"Oh I daresay he does; he is not an ill-natured fellow. It was only so like a cad to go carrying wood about like that," said Ralph.

"Ralph," said grandmother suddenly. "You never saw your uncle Jack, of course; has your father ever told you about him?"

Ralph's face lighted up. "Uncle Jack who was killed in the Crimea?" he said, lowering his voice a little. "Yes, papa has told me how brave he was."

"Brave, and gentle, and good," said grandmother, softly. "Some day, Ralph, I will read you a little adventure of his. He wrote it out to please me not long before his death. I meant to have sent it to one of the magazines for boys, but somehow I have never done so."

"What is it about, grandmother? What is it called?" asked the children all together, Molly adding, ecstatically clasping her hands, "If you tell us stories, grandmother, it'll be *perfect*."

"What is the little story about?" repeated grandmother. "I can hardly tell you what it is about, without telling the whole. The *name* of it — the name your uncle gave to it, was ' That Cad Sawyer.' "

Ralph said nothing, but somehow he had a consciousness that grandmother did not agree with him that carrying a bundle of wood through the streets proved that "a fellow" must certainly be a cad.

CHAPTER VI.

THE APPLE-TREE OF STÉFANOS.

"And age recounts the feats of youth."
                                        THOMSON.

"I WAS the only daughter among nine children,"
began old Marie, when the girls and Ralph had made
her sit down in their own parlour, and they had all
drunk her "good health and many happy returns"
in raspberry vinegar and water, and then teased her
till she consented to tell them her story. " That is
to say, my little young ladies and young Monsieur,
I had eight brothers. Not all my own brothers : my
father had married twice, you see. And always
when the babies came they wanted a little girl, for
in the family of my grandfather too, there were but
three boys, my father and his two brothers, and
never a sister. And so one can imagine how I was
fêted when I came, and of all none was so pleased as
the old ' bon papa,' my father's father. He was already very old: in our family we have been prudent
and not married boy and girl, as so many do now,
and wish often they could undo it again. Before he
had married he had saved and laid by, and for his
sons there was something for each when they too
started in life. For my father there was the cottage
and the little farm at Stéfanos."

66

" Where is Stéfanos, Marie?" interrupted Ralph.

" Not so far, my little Monsieur; nine kilomètres perhaps from Châlet."

" Nine kilomètres; between five and six miles? we must have passed it when we were driving," said Ralph.

" Without doubt," replied Marie. " Well, as I was saying, my father had the paternal house at Stéfanos for his when he married, and my uncles went to the towns and did for themselves with their portions. And the bon papa came, of course, to live with us. He was a kind old man — I remember him well — and he must have had need of patience in a household of eight noisy boys. They were the talk of the country, such fine men, and I, when I came, was such a tiny little thing, you would hardly believe there could be a child so small! And yet there was great joy. 'We have a girl at last,' they all cried, and as for the bon papa he knew not what to do for pleasure.

" ' I shall have a little granddaughter to lead me about when my sight is gone, I shall live the longer for this gift of thine,' he said to my mother, whom he was very fond of. She was a good daughter-in-law to him. 'She shall be called Marie, shall she not? The first girl, and so long looked for. And, Eulalie,' he told my mother, 'this day, the day of her birth, I shall plant an apple-tree, a seedling of the best stock, a "reinette," in the best corner of the orchard, and it shall be her tree. They shall grow together, and to both we will give the best care, and as the one prospers the other will prosper, and when trouble comes to the one, the other will droop and fade till again the storms have passed away. The tree shall be called "le pommier de la petite." '

"My mother smiled; she thought it the fancy of the old man, but she was pleased he should so occupy himself with the little baby girl. And he did as he said : that very day he planted the apple-tree in the sunniest corner of the orchard. And he gave it the best of his care; it was watered in dry weather, the earth about its roots was kept loose, and enriched with careful manuring; no grass or weeds were allowed to cling about it, never was an apple-tree better tended."

Marie paused. "It is not always those that get the most care that do the best in this world," she said, with a sigh. "There was my Louis, our eldest, I thought nothing of the others compared with him! and he ran away to sea and nearly broke my heart."

"Did he ever come back again?" asked the children. Old Marie shook her head.

"Never," she said. "But I got a letter that he had got the curé somewhere in the Amérique du sud — I know not where, I have not learnt all about the geography like these little young ladies — to write for him, before he died of the yellow fever. And he asked me to forgive him all the sorrows he had caused me : it was a good letter, and it consoled me much. That was a long time ago; my Louis would have been in the fifties by now, and my other children were obedient. The good God sends us comfort."

" And about the apple-tree, tell us more, Marie," said Molly. " Did it do well? "

"Indeed yes. Mademoiselle can judge, are not the apples good? Ah, yes, it did well, it grew and it grew, and the first walk I could take with the hand of the bon papa was to the apple-tree. And the first words I could say were 'Mi pommier à Malie.' Before many years there were apples, not so fine at the first, of course, but every year they grew finer and finer, and always they were for me. What we did not eat were sold, and the money given to me to keep for the Carnival, when the bon papa would take me to the town to see the sights."

" And did you grow finer and finer too, Marie? " said Sylvia.

Marie smiled.

" I grew strong and tall, Mademoiselle," she said. " As for more than that it is not for me to say. But *they* all thought so, the father and mother and the eight brothers, and the bon papa, of course, most of all. And so you see, Mademoiselle, the end was I got spoilt."

"But the apple-tree didn't?"

" No, the apple-tree did its work well. Only I was forgetting to tell you there came a bad year. Everything was bad — the cows died, the harvest was poor, the fruit failed. To the last, the bon papa hoped that 'le pommier de la petite' would do well, though nothing else did, but it was not so. There was a good show of blossom, but when it came to the apples, *every one* was blighted. And the strange thing was, my little young ladies and little Monsieur, that that was the year the small-pox came — ah, it was a dreadful year! — and we all caught it."

"*All?*" exclaimed Sylvia.

"Yes, indeed, Mademoiselle — all the seven, that is to say, that were at home. I cannot remember it well — I was myself too ill, but we all had it. I was the worst, and they thought I would die. It was not the disease itself, but the weakness after that nearly killed me. And the poor bon papa would shake his head and say he might have known what was coming, by the apple-tree. And my mother would console him — she, poor thing, who so much needed consoling herself — by saying, 'Come, now, bon papa, the apple-tree lives still, and doubtless by next year it will again be covered with beautiful fruit. Let us hope well that our little one will also recover.' And little by little I began to mend — the mother's words came true — by the spring time I was as well as ever again, and the six brothers too. All of us recovered; we were strong, you see, very strong. And after that I grew so fast — soon I seemed quite a young woman."

"And did the small-pox not spoil your beauty, Marie?" inquired Sylvia with some little hesitation. It was impossible to tell from the old woman's face now whether the terrible visitor had left its traces or not; she was so brown and weather worn — her skin so dried and wrinkled — only the eyes were still fine, dark, bright and keen, yet with the soft far-away look too, so beautiful in an old face.

"No, Mademoiselle," Marie replied naïvely, "that

was the curious part of it. There were some, my neighbour Didier for one, the son of the farmer Larreya — "

" Why, Marie, that's *your* name," interrupted Molly. " ' Marie Larreya,' — I wrote it down the other day because I thought it such a funny name when grandmother told it me."

" Well, well, Molly," said Sylvia, " there are often many people of the same name in a neighbourhood. Do let Marie tell her own story."

" As I was saying," continued Marie, " many people said I had got prettier with being ill. I can't tell if it was true, but I was thankful not to be marked : you see the illness itself was not so bad with me as the weakness after. But I got quite well again, and that was the summer I was sixteen. My eldest brother was married that summer, — he was one of the two sons of my father's first marriage, and he had been away for already some time from the paternal house. He married a young girl from Châlet ; and ah, but we danced well at the marriage ! I danced most of all the girls — there was my old friend Didier who wanted every dance, and glad enough I would have been to dance with him — so tall and straight he was — but for some new friends I made that day. They were the cousins of my brother's young wife — two of them from Châlet, one a maid in a family from Paris, and with them there came a young man who was a servant in the same family. They were pleasant, good-natured girls, and for the young man, there was no harm in him ; but their talk quite turned my silly head. They talked of Châlet and how grandly the ladies there were dressed, and still more of Paris — the two who knew it — till I felt quite ashamed of being only a country girl, and the fête-day costume I had put on in the morning so proudly, I wished I could tear off and dress like my new friends. And when Didier came again to ask me to dance, I pushed him away and told him he tired me asking me so often. Poor Didier! I remember so well how he looked — as if he could not understand me — like our great sheep-dog, that would stare up with his soft sad eyes if ever I spoke roughly to him!

"That day was the beginning of much trouble for me. I got in the way of going to Châlet whenever I could get leave, to see my new friends, who were always full of some plan to amuse themselves and me, and my home where I had been so happy I seemed no longer to care for. I must have grieved them all, but I thought not of it — my head was quite turned.

"One day I was setting off for Châlet to spend the afternoon, when, just as I was leaving, the bon papa stopped me.

"'Here, my child,' he said, holding out to me an apple; 'this is the first of this season's on thy pommier. I gathered it this morning — see, it is quite ripe — it was on the sunny side. Take it; thou mayest, perhaps, feel tired on the way.'

"I took it carelessly.

"'Thanks, bon papa,' I said, as I put it in my pocket. Bon papa looked at me sadly.

"'It is never now as it used to be,' he said. 'My little girl has never a moment now to spare for the poor old man. And she would even wish to leave him for ever; for thou knowest well, my child, I could not live with the thought of thee so far away. When my little girl returned she would find no old grandfather, he would be lying in the cold churchyard.'

"The poor old man held out his arms to me, but I turned away. I saw that his eyes were filled with tears — he was growing so feeble now — and I saw, too, that my mother, who was ironing at the table — work in which I could have helped her — stooped to wipe away a tear with the corner of her apron. But I did not care — my heart was hard, my little young ladies and young Monsieur — my heart was hard, and I would not listen to the voices that were speaking in my conscience.

"'It is too bad,' I said, 'that the chances of one's life should be spoilt for such fancies;' and I went quickly out of the cottage and shut the door. But as I went I saw my poor bon papa lift his head, which he had bent down on his hands, and say to my mother,

"'There will be no more apples this year on the pommier de la petite. Thou wilt see, my daughter, the fortune of the tree will leave it.'

"I heard my mother say something meant to comfort him, but I only hurried away the faster.

"What my grandfather meant about my wishing to leave him was this, — my new friends had put it in my head to ask my parents to consent to my going to Paris with the family in which the two that I told you of were maid and valet. They had spoken of me to their lady; she knew I had not much experience, and had never left home. She did not care for that, she said. She wanted a nice pretty girl to amuse her little boy, and walk out with him. And of course the young man, the valet, told me he knew she could not find a girl so pretty as I anywhere! I would find when I got to Paris, he said, how I would be admired, and then I would rejoice that I had not stayed in my stupid little village, where it mattered not if one had a pretty face or not. I had come home quite full of the idea — quite confident that, as I had always done exactly what I wished, I would meet with no difficulty. But to my astonishment, at the paternal house, one would not hear of such a thing!

" 'To leave us — thou, our only girl — to go away to that great Paris, where one is so wicked — where none would guard thee or care for thee? No, it is not to be thought of,' said my father with decision; and though he was a quiet man who seldom interfered in the affairs of the house, I knew well that once that he had said a thing with decision, it was done with — it would be so.

" And my mother said gently,

" 'How could'st thou ask such a thing, Marie?'

" And the bon papa looked at me with sad reproach; that was worse than all.

" So this day — the day that bon papa had given me the first apple of the season — I was to go to

Châlet to tell my friends it could not be. I felt very cross and angry all the way there.

"'What have I done,' I said to myself, 'to be looked at as if I were wicked and ungrateful? Why should my life be given up to the fancies of a foolish old man like bon papa?'

"And when I got to Châlet and told my friends it was not to be, their regret and their disappointment made me still more displeased.

"'It is too much,' they all said, 'that you should be treated still like a bébé — you so tall and womanly that one might think you twenty.'

"'And if I were thee, Marie,' said one, 'I would go all the same. They would soon forgive thee when they found how well things would go with thee at Paris. How much money thou wouldst gain!'

"'But how could I go?' I asked.

"Then they all talked together and made a plan. The family was to leave Châlet the beginning of the week following, sooner than they had expected. I should ask leave from my mother to come again to say good-bye the same morning that they were to start, and instead of returning to Stéfanos I should start with them for Paris. I had already seen the lady, a young creature who, pleased with my appearance, concerned herself little about anything else, and my friends would tell her I had accepted her offer. And for my clothes, I was to pack them up the evening before, and carry the parcel to a point on the road where the young man would meet me. They would not be many, for my pretty fête costumes, the dress of the country, which were my best possessions, would be of no use in Paris.

"'And once there,' said my friend, 'we will dress thee as thou should'st be dressed. For the journey I can lend thee a hat. Thou could'st not travel with that ridiculous foulard on thy head, hiding all thy pretty hair.'

"I remember there was a looking-glass in the room, and as Odette — that was the girl's name — said this, I glanced at myself. My poor foulard, I had thought it so pretty. It had been the 'nouvel an' of the bon papa! But I would not listen to the voice of my heart. I set out on my return home quite determined to carry out my own way.

"It was such a hot walk that day. How well I remember it! my little young ladies and little Monsieur, you would hardly believe how one can remember things of fifty years ago and more, as if they were yesterday when one is old as I am! The weather had been very hot, and now the clouds looked black and threatening.

"'We shall have thunder,' I said to myself, and I tried to walk faster, but I was tired, and oh, so hot and thirsty. I put my hand in my pocket and drew out the apple, which I had forgotten. How refreshing it was!

"'Poor bon papa.' I said to myself. 'I wish he would not be so exacting. I do not wish to make him unhappy, but what can I do? One cannot be all one's life a little child.'

"Still, softer thoughts were coming into my mind.

I began to wish I had not given my decision, that I had said I would think it over. Paris was so far away; at home they might all be dead before I could hear, the poor bon papa above all; it was true he was getting very old.

"Just then, at a turn in the road, I found myself in face of Didier, Didier Larreya. He was walking fast, his face looked stern and troubled. He stopped suddenly on seeing me; it was not often of late that we had spoken to each other. He had not looked with favour on my new friends, who on their side had made fun of him (though I had noticed the day of the wedding that Odette had been very ready to dance with him whenever he had asked her), and I had said to my silly self that he was jealous. So just now I would have passed him, but he stopped me.

"'It is going to thunder, Marie,' he said. 'We shall have a terrible storm. I came to meet thee, to tell thee to shelter at our house; I told thy mother I would do so. I have just been to thy house.'

"I felt angry for no reason. I did not like his watching me, and going to the house to be told of all my doings. I resented his saying 'thou' to me.

"'I thank you, Monsieur Didier,' I said stiffly, 'I can take care of myself. I have no wish to rest at your house. I prefer to go home,' and I turned to walk on.

"Didier looked at me, and the look in his eyes was very sad.

"'Then it is true,' he said.

"'What is true?'

"'That you are so changed'—he did not say 'thou'—'that you wish to go away and leave us all. The poor bon papa is right.'

"'What has bon papa been saying?' I cried, more and more angry. 'What is it to you what I do? Attend to your own affairs, I beg you, Monsieur Didier Larreya, and leave me mine.'

"Didier stopped, and before I knew what he was doing, took both my hands in his.

"'Listen, Marie,' he said. 'You *must*. You are scarcely more than a child, and I was glad for you to be so. It would not be me that would wish to see you all wise, all settled down like an old woman at your age. But you force me to say what I had not wished to say yet for a long time. I am older than you, eight years older, and I know my own mind. Marie, you know how I care for you, how I have always cared for you, you know what I hope may be some day? Has my voice no weight with you? I do not ask you now to say you care for me, you are too young, but I thought you would perhaps learn, but to think of you going away to Paris? Oh, my little Marie, you would never return to us the same!'

"He stopped, and for a moment I stood still without speaking. In spite of myself he made me listen. He seemed to have guessed that though my parents had forbidden it, I had not yet given up the thoughts of going away, and in spite of my silly pride and my

temper I was much touched by what he said, and the
thought that if I went away he would leave off caring for me came to me like a great shock. I had
never thought of it like that; I had always fancied
that whatever I did I could keep Didier devoted to
me; I had amused myself with picturing my return
from Paris quite a grand lady, and how I would pretend to be changed to Didier, just to tease him. But
now something in his manner showed me this would
not do; if I defied him and my friends now, he
would no longer care for me. Yet — would you
believe it, my little young ladies and young Monsieur? — my naughty pride still kept me back. I
turned from Didier in a rage, and pulled away my
hands.

"'I wish none of your advice or interference,' I
said. 'I shall please myself in my affairs.'

"I hurried away; he did not attempt to stop me,
but stood there for a moment watching me.

"'Good-bye, Marie,' he said, and then he called
after me, 'Beware of the storm.'

"I had still two miles to go. I hurried on, passing
the Larreyas' farm, and just a minute or two after
that the storm began. I heard it come grumbling
up, as if out of the heart of the mountains at first,
and then it seemed to rise higher and higher. I was
not frightened, but yet I saw it was going to be a
great storm — you do not know, my young ladies,
what storms we have here sometimes — and I was so
hot and so tired, and when the anger began to pass
away I felt so miserable. I could not bear to go

home and see them all with the knowledge in my heart of what I intended to do. When I got near to the orchard, which was about a quarter of a mile from the house, I felt, with all my feelings together, as if I could go no farther. The storm seemed to. be passing over — for some minutes there had been no lightning or thunder.

" ' Perhaps after all it will only skirt round about us,' I said. And as I thought this I entered the orchard and sat down on my own seat, a little bench that — now many years ago — the bon papa had placed for me with his own hands beside my pommier.

" I was so tired and so hot and so unhappy, I sat and cried.

" I wish I had not said I would go,' I thought. ' Now if I change one will mock so at me.'

" I leaned my head against the trunk of my tree. I had forgotten about the storm. Suddenly, more suddenly than I can tell, there came a fearful flash of lightning — all about me seemed for a moment on fire — then the dreadful boom of the thunder as if it would shake the earth itself to pieces, and a tearing crashing sound like none I had ever heard before. I screamed and threw myself on the ground, covering my eyes. For a moment I thought I was killed — that a punishment had come to me for my disobedience. ' Oh! I will not go away. I will do what you all wish,' I called out, as if my parents could hear me. ' Bon papa, forgive me. Thy little girl wishes no longer to leave thee;' but no one answered, and

UNDER THE APPLE-TREE. — p. 80.

I lay there in terror. Gradually I grew calmer — after that fearful crash the thunder claps seemed to grow less violent. I looked up at last. What did I see? The tree next to my pommier — the one but a yard or two from my bench — stood black and charred as if the burning hand of a great giant had grasped it; already some of its branches strewed the ground. And my pommier had not altogether escaped; one branch had been struck — the very branch on the sunny side from which bon papa had picked the apple, as he afterwards showed me! That my life had been spared was little less than a miracle." Marie paused. . . .

"I left the orchard, my little young ladies and young Monsieur," she went on after a moment or two, "a very different girl from the one that had entered it. I went straight to the house, and confessed all — my naughty intention of leaving them all, my discontent and pride, and all my bad feelings. And they forgave me — the good people — they forgave me all, and bon papa took me in his arms and blessed me, and I promised him not to leave him while he lived. Nor did I — it was not so long — he died the next year, the dear old man! What would my feelings have been had I been away in Paris!"

Old as she was, Marie stopped to wipe away a tear. "It is nearly sixty years ago, yet still the tears come when I think of it," she said. "He would not know me now if he saw me, the dear bon papa," she added. "I am as old as he was then! How it will be in heaven I wonder often — for friends so changed to meet again? But that we must leave to the good God; without doubt He will arrange it all."

"And Didier, Marie?" said Sylvia, after a little pause. "Did you also make friends with him?"

Marie smiled, and underneath her funny old brown wrinkled skin I almost think she blushed a little.

"Ah yes, Mademoiselle," she said. "That goes without saying. Ah yes — Didier was not slow to make friends again — and though we said nothing about it for a long time, not till I was in the twenties, it came all as he wished in the end. And a good husband he made me."

"Oh!" cried Molly, "I see — then *that's* how your name is 'Larreya' too, Marie."

They all laughed at her.

"But grandmother said you had many more troubles, Marie," said Sylvia. "Long after, when first she knew you. She said you would tell us."

"Ah yes, that is because the dear lady wishes not herself to tell how good she was to me!" said Marie. "I had many troubles after my husband died. I told you my son Louis was a great grief, and we were poor — very poor — I had a little fruit-stall at the market — "

"Like my old woman in Paris," said Molly, nodding her head.

"And there it was the dear lady first saw me," said Marie. "It was all through the apples — bon papa did well for me the day he planted that tree! They were so fine — Madame bought them for the poor gentleman who was ill — and then I came to

tell her my history; and when she took this house
she asked me to be her concierge. Since then I have
no troubles — my daughter married, long ago of
course, but she died, and her husband died, and the
friends were not good for her children, and it was
these I had to provide for — my granddaughters.
But now they are very well off — each settled, and
so good to me! The married one comes with her
bébé every Sunday, and the other, in a good place,
sends me always a part of her wages. And my son
too — he that went to Paris — he writes often. Ah
yes, I am well satisfied! And always my great-
nephews send me the apples — every year — their
father and their grandfather made the promise, and
it has never been broken. And still, my little young
ladies and little Monsieur — still, the old apple-tree
at the paternal house at Stéfanos, is called 'le pommier de la petite.'"

"How nice!" said the children all together.
"Thank you, Marie, thank you so much for telling
us the story."

CHAPTER VII.

GRANDMOTHER'S GRANDMOTHER.

" I'll tell you a story of Jack-o-my-nory,
    And now my story's begun.
I'll tell you another of Jack and his brother,
    And now my story's done."
                            OLD NURSERY RHYME.

MARIE'S story was the subject of much conversation among the children. Sylvia announced her intention of writing it down.

"She tells it so nicely," she said. "I could have written it down beautifully while she was talking, if she would have waited."

"She would not have been able to tell it so nicely if she had known you were waiting to write down every word as she said it," remarked grandmother. "At least in her place I don't think *I* could."

A shriek from Molly here startled them all, or perhaps I should say, *would* have done so. had they been less accustomed to her eccentric behaviour.

"What is the matter now, my dear?" said aunty.

"Oh," said Molly, gasping with eagerness, "grandmother's saying that *reminded* me."

"But what about, my dear child?"

"About telling stories; don't you remember grandmother *dear*, I said you would be *perfect* if you

84

would tell us stories, and you didn't say you wouldn't."

"And what's more, grandmother promised me one," said Ralph.

"*Did* I, my dear boy?"

"Yes, grandmother," said Ralph, looking rather abashed, "don't you remember, grandmother — the day I called Prosper de Lastre a cad? I don't think he's a cad now," he added in a lower voice.

"Ah yes, I remember now," said grandmother. "But do you know, my dears, I am so sorry I cannot find your Uncle Jack's manuscript. He had written it out so well — all I can find is the letter in which he first alluded to the incident, very shortly. However, I remember most of it pretty clearly. I will think it over and refresh my memory with the letter, and some day I will tell it to you."

"Can't you tell it us to-night then, grandmother dear?" said Molly in very doleful tones.

They were all sitting round the fire, for it was early December now, and fires are needed then, even at Châlet! What a funny fire some of you would think such a one, children! No grate, no fender, such as you are accustomed to see — just two or three iron bars placed almost on the floor, which serve to support the nice round logs of wood burning so brightly, but alas for grandmother's purse, so swiftly away! But the brass knobs and bars in front look cheery and sparkling, and then the indispensable bellows are a delightful invention for fidgety fingers like those of Ralph and Molly. How many new "nozzles" grandmother had to pay for her poor bellows that winter I should really be afraid to say! And once, to Molly's indescribable consternation, the bellows got on fire *inside;* there was no outward injury to be seen, but they smoked alarmingly, and internal crackings were to be heard of a fearful and mysterious description. Molly flew to the kitchen, and flung the bellows, as if they were alive, into a pan of water that stood handy. Doubtless the remedy was effectual so far as extinguishing the fire was concerned, but as for the after result on the constitution of the poor bellows I cannot report favourably, as they were never again fit to use. *And,* as this was the fourth pair spoilt in a month, Molly was obliged to give up half her weekly money for some time towards replacing them!

But we are wandering away from the talk by the fire — grandmother and aunty in their low chairs working — the three children lying in various attitudes on the hearthrug, for hearthrug there was, seldom as such superfluities are to be seen at Châlet. Grandmother was too "English" to have been satisfied with her pretty drawing-room without one — a nice fluffy, flossy one, which the children were so fond of burrowing in that grandmother declared she would need a new one by the time the winter was over!

"*Can't* you tell it to us to-night then, grandmother dear?" said Molly.

"I would rather think it over a little first," said grandmother. "You forget, Molly, that old people's

memories are not like young ones. And, as Marie
says, it is very curious how, the older one gets, the
further back things are those that one remembers
the most distinctly. The middle part of my life
is hazy compared with the earlier part. I can
remember the patterns of some of my dresses as a
very little girl — I can remember words said and
trifling things done fifty years ago better than little
things that happened last month."

"How queer!" said Molly. "Shall we all be like
that, grandmother dear, when we get old?"

Grandmother laid down her knitting and looked
at the children with a soft smile on her face.

"Yes, dears, I suppose so. It is the 'common lot.'
I remember once asking *my* grandmother a question
very like that."

"*Your* grandmother!" exclaimed all the children
—Molly adding, "Had *you* ever a grandmother,
grandmother dear?"

"Oh, Molly, how can you be so silly?" said Ralph
and Sylvia, together.

"I'm not silly," said Molly. "It is you that are
silly not to understand what I mean. I am sure
anybody might. Of course I mean can grandmother
remember her — did she know her? Supposing anybody's grandmother died before they were born, then
they wouldn't ever have had one, would they now?"

Molly sat up on the rug, and tossed back her hair
out of her eyes, convinced that her logic was un-
answerable.

"You shouldn't begin by saying 'anybody's grandmother,'" remarked Ralph. "You put anybody in the possessive case, which means, of course, that the grandmother belonged to the anybody, and *then* you make out that the anybody never had one."

Molly retorted by putting her fingers in her ears and shaking her head vehemently at her brother. "Be quiet, Ralph," she said. "What's the good of muddling up what I say, and making my head feel *so* uncomfortable when you know quite well what I *mean?* Please, grandmother dear, will you go on talking as soon as I take my fingers out of my ears, and then he will have to leave off puzzling me."

"And what am I to talk about?" asked grandmother.

"Tell us about your grandmother. If you remember things long ago so nicely, you must remember story sort of things of then," said Molly insinuatingly.

"I really don't, my dear child. Not just at this moment, anyhow."

"Well, tell us *about* your grandmother: what was she like? was she like you?"

Grandmother shook her head.

"That I cannot say, my dear; I have no portrait of her, nor have I ever seen one since I have been grown up. She died when I was about fifteen, and as my father was not the eldest son, few, if any, heirlooms fell to his share. And a good many years before my grandmother's death — at the time of her husband's death — the old home was sold, and she came to live in a curious old-fashioned house, in the little county town a few miles from where we lived.

This old house had belonged to her own family for many, many years, and, as all her brothers were dead, it became hers. She was very proud of it, and even during my grandfather's life they used to come in from the country to spend the worst of the winter there. Dear me! what a long time back it takes us! were my grandmother living now, she would be — let me see — my father would have been a hundred years old by now. I was the youngest of a large family you know, dears. His mother would have been about a hundred and thirty. It takes us back to the middle of George the Second's reign."

"Yes," said Molly so promptly, that every one looked amazed, "George the First, seventeen hundred and fourteen, George the Second, seventeen hundred and twenty-seven, George the Third, seventeen hundred and —"

"When did you learn that — this morning I suppose?" observed Ralph with biting sarcasm.

"No," said Molly complacently, "I always could remember the four Georges. Sylvia will tell you. *She* always remembered the Norman Conquest, and King John, and so when we spoke about something to do with these dates when we were out for a walk Miss Bryce used to be as pleased as pleased with us."

"Is that the superlative of ' very pleased,' my dear Molly?" said aunty.

Molly wriggled.

"History is bad enough," she muttered. "I don't think we need have grammar too, just when I thought we were going to have nice story-talking. Did *you*

like lessons when you were little, grandmother dear?"
she inquired in a louder voice.

"I don't know that I did," said grandmother. "I
was a very tom-boy little girl, Molly. And lessons
were not nearly so interesting in those days as they
are made now."

"Then they must have been — *dreadful*," said Molly
solemnly, pausing for a sufficiently strong word.

"What did you like when you were little, grandmother?" said Sylvia. "I mean, what did you like
best?"

"I really don't know what I liked *best*," said
grandmother. "There were so many nice things.
Haymaking was delicious, so were snow-balling and
sliding; blindman's buff and snapdragon at Christmas
were not bad, nor were strawberries and cream in
summer."

The children drew a long breath.

"Had you all those?" they said. "Oh, what a
happy little girl you must have been!"

"And all the year round," pursued grandmother,
"there was another delight that never palled. When
I look back upon myself in those days I cannot believe that ever a child was a greater adept at it."

"What was that, grandmother?" said the children, opening their eyes.

"*Mischief*, my dears," said grandmother. "The
scrapes I got into of falling into brooks, tearing my
clothes, climbing up trees and finding I could not
get down again, putting my head through window-
panes — ah dear, I certainly had nine lives."

" And what did your grandmother say? Did she
scold you?" asked Molly — adding in a whisper to
Ralph and Sylvia, " Grandmother must have been
an *awfully* nice little girl."

" My grandmother was to outward appearance quiet
and rather cold," replied *their* grandmother. " For
long I was extremely afraid of her, till something
happened which led to my knowing her true character, and after that we were friends for life — till her
death. It is hardly worth calling a story, but I will
tell it to you if you like, children."

" Oh, *please* do," they exclaimed, and Molly's eyes
grew round with satisfaction at having after all in-
veigled grandmother into story telling.

" I told you," grandmother began, " that my grandmother lived in a queer, very old-fashioned house in
the little town near which was our home. It was
such a queer house, I wish you could have seen it,
but long ago it was pulled down, and the ground
where it stood used for shops or warehouses. When
you entered it, you saw no stair at all — then, on
opening a door, you found yourself at the foot of a
very high spiral staircase that went round and round
like a corkscrew up to the very top of the house. By
the by that reminds me of an adventure of my grandmother's which you might like to hear. It happened
long before I was born, but she has often told it me.
Ah, Molly, I see that twinkle in your eyes, my dear,
and I know what it means! You think you have
got grandmother started now — wound up — and that
you will get her to go on and on ; ah well, we shall

see. Where was I? Taking you up the corkscrew
stair. The first landing, if landing it could be called,
it was so small, had several doors, and one of these
led into a little ante-room, out of which opened again
a larger and very pretty drawing-room. It was a
long, rather narrow room, and what I admired in it
most of all were wall cupboards with glass doors,
within which my grandmother kept all her treasures.
There were six of them at least — in two or three
were books, of which, for those days, grandmother
had a good many; another held Chinese and Indian
curiosities, carved ivory and sandal-wood ornaments,
cuscus grass fans, a pair or two of Chinese ladies'
slippers — things very much the same as you may see
some of now-a-days in almost every prettily furnished
drawing-room. And one, or two perhaps, of the cupboards contained treasures which are rarer now than
they were then — the *loveliest* old china! Even I,
child as I was, appreciated its beauty — the tints were
so delicate and yet brilliant. My grandmother had
collected much of it herself, and her taste was excellent. At her death it was divided, and among so
many that it seemed to melt away. All that came
to my share were those two handless cups that are at
the top of that little cabinet over there, and those
were by no means the most beautiful, beautiful as
they undoubtedly are. I was never tired of feasting
my eyes on grandmother's china when I used to be
sent to spend a day with her, which happened every
few weeks. And *sometimes*, for a great treat, she
used to open the wall cupboards and let me handle

some of the things — for it is a curious fact that a child *cannot* admire anything to its perfect satisfaction without touching it too, and looking back upon things now, I can see that despite her cold manner, my grandmother had a very good knowledge of children and a real love and sympathy for them.

"One day — it was a late autumn day I remember, for it was just a few days after my ninth birthday — my birthday is on the fifteenth of November, — my mother told me that my father, having to drive to the town the following day, would take me with him to spend the day with grandmother.

"'And Nelly,' said my mother, 'do try to be very good and behave prettily. I really fear, my dear, that you will never be like a young lady — it is playing so much with your brothers, I suppose, and you know grandmother is very particular. The last time you were there you know you dressed up the cat and frightened poor old Betsy (my grandmother's cook) so. Do try to keep out of mischief this time.'

"'I can't,' I said. 'There is no one to play with there. I would rather stay at home;' and I teased my mother to say I need not go. But it was no good; she was firm about it — it was right that I, the only girl at home, should go to see my grandmother sometimes, and my mother repeated her admonitions as to my behaviour; and as I really loved her dearly I promised to 'try to be very good;' and the next morning I set off with my father in excellent spirits. There was nothing I liked better than a drive with him, especially in rather cold weather, for then he used to tuck me up so beautifully warm in his nice soft rugs, so that hardly anything but the tip of my nose was to be seen, and he would call me his 'little woman' and pet me to my heart's content.

"When we reached my grandmother's I felt very reluctant to descend from my perch, and I said to my father that I wished he would take me about the town with him instead of leaving me there.

"He explained to me that it was impossible — he had all sorts of things to do, a magistrate's meeting to attend, and I don't know all what. Besides which he liked me to be with my grandmother, and he told me I was a silly little goose when I said I was afraid of her.

"My father entered the house without knocking — there was no need to lock doors in the quiet streets of the little old town, where everybody that passed up and down was known by everybody else, and their *business* often known better by the everybody else than by themselves. We went up to the drawing-room, there was nobody there — my father went out of the room and called up the staircase, 'Mother, where are you?'

"Then I heard my grandmother's voice in return.

"'My dear Hugh — is it you? I am so sorry. I cannot possibly come down. It is the third Tuesday of the month. My wardrobe day.'

"'And the little woman is here too. What shall I do with her?' said my father. He seemed to understand, though I did not, what 'wardrobe day' meant.

"'Bring her up here,' my grandmother called back.

'I shall soon have arranged all, and then I can take her downstairs again.'

"I was standing on the landing by my father by this time, and, far from loth to discover what my grandmother was about, I followed him upstairs. You have no idea, children, what a curious sight met me! My grandmother, who was a very little woman, was perched upon a high stool, hanging up on a great clothes-horse ever so many dresses, which she had evidently taken out of a wardrobe, close by, whose doors were wide open. There were several clothes-horses in the room, all more or less loaded with garments, — and oh, what queer, quaint garments some of them were! The clothes my grandmother herself had on — even those I was wearing — would seem curious enough to you if you could see them now, — but when I tell you that of those she was hanging out, many had belonged to *her* grandmother, and mother, and aunts, and great-aunts, you can fancy what a wonderful array there was. Her own wedding dress was among them, and all the coloured silks and satins she had possessed before her widowhood. And more wonderful even than the dresses were a few, not very many, for indeed no room or wardrobe would have held *very* many, bonnets, or 'hats,' as I think they were then always called. Huge towering constructions, with feathers sticking straight up on the top, like the pictures of Cinderella's sisters in old-fashioned fairy-tale books — so enormous that any ordinary human head must have been lost in their depths."

"Did you ever try one on, grandmother?" said Molly.

Grandmother shook her head.

"I should not have been allowed to take such a liberty," she said. "I stood and stared about me in perfect amazement without speaking for a minute or two, till my grandmother got down from her stool, and my father told me to go to speak to her.

"'Are you going away, grandmother?' I said at last, my curiosity overcoming my shyness. 'Are these all your clothes? You will want a great many boxes to pack them in, and what queer ones some of them are!'

"'Queer, my dear,' said my grandmother. 'They are certainly not like what you get now-a-days, if that is what you mean by queer. See here, Nelly, this is your great-grandmother's wedding dress— white Padusoy embroidered in gold — why, child, it would stand alone! And this salmon-coloured satin, with the pea-green slip — will the stuffs they dye now keep their colour like that a hundred years hence?'

"'It's good strong stuff certainly,' said my father, touching it as he spoke. But then he went on to say to my grandmother that the days for such things were past. 'We don't want our clothes to last a century now, mother,' he said. 'Times are hurrying on faster, and we must make up our minds to go on with them and leave our old clothes behind. The world would get too full if everybody cherished by-gone relics as you do.'

"I don't think she much liked his talking so.

She shook her head and said something about revolutionary ideas, which I didn't understand. But my father only laughed; his mother and he were the best of friends, though he liked to tease her sometimes. I wandered about the room, peeping in among the rows of quaint costumes, and thinking to myself what fun it would be to dress up in them. But after a while I got tired, and I was hungry too, so I was very glad when grandmother, having hung out the last dress to air, said we must go down to dinner — my father had left some time before — "

"What did you have for dinner, grandmother?" said Sylvia. "It isn't that I care so much about eating," she added, blushing a little, "but I like to know exactly the sort of way people lived, you know."

"Only I wish you wouldn't interrupt grandmother," said Molly. "I'm *so* afraid it'll be bedtime before she finishes the story."

"Which isn't yet begun — eh, Molly?" said grandmother. "I warned you my stories were sadly deficient in beginning and end, and middle too — in short they are not stories at all."

"Never mind, they're *very* nice," said Molly; "and if I may sit up till this one's done I don't mind your telling Sylvia what you had for dinner, grandmother dear."

"Many thanks for your small majesty's gracious permission," said grandmother. "But as to what we had for dinner, I really can't say. Much the same as you have now, I fancy. Let me see — it was November — very likely a roast chicken and nice pudding."

"Oh!" said Sylvia, in a tone of some disappointment; "go on then, please, grandmother."

"Where was I?" said grandmother. "Oh yes—well, after dinner we went up to the drawing-room, and grandmother, saying she was a good deal tired by her exertions of the morning, sat down in her own particular easy chair by the fire, and, spreading over her face a very fine cambric handkerchief which she kept, I strongly suspect, for the purpose, prepared for her after-dinner nap. It was really a regular institution with her—but I noticed she always made some little special excuse for it, as if it was something quite out of the common. She told me to amuse myself during her forty winks by looking at the treasures in the glass-doored cupboards, which she knew I was very fond of admiring, and she told me I might open the book cupboard if I wanted to take out a book, but on no account any of the others.

"Now I assure you, children, and by your own experience you will believe what I say, that, but for my grandmother's warnings, the idea of opening the glass doors when by myself would never have come into my head. I had often been in the drawing-room alone and gazed admiringly at the treasures without ever dreaming of examining them more closely. I had never even *wished* to do so, any more than one wishes to handle the moon or stars or any other unget-at-able objects. But now, unfortunately, the idea was suggested, it had been put into my head, and there it stayed. I walked round the room gazing in at the cupboards in turn — the book ones did not particularly attract me — long ago I had read, over and over again, the few books in my grandmother's possession that I could feel interested in, and I stood still at last in front of the prettiest cupboard of all, wishing that grandmother had not forbidden my opening it. There were such lovely cups and saucers! I longed to handle them — one in particular that I felt sure I had never seen before. It had a deep rose pink ground, and in the centre there was the sweetest picture of a dear little shepherdess curtseying to an equally dear little shepherd.

"As I gazed at this cup the idea struck me that it would be delicious to dress one of my dolls in the little shepherdess's costume, and, eager to see it more minutely, I opened the glass door, and was just stretching up my hand for the cup, when I again remembered what my grandmother had said. I glanced round at her; she was fast asleep; there was no danger; what harm *could* it do for me to take the cup into my hand for a moment? I stretched up and took it. Yes, it was really most lovely, and the little shepherdess's dress seemed to me a perfect facsimile of the one I had most admired up stairs in my grandmother's wardrobe — a pea-green satin over a pale pink or rather salmon-coloured quilted slip. I determined that Lady Rosabella should have one the same, and I was turning over in my mind the possibilities of getting satin of the particular shades I thought so pretty, when a slight sound in the direction, it seemed to me, of my grandmother's arm-chair, startled me. I turned round hastily — how it was I cannot tell, but so it was — the beautiful cup fell from my hands and lay at my feet in, I was going to say, a thousand fragments."

"Oh!" exclaimed Sylvia and Molly — "oh, grandmother, what *did* you do?"

"First of all," grandmother continued, "first of all I stooped down and picked up the pieces. There were not a thousand of them — not perhaps above a dozen, and after all, grandmother was sleeping quietly, but to all appearance soundly. The sound that had startled me must have been a fancied one, I said to myself, and oh dear, what a terrible pity I had been startled!

"I gathered the bits together in my handkerchief, and stood staring at them in perfect despair. I dared not let myself burst out crying as I was inclined to do, for grandmother would have heard me and asked what was the matter, and I felt that I should sink into the earth with shame and terror if she saw what I had done, and that I had distinctly disobeyed her. My only idea was to conceal the mischief. I huddled the bits up together in my handkerchief, and huddled the handkerchief into my pocket — the first pocket I had ever had, I rather think — and then I looked up to see if the absence of the cup was very conspicuous. I thought not; the saucer was still there, and by pulling one or two of the other pieces of china forward a little, I managed to make it look as if the cup was just accidentally hidden. To reach up to do this, I had to draw forward a chair; in getting down from it again I made some little noise, and I looked round in terror to see if grandmother was awake. No, she was still sleeping soundly. *What* a blessing! I got out of one of the book cupboards a book I had read twenty times at least, and sitting down on a stool by the fire I pretended to read it again, while really all my ideas were running on what I should, what I *could* do. For I had no manner of doubt that before long the accident would be discovered, and I felt sure that my grandmother's displeasure would be very severe. I knew too that my having tried to conceal it would make her far less ready to forgive me, and yet I felt that I *could* not make up my mind to confess it all. I was so miserable that it was the greatest relief to me a minute or two afterwards to hear the hall door open and my father's hearty voice on the stair.

"'I have come to fetch you rather sooner than I said, little woman,' he exclaimed, as he came in, and then he explained that he had promised to drive a friend who lived near us home from the town in our gig, and that this friend being in a hurry, we must leave earlier than usual. My grandmother had wakened up of course with my father's coming in. It seemed to me, or was it my fancy?—that she looked graver than usual and rather sad as she bade us good-bye. She kissed me very kindly, more tenderly than was her habit, and said to my father that he must be sure to bring me again very soon, so that as I was going downstairs with him, he said to me that he was glad to see how fond grandmother was getting of me, and that he would bring me again next week. *I* did not feel at all pleased at this — I felt more unhappy than ever I had done in my life, so that my father, noticing it, asked what was the matter. I replied that I was tired and that I did not care for going to grandmother's, and then, when I saw that this ungracious answer vexed my kind father, I felt more and more unhappy. Every moment as we walked along — we were to meet the carriage at the inn where it had been left — the bits of broken china in my pocket bumped against my leg, as if they would not let themselves be forgotten. I wished I could stop and throw them away, but that was impossible. I trudged along, gloomy and wretched, with a weight on my heart that it seemed to me I would never get rid of. Suddenly — so suddenly that I could hardly believe my own senses — something caught my eye that entirely changed my whole ideas. I darted forward, my father was a few steps in front of me — the footpath was so narrow in the old town that there was often not room for two abreast — *and* — "

Just at this moment the door opened, and grandmother's maid appeared with the tea-tray. Molly gave an impatient shake.

" Oh, *what* a bother!" she said. " I quite forgot about tea. And immediately after tea it is always time for us to go to bed. It is eight o'clock now, oh, grandmother, *do* finish the story to-night."

" And why cannot my little girl ask it without all those shakes and 'bothers'?" said grandmother. She spoke very gently, but Molly looked considerably ashamed.

"Yes, grandmother dear," she replied meekly. Then she got up from the rug and stood by aunty patiently, while she poured out the tea, first "grandmothering" each cup to keep it from slipping about, then warming them with a little hot water, then putting in the beautiful yellow cream, the sugar, and the nice rich brown tea, all in the particular way grandmother liked it done. And during the process, Molly did not once wriggle or twist with impatience, so that when she carried grandmother's tea to her, very carefully and steadily, without a drop spilling over into the saucer in the way grandmother disliked to see, she got a kiss by way of reward, and what was still better perhaps, grandmother looked up and said,

"That's *my* good little woman. There is not much more of what you call 'my story' to tell, but such as it is, you may sit up to hear it, if you like."

CHAPTER VIII.

"O while you live, tell truth."

HENRY IV., Part I.

So in a few minutes they were all settled again,
and grandmother went on.

"We were walking through a very narrow street,
I was telling you — was I not? when I caught sight
of something that suddenly changed my ideas.
'What was this something?' you are all asking, I
see. It was a china cup in a shop window we were
passing, a perfect match it seemed to me of the unfortunate one still lamenting its fate by rattling its
bits in my pocket! It was a shabby little old shop,
of which there were a good many in the town, filled
with all sorts of curiosities, and quite in the front of
the window, as conspicuous as if placed there on purpose, stood the cup. I darted forward to beg my
father to let me wait a moment, but just then, curiously enough, he had met a friend and was standing
talking to him, and when I touched his arm he turned
rather hastily, for, as I told you, he had not been
pleased with my way of replying about my grandmother. And he said to me I must not be so impatient, but wait till he had finished speaking to Mr.

104

"Zwanzig — Twenty Schelling, that Cup." — p. 105.

Lennox. I asked him if I might look in at the shop window, and he said 'Yes, of course I might,' so I flew back, the bits rattle-rattling in my pocket, and stood gazing at the twin-cup. I must tell you that I happened to have in my possession an unusual amount of money just then — ten shillings, actually ten whole shillings, which my father had given me on my birthday, and as I always brought my purse with me when I came into the town, there it was all ready! I looked and looked at the cup till I was satisfied it was a perfect match, then glancing up the street and seeing my father still talking to his friend, I crept timidly into the shop, and asked the price of the pink cup and saucer in the window.

"The old man in the shop was a German; afterwards my grandmother told me he was a Jew, and well accustomed to having his prices beaten down. He looked at me curiously and said to me,

"'Ach! too moch for leetle young lady like you. Zwanzig — twenty schelling, that cup. Old lady bought von, vill come again buy anoder. Zwanzig — twenty schelling.'

"I grew more and more eager. The old lady he spoke of must be my grandmother; I had often heard my father laugh at her for poking about old shops; I felt perfectly certain the cups were exactly alike. I begged the old man to let me have it, and opened my purse to show him all I had — the ten shilling piece, two sixpences and a fourpenny, and a few coppers. That was all, and the old man shook his head. It was too little, 'twenty schelling,' he repeated, or at the very least, to oblige the 'young lady,' fifteen. I said to him I had not got fifteen — eleven and ninepence was everything I possessed, and at last, in my eagerness, I nearly burst into tears. I really do not know if the old man was sorry for me, or if he only thought of getting my money; however that may have been, he took my purse out of my hand and slowly counted out the money. I meanwhile, nearly dancing with impatience, while he repeated 'ninepence, von schelling, zehn schelling! ach vell, most be, most be,' and to my great delight he handed me the precious cup and saucer, first wrapping them up in a dirty bit of newspaper.

"Then he took the ten-shilling piece out of my purse, and handed it back to me, leaving me in possession of my two sixpences, my fourpenny bit, and my five coppers.

"I flew out of the shop thanking the old man effusively, and rushed up the street clutching my treasure, while rattle-rattle went the bones of its companion in my pocket. My father was just shaking hands with Mr. Lennox and turning round to look for me, when I ran up. Mr. Lennox, it appeared, was the gentleman who was to have driven home with us, but something had occurred to detain him in the town, and he was on his way to explain this to my father when we met him.

"My father was rather silent and grave on the way home; he seemed to have forgotten that I had said anything to vex him; some magistrates' business had worried him, and it was that that he had been talking about to Mr. Lennox. He said to me that he was half afraid he would have to drive into the town again the next day, adding, 'It is a pity Lennox did not know in time. By staying a little later, we might have got all done.'

"To his astonishment I replied by begging him to let me come with him again the next day. He said to me, 'Why, Nelly, you were just now saying you did not care for going to see your grandmother, that it was dull, and tired you. What queer creatures children are.'

"I felt my cheeks grow hot, but I replied that I was sorry I had said that, and that I did want very much to go to see my grandmother again. Of course you will understand, children, that I was thinking about the best chance of putting back the cup, or rather its substitute, but my dear father thought I was sorry for having vexed him, and that I wanted to please him by asking to go again, so he readily granted my request. But I felt far from happy that evening at home, when something was said about my wanting to go again, and one of my brothers remarking that I must surely have enjoyed myself very greatly at my grandmother's, my father and mother looked at me kindly and said that their little Nelly liked to please others as well as herself. Oh how guilty I felt! I hated having anything to conceal, for I was by nature very frank. And oh, what a torment the poor cup and saucer were! I got rid of the bits by throwing them behind a hedge, but I could not tell where to hide my purchase, and I was so

terribly afraid of breaking it. It was a relief to my
mind the next morning when it suddenly struck me
that I need not take the saucer too, the cup was
enough, as the original saucer was there intact, and
the cup was much easier to carry by itself.

" When we got to the town my father let me down
at my grandmother's without coming in himself at
all, and went off at once to his business. The door
was open, and I saw no one about. I made my way
up to the drawing-room as quickly and quietly as
possible; to my great satisfaction there was no one
there. I stole across the room to the china cupboard,
drew forward a chair and climbed upon it, and, in
mortal fear and trembling, placed the cup on the
saucer waiting for it. They seemed to match exactly,
but I could not wait to see any more — the sound of
some one coming along the ante-room reached my
ears — I had only just time to close the door of the
cupboard, jump down and try to look as if nothing
were the matter, when my grandmother entered the
room. She came up to me with both her hands out-
stretched in welcome, and a look on her face that I
did not understand. She kissed me fondly, exclaiming,

" ' My own dear little Nelly. I thought you would
come. I knew you would not be happy till you
had —.' But she stopped suddenly. I had drawn a
little back from her, and again I felt my face get red.
Why would people praise me when I did not deserve
it? My grandmother, I supposed, thought I had
come again because I had felt conscious of having

been not particularly gracious the day before — whereas I knew my motive to have been nothing of the kind.

" 'Papa was coming again, and he said I might come. I have nothing to do at home just now. It's holidays,' I said abruptly, my very honesty *now* leading me into misrepresentations, as is constantly the case once one has quitted the quite straight path of candour.

" My grandmother looked pained and disappointed, but said nothing. But *never* had she been kinder. It was past dinner time, but she ordered tea for me an hour earlier than her usual time, and sent down word that the cook was to bake some gridle-cakes, as she knew I was fond of them. And what a nice tea we might have had but for the uncomfortable little voice that kept whispering to me that I did not deserve all this kindness, that I was deceiving my grandmother, which was far worse than breaking twenty cups. I felt quite provoked with myself for feeling so uneasy. I had thought I should have felt quite comfortable and happy once the cup was restored. I had spent all, or very nearly all, my money on it. I said to myself, Who could have done more? And I determined not to be so silly and to think no more about it — but it was no good. Every time my grandmother looked at me, every time she spoke to me — worst of all when the time came for me to go and she kissed me, somehow so much more tenderly than usual, and murmured some words I could not catch, but which sounded like a little prayer, as she

stroked my head in farewell — it was dreadfully hard
not to burst into tears and tell her all, and beg her
to forgive me. But I went away without doing so.

"Half way home a strange thought came suddenly
into my mind. It seemed to express the unhappi-
ness I was feeling. Supposing my grandmother were
to die, supposing I were never to see her again, would
I *then* feel satisfied with my behaviour to her, and
would I still say to myself that I had done all for the
best in spending my money on a new cup? Would
I not then rather feel that it would have been less
grievous to my grandmother to know of my breaking
twenty cups, than to discover the concealment and
want of candour into which my cowardliness had
led me?

"'If grandmother were *dead*, I suppose she would
know all about it,' I said to myself. 'I would not
like to think of that. I would rather have told her
myself.'

"And I startled my father by turning to him suddenly and asking if grandmother was very old. He
replied, 'Not so very. Of course she is not *young*,
but we may hope to have her among us many a day
yet if God wills it, my little woman.'

"I gave a sigh of relief. 'I know she is very
strong,' I said. 'She is very seldom ill, and she can
take quite long walks still.'

"'Thank God for it,' said my father, evidently
pleased with my interest in my grandmother. And
although it was true that already I was beginning to
love her much more than formerly, still my father's

manner gave me again the miserable feeling that I
was gaining credit which I did not deserve.

" More than a week passed after this without my
seeing my grandmother. It was not a happy week
for me. I felt quite unlike my old light-hearted self.
And constantly — just as when one has a tender spot
anywhere, a sore finger for instance, everything seems
to rub against it — constantly little allusions were
made which appeared to have some reference to my
concealment. Something would be said about my
birthday present, and my brothers would ask me if I
had made up my mind what I should buy with it,
or they would tease me about my sudden fancy for
spending two days together with my grandmother,
and ask me if I was not in a hurry to go to see
her again. I grew irritable and suspicious, and more
and more unhappy, and before long those about me
began to notice the change. My father and mother
feared I was ill — 'Nelly is so unlike herself,' I heard
them say. My brothers openly declared ' there was
no fun in playing with me now, I had grown so
cross.' I felt that it was true — indeed both opin-
ions were true, for I really *was* getting ill with the
weight on my mind, which never, night or day,
seemed to leave it.

" At last one day my father told me that he was
going to drive into the little town where my grandmother lived, the next day, and that I was to go with
him to see her. I noticed that he did not ask me, as
usual, if I would like to go ; he just said I must be
ready by a certain hour, and gave me no choice in

the matter. I did not want to go, but I was afraid of making any objection for fear of their asking my reasons, so I said nothing, but silently, and to all appearance I fear, sulkily, got ready as my father desired. We had a very quiet drive; my father made no remarks about my dullness and silence, and I began to be afraid that something had been found out, and that he was taking me to my grandmother's to be ' scolded,' as I called it in my silly little mind. I glanced up at his face as I sat beside him. No, he did not look severe, only grave and rather anxious. Dear father! Afterwards I found that he and my mother had been really *very* anxious about me, and that he was taking me to my grandmother, by her express wish, to see what she thought of the state of matters, before consulting a doctor or trying change of air, or anything of that kind. And my grand-mother had particularly asked him to say nothing more to myself about my own unsatisfactory condi-tion, and had promised him to do her utmost to put things right.

"Well — we got to my grandmother's — my father lifted me out of the carriage, and I followed him up-stairs — my grandmother was sitting in the drawing-room, evidently expecting us. She came forward with a bright kind smile on her face, and kissed me fondly. Then she said to my father she was so glad he had brought me, and she hoped I would have a happy day. And my father looked at me as he went away with a sort of wistful anxiety that made me again have that horrible feeling of not deserving his care and affection. And oh, how I wished the long day alone with my grandmother were over! I could not bear being in the drawing-room, I was afraid of seeming to glance in the direction of the china cupboard; I felt miserable whenever my grandmother spoke kindly to me.

"And how kind she was that day! If ever a little girl *should* have been happy, that little girl was I. Grandmother let me look over the drawers where she kept her beautiful scraps of silk and velvet, ever so many of which she gave me — lovely pieces to make a costume such as I had fancied for Lady Rosabelle, but which I had never had the heart to see about. She let me 'tidy' her best work-box — a *wonderful* box, full of every conceivable treasure and curiosity — and then, when I was a little tired with all my exertions, she made me sit down on a footstool at her feet and talked to me so nicely — all about when *she* was a little girl — fancy that, Molly, your great-great-grandmother ever having been a little girl! — and about the queer legends and fairy tales that in those days were firmly believed in in the far-away Scotch country place where her childhood was spent. For the first time for all these unhappy ten days I began to feel like myself again. Sitting there at my grandmother's feet listening to her I actually forgot my troubles, though I was in the very drawing-room I had learnt so to dread, within a few yards of the cupboard I dared not even glance at.

"There came a little pause in the conversation; I leaned my head against my grandmother's knee.

" 'I wish there were fairies now,' I said. 'Don't you, grandmother?'

" Grandmother said 'no, on the whole she preferred things being as they were.' There were *some* fairies certainly she would be sorry to lose, Princess Sweet-temper, and Lady Make-the-best-of-it, and old Madame Tidy, and, most of all perhaps, the beautiful fairy *Candour*. I laughed at her funny way of saying things, but yet something in her last words made the uneasy feeling come back again. Then my grandmother went on talking in a different tone.

" 'Do you know, Nelly,' she said, 'queer things happen sometimes that one would be half inclined to put down to fairies if one did not know better?'

" I pricked up my ears.

" 'Do tell me what sort of things, grandmother,' I said eagerly.

" 'Well' — she went on, speaking rather slowly and gravely, and very distinctly — 'the other day an extraordinary thing happened among my china cups in that cupboard over there. I had one pink cup, on the side of which was — or is — the picture of a shepherdess curtseying to a shepherd. Now this shepherdess when I bought the cup, which was only a few days ago, was dressed — I am *perfectly* certain of it, for her dress was just the same as one I have upstairs in my collection — in a pale pink or salmon-coloured skirt, looped up over a pea-green slip — the picture of the shepherdess is repeated again on the saucer, and there it still is as I tell you. But the strangest metamorphosis has taken place in the cup. I left it one morning as I describe, for you know I always dust my best china myself. Two days after, when I looked at it again, the shepherdess's attire was changed — she had on no longer the pea-green dress over the salmon, but a *salmon* dress over a *pea-green* slip. Did you ever hear anything so strange, Nelly?'

" I turned away my head, children; I dared not look at my grandmother. What should I say? This was the end of my concealment. It had done *no* good — grandmother must know it all now, I could hide it no longer, and she would be far, far more angry than if at the first I had bravely confessed my disobedience and its consequences. I tried to speak, but I could not. I burst into tears and hid my face.

" Grandmother's arm was round me in a moment, and her kind voice saying, ' Why, what is the matter, my little Nelly?'

" I drew myself away from her, and threw myself on the floor, crying out to grandmother not to speak kindly to me.

" 'You won't love me when you know,' I said. 'You will never love me again. It was *me*, oh grandmother! It was me that changed the cup. I got another for you not to know. I spent all my money. I broke it, grandmother. When you told me not to open the cupboard, I did open it, and I took out the cup, and it fell and was broken, and then I saw another in a shop window, and I thought it was just the same, and I bought it. It cost ten shillings, but I never knew it wasn't quite the same, only now it doesn't matter. You will never love me again, and nobody will. Oh dear, oh dear, what *shall* I do?'

"'Never love you again, my poor dear faithless little girl,' said grandmother. 'Oh, Nelly, my child, how little you know me! But oh, I am so glad you have told me all about it yourself. That was what I was longing for. I did so want my little girl to be true to her own honest heart.'

" And then she went on to explain that she had known it all from the first. She had not been asleep the day that I disobediently opened the cupboard, at least she had wakened up in time to see what had happened, and she had earnestly hoped that I would make up my mind to tell it frankly. That was what had so disappointed her the next day when she had quite thought I had come on purpose to tell it all. Then when my father had come to consult her about the queer state I seemed to be in, she had not felt surprised. She had quite understood it all, though she had not said so to him, and she had resolved to try to win my confidence. She told me too that she had found out from the old German about my buying the cup, whose reappearance she could not at first explain.

"'I went to his shop the very next morning,' she told me, 'to see if he still had the fellow to the cup I had bought, as I knew he had two of them, and he told me the other had been bought by a little girl. Ten shillings was too much to give for it, Nelly, a great deal too much for you to give, and more than the cup was really worth. It was not a very valuable cup, though the colour was so pretty that I was tempted to buy it to place among the others.'

" 'I don't mind about the money, grandmother,' I replied. 'I would have given ever so much more if I had had it. You will keep the cup now?' I added. 'You won't make me take it back to the old man? And oh, grandmother, will you really forgive me?'

"She told me she had already done so, fully and freely, from the bottom of her heart. And she said she would indeed keep the cup, as long as she lived. and that if ever again I was tempted to distrust her I must look at it and take courage. And she explained to me that even if there had been reason for my fears, 'even if I had been a very harsh and severe grandmother, your concealment would have done no good in the end,' she said. 'It would have been like the first little tiny seed of deceit, which might have grown into a great tree of evil, poisoning all your life. Oh, Nelly, never *never* plant that seed, for once it has taken root who can say how difficult it may be to tear it up?'

"I listened with all my attention; I could not help being deeply impressed with her earnestness, and I was so grateful for her kindness that her advice found good soil ready to receive it. And how many, many times in my life have I not recalled it! For, Ralph and Sylvia and Molly, my darlings, remember this — even to the naturally frank and honest there come times of sore temptation in life, times when a

little swerving from the straight narrow path of up-
rightness would seem to promise to put all straight
when things have gone wrong, times when the cost
seems so little and the gain so great. Ah! yes,
children, we need to have a firm anchor to hold
by at these times, and woe for us then if the little
evil seed has been planted and has taken root in our
hearts."

Grandmother paused. The children too were
silent for a moment or two. Then Sylvia said
gently,

"Did you tell your father and mother all about it,
grandmother?"

"Yes," said grandmother, "I did — all about it.
I told them everything. It was my own choice. My
grandmother left it to myself. She would not tell
them; she would leave it to me. And, of course, I
did tell them. I could not feel happy till I had done
so. They were very kind about it, *very* kind, but
still it was to my grandmother I felt the most grateful and the most drawn. From that time till her
death, when I was nearly grown up, she was my
dearest counsellor and guide. I had no concealment
from her — I told her everything. For her heart
was so wonderfully young; to the very last she was
able to sympathise in all my girlish joys, and sorrows,
and difficulties."

"Like you, grandmother dear," said Molly, softly
stroking her grandmother's hand, which she had taken
in hers. "She must have been just like you."

They all smiled.

"And when she died," pursued grandmother gently, almost as if speaking to herself, "when she died and all her things were divided, I begged them to give me the pink cup. I might have had a more valuable one instead, but I preferred it. It is one of those two over there on the little cabinet."

Molly's eyes turned eagerly in the direction of the little cabinet. "Grandmother dear," she said, solemnly, "when you die — I don't *want* you to die, you know of course, but when you *do* die, I wish you would say that *I* may have that cup — will you? To remind me, you know, of what you have been telling us. I quite understand how you mean: that day all my brooches were broken, I did awfully want not to tell you about them all, and I might forget, you see, about the little bad seed and all that, that you have been telling us so nicely. Please, grandmother dear, *may* I have that cup when you die?"

"Molly," said Sylvia, her face growing very red, "it is perfectly horrible of you to talk that way. I am quite ashamed of you. Don't mind her, grandmother. She just talks as if she had no sense sometimes. How *can* you, Molly?" she went on, turning again to her sister, "how *can* you talk about dear grandmother dying? *Dear* grandmother, and you pretend to love her."

Molly's big blue eyes opened wide with astonishment, then gradually they grew misty, and great tears welled up to their surface.

"I don't *pretend* — I *do* love her," she said. "And I don't *want* you to die, grandmother dear, do I?

only we all must die some time. I didn't mean to talk horribly. I think you are very unkind, Sylvia."

"Children, children," said grandmother's gentle voice, "I don't like these words. I am sure Molly did not mean anything I would not like, Sylvia dear, but yet I know how *you* mean. Don't be in such a hurry to judge each other. And about the cup, Molly, I'll consider, though I hope and believe you will not need it to remind you of the lesson I want to impress on you by the story of my long-ago troubles. Now kiss each other, dears, and kiss me, for it is quite bed-time. Good-night, my little girls. Ralph, my boy, open the door for your sisters, and pleasant dreams to you all."

CHAPTER IX.

RALPH'S CONFIDENCE.

" Sad case it is, as you may think
  For very cold to go to bed;
  And then for cold not sleep a wink."
                    WORDSWORTH's *Goody Blake.*

"GRANDMOTHER," said Ralph, when they were all sitting at breakfast the next morning, "didn't you say that your grandmother once had an adventure that we might like to hear? It was at the beginning of the story you told us — I think it was something about the corkscrew staircase. I liked the story awfully, you know, but I'm fearfully fond of adventures."

Grandmother smiled.

"I remember saying something about it," she said, "but it is hardly worth calling an adventure, my boy. It showed her courage and presence of mind, however. She was a very brave little woman."

"Presence of mind," repeated Ralph. "Ah yes! that's a good thing to have. There's a fellow at our school who saved a child from being burnt to death not long ago. It was his little cousin where he lives. It wasn't he that told me about it, he's too modest, it was some of the other fellows."

"Who is he? what's his name?" asked Molly.

121

"Prosper de Lastre," repeated Ralph. "He's an awful good fellow every way."

"Prosper de Lastre!" repeated Molly, who possessed among other peculiarities that of a sometimes most inconveniently good memory. "Prosper de Lastre! I do believe, Ralph, that's the very boy you called a cad when you first went to school."

Ralph's face got very red, and he seemed on the verge of a hasty reply. But he controlled himself.

"Well, and if I did," he said somewhat gruffly, "a fellow may be mistaken, mayn't he? I don't think him a cad *now*, and that's all about it."

Molly was preparing some rejoinder when grandmother interrupted her.

"You are quite right, Ralph, *quite* right not to be above owning yourself mistaken. Who *can* be above it really? not the wisest man that ever lived. And Molly, my dear little girl, why can you not learn to be more considerate? Do you know what 'tact' is, Molly? Did you ever hear of it?"

"Oh yes, grandmother dear," said Molly serenely. "It means — it means — oh I don't quite know, but I'm sure I do know."

"Think of it as meaning the not saying or doing to another person whatever in that other's place you would not like said or done to you — that is *one* meaning of tact anyway, and a very good one. Will you try to remember it, Molly?"

Molly opened her eyes.

"Yes, grandmother dear, I will try. But I *think* all that will be rather hard to remember, because you see people don't feel the same. My head isn't twisty-turny enough to understand things like that, quickly. I like better to go bump at them, quite straight."

" Without, in nine cases out of ten, the faintest idea what you are going to go bump straight at," said aunty, laughing. " Oh, Molly, you are irresistible!' "

The laughing at her had laughed back Ralph's good humour anyway, and now he returned to the charge.

" Twisty-turny is like a cockscrew, grandmother," he said slyly, " and once there was an old house with a cockscrew stair —"

" Yes," said grandmother, " and in that old house there once lived an old lady, who, strange to say, was not always old. She was not very old at the time of the 'adventure.' You remember, children, my telling you that during her husband's life, my grandmother and he used to spend part of the winter in the old house where she afterwards ended her days. My grandfather used to drive backwards and forwards to his farms, of which he had several in the neighbourhood, and the town was a sort of central place for the season of bad weather and short days. Sometimes he used to be kept rather late, for besides his own affairs, he had, like his son, my father, a good deal of magistrate's business to attend to. But . however late he was detained my grandmother always sat up for him, generally in a little sitting-room she had on the storey above the long drawing-room I have described to you, almost, that is to say, at the top of the house, from attic to basement of which ran the long 'twisty-turny, corkscrew staircase.' One evening, about Christmas time it was, I think, my grandfather was very late of coming home. My grandmother was not uneasy, for he had told her he would be late, and she had mentioned it to the servants, and told them they need not sit up. So there she was, late at night, alone, sewing most likely — ah girls, I wish I could show you some of her sewing — in her little parlour. She was not the least nervous, yet it was a little 'eerie' perhaps, sitting up there alone so late, listening for her husband's whistle — he always whistled when he was late, so that she might be *sure* it was he, when she went down to open the door at his knock — and more than once she looked at the clock and wished he would come. Suddenly a step outside the room, coming up the stair, made her start. She had hardly time to wonder confusedly if it could be my grandfather, knowing all the time it could *not* be he — the doors were all supposed to be locked and barred, and could only be opened from the inside — when the door was flung open and some one looked in. Not my grandfather certainly; the man who stood in the doorway was dressed in some sort of rough workman's clothes, and his face was black and grimy. That was all she had time to catch sight of, for, not expecting to see her there, the intruder, startled, turned sharply round and made for the stair. Up jumped my little grandmother; she took it all in in an instant, and saw that her only chance was to take advantage of his momentary surprise and start at seeing her. Up she jumped and rushed bravely after him, making all the clatter she could. Downstairs he flew, imagining very probably in his fright that two or three people instead of one little woman were at his heels, and downstairs, round and round the corkscrew staircase, she flew after him. Never afterwards, she has often since told me, did she quite lose the association of that wild flight, never could she go downstairs in that house without the feeling of the man before her, and seeming to hear the rattle-rattle of a leathern apron he was wearing, which clattered against the banisters as he ran. But she kept her head to the end of the chase; she followed him — all in the dark, remember — down to the bottom of the staircase, and, guided by the clatter of his apron, through a back kitchen in the basement which opened into a yard — there she stopped — she heard him clatter through this cellar, banging the door — which had been left open, and through which he had evidently made his way into the house — after him, as if to prevent her following him farther. Poor thing, she certainly had no wish to do so; she felt her way to the door and felt for the key to lock it securely. But alas, when she pushed the door closely to, preparatory to locking it, it resisted her. Some one or something seemed to push against her from the outside. Then for the first time her courage gave way, and thinking that the man had returned, with others perhaps, she grew sick and faint with fright. She sank down helplessly on the

floor for a moment or two. But all seemed quiet;
her courage and common sense returned; she got up
and felt all about the door carefully, to try to
discover the obstacle. To her delight she found that
some loose sand or earth driven into a little heap on
the floor was what prevented the door shutting.
She smoothed it away with her hand, closed the door
and locked it firmly, and then, faint and trembling,
but safe, made her way back to the little room where
her light was burning. You can fancy how glad she
was, a very few moments afterwards, to hear my
grandfather's cheerful whistle outside."

"But," interrupted Molly, her eyes looking bigger
and rounder than usual, "but suppose the man had
been waiting outside to catch him — your grandfather
— grandmother, when he came in?"

"But the man wasn't doing anything of the sort,
my dear Molly. He had gone off in a fright, and
when my grandmother thought it over coolly, she
felt convinced that he was not a regular burglar, and
so it turned out. He was a man who worked at a
smithy near by, and this was his first attempt at
burglary. He had heard that my grandfather was to
be out late, through one of the servants, whom he had
persuaded not to lock the door, on the pretence that
he might be passing and would look in to say good-
night. It all came out afterwards."

"And was he put in prison?" said Molly.

"No," said grandmother. "The punishments for
housebreaking and such things in those days were
so frightfully severe, that kind-hearted people often

refrained from accusing the wrong-doers. This man had been in sore want of money for some reason or other; he was not a dishonest character. I believe the end of it was that my grandfather forgave him, and put him in the way of doing better."

"That was very nice," said Molly, with a sigh of relief.

"Good-bye," said Ralph, who was just then strapping his books together for school. "Thank you for the story, grandmother. If it is fine this afternoon," he added, "may I stay out later? I want to go a walk into the country."

"Certainly, my boy," said grandmother. "But you'll be home by dinner."

"All right," said Ralph, as he marched off.

"And grandmother, please," said Sylvia, "may Molly and I go out with Marcelline this afternoon to do some shopping? The pretty Christmas things are coming in now, and we have lots to do."

"Certainly, my dears," said grandmother again, and about two o'clock the little girls set off, one on each side of good-natured Marcelline, in high spirits, to do their Christmas shopping.

Grandmother watched them from the window, and thought how pretty they looked, and the thought carried her back to the time — not so very long ago did it seem to her now — when their mother had been just as bright and happy as they — the mother who had never lived to see them more than babies. Grandmother's eyes filled with tears, but she smiled through the tears.

> "God is good and sends new blessings
> When the old He takes away,"

she whispered to herself. It was a blessing, a very
great blessing and pleasure to have what she had so
often longed for, the care of her dear little granddaughters herself.

"And Ralph," she added, "I cannot help feeling
the responsibility with him even greater. An old
woman like me, can I have much influence with a
boy? But he is a dear boy in many ways, and I was
pleased with the way he spoke yesterday. It was
honest and manly. Ah! if we could teach our boys
what *true* manliness is, the world would be a better
place than it is."

The days were beginning to close in now. By
four o'clock or half-past it was almost dark, and, once
the sun had gone down, cold, with a peculiar biting
coldness not felt farther north, where the temperature
is more equable and the contrasts less sudden.

Grandmother put on her fur-lined cloak and set
off to meet the little market-women. Once, twice,
thrice she walked to the corner of the road—they
were not to be seen, and she was beginning to fear
the temptations of the shops had delayed them unduly,
when they suddenly came in view; and the moment
they caught sight of her familiar figure off they set,
as if touched at the same instant by an electric thrill,
running towards her like two lapwings.

"Dear grandmother, how good of you to come to
meet us," said Sylvia. "We have got such nice
things. They are in Marcelline's basket," nodding

back towards Marcelline, jogging along after them in her usual deliberate fashion.

"*Such* nice things," echoed Molly. "But oh, grandmother dear, you don't know what we saw. We met Ralph in the town, and I'm sure he didn't want us to see him, for what *do* you think he was doing?"

A chill went through poor grandmother's heart. In an instant she pictured to herself all manner of scrapes Ralph might have got into. Had her thoughts of him this very afternoon been a sort of presentiment of evil? She grew white, so white that even in the already dusky light, Sylvia's sharp eyes detected it, and she turned fiercely to Molly, the heedless.

"You naughty girl," she said, "to go and frighten dear little grandmother like that. And only this very morning or yesterday grandmother was explaining to you about tact. Don't be frightened, dear grandmother. Ralph wasn't doing anything naughty, only I daresay he didn't want us to see."

"But what *was* he doing?" said grandmother, and Molly, irrepressible still, though on the verge of sobs, made answer before Sylvia could speak.

"He was carrying wood, grandmother dear," she said — "big bundles, and another boy with him too. I think they had been out to the little forests to fetch it. It was fagots. But I *didn't* mean to frighten you, grandmother; I *didn't* know it was untact to tell you — I have been thinking all day about what you told me."

"Carrying wood?" repeated grandmother, relieved, though mystified. "What can he have been doing that for?"

"I think it is a plan of his. I am sure it is nothing naughty," said Sylvia, nodding her head sagely. "And if Molly will just leave it alone and say *nothing* about it, it will be all right, you will see. Ralph will tell you himself, I'm sure, if Molly will not tease."

"I won't, I promise you I won't," said Molly; "I won't say anything about it, and if Ralph asks me if we saw him I'll screw up my lips as tight as tight, and not say a single word."

"As if that would do any good," said Sylvia contemptuously; "it would only make him think we had seen him, and make a fuss. However, there's no fear of Ralph asking you anything about it. You just see him alone when he comes in, grandmother."

"Oh dear, oh dear," sighed Molly, as they returned to the house, "I shall never understand about tact, never. We've got our lessons to do for to-morrow, Sylvia, and the verbs are very hard."

"Never mind, I'll help you," said Sylvia goodnaturedly, and grandmother was pleased to see them go upstairs to their little study with their arms round each other's waists as usual — the best of friends.

Half an hour later, Ralph made his appearance. He looked rather less tidy than his wont — for as a rule Ralph was a particularly tidy boy — his hair was

IN THE COPPICE. — p. 131.

tumbled, and his hands certainly could not have been described as *clean*.

"Well, Ralph, and what have you been doing with yourself?" said grandmother, as he came in.

Ralph threw himself down on the rug.

"My poor rug," thought grandmother, but she judged it wiser not, at that moment, to express her misgivings aloud.

Ralph did not at once reply. Then —

"Grandmother," he said, after a little pause.

"Well, my boy?"

"You remember my calling one of the boys in my class a cad — what Molly began about last night?"

"Well, my boy?" said grandmother again.

"Do you remember what made me call him a cad? It was that I met him carrying a great bundle of wood — little wood they call it — along the street one day. Well, just fancy, grandmother, *I've* been doing it too. That's what I wanted to stay later for this afternoon."

Grandmother's heart gave a bound of pleasure at her boy's frankness. "Sensible child Sylvia is," she said to herself. But aloud she replied with a smile,

"Carrying wood! what did you do that for, and where did you get it?"

"I'll tell you, I'll tell you all about it," said Ralph. "We went out after school to a sort of little coppice where there is a lot of that nice dry brushwood that anybody may take. Prosper knew the place, and

took me. It was to please him I went. He does it
every Thursday; that is the day we are let out of
school early."

"And what does he do it for?" asked grandmother. "Is he — are his people so very poor that
he has to do it? I thought all the boys were of
a better class," she added, with some inward misgiving as to what Mr. Heriott might say as to his son's
present companions.

"Oh, so they are — at least they are not what you
would call poor," said Ralph. "Prosper belongs to
quite rich people. But he's an orphan; he lives
with his uncle, and I suppose he's not rich — Prosper
himself, I mean — for he says his uncle's always telling him to work hard at school, as he will have to
fight his way in the world. He has got a little room
up at the top of the house, and that's what put it into
his head about the wood. There's an old woman,
who was once a sort of a lady, who lives in the next
room to his. You get up by a different stair; it's
really a different house, but once, somehow, the top
rooms were joined, and there's still a door between
Prosper's room and this old woman's, and one morning
early he heard her crying — she was really *crying*,
grandmother, she's so old and shaky, he says — because
she couldn't get her fire to light. He didn't know what
she was crying for at first, but he peeped through the
keyhole and saw her fumbling away with damp paper
and stuff that wouldn't light the big logs. So he
thought and thought what he could do — he hasn't
any money hardly — and at last he thought he'd go

and see what he could find. And he found a *beautiful* place for brushwood, and he carried back all he could, and since then every Thursday he goes out to that place. But, of course, one fellow alone can't carry much, and you should have seen how pleased he was when I said I'd go with him. But I thought I'd better tell you. You don't mind, grandmother?"

Grandmother's eyes looked very bright as she replied. "*Mind*, my Ralph? No, indeed. I am only glad you should have so manly and self-denying an example as Prosper's, and still more glad that you should have the right feeling and moral courage to follow it. Poor old woman! is she quite alone in the world? She must be very grateful to her little next-door neighbour."

"I don't know that she is—at least not so very," said Ralph. "The fun of it was, that for ever so long she didn't know where the little wood came from. Prosper found a key that opened the door, and when she was out he carried in the fagots, and laid the fire all ready for her with some of them; and when she came in he peeped through the key-hole. She was so surprised, she couldn't make it out. And the wood he had fetched lasted a week, and then he got some more. But the next time she found him out."

"And what did she say?"

"At first she was rather offended, till he explained how he had got it; and then she thanked him, of course, but not so very much, I fancy. He always says old people are grumpy—doesn't 'grogneur' mean

grumpy, grandmother?—that they can't help it, and
when his old woman is grumpy he only laughs a little. But *you're* not grumpy, grandmother, and you're
old; at least getting rather old."

"Decidedly old, my boy. But why should I be
grumpy? And how do you know I shouldn't be so
if I were living up alone in an attic, with no children
to love and cheer me, my poor old hands swollen
and twisted with rheumatism, perhaps, and very
little money. Ah, what a sad picture! Poor old
woman, I must try to find out some way of helping
her."

"She washes lace for ladies, Prosper says," said
Ralph, eagerly. "Perhaps if you had some lace to
wash, grandmother."

"I'll see what I can do," said grandmother. "You
get me her name and address from Prosper. And,
Ralph, we might think of something for a little
Christmas present for her, might we not? You must
talk to your friend about it. I suppose his relations
are not likely to interest themselves in his protégée?"

"No," said Ralph. "His aunt is young, and
dresses very grandly, and I don't think she takes
much notice of Prosper himself. Oh no, *you* could
do it much better than any one else, grandmother;
find out all about her and what she would like—in
a nice sort of way, you know."

Grandmother drew Ralph to her and kissed him.
"My own dear boy," she said.

Ralph got rather red, but his eyes shone with
pleasure nevertheless. "Grandmother," he said, half

shyly, "I've had a lesson about not calling fellows cads in a hurry, but all the same you won't forget about telling us the story of Uncle Jack's cad, will you?"

"What a memory you have, Ralph," said grandmother. "You're nearly as bad for stories as Molly. No, I haven't forgotten. As well as I could remember, I have written out the little story — I only wish I had had it in your uncle's own words. But such as it is, I will read it to you all this evening."

Grandmother went to her Davenport, and took out from one of the drawers some sheets of ruled paper, which she held up for Ralph to see. On the outside one he read, in grandmother's neat, clear handwriting, the words —

CHAPTER X.

— "THAT CAD SAWYER."

"I do not like thee, Doctor Fell,
The reason why I cannot tell."
OLD RHYME.

AND grandmother of course kept her promise.
That evening she read it aloud.

"They were Ryeburn boys — Ryeburn boys to
their very heart's core — Jack and his younger brother
Carlo, as somehow he had got to be called in the
nursery, before he could say his own name plainly."

"That's Uncle Charlton, who died when he was
only about fifteen," whispered Sylvia to Ralph and
Molly; "you see grandmother's written it out like a
regular story — not saying 'your uncle this' or 'your
uncle that,' every minute. Isn't it nice?"

Grandmother stopped to see what all the whispering was about.

"We beg your pardon, grandmother, we'll be quite
quiet now," said the three apologetically.

"They had been at school at Ryeburn since they
were quite little fellows, and they thought that nowhere in the world was there a place to be compared
with it. Holidays at home were very delightful, no
doubt, but school-days were delightful too. But for
the sayings of good-byes to the dear people left at
home — father and mother, big sister and little one,
136

I think Jack and Carlo started for their return journey
to school at the end of the midsummer holidays *very*
nearly as cheerfully as they had set off for home eight
weeks previously, when these same delightful holidays had begun. Jack had not very many more half-
years to look forward to: he was to be a soldier, and
before long must leave Ryeburn in preparation for
what was before him, for he was fifteen past. Carlo
was only thirteen and small of his age. He *had*
known what it was to be homesick, even at Ryeburn,
more than three years ago, when he had first come
there. But with a big brother — above all a big
brother like Jack, great strong fellow that he was,
with the kindest of hearts for anything small or weak
— little Carlo's preliminary troubles were soon over.
And now at thirteen he was very nearly, in his way,
as great a man at Ryeburn as Jack himself. Jack
was by no means the cleverest boy at the school, far
from it, but he did his book work fairly well, and
above all honestly. He was honesty itself in everything, scorned crooked ways, or whatever he considered meanness, with the exaggerated scorn of a
very young and untried character, and, like most
boys of his age, was inclined, once he took up a prejudice, to carry it to all lengths.

" There was but one cloud over their return to
school this special autumn that I am telling you of,
and that was the absence of a favourite master — one
of the younger ones — who, an unexpected piece of
good luck having fallen to his share, had left Ryeburn
the end of the last half.

" 'I wonder what sort of a fellow we shall have instead of Wyngate,' said Jack to Carlo, as the train slackened for Ryeburn station.

" 'We shan't have any one as nice, that's certain,' said Carlo, lugubriously. 'There couldn't be any one as nice, could there?'

" But their lamentations over Mr. Wyngate were forgotten when they found themselves in the midst of their companions, most of whom had already arrived. There were such a lot of things to tell and to ask; the unfortunate 'new boys' to glance at with somewhat supercilious curiosity, and the usual legendary caution as to 'chumming' with them, till it should be proved what manner of persons they were; the adventures of the holidays to retail to one's special cronies; the anticipated triumphs in cricket and football and paper-chases of the forthcoming 'half' to discuss. Jack and Carlo soon found themselves each the centre of his particular set, too busy and absorbed in the present to give much thought to the past. Only later that evening, when prayers were over and supper-time at hand, did the subject of their former teacher and his successor come up again.

" A pale, thin, rather starved-looking young man came into the school-room desiring them to put away their books, which they were arranging for next morning. His manner was short but ill-assured, and he spoke with a slightly peculiar accent. None of the boys seemed in any hurry to obey him.

" 'Cod-faced idiot!' muttered one.

" 'French frog!' said another.

"'Is that the new junior?' said Jack, looking up from the pile of books before him.

"'Yes; did you ever see such a specimen?' replied a tall boy beside him, who had arrived the day before. 'And what a fellow to come after Wyngate too.'

"'He can't help his looks,' said Jack quietly; 'perhaps he's better than they are.'

"'Hallo, here's old Berkeley going to stick up for that nice specimen Sawyer!' called out the boy, caring little apparently whether Mr. Sawyer, who had only just left the room, was still within ear-shot or not.

"Jack took it in good part.

"'I'm not "sticking up" for him, nor "not sticking up" for him,' he said. 'All I say is, wait a bit till you see what sort of a fellow he is himself, whatever his looks are.'

"'And most assuredly they're *not* in his favour,' replied the tall boy.

"From this Jack could not honestly dissent; Mr. Sawyer's looks were not, in a sense, in his favour. It was not so much that he was downright ugly — perhaps that would have mattered less — but he was *poor* looking. He had no presence, no self-assertion, and his very anxiety to conciliate gave his manner a nervous indecision, in which the boys saw nothing but cause for ridicule. He did not understand his pupils, and still less did they understand him. But all the same he was a capital teacher, patient and painstaking to the last degree, clear-headed himself,

and with a great power, when he forgot his nervousness in the interest of his subject, of making it clear
to the apprehensions of those about him. In class
it was impossible for the well-disposed of his pupils
not to respect him, and in time he might have fought
his way to more, but for one unfortunate circumstance — the unreasonable and unreasoning prejudice
against him throughout the whole school.

" Now our boys — Jack and Carlo — Jack, followed
by Carlo, perhaps I should say, for whatever Jack
said Carlo thought right, wherever Jack led Carlo
came after — to do them justice, I must say, did not
at once give in to this unreasonable prejudice. Jack
stuck to his resolution to judge Sawyer by what he
found him to be on further acquaintance, not to fly
into a dislike at first sight. And for some time nothing occurred to shake Jack's opinion that not im-
probably the new master was better than his looks.
But Sawyer was shy and reserved; he liked Jack,
and was in his heart grateful to him for his respectful
and friendly behaviour, and for the good example
he thereby set to his companions, only, unfortunately,
the junior master was no hand at expressing his
appreciation of such conduct. Unfortunately too,
Jack's lessons were not his strong point, and Mr.
Sawyer, for all his nervousness, was so rigorously, so
scrupulously honest that he found it impossible to
pass by without comment some or much of Jack's
unsatisfactory work. And Jack, though so honest
himself, was human, and *boy*-human, and it was not
in boy-human nature to remain perfectly unaffected

by the remarks called forth by the new master's frequent fault-finding.

"'It's just that you're too civil to him by half,' his companions would say. 'He's a mean sneak, and thinks he can bully you without your resenting it. *Wynyate* would never have turned back those verses.'

"Or it would be insinuated how partial Sawyer was to little Castlefield, 'just because he's found out that Castle's father's so rich'—the truth being that little Castlefield, a delicate and precocious boy, was the cleverest pupil in the school, his tasks always faultlessly prepared, and his power of taking in what he was taught wonderfully great, though, fortunately for himself, his extreme good humour and merry nature made it impossible for his companions to dislike him or set him down as a prig.

"Jack laughed and pretended—believed indeed —that he did not care.

"'I don't want him to say my verses are good if they're not good,' he maintained stoutly. But all the same he did feel, and very acutely too, the mortification to which more than once Mr. Sawyer's uncompromising censure exposed him, little imagining that the fault-finding was far more painful to the teacher than to himself, that the short, unsympathising manner in which it was done was actually the result of the young man's tender-hearted reluctance to cause pain to another, and that other the very boy to whom of all in the school he felt himself most attracted.

"And from this want of understanding his master's real feelings towards him arose the first cloud of prejudice to dim Jack's reasonable judgment.

"Now at Ryeburn, as was in those days the case at all schools of old standing, there were legends, so established and respected that no one ever dreamed of calling them into question; there were certain customs tolerated, not to say approved of, which yet, regarded impartially, from the outside as it were, were open to objection. Among these, of which there were several, were one or two specially concerning the younger boys, which came under the junior master's direction, and of them all, none was more universally practised than the feat of what was called 'jumping the bar.' The 'bar' — short in reality for 'barrier' — was a railing of five or six feet high, placed so as to prevent any of the junior boys, who were late in the morning, from getting round by a short cut to the chapel, where prayers were read, the proper entrance taking them round the whole building, a matter of at least two minutes' quick walking. Day after day the bar was 'jumped,' day after day the fact was ignored; on no boy's conscience, however sensitive, would the knowledge of his having made his way into chapel by this forbidden route have left any mark. But alas, when Mr. Sawyer came, things struck him in a different light.

"I cannot go into the question of how far he was wrong and how far right. He meant well, of that there is no doubt, but as to his judiciousness in the matter, that is another affair altogether. He had never been at a great English school before; he was conscientious to the last degree, but inexperienced. And I, being only an old woman, and never having been at school at all, do not feel myself able to give an opinion upon this or many other matters of which I, like poor Mr. Sawyer, have no experience. I can only, children, 'tell the tale as 'twas told to me,' and not even that, for the telling to me was by an actor in the little drama, and I cannot feel, therefore, that in this case the 'tale will gain by the telling,' but very decidedly the other way.

"To return, however, to the bar-jumping — of all the boys who made a practice of it, no one did so more regularly than Carlo, 'Berkeley minor.' He was not a lazy boy in the morning; many and many a time he would have been quite soon enough in the chapel had he gone round the proper way; but it became almost a habit with him to take the nominally forbidden short cut — so much a habit that Mr. Wyngate, who was perfectly aware of it, said to him jokingly one day, that he would take it as a personal favour, if, *for once*, Carlo would gratify him by coming to chapel by the regular entrance. As for being *blamed* for his bar-jumping, such an idea never entered Carlo's head; he would almost as soon have expected to be blamed for eating his breakfast, and, naturally enough, when Mr. Sawyer's reign began, it never occurred to him to alter his conduct. For some time things went on as usual, Mr. Sawyer either never happening to see Carlo's daily piece of gymnastics, or not understanding that it was prohibited.

But something occurred at last, some joke on the subject, or some little remark from one of the other masters, which suddenly drew the new 'junior's' attention to the fact. And two or three mornings afterwards, coming upon Carlo in the very act of bar-jumping, Mr. Sawyer ventured mildly, but in reality firmly, to remonstrate.

"'Berkeley,' he said, in his nervous, jerky fashion, 'that is not the *proper* way from your schoolroom to chapel, is it?'

"Carlo took this remark as a good joke, after the manner of Mr. Wyngate's on the same subject.

"'No, sir,' he replied mischievously, 'I don't suppose it is.'

"'Then,' said Mr. Sawyer, stammering a very little, as he sometimes did when more nervous than usual, 'then will you oblige me for the future by coming the proper way?'

"He turned away before Carlo had time to reply, if indeed he had an answer ready, which is doubtful, for he could not make up his mind if Mr. Sawyer was in earnest or not. But by the next morning all remembrance of the junior master's remonstrance had faded from Carlo's thoughtless brain. Again he went bar-jumping to chapel, and this time no Mr. Sawyer intercepted him. But two mornings later, just as he had successfully accomplished his jump, he perceived in front of him the thin, uncertain-looking figure of the junior master.

"'Berkeley,' he said gravely, 'have you forgotten what I said to you two or three days ago?'

"Carlo stared. The fact of the matter was that he *had* forgotten, but as his remembering would have made no difference, considering that he had never had the slightest intention of taking any notice of Mr. Sawyer's prohibition, his instinctive honesty forbade his giving his want of memory as an excuse.

"'No,' he replied, 'at least I don't know if I did or not. But I have always come this way — lots of us do — and no one ever says anything.'

"'But *I* say something now,' said Mr. Sawyer, more decidedly than he had ever been known to speak, 'and that is to forbid your coming this way. And I expect to be obeyed.'

"Carlo made no reply. This time there was no mistaking Mr. Sawyer's meaning. It was mortifying to have to give in to the 'mean little sneak,' as Carlo mentally called the new master; still, as next morning he happened to be in particularly good time he went round the proper way. The day after, however, he was late, decidedly late for once, and, throwing to the winds all consideration for Mr. Sawyer or his orders, Carlo jumped the bar and made his appearance in time for prayers. He had not known that he was observed, but coming out of chapel Mr. Sawyer called him aside.

"'Berkeley,' he said, 'you have disobeyed me again. 'If this happens once more I shall be obliged to report you.'

"Carlo stared at him in blank amazement.

"'Report me?' he said. Such a threat had never, been held out to either him or Jack through all their

Ryeburn career. They looked upon it as next worst to being expelled. For reporting in Ryeburn parlance meant a formal complaint to the head-master, when a boy had been convicted of aggravated disobedience to the juniors. And its results were very severe; it entirely prevented a boy's in any way distinguishing himself during the half-year: however hard a 'reported' boy might work, he could gain no prize that term. So no wonder that poor Carlo repeated in amazement,

" ' *Report* me?'

" ' Yes,' said Sawyer. 'I don't want to do it, but if you continue to disobey me, I must,' and he turned away.

" Off went Carlo to his cronies with his tale of wrongs. The general indignation was extreme.

" ' I'd like to see him dare to do such a thing,' said one.

" ' I'd risk it, Berkeley, if I were you,' said another. 'Anything rather than give in to such a cowardly sneak.'

" In the midst of the discussion up came Jack, to whom, with plenty of forcible language, his brother's woes were related. Jack's first impulse was to discredit the sincerity of Mr. Sawyer's intention.

" ' He'd never *dare* do such a thing as report you for nothing worse than bar-jumping,' he exclaimed.

" But Carlo shook his head.

" ' He's mean enough for anything,' he replied. ' I believe he'll do it fast enough if ever he catches me bar-jumping again.'

"'Well, you'll have to give it up then,' said Jack. 'It's no use hurting yourself to spite him,' and as Carlo made no reply, the elder brother went away, satisfied that his, it must be confessed, not very exalted line of argument, had had the desired effect.

"But Carlo's silence did *not* mean either consent or assent. When Jack had left them the younger boys talked the whole affair over again in their own fashion and according to their own lights — the result being that the following morning, with the aggravation of a whoop and a cry, Carlo defiantly jumped the bar on his way to chapel for prayers.

"When Jack came to hear of it, as he speedily did, he was at first very angry, then genuinely distressed.

"'You will only get what you deserve if he does report you,' he said to Carlo in his vexation, and when Carlo replied that he didn't see that he need give up what he had always done 'for a cad like that,' Jack retorted that if he thought Sawyer a cad he should have acted accordingly, and not trusted to *his* good feeling or good nature. But in his heart of hearts Jack did not believe the threat would be carried out, and, unknown to Carlo, he did for his brother what he would never have done for himself. As soon as morning school was over he went to Mr. Sawyer to beg him to reconsider his intention, explaining to the best of his ability the extenuating circumstances of the case — the tacit indulgence so long accorded to the boys, Carlo's innocence, in the first place, of any intentional disobedience.

"Mr. Sawyer heard him patiently; whether his arguments would have had any effect, Jack, at that time at least, had not the satisfaction of knowing, for when he left off speaking Mr. Sawyer replied quietly,

"'I am very sorry to seem severe to your brother, Berkeley, but what I have done I believed to be my duty. I have *already* reported him.'

"Jack turned on his heel and left the room without speaking. Only as he crossed the threshold one word of unutterable contempt fell from between his teeth. '*Cad*,' he muttered, careless whether Sawyer heard him or not.

"And from that moment Jack's championship of the obnoxious master was over; and throughout the school he was never spoken of among the boys, big and little, but as 'that cad Sawyer.'

"Though, after all, the 'reporting' turned out less terrible than was expected. How it was managed I cannot exactly say, but Carlo was let off with a reprimand, and new and rigorous orders were issued against 'bar-jumping' under any excuse whatever.

"I think it probable that the 'authorities' privately pointed out to Mr. Sawyer that there might be such a thing as over-much zeal in the discharge of his duties, and if so I have no doubt he took it in good part. For it was not zeal which actuated him — it was simple conscientiousness, misdirected perhaps by his inexperience. He could not endure hurting any one or anything, and probably his very knowledge of his weakness made him afraid of himself. Be that

as it may, no one concerned rejoiced more heartily
than he at Carlo's acquittal.

"But it was too late — the mischief was done.
Day by day the exaggerated prejudice and suspicion
with which he was regarded became more apparent.
Yet he did not resent it — he worked on, hoping that
in time it might be overcome, for he yearned to be
liked and trusted, and his motives for wishing to do
well at Ryeburn were very strong ones.

"And gradually, as time went on, things improved
a little. Now and then the better-disposed of the boys
felt ashamed of the tacit disrespect with which one so
enduring and inoffensive was treated; and among
these better-disposed I need hardly say was our Jack.

"It was the end of October. But a few days were
wanting to the anniversary so dear to schoolboy
hearts — that of Gunpowder Plot. This year the
fifth of November celebration was to be of more than
ordinary magnificence, for it was the last at which
several of the elder boys, among them Jack, could
hope to be present. Fireworks committees were
formed and treasurers appointed, and nothing else
was spoken of but the sums collected and promised,
and the apportionment thereof in Catherine wheels,
Chinese dragons, and so on. Jack was one of the
treasurers. He had been very successful so far, but
the sum total on which he and his companions had
set their hearts was still unattained. The elder boys
held a committee meeting one day to consider ways
and means, and the names of all the subscribers were
read out.

"'We *should* manage two pounds more; we'd do then,' said one boy.

"'Are you sure everybody's been asked?' said another, running his eye down the lists. 'Bless me, Sawyer's not in,' he added, looking up inquiringly.

"'No one would ask him,' said the first boy, shrugging his shoulders.

"A sudden thought struck Jack.

"'I'll tell you what, *I'll* do it,' he said, 'and, between ourselves, I shouldn't much wonder if he comes down handsomely. He's been very civil of late — I rather think he'd be glad of an opportunity to do something obliging to make up for that mean trick of his about Carlo, and what's more,' he added mysteriously, 'I happen to know he's by no means short of funds just now.'

"They teased him to say more, but not another word on the subject could be got out of Jack. What he knew was this — that very morning when the letters came, he had happened to be standing beside Mr. Sawyer, who, with an eager face, opened one that was handed to him. He was nervous as usual, more nervous than usual probably, and perhaps his hands were shaking, for as he drew his letter hastily out of the envelope, something fluttered to the ground at Jack's feet.

"It was a cheque for twenty pounds, and conspicuous on the lowest line was the signature of a well-known publishing firm. Instinctively Jack stooped to pick it up and handed it to its owner — it had been impossible for him not to see what he did, but he had thought no more about it, beyond a passing wonder in his own mind, as to 'what on earth Sawyer got to write about,' and had forgotten all about it till the meeting of the fireworks committee recalled it to his memory.

" But it was with a feeling of pleasant expectancy, not unmixed with some consciousness of his own magnanimity in 'giving old Sawyer a chance again,' that Jack made his way to the junior master's quarters, the list of subscribers in his hand.

" He made a pleasant picture, as, in answer to the ' come in ' which followed the knock at the door, he opened it and stood on the threshold of Mr. Sawyer's room — his bright, honest, blue-eyed, fair-haired ' English boy' face smiling in through the doorway. With almost painful eagerness the junior master bade him welcome; he liked Jack so much, and would so have rejoiced could the attraction have been mutual. And this was the first time that Jack had voluntarily sought Mr. Sawyer in his own quarters since the bar-jumping affair. Mr. Sawyer's spirits rose at the sight of him, and hope again entered his heart — hope that after all, his position at Ryeburn, which he was beginning to fear it was nonsense to attempt to retain, in face of the evident dislike to him, might yet alter for the better.

" 'I have not a good way with them — that must be it,' he had said to himself sadly that very morning. ' I never knew what it was to be a boy myself, and therefore I suppose I don't understand boys. But if they could but see into my heart and read there how earnestly I wish to do my best by them, surely we could get on better together.'

"'Well, Berkeley — glad to see you — what can I do for you?' said Sawyer, with a little nervous attempt at off-hand friendliness of manner, in itself infinitely touching to any one with eyes to take in the whole situation and judge it and him accordingly. But those eyes are not ours in early life, more especially in *boy*-life. We must have our powers of mental vision quickened and cleared by the magic dew of sad experience — experience which alone can give sympathy worth having, ere we can understand the queer bits of pathos we constantly stumble upon in life, ere we can begin to judge our fellows with the large-hearted charity that alone can illumine the glass through which for so long we see so *very* 'darkly.'

"'I have come to ask you for a subscription for the fifth of November fireworks, Mr. Sawyer,' said Jack, plunging, as was his habit, right into the middle of things, with no beating about the bush. 'We've asked all the other masters, and every one in the school has subscribed, and I was to tell you, sir, from the committee that they'll be very much obliged by a subscription — and — and I really think they'll all be particularly pleased if you can give us something handsome.'

"The message was civil, but hardly perhaps, coming from pupils to a master, 'of the most respectful,' as French people say. But poor Sawyer understood it — in some respects his perceptions were

almost abnormally sharp; he read between the lines
of Jack's rough-and-ready, boy-like manner, and
understood perfectly that here was a chance for him
— a chance in a thousand, of gaining some degree of
the popularity he had hitherto so unfortunately failed
to obtain. And to the bottom of his heart he felt
grateful to Berkeley — but alas!

" He grew crimson with vexation.

" 'I am dreadfully sorry, Berkeley,' he said, 'dreadfully sorry that I cannot respond as I would like to
your request. At this moment unfortunately, I am
very peculiarly out of pocket. Stay.' — with a
momentary gleam of hope, ' will you let me see the
subscription list. How — how much do you think
would please the boys?'

" 'A guinea wouldn't be — would please them very
much, and of course two would be still better,' said
Jack drily. Already he had in his own mind pronounced a final verdict upon Mr. Sawyer, already he
had begun to tell himself what a fool he had been
for having anything more to do with him, but yet,
with the British instinct of giving an accused man a
fair chance, he waited till all hope was over.

" 'A guinea, two guineas!' repeated Mr. Sawyer
sadly. ' It is perfectly impossible;' and he shook
his head regretfully but decidedly. ' Half-a-crown,
or five shillings perhaps, if you would take it,' he
added hesitatingly, but stopped short on catching
sight of the hard, contemptuous expression that overspread Jack's face, but a moment ago so sunny.

" 'No thank you, sir,' he replied. ' I should be

very sorry to take *any* subscription from you, knowing what I do, and so would all my companions.
You're a master, sir, and I'm a boy, but I can tell
you I wish you *were* a boy that I might speak out.
I couldn't help seeing what came to you by post this
morning — you know I couldn't — and yet on the
face of that you tell me you're too hard-up to do
what I came to ask like a gentleman — and what
would have been for your good in the end too. I'm
not going to tell what came to my knowledge by
accident; you needn't be afraid of that, but I'd be
uncommonly sorry to take *anything* from you for our
fireworks.'

" And again Jack turned on his heel, and in hot
wrath left the under-master, muttering again between
his set teeth as he did so the one word 'cad.'

"'Jack,' Mr. Sawyer called after him, but either
he did not call loud enough or Jack would not take
any notice of his summons, for he did not return.
What a pity! Had he done so, Mr. Sawyer, who
understood him too well to feel the indignation a
more superficial person would have done at his
passionate outburst, had it in his heart to take the
hasty, impulsive, generous-spirited lad into his confidence and what might not have been the result?
What a different future for the poor under-master,
had he then and there and for ever won from the
boy the respect and sympathy he so well deserved!

" Jack returned to his companions gloomy but
taciturn. He gave them to understand that his
mission had failed, and that henceforth he would

have nothing to say to Sawyer that he could help, and that was all. He entered into no particulars, but there are occasions on which silence says more than words, and from this time no voice was ever raised in the junior master's defence — throughout the school he was never referred to except as 'the cad,' or 'that cad Sawyer.'

"And alone in his own room, Mr. Sawyer, sorrowful but unresentful still, was making up his mind that his efforts had been all in vain. 'I must give it up,' he said. 'And both for myself and the boys the sooner the better, before there is any overt disrespect which would *have* to be noticed. It is no use fighting on. I have not the knack of it. The boys will never like me, and I may do harm where I would wish to do good. I must try something else.'

"Two or three weeks later — a month perhaps — the boys were one day surprised by the appearance of a strange face at what had been Mr. Sawyer's desk. And on inquiry the new comer proved to be a young curate accidentally in the neighbourhood, who had undertaken to fill for a few weeks the under-master's vacant place. The occurrence made some sensation — it was unusual for any change of the kind to take place during a term. 'Was Sawyer ill?' one or two of the boys asked, as there came before them the recollection of the young man's pale and careworn face, and they recalled with some compunction the Pariah-like life that for some time past had been his.

"No, he was not ill, they were informed, but he had requested the head-master to supply his place and let him leave, for private reasons, as soon as possible.

"What were the private reasons? The head-master and his colleagues had tried in vain to arrive at them. Not one syllable of complaint had fallen from the junior master's lips. He had simply re-peated that, though sorry to cause any inconvenience, it was of importance to him to leave at once.

"'At least,' he said to himself, 'I shall say nothing to get any of them into trouble after I am gone.'

"And he had begged, too, that no public intimation of his resignation should be given.

"But one or two of the boys had known it before it actually occurred — and among them the Berkeley brothers. Late one cold evening, for winter had set in very early that year, Mr. Sawyer had stopped them on their way across the courtyard to their own rooms.

"'Berkeley,' he had said, 'I am leaving early to-morrow morning. I should like to say good-bye and shake hands with you before I go. I have not taken a good way with you boys, somehow, and — and the prejudice against me has been very strong. But some day — when you are older perhaps, you may come to think it possible you have misunderstood me. Be that as it may, there is not and never has been any but good feeling towards you on my part.'

"He held out his hand, but a spirit of evil had taken possession of Jack — a spirit of hard, unforgiv-ing prejudice.

"'Good-bye, Mr. Sawyer,' he said, but he stalked on

without taking any notice of the out-stretched hand, and Carlo, echoing the cold 'Good-bye, Mr. Sawyer,' followed his example.

"But little Carlo's heart was very tender. He slept ill that night, and early, very early the next morning he was up and on the watch. There was snow on the ground, snow, though December had scarcely set in, and it was very cold.

" Carlo shivered as he hung about the door leading to Mr. Sawyer's room, and he wondered why the fly which always came for passengers by the early London train had not yet made its appearance, little imagining that not by the comfortable express, but third class in a slow 'parliamentary' Mr. Sawyer's journey was to be accomplished. And, when at last the thin figure of the under-master emerged from the doorway, it went to the boy's heart to see that he himself was carrying the small black bag which held his possessions.

" ' I have come to wish you good-bye again, sir,' said Carlo, 'and I am sorry I didn't shake hands last night. And — and — I believe Jack would have come too, if he'd thought of it.'

" Mr. Sawyer's eyes glistened as he shook the small hand held out to him.

" 'Thank you, my boy,' he said earnestly, 'how much I thank you you will never know.'

" 'And is that all your luggage?' asked Carlo, half out of curiosity, half by way of breaking the melancholy of the parting, which somehow gave him a choky feeling about the throat.

"'Oh no,' said Mr. Sawyer, entering into the boy's shrinking from anything like a scene, 'oh no, I sent on my box by the carrier last Saturday. It would have been *rather* too big to carry.' He spoke in his usual commonplace tone, more cheerful, less nervous perhaps than its wont. Then once more, with a second hearty shake of the hand,

"'Good-bye again, my boy, and God bless you.' And Carlo, his eyes dim in spite of his intense determination to be above such weakness, stood watching the dark figure, conspicuous against the white-sheeted ground and steel-blue early morning winter sky.

"'I wonder if we've been right about him,' he said to himself. 'I'm glad I came, any way.'

"And there came a day when others beside little Carlo himself were glad, oh so glad, that he had 'come' that snowy morning to bid the solitary traveller God-speed."

"Good-bye again, my Boy, and God bless you!" — p. 158.

CHAPTER XI.

"THAT CAD SAWYER." — PART II.

"Did the road wind uphill all the way?
Yes to the very end."
CHRISTINA ROSSETTI.

GRANDMOTHER'S voice had faltered a little now and then during the latter part of her reading. The children looked at each other significantly.

" Uncle Carlo *died* you know," whispered Sylvia again to Ralph and Molly.

" And uncle Jack too," said Ralph.

" Yes, but much longer after. Uncle *Carlo* was only a boy when he died," said Molly, as if the fact infinitely aggravated the sorrow in his case.

Their whispering did not interrupt their grandmother this time. She had already paused.

" I think, dears," she said, " I had better read the rest to-morrow evening. There is a good deal more of it, and my voice gets tired after a while."

" Couldn't I read it for you, mother dear?" said aunty.

Grandmother smiled a little rougishly. " No, my dear, thank you," she said. " I think I like best to read myself what I have written myself. And you, according to that, will have your turn soon, Laura."

159

"*Mother!* how did you find out what I was doing?" exclaimed aunty.

"A little bird told me, of course," said grandmother, smiling. "You know how clever my little birds are."

During this mysterious conversation the children had sat with wide open eyes and puzzled faces. Suddenly a light broke upon Sylvia.

"I know, I know," she cried. "*Aunty's* writing a story for us too. Oh, you delightful aunty!"

"Oh you beautiful aunty! oh you delicious aunty!" echoed Molly. "Why don't you say something too, Ralph?" she exclaimed, turning reproachfully to her brother. "You like stories just as much as we do —you know you do."

"But you and Sylvia have used up all the adjectives," said Ralph. "What *can* I call aunty, unless I say she's a very jolly fellow?"

"Reserve your raptures, my dears," said aunty, "'The proof of the pudding's in the eating,' remember. Perhaps you may not care for my story when you hear it. I am quite willing to wait for your thanks till you have heard it."

"But any way, aunty dear, we'll thank you for having *tried*," said Molly encouragingly. "I daresay it won't be *quite* as nice as grandmother's. You see you're so much younger, and then I don't think anybody *could* tell stories like her, could they? But, grandmother dear," she went on, "would you mind telling me one thing? When people write stories how do they know all the things they tell? How do

you know what poor Mr. Sawyer said to himself
when he was alone in his room that day? Did he
ever tell anybody? I know the story's true, because
uncle Jack told it you himself, only I can't make
out how you got to know all those bits of it, like."

"What a goose you are, Molly!" exclaimed both
Ralph and Sylvia. "How could any stories ever be
written if people went on about them like that?"

But Molly's honest puzzled face made grandmother
smile.

"I know how you mean, dear," she said, "I used
to think like that myself. No, I don't know *exactly*
the very words Mr. Sawyer said to himself, but,
judging from my knowledge of the whole story, I put
myself, as it were, in his place, and picture to myself
what I would have said. I told you I had altered it
a little. When your uncle wrote it out it was all
in the first person, but not having been an eye-witness,
as he was, it seemed to me I could better give the
spirit of the story by putting it into this form. Do
you understand at all better, dear? When you have
heard the whole to the end you will do so, I think.
All the part about Carlo I had from his own lips."

"Thank you, grandmother dear. I think I understand," said Molly, and she was philosophical enough
to take no notice of the repeated whisper which
reached her ears alone, "Oh, you *are* a goose!"

It was not till the next evening that grandmother
went on with the second part of her story.

"What do all those stars mean?" asked Molly,
peeping over her grandmother's shoulder before she

began to read. "Look Sylvia, how funny!" and she pointed to a long row of   *   *   *   * at the end of the first part of the manuscript.

"They mean that some length of time has elapsed between the two parts of the story," said grandmother.

"Oh, I see. And each star counts for a year, I suppose. Let me see; one, two, three —"

"Molly, *do* be quiet, and let grandmother go on," said Ralph and Sylvia, their patience exhausted.

"No, they are not counted like that," said grandmother. "Listen, Molly, and you will hear for yourself."

"The first part of my little story finished in the snow — on a cold December morning in England. The second part begins in a very different scene and many, many miles away from Ryeburn. Three or four years have passed. Some of those we left boys are now men — many changes have taken place. Instead of December, it is August. Instead of England we have a far-away country, which till that time, when the interest of the whole world was suddenly concentrated on it, had been but little known and still less thought of by the dwellers in more civilised lands. It is the Crimea, children, and the Crimea on a broiling, stifling August day. At the present time when we speak and think of that dreadful war and the sufferings it entailed, it is above all the *winters* there that we recall with the greatest horror — those terrible 'Crimean winters.' But those who went through it all have often assured me that the

miseries of the summers — of some part of them at
least — were in their way quite as great, or worse.
What could be much worse? The suffocating heat:
the absence, or almost total absence, of shade; the
dust and the dirt, and the poisonous flies; the foul
water and half-putrid food? Bad for the sound ones,
or those as yet so — and oh, how intolerably dreadful
for the sick!

" 'What could be much worse?' thought Jack
Berkeley to himself, as after a long killing spell in
the trenches he at last got back to his tent for a few
hours' rest.

" 'My own mother wouldn't know me,' he said to
himself, as out of a sort of half melancholy mischief
he glanced at his face in the little bit of cracked
looking-glass which was all he had to adorn himself
by. He was feeling utterly worn out and depressed
— so many of his friends and companions were dead
or dying — knocked down at that time quite as much
by disease as by Russian bullets — in many cases the
more terrible death of the two. And things in general
were looking black. It was an anxious and weariful
time.

" Jack threw himself on the bed. He was too
tired to undress. All he longed for was coolness and
sleep — the first the less attainable of the two, for the
thin sides of his tent were as powerless to keep out
the scorching heat as the biting cold, and it was not
till many more months of both heat and cold had
passed that any better shelter was provided for him
or his fellows.

"But heat and flies notwithstanding Jack fell asleep, and had slept soundly for an hour or two when he was suddenly awakened by a voice calling him by name.

"'Berkeley,' it said, 'you are Berkeley of the 300th, aren't you? I am sorry to awaken you if you're not, but I couldn't see your servant about anywhere to ask. There's a poor fellow dying, down at Kadikoi, asking for Berkeley — Jack Berkeley of the 300th.'

"'Yes, that's me,' said Jack, rubbing his eyes with his smoke-begrimed hands, which he had neither had energy nor water to wash before he fell asleep. 'That's me, sure enough. Who is it? What does he want?'

"'I don't know who he is,' replied the other. 'I didn't hear his name. He's not one of us. He's a poor devil who's out here as a correspondent to some paper — I forget which — he's only been out a short time. He's dying of dysentery — quite alone, near our quarters. I'm Montagu of the 25th Hussars — Captain Montagu, and our doctor, who's looking after him, sent in for me, knowing I'd been at Rye-burn, as the poor fellow said something about it. But it must have been after my time. I left in '48.'

"'I don't think I remember you,' said Jack meditatively. 'But you may have been among the upper boys when I was one of the small ones.'

"'Sure to have been,' said Captain Montagu. 'But about this poor fellow. He was so disappointed when he found I was a stranger to him that I said

I'd try to find some other Ryeburn boy who might remember him. And some one or other mentioned you, so I came over to look you up.'

"'Very good of you,' said Jack, who was still, however, feeling so sleepy that he could almost have wished Captain Montagu had *not* been so good. 'Shall I go back with you to Kadikoi? Very likely it's some one I did not know either, still one can but try.'

"'You're very tired,' said Montagu, sympathisingly. 'I am sorry to give you such a long walk. But the doctor said he couldn't last long, and the poor fellow seemed so eager when he heard your name.'

"'Oh, he *does* know me then?' said Jack, his interest reviving. 'I didn't understand.'

"'Oh yes. I mentioned your name when I heard it, and he said at once if it was *Jack* Berkeley he would extremely like to see him. It was stupid of me not to ask his name.'

"'I'll be ready to go with you in a moment,' said Jack, after frantic efforts discovering in a bucket a very small reserve of water with which he managed to wash his face clear of some part of its grimy covering. 'My servant's gone to Balaclava to see what he could get in the way of food for a change from these dreadful salt rations. He brought me a bottle of porter the other day; it cost three shillings, but I never enjoyed anything so much in my life.'

"'I can quite believe it,' said Captain Montagu feelingly. 'Your servant must be worth his weight in gold.'

"In another minute they were on their way. The sun was beginning to sink, fortunately; it was not *quite* so hot as a few hours previously. But it was quite as dusty, and the walking along a recently and roughly made track, not worthy the name of road, was very tiring. It was fully five miles to Kadikoi — five miles across a bare, dried-up country, from which all traces of the scanty cultivation it had ever received were fast disappearing under the present state of things. There was not a tree, hardly a stunted shrub, to be seen, and the ground — at best but a few inches of poor soil above the sterile rock, felt hard and unyielding as well as rough. It was a relief of its kind at last to quit the level ground for the slope leading down to Balaclava, where, though they were too small to afford anything in the shape of shade, the sight of some few, starved-looking bushes and some remains of what might once have been grass, refreshed the eye, at once wearied and dazzled by the glare and monotony of the sun-dried plain.

"The tent to which Captain Montagu led the way stood by itself on some rising ground, a little behind the row of nondescript hovels or mud huts representing what had been the little hamlet of Kadikoi. It looked wretched enough as the two young men made their way in, but everywhere looked wretched, only the bareness and comfortlessness impressed one doubly when viewed in connection with physical suffering that would have been hard to endure even with all the alleviations and tenderness of friends and home about one.

"The doctor was just leaving the tent—his time was all too precious to give much of it where it was evident that his skill could be of no avail—but before going he had done what he could for the sick man's comfort, and he lay now, pale, worn, and wan, but no longer in pain, and by the bedside—a low narrow camp stretcher—sat a young soldier, holding from time to time a cup of water to the dry lips of the dying man. Clumsy he might be, but there was no lack of tenderness in his manner or expression.

"'That's one of our men that the doctor sent in,' whispered Montagu; 'the poor fellow there had been lying alone for two or three days, and no one knew. His Greek servant—scoundrels those fellows are—had deserted him.'

"Jack cautiously approached the bed.

"'This is Mr. Berkeley—Jack Berkeley of the 300th, whom you said you would like to see,' said Captain Montagu gently, stepping in front of Jack.

"The sick man's eyes lightened up, and a faint flush rose in his cheeks. He was very fair, and lying there looked very young, younger somehow than Jack had expected. *Had* he ever seen him before? There was nothing remarkable about the face except its peculiarly gentle and placid expression—yet it was a face of considerable resolution as well, and there were lines about the mouth which told of endurance and fortitude, almost contradicting the wistfulness of the boyish-looking blue eyes. Jack grew more and more puzzled. *Something* seemed familiar to him, yet—

" ' How good, how very good of you to come. Do
you remember me, Berkeley?' said the invalid, feebly
stretching out a thin hand, which Jack instinctively
took and held gently in his own strong grasp.

" Jack hesitated. A look of disappointment overspread the pale face.

" 'I am afraid you don't know me. Perhaps you
would not have come if you had understood who it was.'

" 'I did not hear your name,' said Jack, very gently,
' but, of course, hearing you wished to see me —' he
hesitated. 'Were we at Ryeburn together?'

" 'Yes,' said the dying man. 'My — my name is
Sawyer — Philip Sawyer — but you only knew my
surname, of course.'

" Jack understood it all. Even before the name
was mentioned, the slight nervous stammer, the faint
peculiarity of accent, had recalled to his memory the
poor young junior master, whose short, apparently
unsuccessful, Ryeburn career had left its mark on the
lives of others besides his own.

" *Jack* understood — not so the sick man. He was
surprised and almost bewildered by the eagerness with
which his visitor received his announcement.

" 'Sawyer, Mr. Sawyer!' he exclaimed. 'You cannot imagine how glad I am to see you again. I don't
mean — I am terribly sorry to see you like this — but
I have so often wished to find you, and I could never
succeed in doing so.'

" He turned as he spoke to Captain Montagu.

" 'I'll stay with him for an hour or two — as long
as I can,' he said. 'I think, —' he added, glancing

at the extempore sick-nurse, and hesitating a little.
Captain Montagu understood the glance.

" ' Come, Watson,' he said to the young soldier,
' Mr. Berkeley will sit with — with Mr. — '

" ' Sawyer,' said Jack.

— " ' With Mr. Sawyer for a while. Shall he return
in an hour, Berkeley?'

" ' Thank you, yes,' said Jack, and then he found
himself alone with his old master.

" ' You said you tried to trace me after I left Ryeburn,' said Sawyer. ' Will you tell me why? There
was no special reason for it, was there? I know I
was disliked, but the sort of enmity I incurred must
soon have died out. I was too insignificant for it to
last. And the one great endeavour I made was to
injure no one. That was why I left hurriedly —
before I should be forced to make any complaints.'

" He stopped — exhausted already by what he had
said. ' And I have so much to say to him,' he whispered regretfully to himself.

" ' I know,' said Jack sadly. 'I understood it all
before you had left many months.'

" Mr. Sawyer looked pleased but surprised.

" ' It is very kind of you to speak so,' he said. ' I
remember that dear little brother of yours when he
came to see me off that last morning — I remember
his saying, ' I'm sure Jack would have come if he had
thought of it.' You don't know what a comfort the
remembrance of that boy has been to me sometimes.
You must tell him so. Dear me — he must be nearly
grown up. Is he too in the army?'

" 'No, oh no,' said Jack. 'He — he died the year after you knew him.'

"Sawyer's eyes looked up wistfully in Jack's face. 'Dead?' he said. 'That dear boy?'

" 'Yes,' Jack went on. 'It was of scarlet fever. It was very bad at Ryeburn that half. We both had it, but I was soon well again. It was not till Carlo was ill that he told me of having run over to wish you good-bye that morning — he had been afraid I would laugh at him for being soft-hearted — what a young brute I was — forgive my speaking so, Sawyer, but I can't look back to that time without shame. What a life we led you, and how you bore it! You were too good for us.'

"Sawyer smiled. 'No,' he said. 'I cannot see it that way. I had not the knack of it — I was not fit for the position. The boys were very good boys, as boys go. It would have been inexcusable of me to have made them suffer for what, after all, was an unfortunate circumstance only. I had attempted what I could not manage. And Carlo — he is dead —somehow, perhaps because I am so near death my-self, it does not shock or startle me. Dear little fellow that he was!'

" 'And while he was ill he was constantly talking about you. It seemed that the only thing on his con-science, poor little chap, that he had joined at all in our treatment of you. And he begged me — I would have promised him anything, but by that time I saw it plainly enough for myself — to try to find you and ask you to forgive us both. But I little thought

it would have been like this — I had fancied sometimes — ' Jack hesitated, and the colour deepened in
his sunburnt cheeks.

" ' What?' said Mr. Sawyer. 'Do not be afraid
of my misunderstanding anything you say.'

" ' I had hoped perhaps that if I found you again I
might be able to be of some use to you. And now it
is too late. For you see we owe you some reparation
for indirectly forcing you to leave Ryeburn — you
might have risen there — who knows? I can see
now what a capital teacher you were.'

" Mr. Sawyer shook his head.

" ' I know I could teach,' he said, ' but that was all.
I did not understand boys' ways. I never was a
boy myself. But put all this out of your mind,
Berkeley, for ever. In spite of all the disappointment, I was very happy at Ryeburn. The living
among so many healthy-minded happy human beings
was a new and pleasant experience to me. Short as
it was, no part of my life has left a pleasanter remembrance. You say you would like to do something for
me. Will you write to my mother after I am gone,
and tell her? Tell her how little I suffered, and how
good every one was to me, a perfect stranger. Will
you do this?'

" Jack bent his head. 'Willingly,' he said.

" ' You will find her address in this book,' he went
on, handing a thick leather pocket-book to Jack.
' Also a sort of will — roughly drawn up, but correctly
— leaving her all I have, and the amount of that, and
the Bank it is in — all is noted. I have knocked

about so — since I was at Ryeburn I have tried so
many things and been in so many places, I have
learnt to face all eventualities.   I was so pleased to
get the chance of coming out here —'

"He stopped again.

"'You must not tire yourself so,' said Jack.

"'What does it matter ?   I can die so much more
easily if I leave things clear — for, trifling as they are,
my poor mother's comfort depends on them.   And
I am so glad too for you to understand about me,
Berkeley.   That day — it went to my heart to have
to refuse you about the subscription for the fireworks.'

"'Don't speak of it.   I know you had some good
motive,' said Jack.

"'Necessity — sheer, hard necessity,' said poor
Sawyer.   'The money I had got that morning was
only just in time to save my younger brother from
life-long disgrace, perhaps imprisonment.'

"Then painfully —'in short and broken sentences
— he related to Jack the history of his hard, sad, but
heroic life.   *He* did not think it heroic — it seemed to
him, in his single-minded conscientiousness, that he
had done no more than his duty, and that but im-
perfectly.   He had given his life for others, and,
hardest of all, for others who had little appreciated
his devotion.

"'My father died when I was only about twelve,'
he said.   'He had been a clergyman, but his health
failed, and he had to leave England and take a small
charge in Switzerland.   There he met my mother —

a Swiss, and there I was partly brought up. When
he died he told me I must take his place as head of
the family. I was not so attractive as my brother
and sister; I was shy and reserved. Naturally my
mother cared most for them. I fear she was too in-
dulgent. My sister married badly, and I had to try
to help her. My poor brother, he was always in
trouble and yet he meant well — '

"And so he told Jack the whole melancholy history, entering into details which I have forgotten,
and which, even if I remember them, it would be
only painful to relate. His brother was now in
America — doing well he hoped, thanks of course to
him; his sister's circumstances too had improved.
For the first time in his life Sawyer had begun to
feel his burdens lessening, when he was brought face
to face with the knowledge that all in this world
was over for him. Uncomplainingly he had, through
all these long years, borne the heat and burden of
the day ; rest for him was to be elsewhere, not here.
But as he had met life, so he now met death — calmly
and unrepiningly, certain that hard as it had been,
hard as it seemed now, it must yet be for the best —
the solving of the riddle he left to God.

"And his last thought was for others — for the
mother who had so little appreciated him, who required to lose him, perhaps, to bring home to her his
whole value.

"'I have always foreseen the possibility of this,'
he said, ' and prepared for it as best I could. Besides
the money I have confided to you, I insured my life,

most fortunately, last year. She will have enough
to get on pretty comfortably — and tell her,' he hesitated, 'I don't think she will miss me very much. I
have never had the knack of drawing much affection
to myself. But tell her I was quite satisfied that it
is all for the best, and Louis may yet return to cheer
her old age.'

"Jack stayed till he could stay no longer. Then,
with a grasp of the hand which meant more than
many words, he left his new, yet old friend, promising to be down again at Kadikoi first thing in the
morning. 'But take the papers with you, Berkeley,
the papers and the pocket-book, in case, you know —'
were Sawyer's last words to him.

"Jack was even earlier the next day than he had
expected. But when he got to the tent the canvas
door was drawn to.

"'Asleep?' he said to the doctor of the 25th Hussars, who came up at that moment, recognising him.

"'Yes,' said the doctor, bending his head rever-
ently, as he said the word.

"He unfastened the door, and signed to Jack to
follow him. Jack understood — yes, asleep indeed.
There he lay — all the pain and anxiety over, and as
the two men gazed at the peaceful face, there came
into Jack's mind the same words which his mother
had whispered over the dead face of his little brother,

"'Of such is the kingdom of Heaven.'"

CHAPTER XII.

A CHRISTMAS ADVENTURE.

" With bolted doors and windows wedged,
   The care was all in vain ;
For there were noises in the night
   Which nothing could explain."

GRANDMAMMA AND THE FAIRIES.

THE children had gone quietly to bed the evening before when grandmother had finished the reading of her story. They just kissed her and said, " Thank you, *dear* grandmother," and that was all. But it was all she wanted.

" I felt, you know," said Molly to Sylvia when they were dressing the next morning, " I felt a sort of feeling as if I'd been in church when the music was *awfully* lovely. A beautiful feeling, but strange too, you know, Sylvia? *Particularly* as Uncle Jack died too. When did he die ? Do you know, Sylvia? Was it at that place ? "

" What place ? " said Sylvia curtly. When her feelings were touched she had a way of growing curt and terse, sometimes even snappish.

" That hot place — without trees, and all so dusty and dirty — Kadi — Kadi — I forget."

" Oh! you stupid girl. Kadikoi was only one little wee village. You mean the Crimea — the

175

Crimea is the name of all the country about there — where the war was."

"Yes, of course. I *am* stupid," said Molly, but not at all as if she had any reason to be ashamed of the fact. "Did he never come home from the Crimea?"

"No," said Sylvia, curtly again, "he never came home."

For an instant Molly was silent. Then she began again.

"Well, I wonder how the old lady, that poor nice man's mother, I mean — I wonder how she got the money and all that, that Uncle Jack was to settle for her. Shall we ask grandmother, Sylvia?"

"No, of course not. What does it matter to us? Of course it was all properly done. If it hadn't been, how would grandmother have known about it?"

"I never thought of that. Still I would like to know. I think," said Molly meditatively, "I think I could get grandmother to tell without exactly asking — for fear, you know, of seeming to remind her about poor Uncle Jack."

"You'd much better not," said Sylvia, as she left the room.

But once let Molly get a thing well into her head, "trust her," as Ralph said, "not to let it out again till it suited her."

That very evening when they were all sitting together again, working and talking, all except aunty, busily writing at her little table in the corner, Molly began.

"Grandmother dear," she said gently, "wasn't the old lady *dreadfully* sorry when she heard he was dead?"

For a moment grandmother stared at her in bewilderment — her thoughts had been far away. "What are you saying, my dear?" she asked.

Sylvia frowned at Molly across the table. Too well did she know the peculiarly meek and submissive tone of voice assumed by Molly when bent on — had the subject been any less serious than it was, Sylvia would have called it "mischief."

"Molly," she said reprovingly, finding her frowns calmly ignored.

"What is it?" said Molly sweetly. "I mean, grandmother dear," she proceeded, "I mean the mother of the poor nice man that uncle was so good to. Wasn't she *dreadfully* sorry when she heard he was dead?"

"I think she was, dear," said grandmother unsuspiciously. "Poor woman, whatever her mistakes with her children had been, I felt dreadfully sorry for her. I saw her a good many times, for your uncle sent me home all the papers and directions — 'in case,' as poor Sawyer had said of himself — so my Jack said it."

Grandmother sighed; Sylvia looked still more reproachfully at Molly; Molly pretended to be threading her needle.

"And I got it all settled as her son had wished. He had arranged it so that she could not give away the money during her life. Not long after, she went to America to her other son, and I believe she is still living. He got on very well, and is now a rich man. I had letters from them a few years ago — nice letters. I think it brought out the best of them — Philip Sawyer's death I mean. Still — oh no — they did not care for him, alive or dead, as such a man deserved."

"What a shame it seems!" said Molly. "When *I* have children," she went on serenely, "I shall love them all alike — whether they're ugly or pretty, if *anything* perhaps the ugliest most, to make up to them, you see."

"I thought you were never going to marry," said Ralph. "For you're never going to England, and you'll never marry a Frenchman."

"Englishmen might come here," replied Molly. "And when you and Sylvia go to England, you might take some of my photographs to show."

This was too much. Ralph laughed so that he rolled on the rug, and Sylvia nearly fell off her chair. Even grandmother joined in the merriment, and aunty came over from her corner to ask what it was all about.

"I have finished my story," she said. "I am so glad."

"And when, oh, when will you read it?" cried the children.

"On the evening of the twenty-second of December. I fixed that while I was writing it, for that was the day it happened on," said aunty. "That will be next Monday, and this is Friday. Not so very long to wait. And after all it's a very short story — not nearly so long as grandmother's."

"Never mind, we'll make it longer by talking about it," said Molly. "That's how I did at home when I had a very small piece of cake for tea. I took one bite of cake to three or four of bread and butter. It made it seem much more."

"I can perfectly believe that *you* will be ready to provide the necessary amount of 'bread and butter' to eke out my story," said aunty gravely.

And Molly stared at her in such comical bewilderment as to what she meant, that she set them all off laughing again.

Monday evening came. Aunty took her place at the table in front of the lamp, and having satisfied herself that Molly's wants in the shape of needles and thread, thimble, etc., were supplied for the next half-hour at least, she began as follows : —

"A Christmas Adventure."

"On the twenty-second of December, in the year eighteen hundred and fifty —" "No," said aunty, stopping short, "I can't tell you the year. Molly would make all sorts of dreadful calculations on the spot, as to my exact age, and the date at which the first grey hairs might be looked for — I will only say eighteen hundred and *something*."

"*Fifty* something," said Molly promptly. "You did say that, aunty."

" Terrible child!" said aunty. "Well, never mind, I'll begin again. "On the twenty-second of December, in a certain year, I, Laura Berkeley, set out with my elder sister Mary, on a long journey. We were then living on the western coast of England, or Wales rather; we had to cross the whole country, for our destination was the neighbourhood, a few miles inland, of a small town on the *eastern* coast. Our journey was not one of pleasure — we were not going to spend 'a merry Christmas' with near and dear friends and relations. We were going on business, and our one idea was to get it accomplished as quickly as possible, and hurry home to our parents again, for otherwise their Christmas would be quite a solitary one. And as former Christmases — before we children had been scattered, before there were vacant chairs round the fireside — had been among the happiest times of the year in our family, as in many others, we felt doubly reluctant to risk spending it apart from each other, we four — all that were left now!

"'It is dreadfully cold, Mary,' I said, when we were fairly off, dear mother gazing wistfully after us, as the train moved out of the station and her figure on the platform grew smaller and smaller, till at last we lost sight of it altogether. 'It is dreadfully cold, isn't it?'

" We were tremendously well wrapped up — there were hot-water tins in the carriage, and every comfort possible for winter travellers. Yet it was true. It was, as I said, bitterly cold.

"'Don't say that already, Laura,' said Mary

anxiously, 'or I shall begin to wish I had stood out against your coming with me.'

" 'Oh, dear Mary, you couldn't have come alone,' I said.

" I was only fifteen. My accompanying Mary was purely for the sake of being a companion to her, though in my own mind I thought it very possible that, considering the nature of the ' business' we were bent upon, I might prove to be of practical use too. I must tell you what this same ' business' was. It was to choose a house. Owing to my father's already failing health, we had left our own old home more than a year before, and till now we had been living in a temporary house in South Wales. But my father did not like the neighbourhood, and fancied the climate did not suit him, and besides this we could not have had the house after the following April, had we wished it. So there had been great discussions about what we should do, where we should go rather, and much consultation of advertisement sheets and agents' lists. Already Mary had set off on several fruitless expeditions in quest of delightful ' residences' which turned out very much the reverse. But she had never before had to go such a long way as to East Hornham, which was the name of the post-town near which were two houses to let, each seemingly so desirable that we really doubted whether it would not be difficult to resist taking *both*. My father had known East Hornham as a boy, and though its neighbourhood was not strikingly pictu-resque, it was considered to be eminently healthy, and

he was full of eagerness about it, and wishing he
himself could have gone to see the houses.   But that
was impossible — impossible too for my mother to
leave him even for three days; there was nothing
for it but for Mary to go, and at once.   Our decision
in the case of one of the houses must not be delayed
a day, for a gentleman had seen it and wanted to
take it, only as the agent in charge of it considered
that we had ' the first refusal,' he had written to beg
my father to send some one to see it at once.

"And thus it came about that Mary and I set off
by ourselves in this dreary fashion only two days
before Christmas!   Mother had proposed our taking
a servant, but as we knew that the only one who
would have been any use to us was the one of *most*
use to mother, we declared we should much prefer
the ' independence ' of going by ourselves.

"By dint of much examination of Bradshaw we
had discovered that it was possible, just possible, to
get to East Hornham the same night about nine
o'clock.

"' That will enable us to get to bed early, after
we have had some supper, and the next day we can
devote to seeing the two houses, one or other of
which *must* suit us,' said Mary, cheerfully.   'And
starting early again the next day we may hope to
be back with you on Christmas eve, mother dear.'

"The plan seemed possible enough, — one day
would suffice for the houses, as there was no need as
yet to go into all the details of the apportionment of
rooms, and so on.   That would be time enough in

the spring, when we proposed to stay at East Hornham for a week or two at the hotel there, and arrange
our new quarters at leisure. It was running it rather
close, however; the least hitch, such as failing to
catch one train out of the many which Mary had
cleverly managed to fit in to each other, would throw
our scheme out of gear; so mother promised not to
be anxious if we failed to appear, and we, on our
part, promised to telegraph if we met with any detention.

"For the first half — three-quarters, I might say —
of our journey we got on swimmingly. We caught
all the trains; the porters and guards were civility
itself; and as our only luggage was a small hand-bag
that we carried ourselves, we had no trouble of any
kind. When we got to Fexel Junction, the last important station we were to pass, our misfortunes
began. Here, by rights, we should have had a full
quarter of an hour to wait for the express which
should drop us at East Hornham on its way north;
but when the guard heard our destination he shook
his head.

"'The train's gone,' he said. 'We are more than
half an hour late.'

"And so it proved. A whole hour and a half had
we to sit shivering, in spite of the big fire, in the
Fexel waiting-room, and it was eleven at night before,
in the slowest of slow trains, we at last found ourselves within a few miles of East Hornham.

"Our spirits had gone down considerably since
the morning. We were very tired, and that has *very*

much more to do with people's spirits than almost any one realises.

"'It wouldn't matter if we were going to friends,' said Mary. 'But it does seem very strange and desolate — we two poor things, two days before Christmas, arriving at midnight in a perfectly strange place, and nowhere to go to but an inn.'

"'But think how nice it will be, getting home to mother again — particularly if we've settled it all nicely about the house,' I said.

"And Mary told me I was a good little thing, and she was very glad to have me with her. It was not usual for me to be the braver of the two, but you see I felt my responsibilities on this occasion to be great, and was determined to show myself worthy of them.

"And when we did get to the inn, the welcome we received was worthy of Dr. Johnson's praise of inns in general. The fire was so bright, the little table so temptingly spread that the spirits — seldom long depressed — of one-and-twenty and fifteen rose at the sight. For we were hungry as well as tired, and the cutlets and broiled ham which the good people had managed to keep beautifully hot and fresh for us — possibly they were so accustomed to the railway eccentricities that they had only cooked them in time for our arrival by the later train, for we were told afterwards that no one ever *did* catch the express at Fexel Junction, — the cutlets and ham, as I was saying, and the buttered toast, and all the other good things, were *so* good that we made an excellent supper, and slept the sleep of two tired but perfectly healthy young people till seven o'clock the next morning.

"We awoke refreshed and hopeful. But alas! when Mary pulled up the blind what a sight met her eyes! snow — snow everywhere.

"'What *shall* we do?' she said. 'We can never judge of the houses in this weather. And how are we to get to them? Dear me! how unlucky!'

"'But it has left off, and it can't be very thick in these few hours,' I said. 'If only it keeps off now, we could manage.'

"We dressed quickly, and had eaten our breakfast by half-past eight; for at nine, by arrangement, the agent was to call for us to escort us on our voyage of discovery. The weather gave promise of improving, a faint wintry sunshine came timidly out, and there seemed no question of more snow. When Mr. Turner, the agent, a respectable fatherly sort of man, made his appearance, he altogether pooh-poohed the idea of the roads being impassable; but he went on to say that, to his great regret, it was perfectly impossible for him to accompany us. Mr. H——, Mr. Walter H——, that is to say, the younger son of the owner of the Grange, the larger of the two houses we were to see, had arrived unexpectedly, and Mr. Turner was obliged to meet him about business.

"'I have managed the business about here for them since they left the Grange, and Mr. Walter is only here for a day,' said the communicative Mr. Turner. 'It is most unfortunate. But I have engaged a comfortable carriage for you, Miss Berkeley, and a driver who knows the country thoroughly, and is a very steady man. And, if you will allow me, I will call in this evening to hear what you think of the houses — which you prefer.' He seemed to be quite sure we should fix for one or other.

" 'Thank you, that will do very well,' said Mary, — not in her heart, to tell the truth, sorry that we were to do our house-hunting by ourselves. 'We shall get on quite comfortably, I am sure, Mr. Turner. Which house shall we go to see first?'

" 'The farthest off, I would advise,' said Mr. Turner. 'That is Hunter's Hall. It is eight miles at least from this, and the days are so short.'

" 'Is that the old house with the terraced garden?' I asked.

"Mr. Turner glanced at me benevolently.

" 'Oh no, Miss,' he said. 'The terraced garden is at the Grange. Hunter's Hall is a nice little place, but much smaller than the Grange. The gardens at the Grange are really quite a show in summer.'

" 'Perhaps they will be too much for us,' said Mary. 'My father does not want a very large place, you understand, Mr. Turner — not being in good health he does not wish to have the trouble of looking after much.'

" 'I don't think you would find it too much,' said Mr. Turner. 'The head gardener is to be left at Mr. H——'s expense, and he is very trustworthy. But I can explain all these details this evening if you will allow me, after you have seen the house,' and, so saying, the obliging agent bade us good morning.

" 'I am sure we shall like the Grange the best,' I said to Mary, when, about ten o'clock, we found ourselves in the carriage Mr. Turner had provided for us, slowly, notwithstanding the efforts of the two fat horses that were drawing us, making our way along the snow-covered roads.

" 'I don't know,' said Mary. 'I am afraid of its being too large. But certainly Hunter's Hall is a long way from the town, and that is a disadvantage.'

" A *very* long way it seemed before we got there.

" 'I could fancy we had been driving nearly twenty miles instead of eight,' said Mary, when at last the carriage stopped before a sort of little lodge, and the driver informed us we must get out there, there being no carriage drive up to the house.

" 'Objection number one,' said Mary, as we picked our steps along the garden path which led to the front door. 'Father would not like to have to walk along here every time he went out a drive. Dear me!' she added, 'how dreadfully difficult it is to judge of any place in snow! The house looks so dirty, and yet very likely in summer it is a pretty bright white house.'

" It was not a bad little house : there were two or three good rooms downstairs and several fairly good upstairs, besides a number of small inconvenient rooms that might have been utilised by a very large family, but would be no good at all to us. Then the kitchens were poor, low-roofed, and straggling.

" 'It might do,' said Mary, doubtfully. 'It is more the look of it than anything else that I dislike. It does not look as if gentle-people had lived in it— it seems like a better-class farm-house.'

" And so it proved to be, for on inquiry we learnt from the woman who showed us through, that it never had been anything but a farm-house till the present owner had bought it, improved it a little, and furnished it in a rough-and-ready fashion for a summer residence for his large family of children.

" ' We should need a great deal of additional furniture,' said Mary. ' Much of it is very poor and shabby. The rent, however, is certainly very low — to some extent that would make up.'

" Then we thanked the woman in charge, and turned to go. ' Dear me!' said Mary, glancing at her watch, ' it is already half-past twelve. I hope the driver knows the way to the Grange, or it will be dark before we get there. How far is it from here to East Hornham?' she added, turning again to our guide.

" ' Ten miles good,' said the woman.

" ' I thought so,' said Mary. ' I shall have a crow to pluck with that Mr. Turner for saying it was only eight. And how far to the Grange?'

" ' Which Grange, Miss? There are two or three hereabouts.'

" Mary named the family it belonged to.

" ' Oh it is quite seven miles from here, though not above two from East Hornham.'

" ' Seven and two make nine,' said Mary. ' Why didn't you bring us here past the Grange? It is a shorter way,' she added to the driver, as we got into the carriage again.

" The man touched his hat respectfully, and replied that he had brought us round the other way that we might see more of the country.

" We laughed to ourselves at the idea of seeing the country, shut up in a close carriage and hardly daring to let the tips of our noses peep out to meet the bitter, biting cold. Besides, what was there to see ? It was a flat, bare country, telling plainly of the near neighbourhood of the sea, and with its present mantle of snow, features of no kind were to be discerned. Roads, fields, and all were undistinguishable.

" ' I wonder he knows his way,' we said to each other more than once, and as we drove on farther we could not resist a slight feeling of alarm as to the weather. The sky grew unnaturally dark and gloomy, with the blue-grey darkness that so often precedes a heavy fall of snow, and we felt immensely relieved when at last the carriage slackened before a pair of heavy old-fashioned gates, which were almost immediately opened by a young woman who ran out from one of the two lodges guarding each a side of the avenue.

" The drive up to the house looked very pretty even then — or rather as if it would be exquisitely so in spring and summer time.

" ' I'm sure there must be lots and lots of primroses and violets and periwinkles down there in those woody places,' I cried. ' Oh Mary, Mary, do take this house.'

" Mary smiled, but I could see that she too was pleased. And when we saw the house itself the pleasant impression was not decreased. It was built of nice old red stone, or brick, with grey mullions and gables to the roof. The hall was oak wainscotted all round, and the rooms that opened out of it were home-like and comfortable, as well as spacious. Certainly it was too large, a great deal too large, but then we could lock off some of the rooms.

"'People often do so,' I said. 'I think it is a delicious house, don't you, Mary?'

"One part was much older than the other, and it was curiously planned, the garden, the terraced garden behind which I had heard of, rising so, that after going upstairs in the house you yet found yourself on a level with one part of this garden, and could walk out on to it through a little covered passage. The rooms into which this passage opened were the oldest of all — one in particular, tapestried all round, struck me greatly.

"'I hope it isn't haunted,' I said suddenly. Mary smiled, but the young woman looked grave.

"'You don't mean to say it is?' I exclaimed.

"'Well, Miss, I was housemaid here several years, and I certainly never saw nor heard nothing. But the young gentlemen did used to say things like that for to frighten us, and for me I'm one as never likes to say as to those things that isn't for us to understand.'

"'I do believe it is haunted,' I cried, more and more excited, and though Mary checked me I would not leave off talking about it.

"We were turning to go out into the gardens when an exclamation from Mary caught my attention.

"'It is snowing again and *so* fast,' she said, 'and just see how dark it is.'

"''Twill lighten up again when the snow leaves off, Miss,' said the woman. 'It is not three o'clock yet. I'll make you a bit of fire in a minute if you like, in one of the rooms. In here —' she added, opening the door of a small bedroom next to the tapestry room, 'it'll light in a minute, the chimney can't be cold, for there was one yesterday. I put fires in each in turns.'

"We felt sorry to trouble her, but it seemed really necessary, for just then our driver came to the door to tell us he had had to take out the horses and put them into the stable.

"'They seemed dead beat,' he said, 'with the heavy roads. And besides it would be impossible to drive in the midst of such very thick falling snow. 'Twould be better to wait an hour or two, till it went off. There was a bag in the carriage — should he bring it in?'

"We had forgotten that we had brought with us some sandwiches and buns. In our excitement we had never thought how late it was, and that we must be hungry. Now, with the prospect of an hour or two's enforced waiting with nothing to do, we were only too thankful to be reminded of our provisions. The fire was already burning brightly in the little room — 'Mr. Walter's room' the young woman called it — 'That must be the gentleman that was to be with Mr. Turner to-day,' I whispered to Mary — and she very good-naturedly ran back to her own little house

to fetch the necessary materials for a cup of tea for
us.

"'It is a fearful storm,' she informed us when she
ran back again, white from head to foot, even with
the short exposure, and indeed from the windows we
could see it for ourselves. 'The snow is coming that
thick and fast, I could hardly find my own door,' she
went on, while she busied herself with preparations
for our tea. 'It is all very well in summer here, but
it is lonesome-like in winter since the family went
away. And my husband's been ill for some weeks
too—I have to sit up with him most nights. Last
night, just before the snow began, I did get such a
fright—all of a sudden something seemed to come
banging at our door, and then I heard a queer
breathing like. I opened the door, but there was
nothing to be seen, but perhaps it was that that made
me look strange when Miss here,' pointing to me,
'asked me if the house was haunted. Whatever it was
that came to our door certainly rushed off this way.'

"'A dog, or even a cat, perhaps,' said Mary.

"The woman shook her head.

"'A cat couldn't have made such a noise, and
there's not a dog about the place,' she said.

"I listened with great interest—but Mary's
thoughts were otherwise engaged. There was not a
doubt that the snow-storm, instead of going off, was
increasing in severity. We drank our tea and ate
our sandwiches, and put off our time as well as we
could till five o'clock. It was now of course perfectly
dark but for the light of the fire. We were glad

when our friend from the lodge returned with a couple of tallow candles, blaming herself for having forgotten them.

" 'I really don't know what we should do,' said Mary to her. 'The storm seems getting worse and worse. I wonder what the driver thinks about it. Is he in the house, do you know?'

" 'He's sitting in our kitchen, Miss,' replied the young woman. 'He seems very much put about. Shall I tell him to come up to speak to you?'

" 'Thank you, I wish you would,' said Mary. 'But I am really sorry to bring you out so much in this dreadful weather.'

" The young woman laughed cheerfully.

" 'I don't mind it a bit, Miss,' she said ; 'if you only knew how glad I shall be if you come to live here. Nothing'd be a trouble if so be as we could get a kind family here again. 'Twould be like old times.'

" She hastened away, and in a few minutes returned to say that the driver was downstairs waiting to speak to us—"

"Laura, my dear," said grandmother, "do you know it is a quarter to ten. How much more is there?"

Aunty glanced through the pages—

"About as much again," she said. "No, scarcely so much."

"Well then, dears, it must wait till to-morrow," said grandmother.

" Oh, grandmother!" remonstrated the children.

"Aunty said it was a shorter story than yours, grandmother," said Molly in a half reproachful voice.

"And are you disappointed that it isn't?" said aunty, laughing. "I really didn't think it was so long as it is."

"Oh! aunty, I only wish it was *twenty* times as long," said Molly. "I shouldn't mind hearing it all over again this minute, only you see I do dreadfully want to hear the end. I am sure they had to stay there all night, and that something frightens them. Oh it's 'squisitely delicious," she added, "jigging" up and down on her chair.

"You're a 'squisitely delicious little humbug," said aunty, laughing. "Now good night all three of you and get to bed as fast as you can, as I don't want 'grandmother dear' to scold me for your all being tired and sleepy to-morrow."

CHAPTER XIII.

A CHRISTMAS ADVENTURE. — PART II.

"And as for poor old Rover,
I'm sure he meant no harm."
OLD DOGGIE.

"MOLLY is too sharp by half," said aunty, the following evening, when she was preparing to go on with her story. "We *had* to stay there all night — that was the result of Mary's conversation with the driver, the details of which I may spare you. Let me see, where was I? 'The driver scratched his head,' — no, — ah, here it is! 'He was waiting downstairs to speak to us;' and the result of the speaking I have told you, so I'll go on from here —

"It was so cold downstairs in the fireless, deserted house, that Mary and I were glad to come upstairs again to the little room where we had been sitting, which already seemed to have a sort of home-like feeling about it. But once arrived there we looked at each other in dismay.

"'Isn't it dreadful, Mary?' I said.

"'And we shall miss the morning train from East Hornham — the only one by which we can get through the same day — that is the worst of all,' she said.

"'Can't we be in time? It is only two or three miles from here to East Hornham,' I said.

105

" 'Yes, but you forget I *must* see Mr. Turner again. If I fix to take this house, and it seems very likely, I must not go away without all the particulars for father. There are ever so many things to ask. I have a list of father's, as long as my arm, of questions and inquiries.'

" 'Ah, yes,' I agreed; 'and then we have to get our bag at the hotel, and to pay our bill there.'

" 'And to choose rooms there to come to at first,' said Mary. 'Oh yes, our getting away by that train is impossible. And then the Christmas trains are like Sunday. Even by travelling all night we cannot get home, I fear. I must telegraph to mother as soon as we get back to East Hornham.'

" The young woman had not returned. We were wondering what had become of her when she made her appearance laden with everything she could think of for our comfort. The bed, she assured us, could not be damp, as it had been 'to the fire' all the previous day, and she insisted on putting on a pair of her own sheets, coarse but beautifully white, and fetching from another room additional blankets, which in their turn had to be subjected to 'airing,' or 'firing' rather. To the best of her ability she provided us with toilet requisites, apologising, poor thing, for the absence of what we 'of course, must be used to,' — as she expressed it, in the shape of fine towels, perfumed soap, and so on. And she ended by cooking us a rasher of bacon and poached eggs for supper, all the materials for which refection she had brought from her own cottage. She was so kind that I shrank from suggesting to Mary the objection to the proposed arrangement, which was all this time looming darkly before me. But when our friend was about to take her leave for the night I could keep it back no longer.

"'Mary,' I whispered, surprised and somewhat annoyed at my sister's calmness, 'are you going to let her go away? You and I *can't* stay here all night alone.'

"'Do you mean that you are frightened, Laura dear?' she said kindly, in the same tone. 'I don't see that there is anything to be frightened of; and if there were, what good would another girl — for this young woman is very little older than I — do us?'

"'She knows the house, any way, and it wouldn't seem so bad,' I replied, adding aloud, 'Oh, Mrs. Atkins' — for I had heard the driver mention her name — 'can't you stay in the house with us? We shall feel so dreadfully strange.'

"'I would have done so most gladly, Miss,' the young woman began, but Mary interrupted her.

"'I know you can't,' she said; 'your husband is ill. Laura, it would be very wrong of us to propose such a thing.'

"'That's just how it is,' said Mrs. Atkins. 'My husband has such bad nights he can't be left, and there's no one I could get to sit with him. Besides, it's such a dreadful night to seek for any one.'

"'Then the driver,' I said; 'couldn't he stay somewhere downstairs? He might have a fire in one of the rooms.'

"Mrs. Atkins wished it had been thought of before. 'Giles,'—which it appeared was the man's name—would have done it in a minute, she was sure, but it was too late. He had already set off to seek a night's lodging and some supper, no doubt, at a little inn half a mile down the road.

"'An inn?' I cried. 'I wish we had gone there too. It would have been far better than staying here.'

"'Oh, it's a very poor place—"The Drover's Rest," they call it. It would never do for you, Miss,' said Mrs. Atkins, looking distressed that all her efforts for our comfort appeared to have been in vain. 'Giles might ha' thought of it himself,' she added, 'but then you see it would never strike him but what here—in the Grange—you'd be as safe as safe. It's not a place for bunglaries and such like, hereabouts.'

"'And of course we shall be quite safe,' said Mary. 'Laura dear, what has made you so nervous all of a sudden?'

"I did not answer, for I was ashamed to speak of Mrs. Atkins' story of the strange noises she had heard the previous night, which evidently Mary had forgotten, but I followed the young woman with great eagerness, to see that we were at least thoroughly well defended by locks and bolts in our solitude. The tapestry room and that in which we were to sleep could be locked off from the rest of the empty house, as a door stood at the head of the little stair leading up to them—so far, so well. But Mrs.

Atkins proceeded to explain that the door at the *out-side* end of the other passage, leading into the garden, could not be locked except from the outside.

"'I can lock you in, if you like, Miss,' she said, 'and come round first thing in the morning;' but this suggestion did not please us at all.

"'No, thank you,' said Mary, 'for if it is fine in the morning I mean to get up very early and walk round the gardens.'

"'No, thank you,' said I, adding mentally, 'Supposing we *were* frightened it would be too dreadful not to be able to get out.' — 'But we can lock the door from the tapestry room into the passage, from our side, can't we?' I said, and Mrs. Atkins replied 'Oh yes, of course you can, Miss,' turning the key in the lock of the door as she spoke. 'Master never let the young gentlemen lock the doors when they were boys,' she added, 'for they were always breaking the locks. So you see, Miss, there's a hook and staple to this door, as well as the lock.'

"'Thank you, Mrs. Atkins,' said Mary, 'that will do nicely, I am sure. And now we must really not keep you any longer from your husband. Good night, and thank you very much.'

"'Good night,' I repeated, and we both stood at the door of the passage as she made her way out into the darkness. The snow was still falling very heavily, and the blast of cold wind that made its way in was piercing.

"'Oh, Mary, come back to the fire,' I cried. 'Isn't it *awfully* cold? Oh, Mary dear,' I added, when we had both crouched down beside the welcome warmth for a moment, 'won't it be *delicious* to be back with mother again? We never thought we'd have such adventures, did we? Can you fancy this house ever feeling *home-y*, Mary? It seems so dreary now.'

"'Yes, but you've no idea how different it will seem even to-morrow morning, if it's a bright day,' said Mary. 'Let's plan the rooms, Laura. Don't you think the one to the south with the crimson curtains will be best for father?'

"So she talked cheerfully, more, I am sure — though I did not see it at the time — to encourage me than to amuse herself. And after awhile, when she saw that I was getting sleepy, she took a candle into the outer room, saying she would lock the door and make all snug for the night. I heard her, as I thought, lock the door, then she came back into our room and also locked the door leading from it into the tapestry room.

"'You needn't lock that too,' I said sleepily; 'if the tapestry door is locked, we're all right!'

"'I think it's better,' said Mary quietly, and then we undressed, so far as we could manage to do so in the extremely limited state of our toilet arrangements, and went to bed.

"I fell asleep at once. Mary, she afterwards told me, lay awake for an hour or two, so that when she did fall asleep her slumber was unusually profound. I think it must have been about midnight when I woke suddenly, with the feeling — the indescribable feeling — that something had awakened me. I listened, first of all with *only* the ear that happened to be uppermost — then, as my courage gradually returned again, I ventured to move slightly, so that both ears were uncovered. No, nothing was to be heard. I was trying to compose myself to sleep again, persuading myself that I had been dreaming. when again — yes most distinctly — there *was* a sound. A sort of shuffling, scraping noise, which seemed to come from the direction of the passage leading from the tapestry room to the garden. Fear made me selfish. I pushed Mary, then shook her gently, then more vigorously.

"'Mary,' I whispered. 'Oh, Mary, *do* wake up. I hear such a queer noise.'

"Mary, poor Mary awoke, but she had been very tired. It was a moment or two before she collected her faculties.

"'Where are we? What is it?' she said. Then she remembered. 'Oh yes — what is the matter, Laura?'

"'Listen,' I said, and Mary, calmly self-controlled as usual, sat up in bed and listened. The sound was quite distinct, even louder than I had heard it.

"'Oh, Mary!' I cried. 'Somebody's trying to get in. Oh, Mary, what *shall* we do? Oh, I am so frightened. I shall die with fright. Oh, I wish I had never come?'

"I was on the verge of hysterics, or something of the kind.

"Mary, herself a little frightened, as she afterwards confessed — in the circumstances what young girl could have helped being so?—turned to me quietly. Something in the very tone of her voice seemed to soothe me.

"'Laura dear,' she said gravely, 'did you say your prayers last night?'

"'Oh yes, oh yes, indeed I did. But I'll say them again now if you like,' I exclaimed.

"Even then, Mary could hardly help smiling.

"'That isn't what I meant,' she said. 'I mean, what is the *good* of saying your prayers if you don't believe what you say?'

"'But I do, I do,' I sobbed.

"'Then why are you so terrified? You asked God to take care of you. When you said it you believed He would. Why not believe it now? *Now*, when you are tried, is the time to show if you do mean what you say. I am sure God *will* take care of us. Now try, dear, to be reasonable, and I will get up and see what it is.'

"'But don't leave me, and I will try to be good,' I exclaimed, jumping out of bed at the same moment that she did, and clinging to her as she moved. 'Oh, Mary, don't you think perhaps we'd better go back to bed and put our fingers in our ears, and by morning it wouldn't seem anything.'

"'And fancy ever after that there had been something mysterious, when perhaps it is something quite simple,' said Mary. 'No, I shouldn't like that at all. Of course I won't do anything rash, but I would like to find out.'

"'The fire, fortunately, was not yet quite out.

Mary lighted one of the candles with a bit of paper from a spark which she managed to coax into a flame. The noise had, in the meantime, subsided, but just as we had got the candle lighted, it began again.

" ' Now,' said Mary, ' you stay here, Laura, and I'll go into the next room and listen at the passage door.' She spoke so decidedly that I obeyed in trembling. Mary armed herself with the poker, and, unlocking our door, went into the tapestry room, first lighting the second candle, which she left with me. She crossed the room to the door as she had said. I thought it was to listen ; in reality her object was to endeavour to turn the key in the lock of the tapestry room door, which she had *not* been able to do the night before, for once the door was shut the key would not move, and she had been obliged to content herself with the insecure hold of the hook and staple. Now it had struck her that by inserting the poker in the handle of the key she might succeed in turning it, and thus provide ourselves with a double defence. For if the intruder — dog, cat, whatever it was — burst the outer door and got into the tapestry room, my fears, she told me afterwards, would, she felt sure, have become uncontrollable. It was a brave thing to do — was it not? She deserved to succeed, and she did. With the poker's help she managed to turn the key, and then with a sigh of relief she stood still for a moment listening. The sounds continued — whatever it was it was evidently what Mrs. Atkins had heard the night before —a shuffling, rushing-about sound, then a sort of impatient breathing. Mary came back to me somewhat reassured.

"'Laura,' she said, 'I keep to my first opinion. It is a dog, or a cat, or some animal.'

"'But suppose it is a *mad* dog?' I said, somewhat unwilling to own that my terrors had been exaggerated.

"'It is possible, but not probable,' she replied. 'Any way it can't get in here. Now, Laura, it is two o'clock by my watch. There is candle enough to last an hour or two, and I will make up the fire again. Get into bed and *try* to go to sleep, for honestly I do not think there is any cause for alarm.'

"'But Mary, I *can't* go to sleep unless you come to bed too, and if you don't, I can't believe you think it's nothing,' I said. So, to soothe me, she gave up her intention of remaining on guard by the fire, and came to bed, and, wonderful to relate, we both went to sleep, and slept soundly till — what o'clock do you think?

"It was *nine* o'clock when I awoke; Mary was standing by me fully dressed, a bright frosty sun shining into the room, and a tray with a cup of tea and some toast and bacon keeping hot by the fire.

"'Oh, Mary!' I cried, sitting up and rubbing my eyes.

"'Are you rested?' she said. 'I have been up since daylight — not so very early *that*, at this season — Mrs. Atkins came and brought me some breakfast, but we hadn't the heart to waken you, you poor child.'

"'And oh, Mary, what about the noise? Did she hear it?'

"'She wasn't sure. She half fancied she did, and then she thought she might have been imagining it from the night before. But get up, dear. It is hopeless to try for the early train; we can't leave till to-night, or to-morrow morning; but I am anxious to get back to East Hornham and see Mr. Turner. And before we go I'd like to run round the gardens.'

"'But, Mary,' I said, pausing in my occupation of putting on my stockings, 'are you still thinking of taking this house?'

"'Still!' said Mary. 'Why not?'

"'Because of the noises. If we can't find out what it is, it would be very uncomfortable. And with father being so delicate too, and often awake at night!'

"Mary did not reply, but my words were not without effect. We ran round the gardens as she had proposed — they were lovely even then — took a cordial farewell of Mrs. Atkins, and set off on our return drive to East Hornham. I must not forget to tell you that we well examined that part of the garden into which the tapestry room passage led, but there were no traces of footsteps, the explanation of which we afterwards found to be that the snow had continued to fall till much later in the night than the time of our fright.

"Mr. Turner was waiting for us in considerable anxiety. We had done, he assured us, the most sensible thing possible in the circumstances. He had not known of our non-arrival till late in the evening, and, but for his confidence in Giles, would have set off even then. As it was, he had sent a messenger to Hunter's Hall, and was himself starting for the Grange.

"Mary sent me out of the room while she spoke to him, at which I was not over well pleased. She told him all about the fright we had had, and that, unless its cause were explained, it would certainly leave an uncomfortable feeling in her mind, and that, considering our father's invalid state, till she had talked it over with our mother she could not come to the decision she had hoped.

"'It may end in our taking Hunter's Hall,' she said, 'though the Grange is far more suitable.'

"Mr. Turner was concerned and perplexed. But Mary talked too sensibly to incline him to make light of it.

"'It is very unfortunate,' he said; 'and I promised an answer to the other party by post this evening. And you say, Miss Berkeley, that Mrs. Atkins heard it too. You are *sure*, Miss, you were not dreaming?'

"'*Quite* sure. It was my sister that heard it, and woke me,' she replied; 'and then we both heard it.'

"Mr. Turner walked off, metaphorically speaking, scratching his head, as honest Giles had done literally in his perplexity the night before. He promised to call back in an hour or two, when he had been to the station and found out about the trains for us.

"We packed our little bag and paid the bill, so

that we might be quite ready, in case Mr. Turner
found out any earlier train by which we might get
on, for we had telegraphed to mother that we should
do our best to be back the next day. I was still so
sleepy and tired that Mary persuaded me to lie down
on the bed, in preparation for the possibility of a
night's journey. I was *nearly* asleep when a tap
came to the door, and a servant informed Mary that
a gentleman was waiting to speak to her.

"'Mr. Turner,' said she carelessly, as she passed
into the sitting-room.

"But it was not Mr. Turner. In his place she
found herself face to face with a very different person — a young man, of seven or eight and twenty,
perhaps, tall and dark — dark-haired and dark-eyed
that is to say — grave and quiet in appearance, but
with a twinkle in his eyes that told of no lack of
humour.

"'I must apologise for calling in this way, Miss
Berkeley,' he said at once, 'but I could not help
coming myself to tell how *very* sorry I am about the
fright my dog gave you last night at the Grange. I
have just heard of it from Mr. Turner.'

"'Your dog?' repeated Mary, raising her pretty
blue eyes to his face in bewilderment.

"'Yes,' he said, 'he ran off to the Grange — his
old home, you know — oh, I beg your pardon! — I
am forgetting to tell you that I am Walter H——,
— in the night, and must have tried to find his way
into my room in the way he used to do. I always
left the door unlatched for him.'

" Instead of replying, Mary turned round and flew straight off into the room where I was.

" 'Oh, Laura,' she exclaimed, 'it *was* a dog; Mr. Walter H—— has just come to tell us. Are you not delighted? Now we can fix for the Grange at once, and it will be all right. Come quick, and hear about it.'

" I jumped up, and, without even waiting to smooth my hair, hurried back into the sitting-room with Mary. Our visitor, very much amused at our excitement, explained the whole, and sent downstairs for 'Captain,' a magnificent retriever, who, on being told to beg our pardon, looked up with his dear pathetic brown eyes in Mary's face in a way that won her heart at once. His master, it appeared, had been staying at East Hornham the last two nights with an old friend, the clergyman there. Both nights, on going to bed late, he had missed 'Captain,' whose usual habit was to sleep on a mat at his door. The first night he was afraid the dog was lost, but to his relief he reappeared again early the next morning; the second night, also, his master happening to be out late at Mr. Turner's, with whom he had a good deal of business to settle, the dog had set off again on his own account to his former quarters, with probably some misty idea in his doggy brain that it was the proper thing to do.

" 'But how did you find out where he had been?' said I.

" 'I went out early this morning, feeling rather anxious about "Captain,"' said our visitor; 'and I met him coming along the road leading from the Grange. Where he had spent the night after failing to get into his old home I cannot tell; he must have sheltered somewhere to get out of the snow and the cold. Later this morning I walked on to the Grange, and, hearing from Ruth Atkins of your fright and her own, I put 'two and two together,' and I think the result quite explains the noises you heard.'

"'Quite,' we both said; 'and we thank you so much for coming to tell us.'

"'It was certainly the very least I could do,' he said; 'and I thank you very much for forgiving poor old Captain.'

"So we left East Hornham with lightened hearts, and, as our new friend was travelling some distance in our direction, he helped us to accomplish our journey much better than we could have managed it alone. And after all we *did* get back to our parents on Christmas day, though not on Christmas eve."

Aunty stopped.

"Then you did take the Grange, aunty?" said the children.

Aunty nodded her head.

"And you never heard any more noises?"

"Never," said aunty. "It was the pleasantest of old houses; and oh, we were sorry to leave it, weren't we, mother?"

"Why did you leave it, grandmother dear?" said Molly.

" When your grandfather's health obliged him to spend the winters abroad; then we came here," said grandmother.

" Oh yes," said Molly, adding after a little pause, " I *would* like to see that house."

Aunty smiled. " Few things are more probable than that you will do so," she said, " provided you can make up your mind to cross the sea again."

" Why? how do you mean, aunty?" said Molly, astonished, and Ralph and Sylvia listened with eagerness to aunty's reply.

" Because," said aunty, — then she looked across to grandmother. " Won't you explain to them, mother?" she said.

" Because, my darlings, that dear old house will be your home — your happy home, I trust, some day," said grandmother.

" Is my father thinking of buying it?" asked Ralph, pricking up his ears.

" No, my boy, but some day it will be his. It is your uncle's now, but he is *much* older than your father, and has no children, so you see it will come to your father some day — sooner than we have thought, perhaps, for your uncle is too delicate to live in England, and talks of giving it up to your father."

" But *still* I don't understand," said Ralph, looking puzzled. " Did my *uncle* buy it?"

" No, no. Did you never hear of old Alderwood Grange?"

" Alderwood," said Ralph. " Of *course*, but we

never speak of it as 'The Grange,' you know, and I have never seen it. It has always been let since I can remember. I never even heard it described. Papa does not seem to care to speak of it."

"No, dear," said aunty. "The happiest part of his life began there, and you know how all the light seemed to go out of his life when your mother died. It was there he — Captain's master — got to know her, the 'Mary' of my little adventure. You understand it all now? He was a great deal in the neighbourhood — at the little town I called East Hornham — the summer we first came to Alderwood. And there they were married; and there, in the peaceful old churchyard, your dear mother is buried."

The children listened with sobered little faces. "Poor papa!" they said.

"But some day," said grandmother, "some day I hope, when you three are older, that Alderwood will again be a happy home for your father. It is what your mother would have wished, I know."

"Well then, you and auntie must come to live with us there. You must. Promise now, grandmother dear," said Molly.

Grandmother smiled, but shook her head gently.

"Grandmother will be a *very* old woman by then, my darling," she said, "and perhaps — "

Molly pressed her little fat hand over grandmother's mouth.

"I know what you're going to say, but you're *not* to say it," she said. "And *every* night, grandmother dear, I ask in my prayers for you to live to be a hundred."

Grandmother smiled again.

" Do you, my darling?" she said. " But remember, whatever we *ask*, God knows best what to *answer*."

CHAPTER XIV.

HOW THIS BOOK CAME TO BE WRITTEN.

" Ring out ye merry, merry bells,
　Your loudest, sweetest chime ;
Tell all the world, both rich and poor,
　'Tis happy Christmas time."

" GRANDMOTHER," said Ralph, at breakfast on
what Molly called " the morning of Christmas Eve,"
" I was going to ask you, only the story last night
put it out of my head, if I might ask Prosper to
spend to-morrow with us. His uncle and aunt are
going away somewhere, and he will be quite alone.
Besides he and I have made a plan about taking the
shawl to the old woman quite early in the morning.
You don't know *how* pleased he was when I told him
you had got it for her, grandmother — just as pleased
as if he had bought it for her with his own money."

" Then he is a really unselfish boy," said grandmother. "Certainly you may ask him. I had thought
of it too, but somehow it went out of my head. And,
as well as the shawl, I shall have something to send
to Prosper's old friend. She must have a good
dinner for once."

" That'll be awfully jolly," said Ralph. Sylvia and
Molly listened with approval, for of course they had

heard all about the mystery of Ralph's wood-carrying long ago.

"At Christmas time we're to try to make other people happy," said Molly, meditatively. "*I* thought of something that would make a great lot of people happy, if you and aunty would do it, grandmother dear?"

"I don't think you did *all* the thinking. about it, Molly," said Sylvia, with a slight tone of reproach. "I do think I did some."

"Well, I daresay you did. We did it together. It couldn't be for *this* Christmas, but for another."

"But what is it?" asked grandmother.

"It is that you and aunty should make a book out of the stories you've told us, and then you see lots and lots of other children would be pleased as well as us," said Molly. "Of course you'd have to put more to it, to make it enough. I don't *mind* if you put some in about me, grandmother dear, if you would *like* to very much."

"No," said Sylvia, "that would be very stupid. Grandmother couldn't make a book about *us*. We're not uncommon enough. We couldn't be *heroines*, Molly."

"But children don't care about heroines," said Molly. "Children like to hear about other children, just really what they do. Now, don't they, grandmother dear? And *isn't* my plan a good one?"

.　　.　　.　　.　　.　　.　　.　　.　　.

Will *you* answer little Molly's question, children dear? For dear you all are, whoever and wherever you be. Boys and girls, big and little, dark and fair, brown-eyed and blue-eyed, merry and quiet — all of you, dear unknown friends whose faces I may never see, yet all of whom I love. I shall be so glad — so very glad, if this little simple story-book of mine helps to make this Christmas Day a happy and merry one for you all.

THE END.

"WELL, DEARS," SHE SAID, "AND WHAT ARE YOU PLAYING AT?"—p. 3.

— *Frontispiece.*

BY

MRS. MOLESWORTH

AUTHOR OF "CARROTS," "CUCKOO CLOCK," "TELL ME A STORY"

Two small figures, hurrying along hand-in-hand, caught the
attention of several people. — p. 134.

ILLUSTRATED BY WALTER CRANE

New York

MACMILLAN AND CO.

AND LONDON

1893

First Edition September, 1883. Reprinted December, 1883; 1886, 1890.

"It would both have excited your pity, and have done your heart good, to have seen how these two little ones were so fond of each other, and how hand-in-hand they trotted along."

The Renowned History of Goody Two-Shoes.

TWO LITTLE WAIFS.

CHAPTER I.

PAPA HAS SENT FOR US.

"It's what comes in our heads when we
Play at 'Let's-make-believe,'
And when we play at 'Guessing.'"

CHARLES LAMB.

IT was their favourite play. Gladys had invented
it, as she invented most of their plays, and Roger was
even more ready to play at it than at any other, ready
though he always was to do anything Gladys liked or
wanted. Many children would have made it different
— instead of "going over the sea to Papa," they would
have played at what they would do when Papa should
come over the sea to them. But that was not what
they had learnt to look forward to, somehow — they
were like two little swallows, always dreaming of a
sunny fairyland they knew not where, only "over the
sea," and in these dreams and plays they found the
brightness and happiness which they were still too
young to feel should have been in their everyday
baby life.

For "Mamma" was a word that had no real meaning to them. They thought of *her* as of a far-away

1

beautiful angel — beautiful, but a little frightening too; cold and white like the marble angels in church, whose wings looked so soft, till one day Roger touched them, and found them, to his strange surprise, hard and icy, which made him tell Gladys that he thought hens much prettier than angels. Gladys looked a little shocked at this, and whispered to remind him that he should not say that: had he forgotten that the angels lived up in heaven, and were always good, and that Mamma was an angel? No, Roger had not forgotten, and that was what made him think about angels; but they *weren't* pretty and soft like Snowball, the little white hen, and he was sure he would never like them as much. Gladys said no more to him, for she knew by the tone of his voice that it would not take very much to make him cry, and when Roger got "that way," as she called it, she used to try to make him forget what had troubled him.

"Let's play at going to Papa," she said; "I've thought of such a good way of making a ship with the chairs, half of them upside down and half long-ways — like that, see, Roger; and with our hoop-sticks tied on to the top of Miss Susan's umbrella — I found it in the passage — we can make such a great high pole in the middle. What is it they call a pole in the middle of a ship? I can't remember the name?"

Nor could Roger; but he was greatly delighted with the new kind of ship, and forgot all about the disappointment of the angels in helping Gladys to make it, and when it was made, sailing away, away to Papa, "over the sea, over the sea," as Gladys sang in her little soft thin voice, as she rocked Roger gently up and down, making believe it was the waves.

Some slight misgiving as to what Miss Susan would say to the borrowing of her umbrella was the only thing that interfered with their enjoyment, and made them jump up hastily with a "Oh, Miss Susan," as the beginning of an apology, ready on Gladys's lips when the door opened rather suddenly.

But it was not Miss Susan who came in. A little to their relief and a good deal to their surprise it was Susan's aunt, old Mrs. Lacy, who seldom — for she was lame and rheumatic — managed to get as far as the nursery. She was kind and gentle, though rather deaf, so that the children were in no way afraid of her.

"Well, dears," she said, "and what are you playing at?"

"Over the sea, Mrs. Lacy," said Gladys. "Over the sea," repeated Roger, who spoke very plainly for his age. "Going over the sea to Papa; that's what we're playing at, and we like it the best of all our games. This is the ship, you see, and that's the big stick in the middle that all ships have — what is it they call it? I can't remember?"

"The mast," suggested Mrs. Lacy.

"Oh yes, the mast," said Gladys in a satisfied tone; "well, you see, we've made the mast with our hoop-sticks and Miss Susan's umbrella — you don't think Miss Susan will mind, do you?" with an anxious glance of her bright brown eyes; "*isn't* it high, the — the mart?"

" Mast," corrected Mrs. Lacy ; " yes, it's taller than you, little Gladys, though you are beginning to grow very fast! What a little body you were when you came here first," and the old lady gave a sigh, which made Roger look up at her.

" Has you got a sore troat?" he inquired.

" No, my dear ; what makes you think so?"

" 'Cos, when my troat was sore I was always breaving out loud like that," said Roger sympathisingly.

" No, my throat's not sore, dear, thank you," said the old lady. " Sometimes people ' breathe ' like that when they're feeling a little sad."

" And are you feeling a little sad, poor Mrs. Lacy?" said Gladys. " It's not 'cos Miss Susan's going to be married, is it? *I* think we shall be very happy when Miss Susan's married, only p'raps it wouldn't be very polite to say to her, would it?"

" No, it wouldn't be kind, certainly," said the old lady, with a little glance of alarm. Evidently Miss Susan kept her as well as the children in good order. " You must be careful never to say anything like that, for you know Susan has been very good to you and taken great care of you."

" I know," said Gladys ; " but still I like you best, Mrs. Lacy."

" And you would be sorry to leave me, just a little sorry ; I should not want you to be *very* sorry," said the gentle old lady.

Gladys glanced up with a curious expression in her eyes.

" Do you mean — is it that you are sad about? —
has it come at last? Has Papa sent for us, Mrs.
Lacy? Oh Roger, listen! Of course we should be
sorry to leave you and — and Miss Susan. But is it
true, can it be true that Papa has sent for us?"

" Yes, dears, it is true; though I never thought
you would have guessed it so quickly, Gladys. You
are to go to him in a very few weeks. I will tell you
all about it as soon as it is settled. There will be a
great deal to do with Susan's marriage, too, so soon,
and I wouldn't like you to go away without your
things being in perfect order."

" I think they are in very nice order already," said
Gladys. " I don't think there'll be much to do. I
can tell you over all my frocks and Roger's coats if
you like, and then you can think what new ones we'll
need. Our stockings are getting *rather* bad, but
Miss Susan thought they'd do till we got our new
winter ones, and Roger's second-best house shoes
are — "

" Yes, dear," said Mrs. Lacy, smiling, though a
little sadly, at the child's business-like tone; " I
must go over them all with Susan. But not to-day.
I am tired and rather upset by this news."

" Poor Mrs. Lacy," said Gladys again. " But can't
you tell us just a *very* little? What does Papa say?
Where are we to go to? Not all the way to where
he is?"

" No, dear. He is coming home, sooner than he
expected, for he has not been well, and you are to
meet him somewhere — he has not quite fixed where

—in Italy perhaps, and to stay there through the
winter.   It is a good thing, as it had to be, that he
can have you before Susan leaves me, for I am getting too old, dears, to take care of you as I should
like — as I took care of *him* long ago."

For Mrs. Lacy was a very, very old friend of the
children's father.   She had taken care of him as a
boy, and years after, when his children came to
be left much as he had been, without a mother, and
their father obliged to be far away from them, she
had, for love of her adopted son, as she sometimes
called him, taken his children and done her best to
make them happy.   But she was old and feeble,
sometimes for days together too ill to see Gladys and
Roger, and her niece Susan, who kept house for her,
though a very active and clever young lady, did not
like children.   So, though the children were well
taken care of as far as regarded their health, and
were always neatly dressed, and had a nice nursery
and a pleasant garden to play in, they were, though
they were not old enough to understand it, rather
lonely and solitary little creatures.   Poor old Mrs.
Lacy saw that it was so, but felt that she could do
no more; and just when the unexpected letter from
their father came, she was on the point of writing to
tell him that she thought, especially as her niece was
going to be married, some new home must be found
for his two little waifs, as he sometimes called them.

Before Mrs. Lacy had time to tell them any more
about the great news Miss Susan came in.   She
looked surprised to see her aunt in the nursery.

" You will knock yourself up if you don't take
care," she said rather sharply, though not unkindly.
" And my umbrella — my best umbrella ! I declare
it's too bad — the moment one's back is turned."

" It's the mast, Miss Susan," said Gladys eagerly.
" We thought you wouldn't mind. It's the mast of
the ship that's going to take us over the sea to Papa."

Some softer feeling came over Susan as she
glanced at Gladys's flushed, half-frightened face.

" Poor little things ! " she said to herself gently.
" Well, be sure to put it back in its place when you've
done with it. And now, aunt, come down stairs
with me, I have ever so many things to say to you."

Mrs. Lacy obeyed meekly.

" You haven't told them yet, have you, aunt ? "
said Susan, as soon as they were alone.

" Yes, I told them a little," said the old lady.
" Somehow I could not help it. I went upstairs
and found them playing at the very thing — it seemed
to come so naturally. I know you will think it foolish
of me, Susan, but I can't help feeling their going,
even though it is better for them."

" It's quite natural you should feel it," said Susan
in a not unkindly tone. " But still it is a very good
thing it has happened just now. For you know, aunt,
we have quite decided that you must live with us —"

" You are very good, I know," said Mrs. Lacy,
who was really very dependent on her niece's care.

" And yet I could not have asked Mr. Rexford to
have taken the children, who, after all, are no *relations*, you know."

"No," said Mrs. Lacy.

"And then to give them up to their own father is quite different from sending them away to strangers."

"Yes, of course," said the old lady, more briskly this time.

"On the whole," Miss Susan proceeded to sum up, "it could not have happened better, and the sooner the good-byings and all the bustle of the going are over, the better for you and for me, and for all concerned, indeed. And this leads me to what I wanted to tell you. Things happen so strangely sometimes. This very morning I have heard of such a capital escort for them."

Mrs. Lacy looked up with startled eyes.

"An escort," she repeated. "But not yet, Susan. They are not going yet. Wilfred speaks of 'some weeks hence' in his letter."

"Yes; but his letter was written three weeks ago, and, of course, I am not proposing to send them away to-day or to-morrow. The opportunity I have heard of will be about a fortnight hence. Plenty of time to telegraph, even to write, to Captain Bertram to ensure there being no mistake. But anyway we need not decide just yet. He says he will write again by the next mail, so we shall have another letter by Saturday."

"And what is the escort you have heard of?" asked Mrs. Lacy.

"It is a married niece of the Murrays, who is going to India in about a fortnight. They start from here, as they are coming here on a visit the last thing. They go straight to Marseilles."

" But would they like to be troubled with children ? "

" They know Captain Bertram, that is how we came to speak of it.   And Mrs. Murray is sure they would be glad to do anything to oblige him."

" Ah, well," said Mrs. Lacy.   " It sounds very nice. And it is certainly not every day that we should find any one going to France from a little place like this." For Mrs. Lacy's home was in a rather remote and out-of-the-way part of the country.   " It would save expense too, for, as they have no longer a regular nurse, I have no one to send even as far as London with them."

" And young Mrs. ——, I forget her name — her maid would look after them on the journey.   I asked about that," said Susan, who was certainly not thoughtless.

" Well, well, we must just wait for Saturday's letter," said Mrs. Lacy.

" And in the meantime the less said about it the better, *I* think," said Susan.

" Perhaps so; I daresay you are right," agreed Mrs. Lacy.

She hardly saw the children again that day. Susan, who seemed to be in an unusually gracious mood, took them out herself in the afternoon, and was very kind.   But they were so little used to talk to her, for she had never tried to gain their confidence, that it did not occur to either Gladys or Roger to chatter about what nevertheless their little heads and hearts were full of.   They had also, I think, a vague childish notion of loyalty to their old friend in not mentioning the subject, even though she had not told them not to do so. So they trotted along demurely, pleased at having their best things on, and proud of the honour of a walk with Miss Susan, even while not a little afraid of doing anything to displease her.

"They are good little things after all," thought Susan, when she had brought them home without any misfortune of any kind having marred the harmony of the afternoon. And the colour rushed into Gladys's face when Miss Susan sent them up to the nursery with the promise of strawberry jam for tea, as they had been very good.

"I don't mind so much about the strawberry jam," Gladys confided to Roger, "though it *is* very nice. But I do like when any one says we've been very good, don't you?"

"Yes," said Roger; adding, however, with his usual honesty: "I like *bofe*, being praised *and* jam, you know, Gladdie."

"'Cos," Gladys continued, "if we *are* good, you see, Roger, and I really think we must be so if *she* says so, it will be very nice for Papa, won't it? It matters more now, you see, what we are, 'cos of going to him. When people have people of their own they should be gooder even than when they haven't any one that cares much."

"Should they?" said Roger, a little bewildered. "But Mrs. Lacy cares?" he added. Roger was great at second thoughts.

"Ye—s," said Gladys, "she cares, but not dreadfully much. She's getting old, you know. And sometimes — don't say so to anybody, Roger — sometimes I think p'raps she'll soon have to be going to heaven. I think *she* thinks so. That's another reason, you see," reverting to the central idea round which her busy brain had done nothing but revolve all day, " why it's *such* a good thing Papa's sent for us now."

"I don't like about people going to heaven," said Roger, with a little shiver. "Why can't God let them stay here, or go over the sea to where it's so pretty. *I* don't want ever to go to heaven."

"Oh, Roger!" said Gladys, shocked. " Papa wouldn't like you to say that."

"Wouldn't he?" said Roger; " then I won't. It's because of the angels, you know, Gladdie. Oh, do you think," he went on, his ideas following the next link in the chain, "*do* you think we can take Snowball with us when we go?"

"I don't know," said Gladys; and just then Mrs. Lacy's housemaid, who had taken care of them since their nurse had had to leave them some months before, happening to bring in their tea, the little girl turned to her with some vague idea of taking her into their confidence. To have no one but Roger to talk to about so absorbing a matter was almost too much. But Ellen was either quite ignorant of the great news, or too discreet to allow that she had heard it. In answer to Gladys's " feeler " as to how hens travelled, and if one might take them in the carriage with one, she replied matter-of-factly that she believed there were places on purpose for all sorts of live things on the railway, but that Miss Gladys had better ask Miss Susan, who had travelled a great deal more than she, Ellen.

"Yes," replied Gladys disappointedly, "perhaps she has; but most likely not with hens. But have you stayed at home all your life, Ellen? Have you never left your father and mother till you came here?"

Whereupon Ellen, who was a kindly good girl, only a little too much in awe of Miss Susan to yield to her natural love of children, feeling herself on safe ground, launched out into a somewhat rose-coloured description of her home and belongings, and of her visits as a child to the neighbouring market-town, which much amused and interested her little hearers, besides serving for the time to distract their thoughts from the one idea, which was, I daresay, a good thing. For in this life it is not well to think too much or feel too sure of *any* hoped-for happiness. The doing so of itself leads to disappointment, for we unconsciously paint our pictures with colours impossibly bright, so that the *real* cannot but fall short of the imaginary.

But baby Gladys — poor little girl! — at seven it is early days to learn these useful but hard lessons.

She and Roger made up for their silence when they went to bed, and you, children, can better imagine than I can tell the whispered chatter that

went on between the two little cots that stood close
together side by side. And still more the lovely
confusion of happy dreams that flitted that night
through the two curly heads on the two little
pillows.

CHAPTER II.

POOR MRS. LACY.

"For the last time — words of too sad a tone."
AN OLD STORY AND OTHER POEMS.

SATURDAY brought the expected letter, which both Mrs. Lacy and Susan anxiously expected, though with different feelings. Susan hoped that nothing would interfere with the plan she had made for the children's leaving; Mrs. Lacy, even though she owned that it seemed a good plan, could not help wishing that something would happen to defer the parting with the two little creatures whom she had learnt to love as much as if they had been her own grandchildren.

But the letter was all in favour of Susan's ideas. Captain Bertram wrote much more decidedly than he had done before. He named the date at which he was leaving, a very few days after his letter, the date at which he expected to be at Marseilles, and went on to say that if Mrs. Lacy could possibly arrange to have the children taken over to Paris within a certain time, he would undertake to meet them there at any hour of any day of the week she named. The sooner the better for him, he said, as he would be anxious to get back to the south and settle himself there for the

14

winter, the doctor having warned him to run no risk
in exposing himself to cold, though with care he quite
hoped to be all right again by the spring. As to a
maid for the children — Mrs. Lacy having told him
that they had had no regular nurse for some time —
he thought it would be a good plan to have a French
one, and as he had friends in Paris who understood
very well about such things he would look out for
one immediately he got there, if Mrs. Lacy could find
one to take them over and stay a few days, or if she,
perhaps, could spare one of her servants for the time.
And he begged her, when she had made her plans, to
telegraph, or write if there were time, to him at a
certain hotel at Marseilles, "to wait his arrival."

Susan's face had brightened considerably while
reading the letter; for Mrs. Lacy, after trying to do
so, had given it up, and begged her niece to read it
aloud.

"My sight is very bad this morning," she said,
and her voice trembled as she spoke, "and Wilfred's
writing was never very clear."

Susan looked at her rather anxiously — for some
time past it had seemed to her that her aunt was
much less well than usual — but she took the letter
and read it aloud in her firm distinct voice, only
stopping now and then to exclaim: "*Could* anything
have happened better? It is really most fortunate."
Only at the part where Captain Bertram spoke of
engaging a maid for the journey, or lending one of
theirs, her face darkened a little. "Quite unnecessary — foolish expense. Hope aunt won't speak of it

to Ellen," she said to herself in too low a voice for
Mrs. Lacy to hear.

"Well, aunt?" she said aloud, when she had
finished the letter, but rather to her surprise Mrs.
Lacy did not at once reply. She was lying on her
couch, and her soft old face looked very white
against the cushions. She had closed her eyes, but
her lips seemed to be gently moving. What were
the unheard words they were saying? A prayer
perhaps for the two little fledglings about to be taken
from her wing for ever. She knew it was for ever.

"I shall never see them again," she said, loud
enough for Susan to hear, but Susan thought it better
not to hear.

"Well, aunt," she repeated, rather impatiently,
but the impatience was partly caused by real anxiety;
"won't you say what you think of it? *could* anything
have happened better than the Murrays' escort?
Just the right time and all."

"Yes, my dear. It seems to have happened wonderfully well. I am sure you will arrange it all
perfectly. Can you write to Wilfred at once? And
perhaps you had better see Mrs. Murray again. I
don't feel able to do anything, but I trust it all to
you, Susan. You are so practical and sensible."

"Certainly," replied Susan, agreeably surprised to
find her aunt of the same opinion as herself; "I will
arrange it all. Don't trouble about it in the least.
I will see the Murrays again this afternoon or to-
morrow. But in the meantime I think it is better
to say nothing more to the children."

"Perhaps so," said Mrs. Lacy. Something in her voice made Susan look round. She was leaving the room at the moment. "Aunt, what is the matter?" she said.

Mrs. Lacy tried to smile, but there were tears in her eyes.

"It is nothing, my dear," she said. "I am a foolish old woman, I know. I was only thinking"—and here her voice broke again—"It would have been a great pleasure to me," she went on, "if he could have managed it. If Wilfred could have come all the way himself, and I could have given the children up into his own hands. It would not have seemed quite so—so sad a parting, and I should have liked to see him again."

"But you will see him again, dear aunt," said Susan; "in the spring he is sure to come to England, to settle probably, perhaps not far from us. He has spoken of it in his letters."

"Yes, I know," said Mrs. Lacy, "but—"

"But what?"

"I don't want to be foolish; but you know, my dear, by the spring I may not be here."

"Oh, aunt!" said Susan reproachfully.

"It is true, my dear; but do not think any more of what I said."

But Susan, who was well-principled, though not of a very tender or sympathising nature, turned again, still with her hand on the door-handle.

"Aunt," she said, "you have a right to be consulted—even to be fanciful if you choose. You

have been very good to me, very good to Gladys and
Roger, and I have no doubt you were very good to
their father long ago.   If it would be a comfort to
you, let me do it — let me write to Wilfred Bertram
and ask him to come here, as you say, to fetch the
children himself."

Mrs. Lacy reflected a moment.   Then, as had been
her habit all her life, she decided on self-denial.

"No, my dear Susan," she said firmly.   "Thank
you for proposing it, but it is better not.   Wilfred
has not thought of it, or perhaps he has thought of it
and decided against it.   It would be additional expense for him, and he has to think of that — then
it would give *you* much more to do, and you have
enough."

"I don't mind about that," said Susan.

"And then, too," went on Mrs. Lacy, "there is his
health.   Evidently it will be better for him not to
come so far north so late in the year."

"Yes," said Susan, "that is true."

"So think no more about it, my dear, and thank
you for your patience with a silly old woman."

Susan stooped and kissed her aunt, which from
her meant a good deal.   Then, her conscience quite
at rest, she got ready to go to see Mrs. Murray at
once.

"There is no use losing the chance through any
foolish delay," she said to herself.

Two days later she was able to tell her aunt that
all was settled.   Mrs. Murray had written to her
niece, Mrs. Marton, and had already got her answer.

She and her husband would gladly take charge of the children as far as Paris, and her maid, a very nice French girl, who adored little people, would look after them in every way — not the slightest need to engage a nurse for them for the journey, as they would be met by their father on their arrival. The Martons were to spend two days, the last two days of their stay in England, with Mrs. Murray, and meant to leave on the Thursday of the week during which Captain Bertram had said he could meet the children at any day and any hour. Everything seemed to suit capitally.

"They will cross on Friday," said Susan; "that is the Indian mail day, of course. And it is better than earlier in the week, as it gives Captain Bertram two or three days' grace *in case* of any possible delay."

"And will you write, or telegraph — which is it?" asked Mrs. Lacy timidly, for these sudden arrangements had confused her — "at once, then?"

"Telegraph, aunt? No, of course not," said Susan a little sharply, "he will have left ——pore several days ago, you know, and there is no use *telegraphing* to Marseilles. I will write to-morrow — there is *plenty* of time — a letter to wait his arrival, as he himself proposed. Then *when* he arrives he will telegraph to us to say he has got the letter, and that it is all right. You quite understand, aunt?"

"Oh yes, quite. I am very stupid, I know, my dear," said the old lady meekly.

A few days passed. Gladys had got accustomed by this time to the idea of leaving, and no longer felt bewildered and almost oppressed by the rush of questions and wonderings in her mind. But her busy little brain nevertheless was constantly at work. She had talked it all over with Roger so often that he, poor little boy, no longer knew what he thought or did not think about it. He had vague visions of a ship about the size of Mrs. Lacy's drawing-room, with a person whom he fancied his father — a tall man with very black whiskers, something like Mrs. Murray's butler, whom Miss Susan had one day spoken of as quite "soldier-like" — and Roger's Papa was of course a soldier — standing in the middle to hold the mast steady, and Gladys and he with new ulsters on — Gladys had talked a great deal about new ulsters for the journey — waving flags at each side. Flags were hopelessly confused with ships in Roger's mind; he thought they had something to do with making boats go quicker. But he did not quite like to say so to Gladys, as she sometimes told him he was really too silly for a big boy of nearly five.

So the two had become rather silent on the subject. Roger had almost left off thinking about it. His little everyday life of getting up and going to bed, saying his prayers and learning his small lessons for the daily governess who came for an hour every morning, eating his breakfast and dinner and tea, and playing with his toy-horses, was enough for him. He could not for long together have kept his thoughts on the strain of far-away and unfamiliar things, and so long as he knew that he had Gladys at hand, and that nobody (which meant Miss Susan in particular)

was vexed with him, he asked no more of fate! And
when Gladys saw that he was much more interested
in trying to catch sight of an imaginary little mouse
which was supposed to have been nibbling at the tail
of his favourite horse in the toy-cupboard, than in
listening to her wonderings whether Papa had written
again, and *when* Miss Susan was going to see about
their new ulsters, she gave up talking to him in
despair.

If she could have given up *thinking* so much about
what was to come, it would have been better, I daresay. But still it was not to be wondered at that she
found it difficult to give her mind to anything else.
The governess could not make out why Gladys had
become so absent and inattentive all of a sudden, for
though the little girl's head was so full of the absorbing thought, she never dreamt of speaking of it to
any one but Roger. Mrs. Lacy had not told her she
must *not* do so, but somehow Gladys, with a child's
quick delicate instinct of honour, often so little
understood, had taken for granted that she was not
to do so.

"Everything comes to him that has patience to
wait," says the Eastern proverb, and in her own way
Gladys had been patient, when one morning, about
a week after the day on which Susan had told her
aunt that everything was settled, Miss Fern, the
daily governess, at the close of lessons, told her to go
down to the drawing-room, as Mrs. Lacy wanted her.

"And Roger too?" asked Gladys, her heart beating fast, though she spoke quietly.

" Yes, I suppose so," said Miss Fern, as she tied her bonnet-strings.

The children had noticed that she had come into the schoolroom a little later than usual that morning, and that her eyes were red. But in answer to Roger's tender though very frank inquiries, she had murmured something about a cold.

" That was a story, then, what she said about her eyes," thought sharp-witted Gladys. "She's been crying; I'm sure she has." But then a feeling of pity came into her mind. " Poor Miss Fern; I suppose she's sorry to go away, and I daresay Mrs. Lacy said she wasn't to say anything about it to us." So she kissed Miss Fern very nicely, and stopped the rest of the remarks which she saw Roger was preparing.

" Go and wash your hands quick, Roger," she said, " for we must go downstairs. *Mine* are quite clean, but your middle fingers are all over ink."

" Washing doesn't take it away," said Roger reluctantly. There were not many excuses he would have hesitated to use to avoid washing his hands !

" Never mind. It makes them *clean* anyway," said Gladys decidedly, and five minutes later two very spruce little pinafored figures stood tapping at the drawing-room door.

" Come in, dears," said Mrs. Lacy's faint gentle voice. She was lying on her sofa, and the children went up and kissed her.

" *You* has got a cold too — like Miss Fern," said Roger, whose grammar was sometimes at fault, though he pronounced his words so clearly.

"*Roger*," whispered Gladys, tugging at her little brother under his holland blouse. But Mrs. Lacy caught the word.

"Never mind, dear," she said, with a little smile, which showed that she saw that Gladys understood. "Let him say whatever comes into his head, dear little man."

Something in the words, simple as they were, or more perhaps in the tone, made little Gladys suddenly turn away. A lump came into her throat, and she felt as if she were going to cry.

"I wonder why I feel so strange," she thought, "just when we're going to hear about going to Papa? I think it is that Mrs. Lacy's eyes look so sad, 'cos she's been crying. It's much worse than Miss Fern's. I don't care so much for her as for Mrs. Lacy," and all these feelings surging up in her heart made her not hear when their old friend began to speak. She had already said some words when Gladys's thoughts wandered back again.

"It came this morning," the old lady was saying. "See, dears, can you read what your Papa says?" And she held out a pinky-coloured little sheet of paper, not at all like a letter. Gladys knew what it was, but Roger did not: he had never seen a telegram before.

"Is that Papa's writing?" he said. "It's very messy-looking. *I* couldn't read it, I don't think."

"But I can," said Gladys, spelling out the words. "'Ar — arrived safe. Will meet children as you prop —' What is the last word, please, Mrs. Lacy?"

" Propose," said the old lady, " as you propose."
And then she went on to explain that this telegram
was in answer to a letter from Miss Susan to their
father, telling him all she had settled about the journey. " This telegram is from Marseilles," she said;
" that is the town by the sea in France, where your
dear Papa has arrived. It is quite in the south, but
he will come up by the railway to meet you at Paris,
where Mr. and Mrs. Marton — Mrs. Marton is Mrs.
Murray's niece, Gladys — will take you to."

It was a little confusing to understand, but Mrs.
Lacy went over it all again most patiently, for she
felt it right that the children, Gladys especially,
should understand all the plans before starting away
with Mr. and Mrs. Marton, who, however kind, were
still quite strangers to them.

Gladys listened attentively.

" Yes," she said; " I understand now. But how
will Papa know us, Mrs. Lacy? We have grown so,
and — " she went on, rather reluctantly, " I am not
quite sure that I should know him, not just at the
very first minute."

Mrs. Lacy smiled.

" No, dear, of course you could not, after more
than four years! But Mr. Marton knows your Papa."

Gladys's face cleared.

" Oh, that is all right," she said. " That is a very
good thing. But " — and Gladys looked round hesitatingly — " isn't anybody else going with us? I
wish — I wish nurse wasn't married; don't you, Mrs.
Lacy?"

The sort of appeal in the child's voice went to the
old lady's heart.

"Yes, dear," she said. "But Susan thinks it will
be quite nice for you with Léonie, young Mrs. Marton's maid, for your Papa will have a new nurse all
ready. She wrote to tell him that we would not send
any nurse with you."

Gladys gave a little sigh. It took some of the
bloom off the delight of "going to Papa" to have to
begin the journey alone among strangers, and she saw
that Mrs. Lacy sympathised with her.

"It will save a good deal of expense too," the old
lady added, more as if thinking aloud, and half forgetting to whom she was speaking.

"Will it?" said Gladys quickly. "Oh, then, I
won't mind. We won't mind, will we, Roger?" she
repeated, turning to her little brother.

"No, we won't," answered Roger solemnly, though
without a very clear idea of what he was talking
about, for he was quite bewildered by all he had
heard, and knew and understood nothing but that he
and Gladys were going somewhere with somebody to
see Papa.

"That's right," said Mrs. Lacy cheerfully. "You
are a sensible little body, my Gladys."

"I know Papa isn't very rich," said Gladys, encour-
aged by this approval, "and he'll have a great lot
more to pay now that Roger and I are going to be
with him, won't he?"

"You have such very big appetites, do you think?"

"I don't know," said Gladys. "But there are

such lots of things to buy, aren't there? All our
frocks and hats and boots. But oh!" she suddenly
broke off, "won't we have to be getting our things
ready? and *do* you think we should have new
ulsters?"

"They are ordered," said Mrs. Lacy. "Indeed,
everything you will need is ordered. Susan has
been very busy, but everything will be ready."

"When are we to go?" asked Gladys, suddenly
remembering this important question.

The sad look came into Mrs. Lacy's eyes again,
and her voice trembled as she replied: "Next Thursday, my darling."

"Next Thursday," repeated Gladys; and then
catching sight of the tears which were slowly welling
up into Mrs. Lacy's kind eyes — it is so sad to see
an aged person cry! — she suddenly threw her arms
around her old friend's neck, and, bursting out sobbing, exclaimed again: "Next Thursday. Oh, dear
Mrs. Lacy, next Thursday!"

And Roger stood by, fumbling to get out his
pocket-handkerchief, not quite sure if he should also
cry or not. It seemed to him strange that Gladys
should cry just when what she had wanted so much
had come — just when it was all settled about going
to Papa!

CHAPTER III.

A PRETTY KETTLE OF FISH.

"The cab-wheels made a dreary thunder
In their half-awakened ears;
And then they felt a dreamy wonder
Amid their dream-like fears."

LAVENDER LADY.

GLADYS said something of the same kind to herself when, looking round her in the railway carriage on that same Thursday morning, she realised that the long, long looked-forward-to day had come. She and Roger had actually started on their journey to Papa! Yet her eyes were red and her face was pale. Little Roger, too, looked subdued and sober. It had never been so in their plays; in their pretence goings to Papa they were always full of fun and high spirits. It was always a beautiful sunny day to begin with, and to-day, the real day, was sadly dull and dreary, and cold too; the children, even though the new ulsters were in all their glory, shivered a little and drew closer together. The rain was falling so fast that there was no use trying to look out of the window, when fields and trees and farmhouses all seem to fly past in a misty confusion. Mr. Marton was deep in his *Times;* Mrs. Marton, after settling the children in the most comfortable places and doing all

27

she could think of, had drawn a book out of her travelling-bag and was also busy reading. Roger, after a while, grew sleepy, and nodded his head, and then Mrs. Marton made a pillow for him on the arm of the seat, and covered him up with her rug. But Gladys, who was not at all sleepy, sat staring before her with wide open eyes, and thinking it was all very strange, and, above all, not the very least bit like what she had thought it would be. The tears came back into her eyes again when she thought of the parting with Mrs. Lacy. She and Roger had hardly seen their kind old friend the last few days, for she was ill, much more ill than usual, and Susan had looked grave and troubled. But the evening before, she had sent for them to say good-bye, and this was the recollection that made the tears rush back to the little girl's eyes. Dear Mrs. Lacy, how very white and ill she looked, propped up by pillows on the old-fashioned sofa in her room — every article in which was old-fashioned too, and could have told many a long-ago tender little story of the days when their owner was a merry blooming girl; or, farther back still, a tiny child like Gladys herself! For much of Mrs. Lacy's life had been spent in the same house and among the same things. She had gone from there when she was married, and she had come back there a widow and childless, and there she had brought up these children's father, Wilfred, as she often called him even in speaking to them, the son of her dearest friend. All this Gladys knew, for sometimes when they were alone together, Mrs. Lacy would tell her little stories of the past, which left their memory with the child, even though at the time hardly understood; and now that she and Roger were quite gone from the old house and the old life, the thought of them hung about Gladys with a strange solemn kind of mystery.

"I never thought about leaving Mrs. Lacy when we used to play at going," she said to herself. "I never even thought of leaving the house and our own little beds and everything, and even Miss Susan. And Ellen was very kind. I wish she could have come with us, just till we get to Papa," and then, at the thought of this unknown Papa, a little tremor came over the child, though she would not have owned it to any one. "I wonder if it would have cost a very great deal for Ellen to come with us just for a few days. I would have given my money-box money, and so would Roger, I am sure. I have fifteen and sixpence, and he has seven shillings and fourpence. It *could* not have cost more than all that," and then she set to work to count up how much her money and Roger's added together would be. It would not come twice together to the same sum somehow, and Gladys went on counting it up over and over again confusedly till at last it all got into a confusion together, for she too, tired out with excitement and the awakening of so many strange feelings, had fallen asleep like poor little Roger.

They both slept a good while, and Mr. and Mrs. Marton congratulated themselves on having such very quiet and peaceable small fellow-travellers.

"They are no trouble at all," said young Mrs. Marton. "But on the boat we must of course have Léonie with us, in case of a bad passage."

"Yes, certainly," said her husband; "indeed I think she had better be with us from London. They will be getting tired by then."

"They are tired already, poor pets," said Mrs. Marton, who was little more than a girl herself. "They don't look very strong, do they, Phillip?"

Mr. Marton took the cigarette he had just been preparing to enjoy out of his mouth, and turned towards the children, examining them critically.

"The boy looks sturdy enough, though he's small. He's like Bertram. The girl seems delicate; she's so thin too."

"Yes," agreed Mrs. Marton. "*I* don't mind, and no more does Léonie; but I think it was rather hard-hearted of Susan Lacy to have sent them off like that without a nurse of their own. If she had not been so worried about Mrs. Lacy's illness, I think I would have said something about it to her, even at the last. Somehow, till I saw the children, I did not think they were so tiny."

"It'll be all right once we get to Paris and we give them over to their father," said Mr. Marton, who was of a philosophical turn of mind, puffing away again at his cigarette. "It will have saved some expense, and that's a consideration too."

The children slept for some time. When they awoke they were not so very far from London. They felt less tired and better able to look about them and

ask a few modest little questions. And when they
got to London they enjoyed the nice hot cup of tea
they had in the refreshment room, and by degrees
they began to make friends with Léonie, who was
very bright and merry, so that they were pleased to
hear she was to be in the same carriage with them
for the rest of the journey.

"Till you see your dear Papa," said Léonie, who
had heard all the particulars from her young mistress.

"Yes," said Gladys quietly — by this time they
were settled again in another railway carriage — "our
Papa's to be at the station to meet us."

"And we're to have a new nurse," added Roger,
who was in a communicative humour. "Do you
think she'll be kind to us?"

"I'm sure she will," said Léonie, whose heart was
already won.

"She's to teach us French," said Gladys.

"That will be very nice," said Léonie. "It is a
very good thing to know many languages."

"Can you speak French?" asked Roger.

Léonie laughed. "Of course I can," she replied,
"French is my tongue."

Roger sat straight up, with an appearance of great
interest.

"Your tongue," he repeated. "Please let me see
it," and he stared hard at Léonie's half-opened mouth.
"Is it not like our tongues then?"

Léonie stared too, then she burst out laughing.

"Oh, I don't mean tongue like that," she said, "I
mean talking — language. When I was little like

you I could talk nothing but French, just like you now, who can talk only English."

"And can't everybody in France talk English too?" asked Gladys, opening her eyes.

"Oh dear no!" said Léonie.

Gladys and Roger looked at each other. This was quite a new and rather an alarming idea.

"It is a *very* good thing," Gladys remarked at last, "that Papa is to be at the station. If we got lost over there," she went on, nodding her head in the direction of an imaginary France, "it would be even worse than in London."

"But you're not going to get lost anywhere," said Léonie, smiling. "We'll take better care of you than that."

And then she went on to tell them a little story of how once, when she was a very little girl, she had got lost — not in Paris, but in a much smaller town — and how frightened she was, and how at last an old peasant woman on her way home from market had found her crying under a hedge, and had brought her home again to her mother. This thrilling adventure was listened to with the greatest interest.

"How pleased your mother must have been to see you again!" said Gladys. "Does she still live in that queer old town? Doesn't she mind you going away from her?"

"Alas!" said Léonie, and the tears twinkled in her bright eyes, "my mother is no longer of this world. She went away from me several years ago. I shall not see her again till in heaven."

"That's like us," said Gladys. "We've no Mamma. Did you know?"

"But you've a good Papa," said Léonie.

"Yes," said Gladys, rather doubtfully, for somehow the idea of a real flesh-and-blood Papa seemed to be getting more instead of less indistinct now that they were soon to see him. "But he's been away such a very long time."

"Poor darlings," said Léonie.

"And have you no Papa, no little brothers, not any one like that?" inquired Gladys.

"I have some cousins — very good people," said Léonie. "They live in Paris, where we are now going. If there had been time I should have liked to go to see them. But we shall stay no time in Paris — just run from one station to the other."

"But the luggage?" said Gladys. "Mrs. Marton has a lot of boxes. I don't see how you can *run* if you have them to carry. I think it would be better to take a cab, even if it does cost a little more. But perhaps there are no cabs in Paris. Is that why you talk of running to the station?"

Léonie had burst out laughing half-way through this speech, and though she knew it was not very polite, she really could not help it. The more she tried to stop, the more she laughed.

"What is the matter?" said Gladys at last, a little offended.

"I beg your pardon," said Léonie; "I know it is rude. But, Mademoiselle, the idea" — and here she began to laugh again — "of Monsieur and Madame

and me all running with the boxes! It was too
amusing!"

Gladys laughed herself now, and so did Roger.

"Then there are cabs in Paris," she said in a tone
of relief. "I am glad of that. Papa will have one
all ready for us, I suppose. What time do we get
there, Léonie?"

Léonie shook her head.

"A very disagreeable time," she said, "quite, quite
early in the morning, before anybody seems quite
awake. And the mornings are already so cold. I
am afraid you will not like Paris very much at
first."

"Oh yes, they will," said Mrs. Marton, who had
overheard the last part of the conversation. "Think
how nice it will be to see their Papa waiting for
them, and to go to a nice warm house and have
breakfast; chocolate, most likely. Do you like
chocolate?"

"Yes, very much," said Gladys and Roger.

"I think it is not you to be pitied, anyway," Mrs.
Marton went on, for the half-appealing, half-frightened look of the little things touched her. "It's
much worse for us three, poor things, travelling on
all the way to Marseilles."

"That's where Papa's been. Mrs. Lacy showed
it me on the map. What a long way! Poor Mrs.
Marton. Wouldn't Mr. Marton let you stay at Paris
with us till you'd had a rest?"

"We'd give you some of our chocolate," said
Roger hospitably.

"And let poor Phillip, that's Mr. Martin," replied the young lady, "go all the way to India alone?"

The children looked doubtful.

"You could go after him," suggested Roger.

"But Léonie and I wouldn't like to go so far alone. It's nicer to have a man to take care of you when you travel. You're getting to be a man, you see, Roger, already — learning to take care of your sister."

"I *have* growed a good big piece on the nursery door since my birthday," agreed Roger complacently. "But when Papa's there he'll take care of us both till I'm quite big."

"Ah, yes, that will be best of all," said Mrs. Marton, smiling. "I do hope Papa will be there all right, poor little souls," she added to herself. For, though young, Mrs. Marton was not thoughtless, and she belonged to a happy and prosperous family where since infancy every care had been lavished on the children, and somehow since she had seen and talked to Gladys and Roger their innocence and loneliness had struck her sharply, and once or twice a misgiving had come over her that in her anxiety to get rid of the children, and to waste no money, Susan Lacy had acted rather hastily. "Captain Bertram should have telegraphed again," she reflected. "It is nearly a week since he did so. I wish I had made Phillip telegraph yesterday to be sure all was right. The Lacys need not have known anything about it."

But they were at Dover now, and all these fears

and reflections were put out of her head by the bustle
of embarking and settling themselves comfortably,
and devoutly hoping they would have a good passage.
The words meant nothing to Gladys and Roger.
They had never been on the sea since they were
little babies, and had no fears. And, fortunately,
nothing disturbed their happy ignorance, for, though
cold, the sea was very smooth. They were disappointed at the voyage being made in the dark, as
they had counted on all sorts of investigations into
the machinery of the "ship," and Roger had quite
expected that his services would be required to help
to make it go faster, whereas it seemed to them only
as if they were taken into a queer sort of drawing-
room and made to lie down on red sofas, and covered
up with shawls, and that then there came a booming
noise something like the threshing machine at the
farm where they sometimes went to fetch butter and
eggs, and then — and then — they fell asleep, and
when they woke they were being bundled into
another railway carriage! Léonie was carrying
Roger, and Gladys, as she found to her great disgust
— she thought herself far too big for anything of the
kind — was in Mr. Marton's arms, where she struggled
so that the poor man thought she was having an
attack of nightmare, and began to soothe her as if
she were about two, which did not improve matters.

"Hush, hush, my dear. You shall go to sleep
again in a moment," he said. "But what a little
vixen she is!" he added, when he had at last got
Gladys, red and indignant, deposited in a corner.

"I'm too big to be carried," she burst out, half sobbing. "I wouldn't even let *Papa* carry me."

But kind Mrs. Marton, though she could hardly help laughing, soon put matters right by assuring Gladys that lots of people, even quite big grown-up ladies, were often lifted in and out of ships. When it was rough only the sailors could keep their footing. So Gladys, who was beginning to calm down and to feel a little ashamed, took it for granted that it had been very rough, and told Mr. Marton she was very sorry — she had not understood. The railway carriage was warm and comfortable, so after a while the children again did the best thing they could under the circumstances — they went to sleep. And so, I think, did their three grown-up friends.

Gladys was the first to wake. She looked round her in the dim morning light — all the others were still asleep. It felt chilly, and her poor little legs were stiff and numb. She drew them up on to the seat to try to warm them, and looked out of the window. Nothing to be seen but damp flat fields, and trees with a few late leaves still clinging to them, and here and there a little cottage or farmhouse looking, like everything else, desolate and dreary. Gladys withdrew her eyes from the prospect.

"I don't like travelling," she decided. "I wonder if the sun never shines in this country."

A little voice beside her made her look round.

"Gladdie," it said, "are we near that place? Are you *sure* Papa will be there? I'm so tired of these railways, Gladdie."

"So am I," said Gladys sympathisingly. "I should think we'll soon be there. But I'm sure I shan't like Paris, Roger. I'll ask Papa to take us back to Mrs. Lacy's again."

Roger gave a little shiver.

"It's such a long way to go," he said. "I wouldn't mind if only Ellen had come with us, and if we had chocolate for breakfast."

But their voices, low as they were, awakened Léonie, who was beside them. And then Mrs. Marton awoke, and at last Mr. Marton, who looked at his watch, and finding they were within ten minutes of Paris, jumped up and began fussing away at the rugs and shawls and bags, strapping them together, and generally unsettling everybody.

"We must get everything ready," he said. "I shall want to be free to see Bertram at once."

"But there's never a crowd inside the station here," said his wife. "They won't let people in without special leave. We shall easily catch sight of Captain Bertram if he has managed to get inside."

"He's sure to have done so," said Mr. Marton, and in his anxiety to catch the first glimpse of his friend, Mr. Marton spent the next ten minutes with his head and half his body stretched out of the window long before the train entered the station, though even when it arrived there the dim light would have made it difficult to recognise any one.

Had there been any one to recognise! But there was not. The train came to a stand at last. Mr. Marton had eagerly examined the faces of the two

IN ANOTHER MOMENT THE LITTLE PARTY WAS MAKING ITS WAY THROUGH
THE STATION. — p. 39.

or three men, *not* railway officials, standing on the platform, but there was no one whom by any possibility he could for a second have taken for Captain Bertram. Mrs. Marton sat patiently in her place, hoping every instant that "Phillip" would turn round with a cheery "all right, here he is. Here, children!" and oh, what a weight — a weight that all through the long night journey had been mysteriously increasing — would have been lifted off the kind young lady's heart had he done so! But no; when Mr. Marton at last drew in his head there was a disappointed and perplexed look on his good-natured face.

"He's not here — not on the platform, I mean," he said, hastily correcting himself. "He must be waiting outside; we'll find him where we give up the tickets. It's a pity he didn't manage to get inside. However, we must jump out. Here, Léonie, you take Mrs. Marton's bag, I'll shoulder the rugs. Hallo there," to a porter, "that's all right. You give him the things, Léonie. Omnibus, does he say? Bless me, how can I tell? Bertram's got a cab engaged most likely, and we don't want an omnibus for us three. You explain to him, Léonie."

Which Léonie did, and in another moment the little party was making its way through the station, among the crowd of their fellow-passengers. Mr. Marton first, with the rugs, then his wife holding Gladys by the hand, then Léonie and Roger, followed by the porter bringing up the rear. Mrs. Marton's heart was not beating fast by this time; it was al-

most standing still with apprehension. But she said
nothing. On they went through the little gate where
the tickets were given up, on the other side of which
stood with eager faces the few expectant friends who
had been devoted enough to get up at five o'clock to
meet their belongings who were crossing by the night
mail. Mr. Marton's eyes ran round them, then
glanced behind, first to one side and then to the
other as if Captain Bertram could jump up from some
corner like a jack-in-the-box. His face grew graver
and graver, but he did not speak. He led his wife
and the children and Léonie to the most comfortable
corner of the dreary waiting-room, and saying shortly.
" I'm going to look after the luggage and to hunt up
Bertram. He must have overslept himself if he's not
here yet. You all wait here quietly till I come back,"
disappeared in the direction of the luggage-room.

Mrs. Marton did not speak either. She drew
Gladys nearer her, and put her arm round the little
girl as if to protect her against the disappointment
which she *felt* was coming. Gladys sat perfectly
silent. What she was expecting, or fearing, or even
thinking, I don't believe she could have told. She
had only one feeling that she could have put into
words, " Everything is *quite* different from what I
thought. It isn't at all like going to Papa."

But poor little Roger tugged at Léonie, who was
next him.

" What are we waiting here in this ugly house
for?" he said. " Can't we go to Papa and have our
chocolate?"

Léonie stooped down and said something to soothe him, and after a while he grew drowsy again, and his little head dropped on to her shoulder. And so they sat for what seemed a terribly long time. It was more than half an hour, till at last Mr. Marton appeared again.

" I've only just got out that luggage," he said. " What a detestable plan that registering it is! And now I've got it I don't know what to do with it, for —"

" Has he not come?" interrupted his wife.

Mr. Marton glanced at Gladys. She did not seem to be listening.

" Not a bit of him," he replied. " I've hunted right through the station half a dozen times, and it's an hour and a half since the train was due. It cannot be some little delay. It's a pretty kettle of fish and no mistake."

Mrs. Marton's blue eyes gazed up in her husband's face with a look of the deepest anxiety.

" What *is* to be done?" she said.

CHAPTER IV.

"WHAT IS TO BE DONE?"

"That is the question."

HAMLET.

YES, "what was to be done?" That was certainly the question. Mr. Marton looked at his wife for a moment or two without replying. Then he seemed to take a sudden resolution.

"We can't stay here all the morning, that's about all I can say at present," he said. "Come along, we'd better go to the nearest hotel and think over matters."

So off they all set again — Mr. Marton and the rugs, Mrs. Marton and Gladys, Léonie and Roger — another porter being got hold of to bring such of the bags, etc., as were not left at the station with the big luggage. Gladys walked along as if in a dream; she did not even wake up to notice the great wide street and all the carriages, and omnibuses, and carts, and people as they crossed to the hotel in front of the station. She hardly even noticed that all the voices about her were talking in a language she did not understand — she was completely dazed — the only words which remained clearly in her brain were the strange ones which Mr. Marton had made use of — "a pretty kettle of fish and no mistake." "No mistake," that must mean that Papa's not coming to the station was not a mistake, but that there was some reason for it. But "a kettle of fish," what *could* that have to do with it all? She completely lost herself in puzzling about it. Why she did not simply ask Mrs. Marton to explain it I cannot tell. Perhaps the distressed anxious expression on that young lady's own face had something to do with her not doing so.

Arrived at the hotel, and before a good fire in a large dining-room at that early hour quite empty, a slight look of relief came over all the faces. It was something to get warmed at least! And Mr. Marton ordered the hot chocolate for which Roger had been pining, before he said anything else. It came almost at once, and Léonie established the children at one of the little tables, drinking her own coffee standing, that she might attend to them and join in the talking of her master and mistress if they wished it.

Roger began to feel pretty comfortable. He had not the least idea where he was — he had never before in his life been at a hotel, and would not have known what it meant — but to find himself warmed and fed and Gladys beside him was enough for the moment; and even Gladys herself began to feel a very little less stupefied and confused. Mr. and Mrs. Marton, at another table, talked gravely and in a low voice. At last Mr. Marton called Léonie.

"Come here a minute," he said, "and see if you can throw any light on the matter. You are more

at home in Paris than we are. Mrs. Marton and I
are at our wits' end. If we had a few days to spare
it would not be so bad, but we have not. Our berths
are taken, and we cannot afford to lose three pas-
sages."

"Mine too, sir," said Léonie. "Is mine taken
too?"

"Of course it is. You didn't suppose you were
going as cabin-boy, did you?" said Mr. Marton rather
crossly, though I don't think his being a little cross
was to be wondered at. Poor Léonie looked very
snubbed.

"I was only wondering," she said meekly, "if I
could have stayed behind with the poor children
till — "

"Impossible," said Mr. Marton; "lose your passage for a day or two's delay in their father's fetching them. If I thought it was more than that I
would send them back to England," he added, turning to his wife.

"And poor Mrs. Lacy so ill! Oh no, that would
never do," she said.

"And there's much more involved than our pas-
sages," he went on. "It's as much as my appointment is worth to miss this mail. It's just this —
Captain Bertram is either here, or has been detained
at Marseilles. If he's still there, we can look him up
when we get there to-morrow; if he's in Paris, and
has made some stupid mistake, we must get his
address at Marseilles, he's sure to have left it at the
hotel there for letters following him, and telegraph

back to him here. I never did know anything so
senseless as Susan Lacy's not making him give a
Paris address," he added.

"He was only to arrive here yesterday or the day
before," said Mrs. Marton.

"But the friends who were to have a nurse ready
for the children? We should have had *some* address."

"Yes," said Mrs. Marton self-reproachfully. "I
wish I had thought of it. But Susan was so *sure* all
would be right. And certainly, in case of anything
preventing Captain Bertram's coming, it was only
natural to suppose he would have telegraphed, or sent
some one else, or done *something*."

"Well—all things considered," said Mr. Marton,
"it seems to me the best thing to do is to leave the
children here, *even* if we had a choice, which I must
say I don't see! For I don't know how I could send
them back to England, nor what their friends there
might find to say if I did—nor can we—"

"Take them on to Marseilles with us?" interrupted Mrs. Marton. "Oh, Phillip, would not that
be better?"

"And find that their father had just started for
Paris?" replied her husband. "And then think of
the expense. Here, they are much nearer at hand
if they have to be fetched back to England."

Mrs. Marton was silent. Suddenly another idea
struck her. She started up.

"Supposing Captain Bertram has come to the station since we left," she exclaimed. "He may be
there now."

Mr. Marton gave a little laugh.

"No fear," he said. "Every official in the place knows the whole story. I managed to explain it, and told them to send him over here."

"And what are you thinking of doing, then? *Where* can we leave them?"

Mr. Marton looked at his watch.

"That's just the point," he said. "We've only three hours unless we put off till the night express, and that is running it too fine. Any little detention and we might miss the boat."

"We've run it too fine already, I fear," said Mrs. Marton dolefully. "It's been my fault, Phillip — the wanting to stay in England till the last minute."

"It's Susan Lacy's fault, or Bertram's fault, or both our faults for being too good-natured," said Mr. Marton gloomily. "But that's not the question now. I don't think we *should* put off going, for — another reason — it would leave us no time to look up Bertram at Marseilles. Only if we had had a few hours, I could have found some decent people to leave the children with here, some good 'pension,' or — "

"But such places are all so dear, and we have to consider the money too."

"Yes," said Mr. Marton, "we have *literally* to do so. I've only just in cash what we need for ourselves, and I couldn't cash a cheque here all in a minute, for my name is not known. But something must be fixed, and at once. I wonder if it would be any good if I were to consult the manager of this hotel? I — "

"Pardon," said Léonie, suddenly interrupting. "I have an idea. My aunt — she is really my cousin, but I call her aunt — you know her by name, Madame?" she went on, turning to Mrs. Marton. "My mother often spoke of her"—for Mrs. Marton's family had known Léonie's mother long ago when she had been a nurse in England—"Madame Nestor. They are upholsterers in the Rue Verte, not very far from here, quite in the centre of Paris. They are very good people — of course, quite in a little way; but honest and good. They would do their best, just for a few days! It would be better than leaving the dear babies with those we knew nothing of. I think I could persuade them, if I start at once!" She began drawing her gloves on while she was speaking. And she had spoken so fast and confusedly that for a moment or two both Mr. and Mrs. Marton stared at her, not clearly taking in what she meant.

"Shall I go, Madame?" she said, with a little impatience. "There is no time to lose. Of course if you do not like the idea—I would not have thought of it except that all is so difficult, so unexpected."

"Not like it?" said Mr. Marton; "on the contrary I think it's a capital idea. The children would be in safe hands, and at worst it can't be for more than a couple of days. If Captain Bertram has been detained at Marseilles by illness or anything — "

"That's not likely," interrupted Mrs. Marton, "he would have written or telegraphed."

"Well, then, if it's some stupid mistake about the

day, he'll come off at once when we tell him where they are. I was only going to say that, at worst, if he *is* ill, or anything wrong, we'll telegraph to Susan Lacy from Marseilles and she'll send over for them somehow."

"Should we not telegraph to her at once from here?"

Mr. Marton considered.

"I don't see the use," he said at last. "We can tell her nothing certain, nothing that she should act on yet. And it would only worry the old lady for nothing."

"I'm afraid she's too ill to be told anything about it," said Mrs. Marton.

"Then the more reason for waiting. But here we are losing the precious minutes, and Léonie all ready to start. Off with you, Léonie, as fast as ever you can, and see what you can do. Take a cab and make him drive fast," he called after her, for she had started off almost with his first words. "She's a very good sort of a girl," he added, turning to his wife.

"Yes, she always has her wits about her in an emergency," agreed Mrs. Marton. "I do hope," she went on, "that what we are doing will turn out for the best. I really never did know anything so unfortunate, and —"

"Is it all because of the kettle of fish? Did Papa tumble over it? Oh, I *wish* you'd tell me!" said a pathetic little voice at her side, and turning round Mrs. Marton caught sight of Gladys, her hands clasped, her small white face and dark eyes gazing up beseechingly. It had grown too much for her at last, the bewilderment and the strangeness, and the not understanding. And the change from the cramped-up railway carriage and the warm breakfast had refreshed her a little, so that gradually her ideas were growing less confused. She had sat on patiently at the table long after she had finished her chocolate, though Roger was still occupied in feeding himself by tiny spoonfuls. He had never had anything in the way of food more interesting than this chocolate, for it was still hot, and whenever he left it for a moment a skin grew over the top, which it was quite a business to clear away — catching now and then snatches of the eager anxious talk that was going on among the big people. And at last when Léonie hurried out of the room, evidently sent on a message, Gladys felt that she must find out what was the matter and what it all meant. But the topmost idea in her poor little brain was still the kettle of fish.

"If Papa has hurt himself," Gladys went on, "I think it would be better to tell me. I'd so much rather know. I'm not so very little, Mrs. Marton, Mrs. Lacy used to tell me things."

Mrs. Marton stooped down and put her arms round the pathetic little figure.

"Oh, I wish I could take you with me all the way. Oh ! I'm so sorry for you, my poor little pet," she exclaimed girlishly. "But indeed we are not keeping anything from you. I only wish we had anything to tell. We don't know ourselves ; we have no idea why your father has not come."

"But the kettle of fish?" repeated Gladys.

Mrs. Marton stared at her a moment, and then looked up at her husband. He grew a little red.

"It must have been I that said it," he explained. "It is only an expression; a way of speaking, little Gladys. It means when — when people are rather bothered, you know — and can't tell what to do. I suppose it comes from somebody once upon a time having had more fish than there was room for in their kettle, and not knowing what to do with them."

"Then we're the fish — Roger and I — I suppose, that you don't know what to do with?" said Gladys, her countenance clearing a little. "I'm very sorry. But I think Papa'll come soon; don't you?"

"Yes, I do," replied Mr. Marton. "Something must have kept him at Marseilles, or else he's mistaken the day after all."

"I thought you said it was 'no mistake!'" said Gladys.

Mr. Marton gave a little groan.

"Oh, you're a dreadful little person and no — there, I was just going to say it again! That's only an expression too, Gladys. It means, 'to be sure,' or 'no doubt about it,' though I suppose it is a little what one calls 'slang.' But you don't know anything about that, do you?"

"No," said Gladys simply, "I don't know what it means."

"And I haven't time to tell you, for we must explain to you what we're thinking of doing. You tell her, Lilly, I'm going about the luggage," he added,

turning to his wife, for he was dreadfully tender-
hearted, though he was such a big strong young man,
and he was afraid of poor Gladys beginning to cry or
clinging to them and begging them not to leave her
and Roger alone in Paris, when she understood what
was intended.

But Gladys was not the kind of child to do so.
She listened attentively, and seemed proud of being
treated like a big girl, and almost before Mrs. Marton had done speaking she had her sensible little
answer ready.

"Yes, I see," she said. "It is much better for us
to stay here, for Papa might come *very* soon, mightn't
he? Only, supposing he came this afternoon he
wouldn't know where we were?"

"Mr. Marton will give the address at the station,
in case your Papa inquires there, as he very likely
would, if a lady and gentleman and two children
arrived there from England this morning. And he
will also leave the address *here*, for so many people
come here from the station. And when we get to
Marseilles, we will at once go to the hotel where he
was — where he is still, perhaps; if he has left, he is
pretty sure to have given an address."

"And if he's not there — if you can't find him —
what will you do then?" said Gladys, opening wide
her eyes and gazing up in her friend's face.

Mrs. Marton hesitated.

"I suppose if we really could not find your father
at once, we should have to write or telegraph to Miss
Susan."

Gladys looked more distressed than she had yet done.

"Don't do that, please," she said, clasping her hands together in the way she sometimes did, "I'd much rather stay here a little longer till Papa comes. It would be such a trouble to Miss Susan — I know she did think we were a great trouble sometimes — and it would make Mrs. Lacy cry perhaps to have to say good-bye again, and she's so ill."

"Yes, I know she is," said Mrs. Marton, surprised at the little girl's thoughtfulness. "But you know, dear, we'd have to let them know, and then most likely they'd send over for you."

"But Papa's *sure* to come," said Gladys. "It would only be waiting a little, and I don't mind much, and I don't think Roger will, not if I'm with him. Will they be kind to us, do you think, those friends of Léonie's?"

"I'm sure they will; otherwise you know, dear, we wouldn't leave you with them. Of course it will only be for a day or two, for they are quite plain people, with quite a little house."

"I don't mind, not if they're kind to us," said Gladys. "But, oh! I do wish you weren't going away."

"So do I," said Mrs. Marton, who felt really very nearly breaking down herself. The sort of quiet resignation about Gladys was very touching, much more so than if she had burst out into sobs and tears. It was perhaps as well that just at that moment Mr. Marton came back, and saying something in a low voice to his wife, drew her out of the room, where in the passage stood Léonie.

"Back already," exclaimed Mrs. Marton in surprise.

"Oh yes," Léonie replied, "it was not far, and the coachman drove fast. But I thought it better not to speak before the children. It is a very little place, Madame. I wonder if it will do." She seemed anxious and a little afraid of what she had proposed.

"But can they take them? That is the principal question," said Mr. Marton.

"Oh yes," said Léonie. "My aunt is goodness itself. She understands it all quite well, and would do her best; and it would certainly be better than to leave them with strangers, and would cost much less; only — the poor children! — all is so small and so cramped. Just two or three little rooms behind the shop; and they have been used to an English nursery, and all so nice."

"I don't think they have been spoilt in some ways," said Mrs. Marton. "Poor little Gladys seems to mind nothing if she is sure of kindness. Besides, what else *can* we do? And it is very kind of your aunt to consent, Léonie."

"Yes, Madame. It is not for gain that she does it. Indeed it will not be gain, for she must find a room for her son, and arrange his room for the dear children. They have little beds among the furniture, so that will be easy; and all is very clean — my aunt is a good manager — but only — "

Léonie looked very anxious.

"Oh I'm sure it will be all right," said Mr. Marton. "I think we had better take them at once — I've got the luggage out — and then we can see for ourselves."

The children were soon ready. Gladys had been employing the time in trying to explain to poor little Roger the new change that was before them. He did not find it easy to understand, but, as Gladys had said, he did not seem to mind anything so long as he was sure he was not to be separated from his sister.

A few minutes' drive brought them to the Rue Verte. It was a narrow street — narrow, at least in comparison with the wide new ones of the present day, for it was in an old-fashioned part of Paris, in the very centre of one of the busiest quarters of the town; but it was quite respectable, and the people one saw were all well-dressed and well-to-do looking. Still Mr. Marton looked about him uneasily.

"Dreadfully crowded place," he said; "must be very stuffy in warm weather. I'm glad it isn't summer; we *couldn't* have left them here in that case."

And when the cab stopped before a low door leading into a long narrow shop, filled with sofas and chairs, and great rolls of stuffs for making curtains and beds and mattresses in the background, Mr. Marton's face did not grow any brighter. But it did brighten up, and so did his wife's, when from the farther end of the shop, a glass door, evidently leading into a little sitting-room, opened, and an elderly woman, with a white frilled cap and a bright healthy face, with the kindliest expression in the world, came forward eagerly.

"Pardon," she said in French, "I had not thought the ladies would be here so soon. But all will be ready directly. And are these the dear children?" she went on, her pleasant face growing still pleasanter.

"Yes," said Mrs. Marton, who held Gladys by one hand and Roger by the other, "these are the two little strangers you are going to be so kind as to take care of for a day or two. It is very kind of you, Madame Nestor, and I hope it will not give you much trouble. Léonie has explained all to you?"

"Oh yes," replied Madame Nestor, "poor darlings! What a disappointment to them not to have been met by their dear Papa! But he will come soon, and they will not be too unhappy with us."

Mrs. Marton turned to the children.

"What does she say? Is she the new nurse?" whispered Roger, whose ideas, notwithstanding Gladys's explanations, were still very confused. It was not a very bad guess, for Madame Nestor's good-humoured face and clean cap gave her very much the look of a nurse of the old-fashioned kind. Mrs. Marton stooped down and kissed the little puzzled face.

"No, dear," she said, "she's not your nurse. She is Léonie's aunt, and she's going to take care of you for a few days till your Papa comes. And she says she will be very, very kind to you."

But Roger looked doubtful.

"Why doesn't she talk p'operly?" he said, drawing back.

Mrs. Marton looked rather distressed. In the hurry and confusion she had not thought of this other difficulty — that the children would not understand what their new friends said to them! Gladys seemed to feel by instinct what Mrs. Marton was thinking.

"I'll try to learn French," she said softly, "and then I can tell Roger."

Léonie pressed forward.

"Is she not a dear child?" she said, and then she quickly explained to her aunt what Gladys had whispered. The old lady seemed greatly pleased.

"My son speaks a little English," she said, with evident pride. "He is not at home now, but in the evening, when he is not busy, he must talk with our little demoiselle."

"That's a good thing," exclaimed Mr. Marton, who felt the greatest sympathy with Roger, for his own French would have been sadly at fault had he had to say more than two or three words in it.

Then Madame Nestor took Mrs. Marton to see the little room she was preparing for her little guests. It was already undergoing a good cleaning, so its appearance was not very tempting, but it would not have done to seem anything but pleased.

"Anyway it will be *clean*," thought Mrs. Marton, "but it is very dark and small." For though it was the best bedroom, the window looked out on to a

narrow sort of court between the houses, whence but
little light could find its way in, and Mrs. Marton
could not help sighing a little as she made her way
back to the shop, where Mr. Marton was explaining
to Léonie about the money he was leaving with
Madame Nestor.

" It's all I can possibly spare," he said, "and it is
English money. But tell your aunt she is *sure* to
hear in a day or two, and she will be fully repaid for
any other expense she may have."

" Oh dear, yes," said Léonie, " my aunt is not at
all afraid about that. She has heard too much of the
goodness of Madame's family to have any fears about
anything Madame wishes. Her only trouble is
whether the poor children will be happy."

" I feel sure it will not be Madame Nestor's fault
if they are not," said Mrs. Marton, turning to the
kind old woman. It was all she could say, for she
felt by no means sure that the poor little things
would be able to be happy in such strange circumstances. The tears filled her eyes as she kissed
them again for the last time, and it was with a heavy
heart she got back into the cab which was to take
her husband and herself and Léonie to the Marseilles station. Mr. Marton was very little happier
than his wife.

" I wish to goodness Susan Lacy had managed her
affairs herself," he grumbled. " Poor little souls! I
shall be thankful to know that they are safe with
their father."

Léonie was sobbing audibly in her pocket-hand-kerchief.

"My aunt will be very kind to them, so far as she understands. That is the only consolation," she said, amidst her tears.

CHAPTER V.

IN THE RUE VERTE.

"The city looked sad. The heaven was gray."
SONGS IN MINOR KEYS.

"GLADDIE, are you awake?"

These were the first words that fell on Gladys's ears the next morning. I cannot say the first *sounds*, for all sorts of strange and puzzling noises had been going on above and below and on all sides since *ever* so early, as it seemed to her — in reality it had been half-past six — she had opened her eyes in the dark, and wondered and wondered where she was! Still in the railway carriage was her first idea, or on the steamer — once she had wakened enough to remember that she was *not* in her own little bed at Mrs. Lacy's. But no — people weren't undressed in the railway, even though they did sometimes lie down, and then —though the sounds she heard were very queer— she soon felt she was not moving. And bit by bit it all came back to her — about the long tiring journey, and no Papa at the station, and Mr. and Mrs. Marton and Léonie all talking together, and the drive in the cab to the crowded narrow street, and the funny old woman with the frilled cap, and the shop full of chairs and sofas, and the queer unnatural long afternoon after their friends went away, and

59

how glad at last she and Roger were to go to bed
even in the little stuffy dark room. *How* dark it
was! It must still be the middle of the night,
Gladys thought for some time, only that everybody
except herself and Roger seemed to be awake and
bustling about. For the workroom, as Gladys found
out afterwards, was overhead, and the workpeople
came early and were not particular about making a
noise. It was very dull, and in spite of all the little
girl's courage, a few tears *would* make their way up
to her eyes, though she tried her best to force them
back, and she lay there perfectly quiet, afraid of waking Roger, for she was glad to hear by his soft breathing that he was still fast asleep. But she could not
help being glad when through the darkness came the
sound of his voice.

" Gladdie, are you awake ? "

" Yes, dear," she replied, " I've been awake a long
time."

" So have I," said Roger in all sincerity — he had
been awake about three minutes. " It's very dark ;
is it the middle of the night ? "

" No. I don't think so," Gladys replied. " I hear
people making a lot of noise."

" Gladdie," resumed Roger half timidly — Gladys
knew what was coming — " may I get into your
bed ? "

" It's *very* small," said Gladys, which was true,
though even if it had not been so, she would probably have tried to get out of Roger's proposal, for
'she was not half so fond of his early morning visits

as he was. In the days of old "nurse" such doings were not allowed, but after she left, Gladys had not the heart to be very strict with Roger, and now in spite of her faint objection, she knew quite well she would have to give in, in the end.

"So's mine," observed Roger, though Gladys could not see what that had to do with it. But she said nothing, and for about half a minute there was silence in the dark little room. Then again.

"Gladdie," came from the corner, "mayn't I come? If we squeezed ourselves?"

"Very well," said Gladys, with a little sigh made up of many different feelings. "You can come and try."

But a new difficulty arose.

"I can't find my way in the dark. I don't 'amember how the room is in the light," said Roger dolefully. "When I first waked I *couldn't* think where we were. Can't you come for me, Gladdie?"

"How can I find my way if you can't," Gladys was on the point of replying, but she checked herself. She felt as if she could not speak the least sharply to her little brother, for he had nobody but her to take care of him, and try to make him happy. So she clambered out of her bed, starting with the surprise of the cold floor, which had no carpet, and trying to remember the chairs and things that stood in the way, managed to get across the room to the opposite corner where stood Roger's bed, without any very bad knocks or bumps.

"I'm here," cried Roger, as if that was a piece of

news, "I'm standing up in my bed jigging up and
down. Can you find me, Gladdie?"

"I'm feeling for you," Gladys replied. "Yes,
here's the edge of your cot. I would have found
you quicker if you had kept lying down."

"Oh, then, I'll lie down again," said Roger, but a
cry from Gladys stopped him.

"No, no, don't," she said. "I've found you now.
Yes, here's your hand. Now hold mine tight, and
see if you can get over the edge. That's right. Now
come very slowly, round by the wall is best. Here's
my bed. Climb in and make yourself as little as
ever you can. I'm coming. Oh, Roger, what a
squeeze it is!"

"I think it's littler than my bed," said Roger con-
solingly.

"It's not any bigger anyway," replied Gladys,
"we might just as well have stayed in yours."

"Is it because they're poor that the beds is so
very little?" asked Roger in a low voice.

"Oh, no, I don't think so," said Gladys gravely.
"They're very nice beds; I think they're almost
quite new."

"Mine was very comfitable," said Roger. "Do
you think all poor childrens have as nice beds?"

"I'm afraid not," said Gladys solemnly. "I'm
afraid that some haven't any beds at all. But why
do you keep talking about poor children, Roger?"

"I wanted to know about them 'cos, you see,
Gladys, if Papa wasn't never finded and we had to
stay here, *we'd* be poor."

"Nonsense," said Gladys rather sharply, in spite of her resolutions, "it *couldn't* be like that; of course Papa will come in a few days, and — and, even if he didn't, though that's quite nonsense, you know, I'm only saying it to make you see, *even* if he didn't, we'd not stay here."

"Where would we go?" said Roger practically.

"Oh, back to Mrs. Lacy perhaps. I wouldn't mind if Miss Susan was married."

"*I* would rather go to India with *them*," said Roger. Gladys knew whom he meant.

"But we can't, they've gone," she replied.

"Are they *gone*, and Lénie, that nice nurse — are they *gone?*" said Roger, appalled.

"Yes, of course. They'll be nearly at India by now, I daresay."

Roger began to cry.

"Why, you *knew* they were gone. Why do you cry about it now — you didn't cry yesterday?" said Gladys, a little sharply it must be confessed.

"I thought," sobbed Roger, "I thought they'd gone to look for Papa, and that they'd come to take us a nice walk every day, and — and —" He did not very well know *what* he had thought, but he had certainly not taken in that it was good-bye for good to the new friends he had already become fond of. "I'm *sure* you said they were gone to look for Papa," he repeated, rather crossly in his turn.

"Well, dear," Gladys explained, her heart smiting her, "they *have* gone to look for Papa. They thought they'd find him at the big town at the side of the sea

where the ships go to India from, and then they'd
tell him where we were in Paris, and he'd come quick
for us."

"Is this Paris?" asked Roger.

"Yes, of course," replied Gladys.

"I don't like it," continued the little boy. "Do
you, Gladys?"

"It isn't like what I thought," said Gladys; "nothing's like what I thought. I don't think when we
go home again, Roger, that I'll ever play at pretend
games any more."

"How do you mean when we go home?" said
Roger. "Where's home?"

"Oh, I don't know; I said it without thinking.
Roger—"

"What?" said Roger.

"Are you hungry?" asked Gladys.

"A little; are you?"

"Yes, I think I am, a little," replied Gladys.
"I couldn't eat all that meat and stuff they gave us
last night. I wanted our tea."

"And bread and butter," suggested Roger.

"Yes; at home I didn't like bread and butter
much, but I think I would now. I daresay they'd
give it us if I knew what it was called in their talking," said Gladys.

"It wouldn't be so bad if we knew their talking,"
sighed Roger.

"It wouldn't be so bad if it would get light," said
his sister. "I don't know what to do, Roger. It's
hours since they've all been up, and nobody's come to
us. I wonder if they've forgotten we're here."

" There's a little tiny, weeny *inch* of light beginning to come over there. Is that the window?" said Roger.

" I suppose so. As soon as it gets more light I'll get up and look if there's a bell," decided Gladys.

" And if there is?"

" I'll ring it, of course."

" But what would Miss— Oh, Gladys," he burst out with a merry laugh, the first Gladys had heard from him since the journey. " Isn't I silly? I was just going to say, 'What would Miss Susan say?' I quite forgot. I'm not sorry *she's* not here. Are you, Gladdie?"

" I don't know," the little girl answered. Truth to tell, there were times when she would have been very thankful to see Miss Susan, even though she was determined not to ask to go back to England till all hope was gone. " I'm not—" but what she was going to say remained unfinished. The door opened at last, and the frilled cap, looking so exactly the same as yesterday that Gladys wondered if Madame Nestor slept in it, only if so, how did she keep it from getting crushed, appeared by the light of a candle surrounding the kindly face.

" *Bon jour*, my children," she said.

" *That* means 'good-morning,'" whispered Gladys, " I know that. Say it, Roger."

Why Roger was to "say it" and not herself I cannot tell. Some unintelligible sound came from Roger's lips, for which Gladys hastened to apologise.

" He's trying to say 'good-morning' in French,"

she explained, completely forgetting that poor Madame Nestor could not understand her.

"Ah, my little dears," said the old woman — in her own language of course — " I wish I could know what you say. Ah, how sweet they are! Both together in one bed, like two little birds in a nest. And have you slept well, my darlings? and are you hungry?"

The children stared at each other, and at their old hostess.

"Alas," she repeated, "they do not understand. But they will soon know what I mean when they see the nice bowls of hot chocolate."

"Chocolate!" exclaimed both children. At last there was a word they could understand. Madame Nestor was quite overcome with delight.

"Yes, my angels, chocolate," she repeated, nodding her head. " The little servant is bringing it. But it was not she that made it. Oh, no! It was myself who took care it should be good. But you must have some light," and she went to the window, which had a curtain drawn before it, and outside heavy old-fashioned wooden shutters. No wonder in November that but little light came through. It was rather a marvel that at eight o'clock in the morning even a "tiny weeny *inch*" had begun to make its way.

With some difficulty the old woman removed all the obstructions, and then such poor light as there was came creeping in. But first she covered the two children up warmly, so that the cold air when the window was opened should not get to them.

SHE PLACED THE WHOLE ON A LITTLE TABLE WHICH SHE DREW CLOSE TO
THE BED. — p. 67.

" Would not do for them to catch cold, that would be a pretty story," she muttered to herself, for she had a funny habit of talking away about everything she did. Then, when all was air-tight again, there came a knock at the door. Madame Nestor opened it, and took from the hands of an invisible person a little tray with two steaming bowls of the famous chocolate and two sturdy hunches of very " hole-y " looking bread. No butter; that did not come within Madame Nestor's ideas. She placed the whole on a little table which she drew close to the bed, and then wrapping a shawl round the children, she told them to take their breakfast. They did not, of course, understand her words, but when she gave Roger his bowl and a preliminary hunch of bread into his hands, they could not but see that they were expected to take their breakfast in bed.

" But we're not ill," exclaimed Gladys; " we never stay in bed to breakfast except when we're ill."

Madame Nestor smiled and nodded. She had not a notion what Gladys meant, and on her side she quite forgot that the children could not understand her any better than she understood them.

" We never stay in bed to breakfast unless we're *ill*," repeated Gladys more loudly, as if that would help Madame Nestor to know what she meant.

" Never mind, Gladdie — the chocolate's very good," said Roger.

As before, " chocolate " was the only word Madame Nestor caught.

" Yes, take your chocolate," she repeated; " don't

let it get cold," and she lifted Gladys's bowl to give it to her.

"Stupid old thing," murmured Gladys, "why doesn't she understand? I should like to throw the chocolate in her face."

"Oh, Gladdie," said Roger reproachfully, "*think* what a mess it would make on the clean sheets!"

"I was only in fun — you might know that," said Gladys, all the same a little ashamed of herself.

Madame Nestor had by this time left the room with a great many incomprehensible words, but very comprehensible smiles and nods.

"I think breakfast in bed's very good," said Roger. Then came a sadder exclamation. "They've give me a pudding spoon 'stead of a teaspoon. It's *so* big — it won't hardly go into my mouth."

"And me too," said Gladys. "How stupid French people are! We'll have to drink it out of the bowls, Roger. How funny it is not to have tea-cups!"

"*I* think it's best to take it like soup," said Roger; "you don't need to put the spoon so much in your mouth if you think it's soup."

"I don't see what difference that makes," returned Gladys. But anyhow the chocolate and the bread disappeared, and then the children began to wonder how soon they might get up. Breakfast in bed wasn't so bad as long as there was the breakfast to eat, but when it was finished and there was no other amusement at hand they began to find it very tiresome. They had not so very long to wait, however, before Madame Nestor again made her appearance.

"Mayn't we get up?" cried both children, springing up in bed and jumping about, to show how ready they were. The old lady seemed to understand this time, but first she stood still for a moment or two with her head on one side admiring them.

"The little angels!" she said to herself. "How charming they are. Come now, my darlings, and get quickly dressed. It is cold this morning," and she took Roger in her arms to lift him down, while Gladys clambered out by herself. Their clothes were neatly placed in two little heaps on the top of the chest of drawers, which, besides the two beds and two or three chairs, was the only furniture in the room. Madame Nestor sat down on one of the chairs with Roger on her knee and began drawing on his stockings.

"Well done," she said, when one was safely in its place; "who would have thought I was still so clever a nurse!" and she surveyed the stockinged leg with much satisfaction. Roger seemed quite of her opinion, and stuck out the other set of pink toes with much amiability. He greatly approved of this mode of being dressed. Miss Susan had told Ellen he was big enough, at five years old, to put on his stockings himself, and she had also been very strict about sundry other nursery regulations. to which the young gentleman, in cold weather especially, was by no means partial. But he was not to get off as easily as he hoped. His silence, which with him always meant content, caught Gladys's attention, which till now had been taken up with her own stockings, as she had a particular way of her own of arranging them before putting them on.

"Roger," she exclaimed when she turned round
and saw him established on Madame Nestor's motherly lap; "what are you thinking of? You haven't
had your bath."

Roger's face grew red, and the expression of satisfaction fled.

"Need I—?" he was beginning meekly, but Gladys
interrupted him indignantly:

"You dirty little boy," she said. "What would
Miss Susan say?" at which Roger began to cry, and
poor Madame Nestor looked completely puzzled.

"We didn't have a bath last night, you know, because in winter Miss Susan thinks once a day is
enough. But I did think we should have had one,
after the journey too. And anyway this morning we
must have one."

But Madame Nestor only continued to stare.

"What shall I say? How *can* I make her understand?" said Gladys in despair. "Where's the little
basin we washed our faces and hands in yesterday,
Roger?" she went on, looking round the room. "Oh,
I forgot — it was downstairs. There's *no* basin in this
room! What dirty people!" then noticing the puzzled look on Madame Nestor's face, she grew frightened that perhaps she was vexed. "Perhaps she
knows what 'dirty' means," she half whispered to
herself. "Oh dear, I don't mean to be rude, ma'am,"
she went on, "but I suppose you don't know about
children. How *can* I explain?"

A brilliant idea struck her. In a corner of the
room lay the carpet-bag in which Miss Susan had

packed their nightgowns and slippers, and such things
as they would require at once. There were, too, their
sponges; and, as Miss Susan had been careful to point
out, a piece of *soap*, "which you never find in French
hotels," she had explained to Gladys. The little girl
dived into the bag and drew out the sponges and soap
in triumph.

"See, see," she exclaimed, darting back again to
the old lady, and flourishing her treasure-trove,
"that's what I mean! We must have a *bath*," raising
her voice as she went on; "we must be washed and
sponged;" and suiting the action to the word she
proceeded to pat and rub Roger with the dry sponge,
glancing up at Madame Nestor to see if the panto-
mime was understood.

"Ah, yes, to be sure," Madame Nestor exclaimed,
her face lighting up, "I understand now, my little
lady. All in good time — you shall have water to
wash your face and hands as soon as you are dressed.
But let me get this poor little man's things on
quickly. It is cold this morning."

She began to take off Roger's nightgown and to
draw on his little flannel vest, to which *he* would
have made no objection, but Gladys got scarlet with
vexation.

"No, no," she cried, "he must be washed *first*.
If you haven't got a bath, you might anyway let us
have a basin and some water. Roger, you *are* a
dirty boy. You might join me, and then perhaps
she'd do it."

Thus adjured, Roger rose to the occasion. He

slipped off Madame Nestor's knee, and stepping out
of his nightgown began an imaginary sponging of his
small person. But it was cold work, and Madame
Nestor seeing him begin to shiver grew really uneasy,
and again tried to get him into his flannels.

"No, no," said Roger, in his turn — he had left off
crying now — even the cold wasn't so bad as Gladdie
calling him a dirty boy. Besides who could tell
whether, somehow or other, Miss Susan might not
come to hear of it? Gladys might write her a letter.
"No, no," repeated Roger valorously, "we must be
washed *first*."

"You too," said Madame Nestor in despair; "ah,
what children!" But her good-humour did not desert her. Vaguely understanding what they meant
— for recollections began to come back to her mind
of what Léonie's mother used to tell her of the manners and customs of *her* nurseries — she got up, and
smiling still, though with some reproach, at her queer
little guests, she drew a blanket from the bed and
wrapped it round them, and then opening the door
she called downstairs to the little servant to bring a
basin and towel and hot water. But the little
servant did not understand, so after all the poor old
lady had to trot downstairs again herself.

"My old legs will have exercise enough," she said
to herself, "if the Papa does not come soon. However!"

"I'm sure she's angry," whispered Roger to Gladys
inside the blanket, "we needn't have a bath *every*
day, Gladdie."

"Hush," said Gladys sternly. "I'm *not* going to let you learn to be a dirty boy. If we can't have a bath we may at least be *washed*."

"But if Papa's coming for us to-day or to-morrow," Roger said, "the new nurse could wash us. I don't believe Papa's coming for us," he went on as if he were going to cry again. "I believe we're going to stay here in this nugly little house *always* — and it's all a trick. I don't believe we've got any Papa."

Poor Gladys did not know what to say. Her own spirits were going down again, for she too was afraid that perhaps Madame Nestor was vexed, and she began to wonder if perhaps it would have been better to let things alone for a day or two — "If I was sure that Papa would come in a day or two," she thought! But she felt sure of nothing now — everything had turned out so altogether differently from what she had expected that her courage was flagging, and she too, for the first time since their troubles had begun, followed Roger's example and burst into tears.

CHAPTER VI.

AMONG THE SOFAS AND CHAIRS.

"They wake to feel
That the world is a changeful place to live in,
And almost wonder if all is real."

LAVENDER LADY.

So it was rather a woe-begone looking little couple, crouching together in the blanket, that met old Madame Nestor's eyes when, followed by the little servant with the biggest basin the establishment boasted of, and carrying herself a queer-shaped tin jug full of hot water and with a good supply of nice white towels over her arm, she entered the room again.

"How now, my little dears?" she exclaimed; "not crying, surely? Why, there's nothing to cry for!"

Gladys wiped her eyes with the skirt of her little nightgown, and looked up. She did not know what the old woman was saying, but her tone was as kind as ever. It was very satisfactory, too, to see the basin, small as it was, and still more, the plentiful hot water.

"Thank you, ma'am," said Gladys gravely, and nudging Roger to do the same. Everybody, she had noticed the day before, had called the old lady

74

"madame," but that was the French for "ma'am" Léonie had told her, so she stuck to her native colours.

"Thank you," repeated Roger, but without the "ma'am." "It sounds so silly, nobody says it but servants," he maintained to Gladys, and no doubt it mattered very little whether he said it or not, as Madame Nestor didn't understand, though she was quick enough to see that her little guests meant to say something civil and kind. And the washing was accomplished — I cannot say without difficulty, for Roger tried to stand in the basin and very nearly split it in two, and there was a great splashing of water over the wooden floor — on the whole with success.

Poor Madame Nestor! When she had at last got her charges safely into their various garments, she sat down on a chair by the bed and fairly panted!

"It's much harder than cooking a dinner," she said to herself. "I can't think how my cousin Marie could stand it, if they have this sort of business every morning with English children. And five, six of them as there are sometimes! The English are a curious nation."

But she turned as smilingly as ever to Gladys and Roger; and Gladys, seeing that she was tired, and being sensible enough to understand that the kind old woman was really giving herself a great deal of trouble for their sake, went and stood close beside her, and gently stroked her, as she sometimes used to do — when Miss Susan was not there, be it remarked — to Mrs. Lacy.

"I wish I knew how to say 'thank you' in French," said Gladys to Roger. But Madame Nestor had understood her.

"Little dear," she said in her own language, "she thinks I am tired." The word caught Gladys's ear —"fatigued," she interrupted, "I know what that means. Poor Mrs. Nest," she explained to her little brother, "she says she's fatigued. I think we should kiss her, Roger," and both children lifted up their soft fresh rosy lips to the old woman, which was a language that needed no translation.

"Little dears," she repeated again, "but, all the same, I hope we shall soon have some news from the Papa. Ah!" she interrupted herself; "but there is the clock striking nine, and my breakfast not seen to. I must hasten, but what to do with these angels while I am in the kitchen?"

"Take them with you; children are very fond of being in a kitchen when they may," would have seemed a natural reply. But not to those who know what a Paris kitchen is. Even those of large grand houses would astonish many English children and big people, too, who have never happened to see them, and Madame Nestor's kitchen was really no better than a cupboard, and a cupboard more than half filled up with the stove, in and on which everything was cooked. There could be no question of taking the children into the kitchen, and the tiny room behind the shop was very dark and dull. Still it was the only place, and thither their old friend led them, telling them she must now go to cook the breakfast and they must try to amuse themselves; in the afternoon she would perhaps send them out a walk.

Two words in this were intelligible to Gladys.

"We are to be amused, Roger," she said, "and we are to promenade, that means a walk where the band plays like at Whitebeach last summer. I wonder where it can be?"

The glass door which led into the shop had a little curtain across it, but one corner was loose. This Gladys soon discovered.

"See here, Roger," she said, "we can peep into the shop and see if any one comes in. Won't that be fun?"

Roger took his turn of peeping.

"It aren't a pretty shop," he said, "it's all chairs and tables. I'd like a toy-shop, Gladdie, wouldn't you?"

"It wouldn't be much good if we mightn't play with the toys," Gladys replied. "But I'll tell you what, Roger, we might play at beautiful games of houses in there. We could have that corner where there are the pretty blue chairs for our drawing-room, and we might pay visits. Or I might climb in there behind that big sofa and be a princess in a giant's castle, and you might come and fight with the giant and get me out."

"And who'd be the giant?" asked Roger.

"Oh, we can *pretend* him. I can make a dreadful *booing* when I see you coming, and you can pretend you see him. But you must have a sword. What would do for a sword?" she went on, looking round.

"They haven't even a poker! I wish we had Miss Susan's umbrella."

"Here's one!" exclaimed Roger, spying the umbrella of Monsieur Adolphe, Madame Nestor's son, in a corner of the room. It was still rather damp, for poor Adolphe had had to come over in the heavy rain early that morning from the neighbouring inn where he had slept, having, as you know, given up his room to the two little strangers, and his mother would have scolded him had she noticed that he had put it down all dripping, though as the floor was a stone one it did not much matter. And the children were not particular. They screwed up the wet folds and buttoned the elastic, and then shouldering it, Roger felt quite ready to fight the imaginary giant.

There was a little difficulty about opening the door into the shop, and rather *too* little about shutting it, for it closed with a spring, and nearly snapped Roger and his umbrella in two. But he was none the worse save a little bump on his head, which Gladys persuaded him not to cry about. It would never do to cry about a knock when he was going to fight the giant, she assured him, and then she set to work, planning the castle and the way Roger was to come creeping through the forest, represented by chairs and stools of every shape, so that he grew quite interested and forgot all his troubles.

It really turned out a very amusing game, and when it was over they tried hide-and-seek, which would have been famous fun — there were so many hiding-holes among the bales of stuffs and pillows and uncovered cushions lying about—if they had had one or two more to play at it with them! But to playfellows they were little accustomed, so they did not much miss them, and they played away contentedly enough, though quietly, as was their habit. And so it came about that Madame Nestor never doubted that they were in the little back-room where she had left them, when a ring at the front door of the shop announced a customer.

This door was also half of glass, and when it was opened a bell rang. Gladys and Roger were busy looking for new hiding-places when the sudden sound of the bell startled them.

"Somebody's coming in," whispered Gladys; "Roger, let's hide. Don't let them see us; we don't know who they are," and quick as thought she stooped down in a corner, drawing her little brother in beside her.

From where they were they could peep out. Two ladies entered the shop, one young and one much older. The face of the older one Gladys did not distinctly see, or perhaps she did not much care to look at it, so immediately did the younger one seize her fancy. She was very pretty and pleasant looking, with bright brown hair and sweet yet merry eyes, and as she threw herself down on a seat which stood near the door, Gladys was able to see that she was neatly and prettily dressed.

"Aren't you tired, Auntie?" she said to the other lady.

"A little. It is farther than I thought, and we

have not much time. I wonder what colour will be prettiest for the curtains, Rosamond?"

"The shade of blue on that sofa over in the corner is pretty," said the young lady.

Gladys pinched Roger. It was precisely behind the blue-covered sofa that they were hiding.

"I wish they would be quick," said the elder lady. "Perhaps they did not hear the bell."

"Shall I go to the door and ring it again?" asked the one called Rosamond.

"I don't know; perhaps it would be better to tap at the glass door leading into the house. Madame Nestor sits in there, I fancy. She generally comes out at that door."

"I don't fancy she is there now," said the young lady. "You see we have come so early. It has generally been in the afternoon that we have come. Madame Nestor is probably busy about her 'household avocations' at this hour," she added, with a smile.

"I wonder what that means," whispered Gladys. "I suppose it means the dinner."

Just at that moment the door opened, and Madame Nestor appeared, rather in a flutter. She was so sorry to have kept the ladies waiting, and how unfortunate! Her son had just gone to their house with the patterns for the curtains. He would have sent yesterday to ask at what hour the ladies would be at home, but they had all been so busy — an unexpected arrival — and Madame Nestor would have gone on to give all the story of Léonie's sudden visit to beg a shelter for

the two little waifs, had not the ladies, who knew of
old the good dame's long stories, cut her short as
politely as they could.

"We are very hurried," said the one whom the
young lady called "auntie." "I think the best thing
to be done is to get home as quickly as we can, and
perhaps we shall still find your son there; if not, he
will no doubt have left the patterns, so please tell
him to try to come this evening or to-morrow morning
before twelve, for we must have the curtains this
week."

Of course — of course — Madame Nestor agreed
to everything as amiably as possible, and the ladies
turned to go.

"Are you much troubled with mice?" said the
younger lady as they were leaving. "I have heard
queer little noises two or three times over in that
corner near the blue sofa while we were speaking."

Old Madame Nestor started.

"Mice!" she exclaimed. "I hope not. It would
be very serious for us — with so many beautiful stuffs
about. I must make them examine, and if necessary
get a cat. We have not had a cat lately — the last
was stolen, she was such a beauty, and — "

And on the old body would have chattered for
another half-hour, I daresay, had not the ladies again
repeated that they were very hurried and must hasten
home.

The idea of mice had taken hold of Madame Nestor's mind; it made her for the moment forget the
children, though in passing through the little room

where she had left them she had wondered where they were. She hurried into the workroom to relate her fears, and Gladys and Roger, as soon as she had left the shop, jumped up, not sorry to stretch their legs after having kept them still for nearly a quarter of an hour.

"I wonder if she'd be angry at our playing here," said Gladys. "What fun it was hiding and those ladies not knowing we were there! I think they were nice ladies, but I wish they had kept on talking properly. I liked to hear what they said."

"Why doesn't everybody talk properly here if some does?" asked Roger.

"I suppose," said Gladys, though she had not thought of it before, it had seemed so natural to hear people talking as she had always heard people talk — "I suppose those ladies are English. I wish they had talked to *us*, Roger. Perhaps they know Papa."

"They couldn't talk to us when they didn't know us was there," said Roger, with which Gladys could not disagree. But it made her feel rather sorry not to have spoken to the ladies — it would have been very nice to have found some one who could understand what they said.

"I wish we hadn't been hiding," she was going to say, but she was stopped by a great bustle which began to make itself heard in the sitting-room, and suddenly the door into the shop opened, and in rushed Madame Nestor, followed by the servant and two or three of the workpeople.

"Where are they, then? Where can they have gone, the poor little angels?" exclaimed the old lady, while the servant and the others ran after her, repeating:

"Calm yourself, Madame, calm yourself. They cannot have strayed far — they will be found."

Though the children could not understand the words, they could not *mis*understand the looks and the tones, and, above all, the distress in their kind old friend's face. They were still half hidden, though they were no longer crouching down on the floor. Out ran Gladys, followed by Roger.

"Are you looking for us, Mrs. Nest?" she said. "Here we are! We've only been playing at hiding among the chairs and sofas."

Madame Nestor sank down exhausted on the nearest arm-chair.

"Oh, but you have given me a fright," she panted out. "I could not imagine where they had gone," she went on, turning to the others. "I left them as quiet as two little mice in there," pointing to the sitting-room, "and the moment my back was turned off they set."

"It is always like that with children," said Mademoiselle Anna, the forewoman. She was a young woman with very black hair and very black eyes and a very haughty expression. No one liked her much in the workroom — she was so sharp and so unamiable. But she was very clever at making curtains and covering chairs and sofas, and she had very good taste, so Madame Nestor, who was, besides, the kind-

est woman in the world, kept her, though she disliked
her temper and pride.

"Poor little things — we have all been children in
our day," said Madame Nestor.

"That is possible," replied Mademoiselle Anna,
"but all the same, there are children and children.
I told you, Madame, and you will see I was right;
you do not know the trouble you will have with these
two little foreigners — brought up who knows how —
and a queer story altogether it seems to me," she
added, with a toss of her head.

Gladys and Roger had drawn near Madame Nestor.
Gladys was truly sorry to see how frightened their
old friend had been, and she wished she knew how to
say so to her. But when Mademoiselle Anna went
on talking, throwing disdainful glances in their direction, the children shrank back. They could not
understand what she was saying, but they *felt* she
was talking of them, and they had already noticed
her sharp unkindly glances the evening before.

"Why is she angry with us?" whispered Roger.

But Gladys shook her head. "I don't know," she
replied. "She isn't as kind as Mrs. Nest and her
son. Oh I do wish Papa would come for us, Roger!"

"So do I," said the little fellow.

But five minutes after, he had forgotten their
troubles, for Madame Nestor took them into the long
narrow room where she and her son and some of their
workpeople had their meals, and established them at
one end of the table, to have what *she* called their
"breakfast," but what to the children seemed their

dinner. She was very kind to them, and gave them what she thought they would like best to eat, and some things, especially an omelette, they found very good. But the meat they did not care about.

"It's so greasy, I can't eat it," said Gladys, after doing her best for fear Madame Nestor should think her rude. And Roger, who did not so much mind the greasiness of the gravy, could not eat it either because it was cooked with carrots, to which he had a particular dislike. They were not dainty children generally, but the stuffy room, and the different kind of cooking, and above all, perhaps, the want of their usual morning walk, seemed to take away their appetite. And the sight of Mademoiselle Anna's sharp contemptuous face across the table did not mend matters.

"I wish we had some plain cold meat and potatoes," said Gladys, "like what we had at home. I could even like some nice plain bread and butter."

"Not *this* bread," said Roger, who was beginning to look doleful again. "I don't like the taste of this bread."

So they both sat, watching all that was going on, but eating nothing themselves, till Madame Nestor, who had been busy carving, caught sight of them.

"They do not eat, those poor dears," she said to her son; "I fear the food is not what they are accustomed to — but I cannot understand them nor they me. It is too sad! Can you not try to find out what they would like, Adolphe? You who speak English?"

Monsieur Adolphe got very red; he was not generally shy, but his English, which he was rather given to boasting of when there was no need for using it, seemed less ready than his mother had expected. However, like her, he was very kind-hearted, and the sight of the two grave pale little faces troubled him. He went round to their side of the table.

"You not eat?" he said. "Miss and Sir not eat nothing. Find not good?"

Gladys's face brightened. It was something to have some one who understood a little, however little.

"Oh yes," she said timidly, afraid of appearing uncivil, "it is very good; but we are not hungry. We are not accustomed to rich things. Might we —" she went on timidly, "do you think we might have a little bread and butter?"

Monsieur Adolphe hesitated. He found it much more difficult than he had had any idea of to understand what Gladys said, though she spoke very plainly and clearly.

"Leetle — leetle?" he repeated.

"A little bread and butter," said Gladys again. This time he understood.

"Bread and butter; I will go see," he answered, and then he hurried back to his mother, still busy at the side-table.

"They do not seem accustomed to eat meat," he said, "they ask for bread and butter."

"The greedy little things!" exclaimed Mademoiselle Anna, who had got up from her seat on

pretence of handing a plate to Madame Nestor, but
in reality to hear all that was going on. "How can
they be so bold?"

"It is the custom in England," said the old lady.
"My cousin has often told me how the children there
eat so much bread and butter. But I have no fresh
butter in the house. Would not preserves please
them? Here, Françoise," she went on, calling to the
little servant. "Fetch some preserves from the cupboard, and give some with some bread to the poor
little angels."

"What a to-do to be sure!" muttered Anna to
Adolphe. "I only hope your mother will be paid
for the trouble she is giving herself, but I much
doubt it. I believe it is all a trick to get rid of the
two little plagues. English of the good classes do
not leave their children to anybody's tender mercies
in that way!"

"That is true," said Adolphe, who, though he had
a good deal of his mother's kind-heartedness, was
easily impressed by what Anna said. "And they
have certainly a curious accent. I had difficulty in
understanding them. I never heard an accent like
it in English."

"Exactly," said Anna, tossing her head, "they are
little cheats — no one will come for them, and no
money will be sent. You will see — and so will your
mother. But it will be too late. She should have
thought twice before taking on herself such a
charge."

"I am quite of your opinion," said Adolphe.

"Something must be done; my mother must be made to hear reason. If no one comes to fetch them in a day or two we must do something — even if I have to take them myself to the English Embassy."

"Quite right, quite right, Monsieur Adolphe," said Anna spitefully.

But Madame Nestor heard nothing of what they were saying. She was seated quite contentedly beside the children, happy to see them enjoying the bread and jam which they much preferred to the greasy meat, even though the bread tasted a little sour, though she could not persuade them to take any wine.

"It isn't good for children," said Gladys gravely, looking up into her face. But poor Madame Nestor shook her head.

"It is no use, my dears," she said in her own language. "I cannot understand! Dear me — I do wish the Papa would come. Poor dear angels — I fear I cannot make them happy! But at least I can wash up the dishes for Françoise and let her take them out a walk. You will like that — a nice promenade, will you not?"

Gladys jumped up joyfully.

"The promenade, Roger — we're going to hear the band play. Won't that be nice? Come let us go quick and get ready."

Madame Nestor was enchanted.

CHAPTER VII.

THE KIND-LOOKING GENTLEMAN.

" A friendly pleasant face he had,
  They really thought him very nice,
And when adown the street he'd gone
  They nodded to him twice."

CHANCE ACQUAINTANCES.

THEY were soon ready, for though Gladys had had vague thoughts of trying to explain that she would like the big trunk unfastened to get out their "best" things, she gave up the idea when Madame Nestor got down the new ulsters which she evidently thought quite good enough, and proceeded to wrap them both up warmly. It was cold, she said, and thanks to the way she glanced out-of-doors when she made this remark, at the same time carefully covering up their throats with the white silk handkerchiefs they had had for the journey, Gladys understood her.

" We don't look very nice, do we, Roger?" said the little girl, as with her brother's hand in hers, and Françoise, who was short and stout, and wore a big frilled cap, following close behind. " If there are a lot of children where the band plays we shall seem very plain. But I daresay it doesn't matter, and these ulsters are very warm."

For it was very cold. It was one of those gray

sunless days, less uncommon in Paris than some people imagine, and the Rue Verte was narrow and the houses composing it very high, so that *stray* gleams of sunshine did not very easily get into it. The children shivered a little as they stood for a moment hesitating as to which way Françoise meant them to go, and one or two foot-passengers passing hurriedly, as most people do in that busy part of the town, jostled the two little people so that they shrank back frightened.

"Give me your hands, little Sir and little Miss," said the sturdy peasant girl, catching hold of them, placing one on each side of her as she spoke. It went rather against Gladys's dignity, but still in her heart she was glad of Françoise's protection, though even with that they were a good deal bumped and pushed as they made their way along the narrow pavement.

"It will be nicer when we get to the Boulevards," said Françoise; "there the pavement is so much wider."

But Gladys did not understand. She thought the girl said something about *bulls* and *large*, and she looked up half frightened, expecting to see a troop of cattle coming along the street. There was, however, nothing of the kind to be seen.

"It's not like Whitebeach," said Gladys, trying to make Roger hear across Françoise's substantial person. But it was no use. Narrow as the street was, great heavy waggons and lurries came constantly following each other over the stones, so that the noise

"OH DON'T, DON'T CROSS THAT DREADFUL STREET," GLADYS EXCLAIMED. — p. 91.

was really deafening, and it was impossible to hear what was said. By peeping sometimes in front of Françoise and sometimes behind her, Gladys could catch sight of Roger's little figure. He was looking solemn and grave; she could tell that by the way he was walking, even when she did not see his face.

"I'm afraid he's very cold, poor little boy," thought Gladys to herself, quite forgetting her own little red nose and nipped fingers in concern for her brother.

It was a little better after a while when they got out of the narrow street into a much wider one. *Too* wide Gladys thought it, for the rush of carts and carriages and omnibuses and cabs was really frightening. She saw some people venturing to cross over to the other side in the midst of it all — one lady with a little boy, not much bigger than Roger, especially caught her attention. But she shut her eyes rather than watch them get across — which they did quite safely after all — so terrified was she of seeing them crushed beneath some of the monsters on wheels which seemed to the child's excited imagination to be pounding down one after the other on purpose to knock everything out of their way, like some great engines of war. And she squeezed Françoise's hand so tight that the girl turned round in a fright to see if any one was hurting Gladys, when a slight movement to one side made her fancy the little servant was intending to try to cross.

"Oh don't, don't cross that dreadful street," Gladys exclaimed. And Françoise understood what she meant, thanks to her tugs the other way, and set to work assuring her she had no such intention.

"Are you frightened of crossing?" said a voice close beside her — an English voice belonging to a gentleman who had heard her piteous entreaty.

"Yes, dreadfully. I'm sure we'll be killed if she takes us over," replied Gladys, lifting her little white face and troubled eyes to the stranger.

He turned to Françoise and explained to her that it was hardly safe to attempt to cross, especially as the little girl was so frightened. He spoke, of course, in French, which seemed to him as easy as his own language, and Françoise replied eagerly. Then again the stranger turned to Gladys:

"You need not be afraid, my dear little girl," he said, and his kind voice somehow made the tears come to her eyes, "your nurse does not wish to cross. You have not been long here, I suppose — you don't understand French?"

"No," said Gladys, gulping down a sob, "we've — we've only just come."

"Ah well, you'll soon feel more at home, and be able to explain all you mean for yourself. Good-bye," and raising his hat as perhaps an altogether Englishman would not have done to so little a girl, he smiled again, and in another moment had disappeared in the crowd.

"The nurse seems kind enough, but she's rather stupid — just a peasant. And those children look so refined. But they don't seem happy, poor little souls. I wonder who they can be," said the young man to himself as he walked away.

" I wish he was our Papa," said Roger.

" So do I," said Gladys. And then a queer sort of regret came over her that she had not said more to him. " Perhaps he knows Papa, and could have helped us to find him," was the vague thought in her childish brain. It seemed to her that any English-speaking person in this great town of Paris must know " Papa," or something about him.

Françoise walked on; *she* wished for nothing better than a stroll along the Boulevards, even though this was by no means the best part of them, or containing the prettiest shops. But Gladys kept wishing for the " promenade " and the band. At the corner of a side-street she caught sight of a church at a little distance with some trees and green not far from it. It looked quieter and less crowded, and Gladys was seized with a wish to explore in that direction.

She tugged at Françoise.

" Mayn't we go up there ? " she said, pointing in the direction of the trees. Françoise understood her. She was a good-natured girl, and turned with the children as Gladys wished, though it was against her liking to leave the noisy crowded Boulevards for the quieter side-streets.

When they got close to the trees they turned out to be in a little enclosure with railings, a very small attempt at a " square garden," for there were houses round it on all sides, and, cold as it was, a few nurses and children were walking about it and looking cheerful enough, though no doubt they wished they were not so far away from the prettier parts of Paris where the parks and walks for children are so lively and amusing. Gladys looked round with a mixture of approval and disappointment.

"It must be here that the band plays," she said to Roger; "but it isn't here to-day. And it's a very small place for a promenade; not nearly so pretty as it was at Whitebeach. But we might play here if it wasn't so cold. And there are nice benches for sitting on, you see."

"I don't like being here," said Roger, shaking his head. "I'd like to go home."

"Home"—again the word fell sadly on the little mother-sister's ear. But she said nothing to remind Roger of how homeless they were, though she could not help sighing when she thought of the only "going home" there was for them; the little dark bare cheerless bedroom, and the shop filled with sofas and chairs. Poor Madame Nestor doing her best, but understanding so little what a nice bright cosy nursery was like, and still worse, Mademoiselle Anna's sharp eyes flashing angrily at them across the table at meat times!

"Wouldn't you like to have a run, Roger?" said Gladys suddenly. "It would make us feel warmer, and there's a nice straight bit of path here."

Roger made no objection. He let go of Françoise's hand and took his sister's, and by signs Gladys managed to explain to the girl what they meant to do.

"One, two, three, and away," she called out with an attempt at merriment, and off they set. Roger's stumpy little legs could not go as fast as Gladys's longer and thinner ones, but she took care not to let him find that out, and she was rewarded by the colour in his cheeks, and the brighter look in his eyes when they got back to Françoise again.

"That's right," said she good-naturedly, and in her heart I think she too would have enjoyed a run, had it not been beneath her dignity to behave in so childish a manner within sight of the dignified nurses in their big cloaks and caps with streaming ribbons, who were strutting up and down the little enclosure.

But it grew colder and grayer.

"One could almost think it was going to snow," said Françoise, looking up at the sky. Gladys saw her looking up, but did not, of course, understand her words.

"I wonder if she thinks it's going to rain," she said to Roger. "Anyway it's dreadfully cold," and she gave a little shiver.

"We had better go home," said Françoise, for she was so accustomed to talking about everything she did that even the knowledge that she was not understood did not make her silent. And taking a hand of each child, she turned to go. Gladys and Roger did not mind; they felt tired, though they had not walked nearly so far as they often did at home, and cold, and there had been nothing in their walk to raise their poor little spirits, except perhaps the momentary glance of the bright-faced young Englishman.

"That gentleman we met looked very kind, didn't

he?" said Gladys to Roger, when they had got back to the Rue Verte, and Françoise was helping them to take off their boots.

"Yes," said Roger, in his sober little voice, "I wish — "

"What?" said Gladys.

"I wish he was our Papa!" said Roger again, with a sigh.

"He couldn't be," said Gladys, "he's too young."

"He was *much* bigger than you; he was bigger than *her*," persisted Roger, pointing to Françoise, for like many little children he could not separate the idea of age from size, and Gladys knew it was no use trying to explain to him his mistake.

"Anyway, he *isn't* our Papa," she said sadly. "I wonder what we shall do now," she went on.

"Isn't it tea-time?" asked Roger.

"I'm afraid they don't have tea here," said Gladys. "There's some wine and water and some bread on the table in the little room behind the shop. I'm afraid that's meant for our tea."

She was right; for when Françoise took them downstairs Madame Nestor immediately offered them wine and water, and when Gladys did her best to make the old lady understand that they did not like wine, she persisted in putting two or three lumps of sugar into the water in the glasses, which Roger did not object to, as he fished them out before they were more than half melted, and ate instead of drinking them, but which Gladys thought very nasty indeed, though she did not like not to take it as she had already refused the wine.

"I wish I could get out my doll," said she, "I don't know what to play with, Roger."

"I wish I could get my donkey," said Roger. And Madame Nestor saw that they looked dull and dreary, though she did not know what they said. A brilliant idea struck her. "I will get them some of the packets of patterns to look at," she said, "that will amuse them," and off she trotted to the work-room.

"Find me the books of patterns, the prettiest ones, of the silky stuffs for curtains, and some of the cretonnes," she said to one of the young girls sewing there.

Mademoiselle Anna looked up suspiciously.

"Is there some one in the shop?" she said. "Shall I call Monsieur Adolphe? He has just gone to the other workroom."

"No, no, do not trouble yourself," said Madame Nestor. "I only want the patterns to amuse my two little birds in there," and she nodded her head towards the room where the children were.

Anna gave her head a little toss.

"There is no letter about them yet, I suppose," she said.

"Of course not. How could there be?" replied the old lady. "The poor things have been here but one night. I do not see why you should trouble yourself to be so cross about them. You are not *yet* mistress of this house," upon which Anna murmured something about being sorry to see Madame Nestor troubled about the children, that was her only reason, she knew Madame to be so good, etc.

Madame Nestor said no more, for it was seldom she spoke sharply to any one, and, to tell the truth, she was a little afraid of Anna, who some time or other was to be married to Adolphe, and take the place of the old lady, who looked forward then to having some rest in a little home of her own. She did not wish to quarrel with Anna, for she knew she would make a clever and useful wife to her son, but still unkindness to any one, above all to these little helpless strangers, made her really angry.

She made the young workwoman help her to carry the big books of patterns to the little sitting-room, and at sight of them Gladys and Roger started up. They were pleased at the prospect of anything to do, poor little things, even lessons would have been welcome, and they were greatly delighted when, as well as the books, Madame Nestor produced a lot of scraps of cretonne with gay flowers and birds in all colour, and made them understand they might do as they liked with them.

"Let's cut them out," exclaimed Gladys, "we can cut out lovely things and then afterwards we can paste them on white paper and make all sorts of things with them."

But there were no scissors! Gladys opened and shut the middle and forefingers of her right hand repeating "scissors," till Madame Nestor understood and not only lent her a pair of her own, but sent a little way down the street to buy a little pair with blunt ends for Roger, so afraid was she of his cutting himself.

"Oh, how nice," exclaimed both children, jumping up to kiss the kind old woman. "Now we can cut out beautifully, and when we are tired of cutting out we can look at these lovely patterns," said Gladys, as she settled herself and Roger comfortably at the table, and Madame Nestor went off to the workroom again, quite satisfied about them for the time.

"You see there are *some* things to be got really very nice in Paris, Roger," said Gladys in her prim old-fashioned way. "These scissors are really very nice, and I don't think they were dear. Madame Nestor gave the boy a piece like a small sixpence, and he brought her a halfpenny back. That isn't dear."

"What did he bring her a halfpenny for? Do they sell halfpennies in the shops here?" asked Roger, looking very puzzled.

"No, of course not. You're too little to understand. That's what they call 'giving change,'" replied Gladys, wisely. "Ellen told me that once when I went to a shop with her to buy something for Miss Susan. Now, Roger, will you cut out that blue bird, and I'll do these pinky flowers? Then afterwards we can paste them as if the bird was flying out of the flowers; won't that be pretty?"

"I'd rather do the flowers," said Roger. "The bird's nose is so twisty — I can't do it."

"Very well," said Gladys good-naturedly. "Then I'll do it, and you take the flowers. See they go in nice big rounds — you can easily do them."

And for an hour or two the children were as

really happy as they had been for a good while, and
when the thought of their father and what had become of him pressed itself forward on Gladys, she
pushed it back with the happy trust and hopefulness
of children that "to-morrow" would bring good news.

In a part of Paris, at some distance from the Rue
Verte, that very afternoon three people were sitting
together in a pretty drawing-room at "afternoon
tea." They were two ladies — a young, quite young
one, and an older. And the third person was a
gentleman, who had just come in.

"It's so nice to find you at home, and above all at
tea, Auntie," he said to the elder lady. "It is such
a horrid day — as bad as London, except that there's
no fog. You haven't been out, I suppose?"

"Oh yes, indeed we have," replied the young lady.
"We went a long way this morning — walking — to
auntie's upholsterer, quite in the centre of the town.
It looks very grim and uninviting there, the streets
are so narrow and the houses so high."

"I've walked a good way too to-day," said the
young man.

"I am glad to hear it, my boy," said his aunt. "I
have been a little afraid of your studying too hard
this winter, at least not taking exercise enough, and
you being so accustomed to a country life too!"

"I don't look very bad, do I?" said the young man,
laughing. He stood up as he spoke, and his aunt
and sister glanced at him with pride, though they
tried to hide it. He was tall and handsome, and the

expression of his face was particularly bright and pleasant.

"You are very conceited," said his sister. "I am not going to pay you any compliments."

He sat down again, and a more serious look came into his face; for some moments he did not speak.

"What are you thinking about, Walter?" asked his sister.

Walter looked up.

"I was thinking about two little children I met to-day," he said. "Away over on the Boulevard X—— ever so far."

"That is not so very far from where we were this morning," interrupted the aunt.

"They were such tiny things, and they looked so forlorn and so unhappy; I can't get them out of my head," said Walter.

"Did you give them anything? Did they seem quite alone?" asked Rosamond.

Walter laughed.

"You don't understand," he said; "they were not beggars. Bless me! I shouldn't like to encounter that very imperious little lady if she thought I had made you think they were beggars."

"'Imperious little lady,' and 'poor forlorn little things;' what do you mean, Walter?" said Rosamond.

"I mean what I say. They did look forlorn little creatures, and yet the small girl was as imperious as a princess. They were two little English children, newly arrived evidently. for they didn't understand a word of French. And they were being taken care of by a stupid sort of peasant girl turned into a 'bonne.' And the little girl thought the nurse was going to cross the street, and that she and the small boy would be killed, and she couldn't make the stupid owl understand, and I heard them talking English, and so I came to the rescue — that was all."

"It isn't any thing so very terrible," said the aunt. " No doubt they and their bonne will learn to understand each other in a little."

"It wasn't that only," said Walter reflectively; " there was something out of gear, I am sure. The children looked so superior to the servant, and so — so out of their element dragging up and down that rough crowded place, while she gaped at the shop windows. And there was something so pathetic in the little girl's eyes."

" In spite of her imperiousness," said Rosamond teasingly.

" Yes," said Walter, without smiling. " It was queer altogether — the sending them out in that part of the town with that common sort of servant — and their not knowing any French. I suppose the days are gone by for stealing children or that sort of thing; but I could really have fancied there was something of the kind in this case."

Rosamond and her aunt grew grave.

" Poor little things!" they said. " Why did you not ask them who they were or where they came from, or something ? " added Rosamond.

" I don't know. I wish I had," said Walter. " But

I'm not sure that I would have ventured on such a freedom with the little girl, I'm not indeed."

"Then they didn't look *frightened* — the maid did not seem cross to them?"

"Oh no, she was good-natured enough. Just a great stupid. No, they didn't look exactly frightened, except of the horses and carriages; but bewildered and unhappy, and out of their element. And yet so plucky! I'm certain they were well-bred children. I can't make it out."

"Nor can I," said Rosamond. "I wonder if we shall ever hear any more about them."

Curiously enough she dreamt that night that she was again in the furniture shop in the Rue Verte, and that she heard again a noise which she thought to be mice, but that pulling back a chair to see, she came upon two little children, who at once started to their feet, crying: "We're the boy and girl he met. Take us home, do. We're not mice, and we are *so* unhappy."

CHAPTER VIII.

A FALL DOWNSTAIRS.

"Oh! what's the matter? what's the matter?"

GOODY BLAKE.

SOME days passed; they were much the same as the first, except that the children — children-like — grew used to a certain extent to the things and people and manners and ways of the life in which they found themselves. Roger now and then seemed pretty contented, almost as if he were forgetting the strange changes that had come over them: so long as every one was kind to him, and he had Gladys at hand ready, so far as was possible for her, to attend to his slightest wish, he did not seem unhappy. But on the other hand, the least cross word, or one of Mademoiselle Anna's sharp looks, or even the want of things that he liked to eat, would set him off crying in a way he had never done before, and which nearly broke Gladys's heart. For she, though she seemed quiet and contented enough, was in reality very anxious and distressed. She was of an age to understand that something really serious must be the matter for her and Roger to be left with strangers in this way — no letters coming, no inquiries of any kind being made, just as if she and her little brother were forgotten by all the world! She could write

104

a little, and once or twice she said to herself that if
it went on very long she would try to send a letter
to Miss Susan; but then again, when she remembered
how glad that young lady had been to get rid of
them, how she had disliked the idea of their staying
with Mrs. Lacy after her marriage — for all this by
scraps of conversation, remarks of servants, and so
on, Gladys had been quick enough to find out — she
felt as if she would rather do anything, stay anywhere,
rather than ask Miss Susan to take them back. And
then from time to time hope would rise strong in her,
and she would wake in the morning firmly convinced
that "Papa would come to-day" — hopes, alas, only
to be disappointed! She was beginning to understand a little of what was said by those about them.
Madame Nestor was as kind as ever, and her son, who
had taken a great fancy to Roger, was decidedly
kinder than he had been at first. With them alone
Gladys felt she would not have minded anything so
much; but she could see that Anna's dislike to them
increased, and the child dreaded the hours of the
meals, from the feeling of the hard scornful looks
that Anna was then sure to cast on her.

One day she overheard some talking between her
and Madame Nestor. The young woman seemed
angry, and the old one was remonstrating with her.
Gladys heard that they were speaking about money,
and also about some one going away, but that was
all she could make out, though they were talking
quite loud, and did not seem to mind her being there.

"If only Anna was going away," thought Gladys,

"I wouldn't mind anything. I wouldn't mind the not having baths, or tea, or bread and butter, or — or all the things we had at home, if only there was nobody to look so fierce at us. I'd almost rather be Madame Nestor's little servant, like Françoise, if only Anna would go away."

It almost seemed as if her wishes had been overheard by some fairy, for the next morning, when they were called to the second breakfast — which the children counted their dinner — Anna's place was empty! Gladys squeezed Roger's hand under the table, and whispered to him: "She's gone, I do believe she's gone." Then looking up at Madame Nestor she saw her kind old face looking decidedly jollier than usual.

"Yes," she said, nodding her head; "Anna is away. She has gone away for a few days."

Gladys understood her partly but not altogether, but she did not mind. She was only too pleased to find it true, and that was the happiest day they had since they came to the Rue Verte. Madame Nestor sent out to the pastry-cook's near by for some nice little cakes of a kind the children had never tasted before, and which they found delicious, and Monsieur Adolphe said he would get them some roasted chestnuts to eat if they liked them. He found the words in a dictionary which he showed Gladys with great pride, and pointed them out to her, and was quite delighted when she told him how to pronounce them, and added: " I like roast chestnuts *very* much."

" Mademoiselle shall give me some lessons of Eng-

lish," he said to his mother, his round face beaming
with pleasure. "You are quite right, they are little
gentlepeople, there is no doubt of it; and I feel sure
the Papa will come to fetch them in a few days. He
will be very grateful to us for having taken such care
of them — it may be a good thing in the end even
from a business point of view, for I should have no
objection to extend our English connection."

No thought of gain to themselves in any way had
entered Madame Nestor's head; but she was too
pleased to see her son in such a good humour about
the children to say anything to disagree with him.

"He has a good heart, my Adolphe," she said to
herself. "It is only Anna that makes him seem what
he is not; if she would but stay away altogether!
And yet, it would be difficult to find her equal in
other ways."

"Speaking of English," she said aloud, "reminds
me that those English ladies will be getting impatient for their curtains. And the trimming has not
yet come; how slow those makers are! It is a fortnight since they promised it for the end of the week."

"It does not matter much," said Adolphe, "for no
one can make them up properly except Anna. She
should not have gone away just now; she knows there
are several things that require her."

"That is true," said Madame Nestor, and so it was.
Mademoiselle Anna seemed purposely to have chosen
a most inconvenient time for going off on a visit to
her family, and when Madame Nestor reproached her
for this she had replied that with all the money the

Nestors had received for the two little strangers, they could well afford to engage for the time a first-rate workwoman to replace her. This was the conversation Gladys had heard and a little understood. Poor Madame Nestor, wishing to keep up the children's dignity, had told every one that Mr. Marton had left her plenty of money for them, making the most of the two or three pounds which was all he had been able to spare, and of which she had not as yet touched a farthing.

But whether Anna's absence was inconvenient or not, it was very pleasant to most people concerned. Adolphe himself took the children out a walk, and though Gladys was at first not quite sure that it was not a little beneath her dignity to let the young man be her "chaperon," she ended by enjoying it very much. Thanks to his broken English and the few French words she was now beginning to understand, they got on very well; and when he had taken them some way out of Paris — or out of the centre of the town rather — in an omnibus, she was obliged to own that it was by no means the gray, grim, crowded, noisy, stuffy place it had seemed to her those first days in the Rue Verte. Poor little Roger was delighted! The carriages and horses were to him the most beautiful sight the world could show; and as they walked home down the Champs Elysées it was quite difficult to get him along, he wanted so constantly to stand still and stare about him.

"How glad I am we had on our best things!" said Gladys, as she hung up her dark-blue braided serge jacket and dress — for long ago Madame Nestor had been obliged to open the big trunk to get out a change of attire for the children — "aren't you, Roger?" She smoothed down the scarlet breast on her little black felt hat as she spoke. "This hat is very neat, and so is my dress; but still they are very plain compared to the things all the children that we saw had on. Did you see that little girl in green velvet with a sort of very soft fur, like shaded gray fluff, all round it? And another one in a red silky dress, all trimmed with lace, and a white feather as long — as long as — "

"Was it in that pretty big wide street?" asked Roger. "I saw a little boy like me with a 'plendid coat all over gold buttons."

"That was a little page, not a gentleman," said Gladys, rather contemptuously. "Don't you remember Mrs. Ffolliot's page? Only perhaps he hadn't so many buttons. I'd like to go a walk there every day, wouldn't you?"

But their conversation was interrupted by Madame Nestor's calling them down to have a little roll and a glass of milk, which she had discovered they liked much better than wine and water.

"If only there would come a letter, or if Papa would come — oh, if Papa would but come before that Anna comes back again, everything would get all right! I do hope when he does come that Papa will let me give a nice present to Mrs. Nest," thought Gladys to herself as she was falling asleep that night.

The next day was so bright and fine, that when the children saw Monsieur Adolphe putting on his coat to go out early in the morning they both wished they might go with him, and they told him so. He smiled, but told them in his funny English that it could not be. He was going out in a hurry, and only about business — some orders he was going to get from the English ladies.

"English ladies," repeated Gladys.

"Yes; have you not seen them? They were here one day."

"We saw them," said Gladys, smiling, "but they did not see *us*. They thought we were mice," but the dictionary had to be fetched before Adolphe could make out what "mice" meant, even though Roger turned it into "mouses" to make it plainer. And then he had to hurry off — it was a long way, he said, in the Avenue Gérard, close to the Champs Elysées, that those ladies lived.

"Avenue Gérard," repeated Gladys, in the idle way children sometimes catch up a name; "that's not hard to say. We say *avenue* in English too. It means a road with lots of trees. Are there lots of trees where those ladies live, Mr. 'Dolph?"

But "Mr. 'Dolph" had departed.

After these bright days came again some dreary autumn weather. The children "wearied," as Scotch people say, a good deal. They were even glad on the fourth day to be sent out a short walk with Françoise.

"I wonder if we shall see that nice gentleman again if we go up that big street?" said Roger.

"I don't think we shall," said Gladys. "Most likely he doesn't live there. And it's a great many days ago. Perhaps he's gone back to England."

It was indeed by this time nearly a fortnight that the little waifs had found refuge in the Rue Verte.

The walk turned out less disagreeable than their first one with Françoise. They did go up the Boulevard, where the servant had some commissions, but they did not meet the "nice gentleman." They came home, however, in very good spirits; for at the big grocer's shop, where Françoise had bought several things, one of the head men had given them each an orange. And chattering together about how they should eat them — whether it was nicest to suck them, or to cut them with a knife, or to peel them and divide them into what are familiarly called "pigs,"—the two children, with Françoise just behind them, reached the shop in the Rue Verte.

The door stood open — that was a little unusual, but they did not stay to wonder at it, but ran in quickly, eager to show their oranges to their kind old friend. The door leading to the room behind the shop stood open also, and the children stopped short, for the room was full of people, all talking eagerly and seemingly much excited. There were all the workpeople and one or two neighbours, but neither Madame Nestor nor her son. Françoise, who had caught sight of the crowd and already overheard something of what they were saying, hurried forward, telling the children as she passed them to stay where they were, and frightened of they knew not

what, the two little creatures took refuge in their old
corner behind the blue sofa.

"What can it be?" said Gladys.

"P'raps Papa's come," suggested Roger.

Gladys's heart gave a great leap, and she sprang
up, glancing in the direction of the little crowd of
people. But she quickly crouched down again.

"Oh no," she said. "It can't be that. Françoise
would not have told us to stay here. I'm afraid
somebody's ill. It seems more like that."

Her instinct was right. By degrees the talking
subsided, and one or two of the workpeople went off
to their business, and a moment or two after, when
Adolphe Nestor suddenly made his appearance, there
was a general hush, broken only by one or two voices
inquiring "how she was."

"Do you hear that, Roger?" whispered Gladys,
nudging her brother; "they're asking how she is.
That means Mrs. Nest, I'm sure. She must be ill."

Roger said nothing, but listened solemnly.

"Her was quite well when us went out," he observed, after a considerable pause.

"Yes, but sometimes people get ill all of a sudden,"
said Gladys. Then, after a moment, "Roger," she
said, "I think I'll go and ask. I shall be *so* unhappy
if poor Mrs. Nest is ill."

"So will I," said Roger.

They got up from the floor, and hand in hand
crept timidly towards the door. Françoise was still
standing there, listening to Adolphe, who was talking to the two or three still standing there. Fran-

çoise turned at the sound of the children's footsteps, and raised a warning finger. But Gladys put her aside, with what "Walter" would have called her imperious air.

"Let us pass," she said. "I want to speak to Mr. 'Dolph."

The young man heard the sound of his own name.

"What is it?" he said quickly, in French.

"I want to know what's the matter. Is Mrs. Nest ill?" asked Gladys. But she had to repeat her question two or three times before Adolphe understood it. He was flurried and distressed — indeed, his eyes looked as if he had been crying — and that made it more difficult for him to catch the meaning of the child's words. But at last he did so.

"Ah!" he exclaimed. "Yes, there is much the matter. My poor mother — she has fallen downstairs and broken her leg."

Gladys clasped her two hands together.

"Broken her leg," she repeated. "Oh, poor Mrs. Nest! Oh, it must hurt her dreadfully."

At this Roger burst out crying. Adolphe turned round, and picked him up in his arms.

"Poor little fellow," he said, "yes, he, too, is very sorry. What we are to do I know not. Anna away, too. I hope you will be very good and quiet children. Françoise, too, will be so busy — you will do all you can to give no trouble, will you not? I wish we had news of the Papa!" he added, as he turned away.

He did not speak at all unkindly, but he seemed

very much troubled, and with his broken English
it was very difficult for Gladys to follow all he said.

"May I go and see poor Mrs. Nest?" she said
timidly.

"No, no; you cannot see her for a long time,"
replied Adolphe hastily, as he left the room.

"I must send a telegram to Mademoiselle Anna,"
he added to Françoise, and unfortunately for her
peace of mind, Gladys understood him. She turned
away, her lips quivering.

"Come upstairs, dear," she said to her little
brother. "Come to our room and I will take off
your things."

Roger followed her obediently. Françoise had
disappeared into the kitchen, where more than ever
she was needed, as there was no one else to see about
the dinner — so the two little things climbed upstairs
by themselves. It was already growing dusk — the
dull little room looked cheerless, and felt chilly.
Roger looked up into Gladys's eyes as she was un-
fastening his coat.

"Are you crying, Gladdie?" he said, in his little
soft sad tone.

Gladys turned away a moment to wipe her eyes.
If she had not done so she would probably have
burst into a terrible fit of tears, for never had she
felt so miserable and desolate. Her pride, too, was
aroused, for she saw most plainly that she and Roger
were more than ever a sad burden and trouble. But
what could she do? What could any little girl of
seven years old have done in such a case?

The sight of Roger's meek sad face gave her a kind of strength. For his sake she must keep up anyway the appearance of cheerfulness. So she kissed him, and answered quietly:

"I am very sorry for poor Mrs. Nest. She has been so kind to us."

"Yes," said Roger. Then a bright idea struck him. "I'll say my prayers for her to be made better to-night. Will you, Gladdie?"

"Yes," said Gladys, and there was comfort in the thought to her, for it brought with it another. "I'll ask God to help *us*," she thought to herself, "and when I go to bed I'll think and think, and perhaps He'll put something in my head. *Perhaps* I must try to write to Miss Susan."

The loss of Madame Nestor's constant kindness was quickly felt. No one came near the children, and when Gladys crept downstairs there was no light in the little sitting-room — no glasses of milk and plate of rolls waiting for them on the table, as had become a habit. And Roger was cold and hungry! He had asked Gladys to go down and look if there was any "goûter," as they had learnt to call this afternoon luncheon, and when she came up again and told him "no," the poor little fellow, frightened, and cold, and hungry, burst into loud sobbing. Gladys was so afraid it would be heard, and that they would be scolded for disturbing Madame Nestor, that she persuaded Roger to get into bed, where she covered him up warmly. and promised to tell him a story if he would leave off crying.

It was not easy to keep her promise — she felt so on the point of bursting into tears herself that she had to stop every now and then to clear her throat, and she was not sorry when, on one of these occasions, instead of Roger's shrill little voice urging her to "go on. What do you stop for, Gladdie?" she heard by his regular breathing that he had fallen asleep. She had no light, but she felt about to be sure he was well covered, and then, leaning her head on the side of his bed, she tried to " think."

" I would not mind anything so much if Anna was not coming back," she said to herself. " But if she is here, and poor Mrs. Nest shut up in her room, she can do anything she likes to us, for Mr. 'Dolph wouldn't know; and if I told him he'd think I was very naughty to bother him when his mother was ill. I think I must write to Miss Susan — at least, if Anna is *very* unkind, I will — unless — unless — oh, if it *would* but happen for Papa to come to-morrow, or a letter! I'll wait till to-morrow and see — and *perhaps* Anna won't come back, not — not if Papa's in the train — she'd run away if she saw him, if he had Mrs. Nest's cap on, she'd " — and that was all. for before Gladys had settled what she would do, she too, as you see, had fallen asleep.

She slept some time — an hour or two — and she awoke, feeling cold and stiff, though what had awakened her she did not at first know, till again, bringing with it the remembrance of having heard it before, the sound of a voice calling her reached her ears.

"Mademoiselle — Mademoiselle Gladees," it said, "why do you not come? The dinner is all ready, and I have called you so many times." It was Françoise, tumbling up the narrow stair in the dark. Gladys heard her fumbling at the door, and called out "Françoise!" Then Roger woke and started up, trembling. "What is it — what is the matter, Gladdie?" he cried, and Gladys had to soothe and pet him, and say it was only Françoise; and Françoise in the meantime had got into the room, exclaiming at their having no light, and pulling a box of matches from her pocket, struck one, and hunted about till she found a bit of candle.

It was a rather melancholy scene that the end of candle lighted up.

"So — you have been asleep!" exclaimed the servant; "well, perhaps it was the best thing. Well, come down now, Monsieur Adolphe is asking for you," and she would scarcely let them wait to dip their hands in water and smooth their tumbled hair.

"What will become of them when *she* comes back and poor Madame ill in bed, who can say?" the peasant girl muttered to herself as she led them downstairs. "I wish their friends would come to fetch them — I do. It's certainly very strange for rich people to leave their children like that," and Françoise shook her head.

Monsieur Adolphe received the children kindly. He had been a little alarmed when Françoise had told him she could not find them in the sitting-room, for he knew it would trouble his poor mother greatly if she found her little favourites were neglected, for the thought of them was one of the things most troubling the poor woman in the middle of her suffering.

"If but the Papa would come for them," she had already said to her son. "I know not what to do. I think we must ask some advice. Anna dislikes them so; and if she comes back to-morrow — "

"She may not come till the day after," said Adolphe. "Do not trouble yourself about anything just now. The children are all right for the moment."

"And you will be kind to them at dinner, and give them nice pieces. They do not eat much, but they are used to more delicate cooking than ours."

"Reassure yourself. I will do all as you would yourself. And if you keep quiet, my good Mamma, perhaps in a day or two you can see them for yourself. The great thing is to keep quiet, and that will keep down the fever, the doctor says," repeated poor Adolphe, who was really a good and affectionate son.

"Ah, yes," thought poor Madame Nestor, "that is all very well, but at my age," for she was really old — old to be the mother of Adolphe, having married late in life, "at my age one does not break one's leg for nothing. But the good God knows best. If my time has come, so be it. I have no great anxiety to leave behind me, like some poor women, thank Heaven! Only these poor children!"

And thanks to what Madame Nestor had said, and thanks in part, too, to his kind feelings, Adolphe was very friendly to the children at dinner; and in reply to their timid inquiries about his mother, told them that the doctor thought she was going on well, and in a day or two they might see her, if they were very good and quiet. So the meal passed off peacefully.

"After all," thought Adolphe, "they do not cost one much. They eat like sparrows. Still it is a great responsibility — poor little things!"

He took Roger in his arms and kissed him when he said good-night, and Gladys would have gone to bed feeling rather less unhappy, for Françoise put in her head to say she would come in half an hour to help to undress "Monsieur Roger," but for some words she overheard among some of the young work-women, which she understood only too well — that Mademoiselle Anna was returning the next morning!

"I *must* write to Miss Susan," thought the little girl, as she at last fell asleep.

CHAPTER IX.

FROM BAD TO WORSE.

" 'Their hearts were laden
With sorrow, surprise, and fear."
PRINCESS BOPEEP.

NOBODY came to wake the children the next morning. They slept later than usual, and when Gladys woke it was already as light as ever it was in the dull little room. But it was very cold — the weather had turned to frost in the night, which made the air clearer and brighter, and in their own warm rooms at Mrs. Lacy's the children would have rejoiced at the change. Here it was very different.

Gladys lay waiting some time, wondering if no one was coming with their chocolate and bread, forgetting at first all that had happened the day before. By degrees it came back to her mind, and then she was no longer surprised at their being left alone.

"Anna has come back," she thought to herself, "and she won't let them bring us our breakfast."

She got out of bed, glad to see that Roger was still sleeping, and crossed the room, the cold wooden floor striking chill to her bare feet. She reached the door and opened it, peering down the narrow dark staircase.

"Françoise," she called softly, for the kitchen was nearer than the workroom, and she hoped perhaps

120

Françoise would come to her without Anna knowing. But no one answered. She heard voices in the distance — in the kitchen they seemed to be — and soon she fancied that she distinguished the sharp tones of Mademoiselle Anna, ordering about the poor little cook. Gladys quickly but softly shut the door and crossed the room again on tiptoes. She stood for a moment or two hesitating what to do. It was so cold that she felt half inclined to curl herself up in bed again and try to go to sleep! But if Roger woke, as he was sure to do soon — no, the best thing was for her to get dressed as quickly as possible. She bravely sponged herself as well as she could with the cold water, which was now always left in the room in a little jug; "no chance of any *hot* water to-day!" she thought to herself as she remembered how unhappy she had been that first morning at not having a bath, and then went on to dress, though not without a good deal of difficulty, as several of her little under-garments fastened behind. Not till the last button was secured did Roger wake.

"Gladdie," he said in a sleepy tone, "are you dressed? We haven't had our chocolate, Gladdie."

"Never mind, Roger dear," said Gladys. "They're all very busy to-day, you know, so I've got up and dressed quickly, and now I'll go down and bring up your breakfast. Unless you'd rather get up first?"

Roger considered. He was in rather a lazy mood, which was perhaps just as well.

"No," he decided. "I'll have my breakfast first. And you can eat yours beside me, can't you, Gladdie?"

" Yes," said Gladys, " that will be very nice."

She spoke with a cheerfulness she was far from feeling, for in her heart she felt by no means sure of getting any breakfast at all. But just as she was turning to go a slight knocking was heard at the door. It was more like a scratching indeed, as if the person were afraid of being heard outside as well as by those in the room.

" Mademoiselle," came in a loud whisper after the queer rapping had gone on for some time, " are you awake ? Open — I have the hands full."

It was Françoise. Gladys opened. The little servant, her round red face rounder and redder than usual, for she had been all the morning at the kitchen fire, and had besides been passing through unusual excitement, stumped into the room, a bowl, from which the steam of some hot liquid was rising, in one hand, and a plate with a large hunch of bread in the other.

She put them down on the little table and wiped her hot face with her apron.

" Ah, Mademoiselle," she said, " no one would believe it — the trouble I have had to get some breakfast for you ! *She* would not have it — lazy little creatures, she called you — you might come down and get it for yourselves — a piece of dry bread and some dripping soup — that was all she would have given you, and I know you are not used to that. So what did I do but wait till her back was turned — the cross cat — and then in with the milk and a tiny bit of chocolate — all I could find, and here it is ! Hot, at any rate ; but not very good, I fear."

Gladys did not, of course, understand a quarter of the words which Françoise rattled off in her queer Norman-French; but her wits were sharpened by anxiety, and she gathered quite enough of the sense of the little servant's long speech to feel very grateful to her. In her hurry Françoise had poured all the chocolate — or hot milk rather, for there was very little chocolate in the composition — into one bowl; but the children were too hungry to be particular. They drank turn-about, and finished by crumbling up the remains of the bread in the remains of the milk and eating it with the spoon, turn-about also, Françoise standing by, watching them with satisfaction. Suddenly she started.

"I must run down," she said, "or she will be after me again. I wish I could stay to help you to dress Monsieur Roger, but I dare not," and gathering up the dishes in her apron so that they could not be seen, she turned to go.

"Dress him as quickly as you can," she said to Gladys, "and then she cannot say you have given any trouble. But stay — I will see if I cannot get you a little hot water for the poor bébé."

And off she set, to appear again in a minute with a tin jug of hot water which she poured out into the basin at once for fear the absence of the tin jug should be discovered.

"She has eyes on every side of her head," she whispered as she went off again.

Roger's toilet was accomplished more luxuriously than poor Gladys's own, and he was quite bright and happy with no fear of Mademoiselle Anna or any one else, chirping like a little bird, as his sister took him down the narrow staircase to the room behind the shop where they spent the mornings.

"Hush, Roger dear, we must be very quiet because poor Mrs. Nest is ill, you know," she said, when his shrill little voice rose higher and higher, for he had had an exceedingly good night and felt in excellent spirits.

"She can't hear us down here," replied Roger. But Gladys still repeated her "hush," for, in reality, it was Anna who she feared might overhear Roger's chatter. She looked about for something to keep him quiet, but could see nothing. It was warm in the sitting-room — though if Anna could have done so, she would have ordered Françoise not to light the fire for the little plagues, as she called them — but except for that they would have been happier up in their bedroom, where Gladys had discovered a few of Roger's toys in a corner of the big trunk, which, however, Madame Nest had not allowed them to bring down.

"When the Papa comes, I wish him to find all your things in good order," she had said. "The toys might get broken, so while you are here I will find you things to amuse you."

But this morning the bundle of cretonne and cut-out birds and flowers was not to be seen!

"I must tell Roger stories all the morning, I suppose," thought Gladys, and she was just going to propose doing so, when Roger, who had been standing peeping through the glass door which led into the shop, suddenly gave a cry of pleasure.

"Oh, Gladdie," he said, "see what a pretty carriage and two prancey horses at the door!"

Gladys ran to look — the shop door was wide open, for one of the apprentice boys was sweeping it out, and they could see right into the street. The carriage had stopped, as Roger said, and out of it stepped one of two people seated in it. It was the younger of the two ladies that the children had seen that first day in the Rue Verte when they were hidden behind the blue sofa in the corner.

She came forward into the shop.

"Is there no one here?" she said in French.

The apprentice, very dusty and looking rather ashamed, came out of a corner. It was not often that ladies in grand carriages came themselves to the little shop, for though the Nestors had some very good customers, Monsieur Adolphe usually went himself to their houses for orders.

"I will call some one," said the boy, "if Mademoiselle will have the goodness to wait a moment," and he disappeared through a little door in the corner of the shop which led into the workroom another way.

The young lady shivered a little — it was very cold — and then walked about, glancing at the furniture now and then. She seemed to think it too cold to sit down. There was certainly no dearth of chairs!

"I wonder if we should ask her to come in here,"

said Gladys. But before she had time to decide, the
door by which the boy had gone out opened again
and Mademoiselle Anna appeared. She came forward with the most gracious manner and sweetest
smiles imaginable. Gladys, who had never seen her
like that, felt quite amazed.

The young lady received Anna's civilities very
calmly. She had never seen her before, and thought
her rather a vulgar young woman. But when Anna
begged her to come for a moment into the sitting-
room while she went to fetch the patterns the young
lady had come for she did not refuse.

"It is certainly bitterly cold this morning," she
said.

"And we are all so upset — by the sad accident to
our poor dear Madame — Mademoiselle must excuse
us," said Anna, leading the way to the sitting-room
as she spoke.

Rosamond stopped short.

"An accident to that good Madame Nestor. I
am very sorry," she exclaimed.

"Ah, yes," Anna went on in her honeyed tones,
"it is really too sad. It was — but will not Mademoiselle come out of the cold, and I will tell her
about it," she went on, backing towards the glass
door. It opened inwards; the children, very much
interested in watching the little scene in the shop,
and not quite understanding Anna's intention, had
not thought of getting out of the way. Anna opened
the door sharply, as she did everything, and in so
doing overthrew the small person of Roger, whose

ANNA OPENED THE DOOR SHARPLY, AS SHE DID EVERYTHING, AND IN SO
DOING OVERTHREW THE SMALL PERSON OF ROGER. — p. 126.

short fat legs were less agile than the longer and thinner ones of his sister. Gladys sprang away like a kitten, but only to spring back again the next moment, as a doleful cry rose from poor Roger.

"You are not hurt, darling, are you?" she said, as she knelt down to pick him up.

Roger went on crying softly. He preferred to take his time about deciding that he wasn't hurt. And in the meantime the stranger young lady had come into the room and was looking round her in some surprise.

"Has the little boy fallen down?" she asked in French. "Poor little fellow! Are they Madame Nestor's grandchildren?"

"Oh dear, no," replied Anna, casting a contemptuous glance at Gladys and Roger, who, crouching on the floor in the corner of the always dusky little room, could not be very clearly distinguished. "Get up," continued she, turning to them, "get up at once and go to your own room."

Frightened by her tone and by Roger's continued sobbing, Gladys dragged him up from the floor as well as she could, and escaped with him by the door leading upstairs, near to which they happened to be. Something in the sudden change of Anna's tone roused the young lady's suspicions.

"Who are they, then?" she asked again. "And are you sure the little boy is not hurt?"

"He cries for nothing, Mademoiselle—he is always crying. They are children our good Madame has taken in out of charity; it is very difficult to manage

with them just now, poor little things. They have
been so neglected and are so troublesome ; but we
must do our best till our dear Madame gets better,"
and then she went on into a long description of the
accident, how she herself had just gone to spend two
days with her sister, whom she had not seen for years,
when she had been recalled, etc. etc., all told so cleverly that Rosamond went away, thinking that after
all she must be a very good sort of young woman, and
that it was not right to yield to prejudice. Yet still
she could not quite forget the glimpse she had had
of the two little creatures taken in " out of charity,"
and the sound of Roger's stifled sobs.

Gladys and he stayed upstairs till they were called
down to " déjeûner." It was cold, but they minded
the cold less than sharp words and unkind looks.
Gladys wrapped Roger up in a shawl and pulled a
blanket off the bed for herself, and then they both
cuddled down together in a corner, and she told him
all the stories she could think of. By twelve o'clock
they were very hungry, for in spite of Françoise's en-
deavours they had had much less breakfast than usual,
but they had no idea what time it was, and were too
frightened to go down, and there they would have
stayed, all day perhaps, if Adolphe, reminded of them
by his poor mother's constant questions, had not sent
one of the apprentice boys to fetch them down, and
meek and trembling the two poor little things entered
the long narrow room where all the members of the
household were seated round the table.

But there was no kindly welcome for them as at

dinner the day before. Monsieur Adolphe's usually good-humoured face looked worried and vexed.

"Sit down and take your food," he said coldly. "I am very sorry to hear from Mademoiselle Anna how troublesome you have been this morning. I thought you, Mademoiselle, as so much older than your brother, who is really only a baby, would have tried to keep him quiet for the sake of my poor mother."

Gladys's face turned scarlet; at first she could scarcely believe that she had heard aright, for it was very difficult to understand the young man's bad English, but a glance at his face showed her she was not mistaken. She clasped her hands in a sort of despair.

"Oh, Mr. 'Dolph," she said, "how can you think we would be so naughty? It was only that Roger fell down, and that made him cry." ·

"Do not listen to her," said Anna in a hard indifferent tone, "naughty children always make excuses."

But the sight of the real misery in Gladys's face was too much for kind-hearted Adolphe. He noticed, too, that both she and Roger were looking pale and pinched with cold, and he had his own doubts as to Anna's truthfulness, though he was too much under her to venture to contradict her.

"Don't cry, my child," he said kindly. "Try to be very good and quiet the rest of the day, and eat your déjeûner now."

Gladys made a valiant effort to choke down her tears.

"Is Mrs. Nest better to-day?" she asked.

The son shook his head.

"I fear not," he replied sadly; "she has a great deal of fever. And I am, unfortunately, obliged to go into the country for a day or two about some important business."

"You are going away! oh, Mr. 'Dolph, there will, be no one to take care of us," cried Gladys, the tears rushing to her eyes again.

The young man was touched by her distress.

"Oh yes, yes," he said; "they will all be very kind to you. I will speak to them, and I shall be soon back again, and you and my little Roger will be very good, I am sure."

There was nothing more to be said. Gladys tried to go on eating, though her hunger had quite left her, and it was difficult to swallow anything without crying again. Only one thought grew clearer in her mind — "I must write to Miss Susan."

During the rest of the meal Adolphe kept talking to Anna about the work and other things to be seen to while he was away.

"You must be sure to send to-morrow early to put up those curtains at the English ladies' — 9 Avenue Gérard."

"9 Avenue Gérard — that is their new house," said Anna, and the address, which she had already heard twice repeated, caught Gladys's ear.

"And tell the one who goes to ask for the patterns back — those the young lady took away to-day. Oh, by the bye, did she see the children?" asked Adolphe.

"No, you may be sure. That is to say, I hurried them out of the way, forward little things. It was just the moment she was here, that he, the bébé there, chose for bursting out crying," replied Anna.

"I hope she did not go away with the idea they were not kindly treated," said Adolphe, looking displeased.

"She thought nothing about them — she hardly caught sight of them."

"She did not see that they were English — her country-people?"

"Certainly not," replied Anna. "Do you think I have no more sense than to bother all your customers with the history of any little beggars your mother chooses to take in?"

"I was not speaking of all the customers — I was speaking of those English ladies who might have taken an interest in these children, because they too are English — or at least have given us some advice what to do. I have already been thinking of asking them. But now it may be too late if they saw the children crying and you scolding them; no doubt, they will either think they are naughty disagreeable children or that we are unkind to them. Either will do harm. You have made a great mistake."

He got up and left the room, afraid perhaps of saying more, for at this moment he could not afford to quarrel with Anna. Poor man, his troubles seemed to be coming on him all at once! Gladys understood very little of what they were saying, but she saw that Adolphe was not pleased with Made-

moiselle Anna, and it made her fear that Anna would
be still crosser to Roger or her. But she took no
notice of them, and when they had finished she
called Françoise, and told her to take them into the
sitting-room and make up the fire.

"P'raps she's going to be kind now, Gladdie," said
Roger, with the happy hopefulness of his age. But
Gladys shook her head.

Monsieur Adolphe set off that afternoon.

For the first day or two things went on rather
better than Gladys had expected. Anna had had a
fright, and did not dare actually to neglect or ill-treat
the children. So Gladys put off writing to Miss
Susan, which, as you know, she had the greatest
dislike to doing till she saw how things went on.
Besides this same writing was no such easy matter
for her. She had neither pen, ink, nor paper — she
was not sure how to spell the address, and she had
not a halfpenny of money! Very likely if she had
spoken of her idea to Adolphe he would have been
only too glad for her to write, but Anna was a very
different person to deal with.

"If I asked her for paper and a pen she would
very likely scold me — very likely she wouldn't like
me to write while Mr. 'Dolph is away, for fear he
should think she had been unkind and that that had
made me do it," reflected Gladys, whose wits were
much sharpened by trouble. "And I *daren't* make
her angry while we're alone with her."

Thus the letter was deferred. Things might
possibly have gone smoothly till Adolphe's return,

for Anna *wished* to avoid any upset now she saw how strongly the Nestors felt on the subject. But unfortunately bad-tempered people cannot always control themselves to act as their common sense tells them would be best even for themselves. And Mademoiselle Anna had a very bad and violent temper, which often got quite the mastery of her.

So the calm did not last long.

CHAPTER X.

"AVENUE GÉRARD, NO. 9."

"One foot up and the other foot down,
For that is the way to London town.
And just the same, over dale and hill,
'Tis also the way to wherever you will."

OLD RHYME.

IT was a very cold day, colder than is usual in Paris in November, where the winter, though intense while it lasts, seldom sets in before the New Year. But though cold, there had been sufficient brightness and sunshine, though of a pale and feeble kind, to encourage the Mammas of Paris either to take out their darlings themselves or to entrust them to the nurses and maids, and nursery governesses of all nations who, on every fairly fine day, may be seen with their little charges walking up and down what Roger called "the pretty wide street," which had so taken his fancy the day of the expedition with Monsieur Adolphe.

Among all the little groups walking up and down pretty steadily, for it was too cold for loitering, or whipping tops, or skipping-ropes, as in finer weather, two small figures hurrying along hand-in-hand, caught the attention of several people. Had they been distinctly of the humbler classes nobody would have

134

noticed them much, for even in this aristocratic part of the town one sometimes sees quite poor children threading their way among or standing to admire the little richly-dressed pets who, after all, are but children like themselves. And sometimes a burst of innocent laughter, or bright smiles of pleasure, will spread from the rich to the poor, at the sight of Henri's top having triumphed over Xavier's, or at the solemn dignity of the walking doll of five-year-old Yvonne.

But these two little people were evidently not of the lower classes. Not only were they warmly and neatly dressed — though that, indeed, would hardly have settled the question, as it is but very seldom in Paris that one sees the children of even quite humble parents ill or insufficiently clad — but even though their coats and hats were plain and unfashionable, there was about them a decided look of refinement and good-breeding. And yet they were alone!

"Who can they be?" said one lady to another. "Just see how half-frightened and yet determined the little girl looks."

"And how the boy clings to her. They are English, I suppose — English people are so eccentric, and let their children do all sorts of things *we* would never dream of."

"Not the English of the upper classes," replied the first lady, with a slight shade of annoyance. "You forget I am half English myself by my mother's side, so I should know. You take your ideas of the English from anything but the upper classes. I am

always impressing that on my friends. How would
you like if the English judged *us* by the French they
see in Leicester Square, or by the dressmakers and
ladies' maids who go over and call themselves
governesses?"

"I wouldn't *like* it, but I daresay it is often done,
nevertheless," said the other lady good-naturedly.
"But very likely those children do *not* belong to
the upper classes."

"I don't know," said the first lady. She stopped as
she spoke and looked after the children, who had
now passed them, thoughtfully. "No," she went on,
"I don't think they are common children. I fancy
there must be something peculiar about them. Can
they have lost their way? Antoinette," she added
suddenly, turning round. "You may think me very
foolish and eccentric — 'English,' if you like, but I
am going to run after them and see if there is anything the matter. Look after Lili for a moment for
me, please."

Antoinette laughed.

"Do as you please, my dear," she said.

So off hastened, in her rich velvet and furs, the
other lady. It was not difficult to overtake the
children, for the two pairs of legs had trotted a long
way and were growing weary. But when close behind them their new friend slackened her pace. How
was she to speak to them? She did not know that
they were English, or even strangers, and if they
were the former that did not much mend matters, for,
alas! notwithstanding the half British origin she was

rather fond of talking about, the pretty young
mother had been an idle little girl in her time, and
had consistently declined to learn any language but
her own. *Now*, she wished for her Lili's sake to make
up for lost time, and was looking out for an English
governess, but as yet she dared not venture on any
rash attempts. She summoned up her courage, however, and gently touched the little girl on the
shoulder, and all her suspicions that something
unusual was in question were awakened again by
the start of terror the child gave, and the pallid look
of misery, quickly followed by an expression of relief,
with which she looked up in her face.

"I thought it was Anna," she half whispered,
clutching her little brother's hand more tightly than
before.

"Mademoiselle — my child," said the lady, for the
dignity on the little face, white and frightened as it
was, made her not sure how to address her. "Can
I do anything to help you? You are alone — have
you perhaps lost your way?"

The last few words Gladys, for she of course it
was, did not follow. But the offer of help, thanks
to the kind eyes looking down on her, she understood. She gazed for a moment into these same
eyes, and then seeming to gather confidence she
carefully drew out from the pocket of her ulster —
the same new ulster she had so proudly put on for
the first time the day of the journey which was to
have ended with "Papa" and happiness — a little
piece of paper, rather smudgy-looking, it must be

owned, which she unfolded and held up to the lady.
On it were written the words —

"9 Avenue Gérard."

"Avenue Gérard," repeated the lady; "is that
where you want to go? It is not far from here."

But seeing that the child did not take in the
meaning of her words, she changed her tactics.
Taking Gladys by the hand she led her to one side
of the broad walk where they were standing, and
pointing to a street at right angles from the rows of
houses bordering the Champs Elysées.

"Go along there," she said, "and then turn to the
left and you will see the name, 'Avenue Gérard,' at
the corner."

She pointed as she spoke; then she stooped, and
with the sharp point of the tiny umbrella she carried,
traced in lines the directions she had given, in the
gravel on which they were standing. Gladys considered for a moment in silence, then she lifted her
head and nodded brightly.

"I understand," she said, "and thank you *very*
much."

Then taking Roger's hand, which, while speaking
to the lady she had let go, she smiled again, and
whispering something to her brother which made
him pluck off his little cap, the two small pilgrims
set off again on their journey. The lady stood for
a moment looking after them, and I think there were
tears in her eyes.

"I wonder if I could have done more for them,"
she said to herself. "Fancy Lili and Jean by them-

"Go along there," she said, "and then turn to the Left and you will see the Name, 'Avenue Gérard,' at the Corner."— p. 138.

selves like that! But they know where they have
to go to — they are not lost."

"How kind she was," said Gladys, as she led her
little brother in the direction the lady had pointed
out. "It is not far now, Roger, dear — are you *very*
tired?"

Roger made a manful effort to step out more
briskly.

"Not so *very*, Gladdie. But oh, Gladdie, I was
so frightened when I felt you stop and when I saw
your face. Oh, Gladdie, I thought it was *her*."

"So did I," said Gladys with a shiver.

"Would she have put us in prison?" he asked.

"I don't know," said Gladys. "I heard her say
something to Françoise about the police. I don't
know if that means prison. But these ladies won't
let her, 'cos you know, Roger, they're *English*, like
us."

"Is all French peoples naughty?" inquired Roger
meekly.

"No, you silly little boy," giving him a small
shake, "of course not. Think of Mrs. Nest, and
Françoise, and even that lady — oh, I didn't mean to
make you cry. You're not silly — I didn't mean it,
dear."

But Roger could not at once stop his tears, for
they were as much the result of tiredness and excitement as of Gladys's words.

"Gladdie," he went on plaintively, "what will
you do if those ladies aren't kind to us?"

"They'll help me to send a tele — you know what

I mean — a letter in that quick way, to Miss Susan,"
replied Gladys confidently. "That's all I'm going
to ask them. They'd never refuse that."

"And could Miss Susan get here to-day, do you
think?"

Gladys hesitated.

"I don't quite know. I don't know how long it
takes *people* to come that way. But I'm afraid it
costs a good deal. We must ask the ladies. Perhaps
they'll get us a little room somewhere, where Anna
can't find us, till Miss Susan sends for us."

"But," continued Roger, "what will you do if
they're *out*, Gladdie?"

Gladys did not answer. Strange to say, practical
as she was, this possibility had never occurred to her.
Her one idea had been to make her way to the
Avenue Gérard at once, then it had seemed to her
that all difficulties would be at an end.

"What's the good of saying that, Roger?" she
said at last. "If they're out we'll —"

"What?"

"Wait till they come in, I suppose."

"It'll be very cold waiting in the street — like beggars," grumbled Roger. But he said it in a low tone,
not particularly wishing Gladys to hear. Only he
was so tired that he had to grumble a little.

Suddenly Gladys pulled up.

"There it is," she said. "Look up there, Roger;
that's the name, 'Av-e-nue Gér-ard.' It's just a street.
I thought an avenue would have been all trees, like
in the country. Nine — I wonder which is nine?"

Opposite to where they stood was No. 34.   Gladys led Roger on a little bit and looked at the number on the other side.   It was 31, and the next beyond that was 29.

"It's this way.   They get littler this way," she exclaimed.   "Come on, Roger, darling — it's not far."

"But if we've to wait in the street," repeated Roger faintly, for he was now possessed by this new idea.

Gladys said nothing — perhaps she did not hear.

"Twenty-seven, twenty-five, twenty-three," she said, as they passed each house, so intent on reaching No. 9 that she did not even feel frightened. Between seventeen and fifteen there was a long space of hoardings shutting off unbuilt-upon ground — nine seemed a very long time of coming.   But at last — at last!

It was a large, very handsome house, and Gladys, young as she was, said at once to herself that the English ladies, as she had got into the way of calling them, must be *very* very rich.   For she did not understand that in Paris one enormous house, such as the one she was standing before, contains the dwellings of several families, each of which is often as large as a good-sized English house, only without stairs once you have entered, as all the rooms are on one floor.

"I wonder which is the front door," said Gladys. "There seems so many in there."   For the great doors of the entrance-court stood open, and, peeping in, it seemed to her that there was nothing but doors on every side to be seen.

"We must ask," she at last said resolutely, and foraging in her pocket she again drew forth the crumpled piece of paper with "No. 9 Avenue Gérard," and armed with this marched in.

A man started up from somewhere — indeed he had been already watching them, though they had not seen him. He was the porter for the whole house.

"What do you want — whom are you looking for?" he said. At first, thinking they *were* little beggars or something of the kind, for the courtyard was not very light, he had come out meaning to drive them away. But when he came nearer them he saw they were not what he had thought, and he spoke therefore rather more civilly. Still, he never thought of saying "Mademoiselle" to Gladys — no children of the upper classes would be wandering about alone! Gladys's only answer was to hold out the bit of paper.

"Avenue Gérard, No. 9," read the man. "Yes, it is quite right — it is here. But there is no name. Who is it you want?"

"The English ladies," replied Gladys in her own tongue, which she still seemed to think everybody should understand. She had gathered the meaning of the man's words, helped thereto by his gesticulations.

"The English ladies — I don't know their name."

Only one word was comprehensible by the porter.

"English," he repeated, using of course the French word for "English." "It must be the English ladies on the second floor they want. No doubt they are some of the poor English those ladies are so kind to. And yet —" he looked at them dubiously. They didn't quite suit his description. Anyway, there was but one answer to give. "The ladies were out; the children must come again another day."

Gladys and Roger, too, understood the first four words. Their worst fears had come true!

If Gladys could have spoken French she would perhaps have found courage to ask the man to let them come in and wait a little; for as, speechless, still holding poor Roger by the hand, she slowly moved to go, she caught sight of a cheerful little room where a bright fire was burning, the glass door standing half open, and towards which the porter turned.

"That must be his house," thought Gladys in a sort of half-stupid dreamy way. It was no use trying to ask him to let them go in and wait there. There was nowhere for them — he seemed to think they were beggars, and would perhaps call the police if they didn't go away at once. So she drew Roger out into the street again, out of the shelter of the court, where the wind felt rather less piercing, and, without speaking, wandered a few steps down the street they had two minutes ago toiled along so hopefully.

"Where are you going, Gladdie? What are you going to do? I knew they'd be out," said Roger, breaking into one of his piteous fits of crying.

Gladys's heart seemed as if it was going to stop.
What *was* she going to do?

Wait in the street a little, she had said to Roger.
But how could they? The wind seemed to be getting
colder and colder; the daylight even was beginning
to fade a little; they were not only cold, they were
desperately hungry, for they had had nothing to eat
except the little bowl of milk and crust of bread —
that was all Françoise had been able to give them
early that morning. She had been out at the market
when the children ran away from Anna in one of her
terrible tempers, so Gladys had not even been able to
ask her for a few sous with which to get something
to eat. Indeed, had Françoise been there, I daresay
they would have been persuaded by her to wait till
Adolphe came home, for he was expected that evening, though 'they did not know it!

"Roger, *darling*, try not to cry so," said Gladys,
at last finding her voice. "Wait a moment and I'll
try to think. If only there was a shop near, perhaps they'd let us go in; but there are no shops in
this street."

No shops and very few passers-by, at this time of
day anyway. A step sounded along the pavement
just as Gladys had drawn Roger back to the wall of
the house they were passing, meaning to wipe his
eyes and turn up the collar of his coat to keep the
wind from his throat. Gladys looked up in hopes
that possibly, in some wonderful way, the new-comer
might prove a friend in need. But no — it was only
a man in a sort of uniform, and with a black bag

strapped in front. Gladys had seen one like him at
the Rue Verte; it was only the postman. He
glanced at them as he passed; he was a kind-hearted
little man, and would have been quite capable of taking the two forlorn "bébés" home to his good wife
to be clothed and fed — for there are many kind
Samaritans even in careless, selfish big towns like
Paris — but how were they to guess that, or how
was he to know their trouble? So he passed on; but
a house or two farther on he stopped again, being
accosted by a gentleman coming quickly up the street
in the other direction, just as he was turning in to
the courtyard of No. 9.

" There is only a paper for you, sir," he said to the
young man, whom he evidently knew, in answer to
his inquiry. " Will you take it? "

" Certainly," was the reply; and both, after a civil
good-evening, were going on their way when a
sound made them stop. It was Roger — all Gladys's
efforts had been useless, and his temper as well as his
courage giving way he burst into a loud roar. He
was too worn out to have kept it up for long at such
a pitch, but while it lasted it was very effective,
for both the gentleman and the postman turned
back.

" I noticed these children a moment ago," said the
latter. " I wondered if they had lost their way, but
I dared not wait."

" I'll see what it is," said the young man good-
naturedly. But the postman lingered a moment.

" What's the matter? " asked the young man in

French. "What's the little boy crying for?" he
went on, turning to Gladys.

But her answer astonished him not a little. She
stared blankly up in his face without speaking for a
moment. Then with a sort of stifled scream she
rushed forward and caught his hands.

" Oh you're the nice gentleman we met — you are
— *don't* say you're not. You're the English gentleman, aren't you? Oh, will you take care of us —
we're all alone — we've run away."

Walter kept her poor little hands in his, but for
half a moment he did not speak. I think there were
tears in his eyes. He had so often thought of the
little pair he had met on the Boulevards, that somehow he did not seem to feel surprise at this strange
meeting.

" My little girl," he said kindly, " who are you?
Where have you run away from? Not from your
home? I remember meeting you; but you must tell
me more — you must tell me everything before I can
help you or take you where you want to go."

" No. 9 Avenue Gérard; that's where we were
going," replied Gladys confusedly. " But they're
out — the ladies are out."

" And we have to wait in the stre-eet," sobbed Roger.
Walter started.

"9 Avenue Gérard," he said; " how can that be?
Whom do you know there?"

" Some ladies who'll be kind to us, and know what
we say, for they're English. I don't know their
name," answered Gladys.

Walter saw there was but one thing to be done. He turned to the postman.

"I know who they are," he said rapidly in French, with the instinctive wish to save this little lady, small as she was, from being made the subject of a sensational paragraph in some penny paper. "I have seen them before. They had come to see my aunt, who is very kind to her country-people, and were crying because she was out. It will be all right. Don't let yourself be late. I'll look after them."

And relieved in his mind the postman trotted off.

Walter turned to Gladys again.

"*I* live at No. 9," he said. "Those ladies are my aunt and my sister. So the best thing you can do is to come in with me and get warm. And when my aunt comes home you shall tell us all your troubles, and we will see what to do."

"And you won't give us to the police?" asked Gladys, with a sudden misgiving. "We've *not* done anything naughty. Will the ladies come soon?"

For though on the first impulse she had flown to Walter with full confidence, she now somehow felt a little frightened of him. Perhaps his being on such good terms with the postman, whose uniform vaguely recalled a policeman to her excited imagination, or his speaking French so easily and quickly, had made her feel rather less sure of him. "*You* won't give us to the police?" she repeated.

Walter could hardly help smiling.

"*Of course* not," he answered. "Come now, you must trust me and not be afraid. Give me your hand, my little man; or stay, he's very tired, I'll carry him in."

And he lifted Roger in his arms, while Gladys, greatly to her satisfaction, walked quietly beside them, her confidence completely restored.

"He's very polite, and he sees I'm *big*," she said to herself as she followed him into the court, past the porter's bright little room, from whence that person put out his head to wish Walter a respectful "good-evening," keeping to himself the reflection which explains so many mysteries to our friends across the water, that "the English are really very eccentric. One never knows what they will be doing next."

CHAPTER XI.

WALTER'S TEA-PARTY.

"They felt very happy and content and went indoors and sat to the table and had their dinner." — *The Almond Tree.*
BROTHERS GRIMM.

ROSAMOND and her aunt had a good many commissions to do that afternoon. They had not long before this changed their house, and there were still a great many pretty things to choose and to buy for the new rooms. But though it was pleasant work it was tiring, and it was, too, so exceedingly cold that even in the comfortable carriage with its hot-water bottles and fur rugs, the young girl shivered and said to her aunt she would be glad to be at home again, and to get a nice hot cup of tea.

"Yes," said her aunt, "and it is getting late. At this time of year the days seem to close in so suddenly."

"I'm afraid it is going to be a severe winter. I do so dislike severe winters, Auntie," said Rosamond, who had spent some part of her life in a warm climate.

"So do I," said her aunt, with a sigh, "it makes everything so much harder for the poor. I really think it is true that cold is worse to endure than hunger."

"You are so kind, Auntie dear," said Rosamond. "You really seem as if you felt other people's sufferings your own self. I think it is the little children I am most sorry for. Perhaps because I have been such a spoilt child myself! I cannot imagine how it would be possible to live through what some children have to live through. Above all, unkindness and neglect. That reminds me — "

She was going to tell her aunt of the children she had seen at Madame Nestor's, and of the sharp way the young woman in the shop had spoken to them, but just at that moment the carriage turned into the courtyard of their house, and the footman sprung down and opened the door.

"I wonder what put those children in my head just now?" thought Rosamond, as she followed her aunt slowly up the wide thickly-carpeted staircase. "I suppose it was talking of the poor people, though they were not exactly poor."

But a moment or two later she really felt as if her thoughts had taken shape, or that she was dreaming, when she caught sight of the most unexpected picture that presented itself to herself and her aunt on opening the door of their pretty "little drawing-room."

The room was brightly lighted, the fire was burning cheerily — not far from it stood the low afternoon tea-table covered with a white cloth and heaped up with plates of bread-and-butter and cakes — while the tea-urn sang its pleasant murmur. And the group round the table? That was the astonishing part of it. Walter was having a tea-party!

WALTER WAS HAVING A TEA-PARTY! — p. 150.

For an instant — they had opened the door softly and he was very much taken up with his guests — the aunt and niece stood looking on without any one's hearing them. Walter was seated in a big arm-chair, and perched on his knee was a very tiny little boy in an English sailor dress. He was a pretty fair child, with a bright pink flush on his face, and he seemed exceedingly happy and to be thoroughly enjoying the cup of hot but mild tea and slice of cake which his host was pressing on him. And on a small chair just opposite sat a pale-faced dark-eyed little girl with an anxious look on her face, yet at the same time an expression of great content. No wonder; she was only seven years old! Fancy the relief it must have been to delicate little Gladys to find herself again in a room like this — to have the comfort of the delicious fire and the food even, to which she was accustomed — above all, to see Roger safe and happy; if only it would last!

"*This* tea isn't too strong for him, is it, Gladys?" Walter said.

And Gladys leaning forward examined it with a motherly air, that was both pathetic and amusing.

"No, that's quite right. That's just like what he had it at home."

The aunt and niece looked at each other.

"Who *can* they be?" whispered the aunt; but Rosamond, though she had scarcely seen the faces of the children in the Rue Verte, seemed to know by instinct. But before she had time to speak, Walter started up; the whisper, low as it was, had caught his ear and Gladys's too. She too got up from her seat and stood facing the ladies, while her cheeks grew still paler, and the anxious look quite chased away the peaceful satisfaction from her poor little face.

"Auntie!" said Walter, and in his voice too there was a little anxiety, not lost on Gladys. For though he knew his aunt to be as kind as any one could be, still it *was* a rather "cool" thing, he felt, to have brought in two small people he had found in the street without knowing anything whatever about them, and to be giving them tea in her drawing-room. "Auntie," he repeated, "this young lady, Miss Gladys Bertram, and her little brother had come to see you, to ask your help. I found them waiting in the street, the concierge had told them you were out; it was bitterly cold, and they had come a very long way. I brought them in and gave them tea, as you see."

His face had flushed as he spoke, and there was a tone of appeal in his voice; he could not *before* Gladys add what was on his lips: "You are not vexed with me?"

"You did quite right, my dear boy," said his aunt heartily. "Rosamond and I are cold and tired too. We should like a cup of tea also, and then these little friends of ours will tell us all they have to tell."

"I have seen them before," added Walter in a lower tone, going nearer his aunt under pretext of getting her a chair. "You remember the children on the Boulevards I told you about the other day? It is they."

But Gladys, who till then had stood still, gazing at the ladies without speaking, suddenly sprang forward and almost threw herself into "Auntie's" arms.

"Oh, thank you, thank you!" she exclaimed, bursting into tears. "I was just thinking perhaps you'd be vexed with *him*," she pointed to Walter, "and he's been so kind, and it *is* so nice here. Oh, we couldn't, we *couldn't* go back there!" and clasping her new friend still more closely she sobbed as if her overcharged heart would break.

Auntie and Rosamond soothed her with the kindest words they could find, and then Auntie, who always had her wits about her, reminded Gladys that they too were very anxious to have a cup of tea, would she help to pour it out? She evidently knew all about it, whereupon Gladys's sobs and tears stopped as if by magic, and she was again the motherly capable little girl they had seen her on entering the room.

Tea over — before thinking of taking off their bonnets — Auntie and Rosamond, and Walter too, made Gladys tell them all she had to tell. It was a little difficult to follow at first, for, like a child, she mixed up names and events in rather a kaleidoscope fashion. But at last by dint of patience and encouragement and several "beginnings again at the beginning," they got a clear idea of the whole strange and yet simple story, all of which that was known to Gladys herself, you, my little readers, already know, except the history of the last miserable day in the Rue Verte,

when Anna's temper had got the better of her pru-
dence to such an extent as to make Gladys feel they
could bear it no longer. She had struck them both
in her passion that very morning when Françoise
was at the market, and wild with fear, more for
Roger than herself, Gladys had set off to ask help
and advice from the only people she knew of in all
great Paris who could understand her story.

"Except *him*," added Gladys, nodding at Walter,
"but we didn't know where he lived. I couldn't
write to Miss Susan, for I hadn't any paper or en-
velopes. I thought I'd wait till Mr. 'Dolph came
home and that he'd let me write, but I don't know
when he's coming, and I hadn't any money, and if
she — oh! if she had struck Roger again it might
have killed him. He's so little, you know," and
Gladys shuddered.

There was silence for a few moments. Then
Auntie turned to Walter.

"The first thing to be done, it seems to me, is for
you to go to the Rue Verte to tell the Nestors —
Madame Nestor, that is to say — where these little
people are. She will be very uneasy, I fear, poor
woman."

"Anna won't tell her, I don't think," said Gladys.
"Poor Mrs. Nest — she is so kind. I shouldn't like
her to be unhappy."

"And," continued the lady, "you must ask for the
children's clothes."

Gladys's eyes glistened.

"Do you mean, are you going to let us stay here?"

she said; "I mean till to-morrow, perhaps, till Miss Susan can come?"

"Where else could you go, my dears?" said Auntie kindly.

"I don't know; I — I thought perhaps you'd get us a little room somewhere, and Miss Susan would pay it when she comes. I thought perhaps you'd send her a tele—, you know what I mean, and perhaps she could come for us that way. It's so quick, only it costs a great deal, doesn't it?"

Auntie and Rosamond had hard work to prevent themselves laughing at this queer idea of Gladys's, but when her mistake was explained to her, she took it very philosophically.

"Then do you think I should write to Miss Susan to-day?" said Gladys. "*You'll* help me, won't you?" she added, turning to Rosamond. "I don't know very well how to write the address."

"Of course I will help you, dear," said Rosamond, but her aunt interrupted.

"I do not think little Gladys need write to-night," she said. "Indeed, perhaps it may be as well for me to write for her to the lady she speaks of. But now, Walter, you had better go off at once, and bring back the children's belongings with you. What were you going to say, dear?" for Gladys seemed as if she were going to speak.

Gladys's face grew red.

"Anna said once that she would sell our big trunk and all our best clothes — I mean she said Mrs. Nest would — to get money for all we had cost them. But

I'm sure Mrs. Nest wouldn't. And when Papa comes he'll pay everything."

The elder lady looked at Walter.

"Try and bring away everything with you," she said. "Take Louis, so that he may help to carry out the boxes. Do your best anyway."

It turned out easier than Auntie had feared, for Walter found Adolphe Nestor already returned, and in a state of frantic anxiety about the children. Knowing that they could not be in better hands than those in which they had placed themselves, he was only too thankful to let them remain there, and gave Walter all the information he could about Mr. and Mrs. Marton, who had confided the children to his mother's care.

"She can tell you all about the family better than I," he said. "I think even she has the address of Madame Marton's mother, where her cousin was so long nurse. Oh, they are in every way most respectable, and indeed one can see by the children themselves that they are little gentlepeople. There must be something sadly amiss for the father not to have come for them. I fear even that he is perhaps dead."

Then he went on to tell Walter that he had told Anna he could no longer keep her in his employment, and that all was at an end with her.

"And indeed," he said, his round face getting very red, "I think no man would be happy with a wife with such a temper," in which Walter, who at eighteen considered himself very wise, cordially agreed.

Adolphe had not told his mother of the children's flight, for she was still very feverish and excitable; but he said she would be relieved to know where they had found refuge. And then he gave Walter the English money which Mr. Marton had left for their use, and which his mother had kept unbroken.

Walter took it, though reluctantly, but he saw that it would have hurt Adolphe to refuse it; and he also reflected that there were other ways in which the Nestors could be rewarded for their kindness. And so he left the Rue Verte with all the children's belongings safely piled on the top of the cab, and with a much more friendly feeling to the upholsterer than he had expected to have, promising to let him know the result of the inquiries his aunt intended immediately to set on foot; and also assuring him that they should not leave Paris without coming to say good-bye to him and his kind old mother.

When the two tired but happy little people were safely in bed that night, their three new friends sat round the fire to have a good talk about them.

"It is a very strange affair, really," said Walter. "I'm more than half inclined to agree with Nestor that the father must be dead."

"But even then," said Auntie, "the friends in England who had charge of them would have known it, and would have sent to inquire about them."

"That 'Miss Susan,' as they call her, seems to me to have thought of nothing but the easiest way to get rid of them," said Rosamond indignantly. "She should never have let them start without a letter or a telegram of Captain Bertram's being actually in Paris, and, as far as I can make out from little Gladys, she had not got that—only of his arrival at Marseilles and his *intention* of coming."

"Did Gladys mention Marseilles? Does she know where it is?" asked Walter.

"Yes, she said the old lady whom they were very fond of showed it to her on the map, and explained that it was the town in France 'at which the big ships from India stopped.' Gladys is quite clear about all that. She is a very clever child in some ways, though in others she seems almost a baby."

"Nothing about her would surprise me after her managing to find her way here," said Auntie. "Just fancy her leading that baby, Roger, all the way here from the Rue Verte!"

"Do you know how she did?" said Rosamond. "She tore a little piece of paper off the edge of a newspaper and wrote the address, 'Avenue Gérard 9,' on it with an end of pencil she found lying about; and she showed this bit of paper to anybody 'kind-looking' whom they met, and thus she got directed. Was it not a good idea? She said if she had *asked* the way the French people would not have understood her speaking."

"Then what do you decide to do, Auntie?" said Walter. "Shall I telegraph in the morning to this Miss Susan, or will you write?"

Auntie hesitated.

"*I* don't see how you can do either with much chance of it reaching her," said Rosamond. "Gladys, you know, said she was going to be married."

"Well, supposing in the first place," said Auntie, "we were to telegraph to the principal hotels at Marseilles and ask if Captain Bertram is there — it would do no harm — it is just possible that by some mistake he is all this time under the belief that the children are still in England."

"That's not likely," said Walter; "no one would stay on at a hotel in Marseilles all this time for no reason — three weeks, it must be. But it's not a bad idea to telegraph there first."

"Gladys would be so pleased if it proved not to be necessary to send to 'Miss Susan' at all," said Rosamond, who seemed to have obtained the little girl's full confidence.

"Well, we shall see," said Auntie. "In the meantime the children are safe, and I hope happy."

"Mr. and Mrs. Marton must be in India by this time," said Walter. "*They* don't seem to have been to blame in the least — they did the best they could. It might be as well to write to them if we had their address."

"Perhaps old Madame Nestor may have it," said Rosamond. "The maid — her niece or cousin, whichever it is — may have left it with her."

"We can ask," said Auntie. "But it would take a good while to hear from India, and very likely they would have very little to tell, for there is one thing that strikes me," she went on thoughtfully, "which is, the *Martons* cannot have thought there was anything wrong when they got to Marseilles, otherwise they would have written or telegraphed to the Rue Verte, and certainly to the friends in England."

She looked up as if to read in the faces of her two young companions how this struck them.

"That's true," said Walter.

"But it only adds to the mystery," said Rosamond.

"Supposing," said Walter, "that the address has been lost — that of the Nestors, I mean — and that all this time Captain Bertram is hunting up and down Paris for his children?"

"That does not seem to me likely," said Auntie. "He would have telegraphed back to England."

"Where it wouldn't have been known, Rosamond," said Walter. "Rather to Mr. Marton in India."

"If he had *his* address," said Walter again.

"Well, anyway *that* could be got in England," said Auntie, a little impatiently. "No, no, Walter, it can't be that. Why, supposing Captain Bertram were here looking for his children, the *police* could have found them for him in a couple of days. No; I very much fear there is more wrong than a mere mistake. Poor little dears — they still seem to have such unbounded faith in 'Papa's coming.' I only trust no harm has come over him, poor man."

Walter telegraphed the next morning in his aunt's name to the two principal hotels at Marseilles, to inquire if Captain Bertram was or had been there. From one came back the answer, "No such name known." From the other the information that Captain Bertram had not yet returned from Nice, and that letters and his luggage were waiting for him at the hotel.

"Just read this, aunt," he said, hurrying into the

drawing-room, and Auntie did so. Then she looked up.

"It is as I feared, I feel sure," she said. "Walter, you must go to Nice yourself, and make inquiries."

"I shall start to-night," said the young fellow readily.

"Stay a moment," said Auntie again. "We have the *Times* advertisements for the last few days; it may be as well to look over them."

"And the Saturday papers, with all the births, marriages, and deaths of the week put in at once," said Rosamond. "You take the *Times*," she added to her brother, going to a side-table where all the papers were lying in a pile, "and I'll look through the others."

For a few moments there was silence in the room. Gladys and Roger were very happy with some of their toys, which they had been allowed to unpack in the dining-room. "Bertram, Bertram, no, I see nothing. And there's no advertisement for two lost cherubs in the agony columns either," said Walter.

Suddenly Rosamond gave a little exclamation.

"Have you found anything?" asked Auntie.

"Nothing about Captain Bertram," she replied. "But I think this must be the old lady they lived with. 'Alicia, widow of the late Major-General Lacy,' etc. etc., 'at Market-Lilford on the 16th November, aged 69.' I am sure it is she, for Gladys's second name is 'Alicia,' and she told me it was 'after Mrs. Lacy.'"

"Poor old lady — she must have been very kind

and good. That may explain 'Miss Susan's' apparent indifference. It was fully a fortnight ago, you see."

"Must I tell Gladys?" said Rosamond.

"Not yet, I think," said Auntie. "We may have worse to tell her, poor child."

"I don't know that it *would* be worse," said the young girl. "They can't remember their father."

"Still, they have always been looking forward to his coming. If it ends in *good* news, it will make them — Gladys especially — very happy."

"As for Roger, perfect happiness is already his," said Rosamond. "He asks no more than weak tea and bread-and-butter, Gladys always at hand, a good fire, and nobody to scold him."

CHAPTER XII.

PAPA AT LAST.

" And now, indeed, there lacked nothing to their happiness as
long as they lived."— *The Golden Bird.*

BROTHERS GRIMM.

WALTER went off to Nice that night. The children
were not told distinctly the object of his journey.
They were allowed to know that he might be passing
near " the big town by the sea," which poor Mrs.
Lacy, in her kind anxiety to make all clear, had
pointed out to Gladys on the map; but that was all,
for Auntie wished to save them any more of the
nervous suspense and waiting of which they had had
so much. She wished, too, to save them any suffering that could be avoided, from the fear of the sorrow, really worse than any they had yet known,
which she often dreaded might be in store for them.

" Let us make them as happy as ever we can for
these few days," she said to Rosamond. " Nothing
like happiness for making children strong and well,
and they will soon forget all their past troubles."

And Rosamond was only too ready to give her
assistance to the kind plan, so that in all their lives
Gladys and Roger had never been so much made of.
The ladies were too wise to overdo it; they found
too that it was very easy to amuse these simple little

163

creatures, who had never known since they were born the slightest approach to "spoiling" or indulgence. Everything pleased them. The mere living in the pretty luxurious house — the waking up in the morning to the sight of the bright dainty room, where already a cheerful little fire would be blazing, for the weather continued exceedingly cold. The tempting "little breakfast" of real bread-and-butter and tea — for both Gladys and Roger found they had got very tired of chocolate — the capacious bath and abundance of hot water — above all, the kind and loving and gentle looks and words which surrounded them — all these would have been enough to make them happy. And a drive in Auntie's beautiful carriage, either into the centre of the town "to see the shops," or now and then to visit one of the wonderful old churches with their mysterious height of roof and softly brilliant windows, and *sometimes*, still better, the beautiful swelling organ music which seemed to them to come from nowhere, yet to be everywhere. Ah! those expeditions were a delight Gladys had never even dreamt of, and which little Roger could scarcely take in. They very much changed their opinion of Paris in those days, and no longer called it "an ugly dirty town," as it had seemed to them in their first experience at the Rue Verte.

"And when Papa comes, we'll take him to see all these beautiful places, won't we?" said Gladys, for with rest and peace of mind had come back all her pretty childish hope and trust in that " coming."

" Yes, dear," said Rosamond. But then she began quickly to speak to the little girl of the pretty colours of the still remaining beech leaves in the Bois de Boulogne, through which for a change they were that day driving. For she could not reply with any confidence in her tone, and she did not want the child to find out her misgiving. Walter had been gone three days and had written twice — once a hurried word to tell of his arrival, once the following day to tell of failure. He had been to two or three of the hotels but had found no traces of Captain Bertram, but there still remained several others, and he hoped to send by his next letter if not good yet anyway more certain news.

So Auntie still put off writing to "Miss Susan," for though since seeing the announcement of Mrs. Lacy's death she did not blame her as much as at first, she yet could not feel it probable that the young lady was suffering great anxiety.

" In any case I had better wait till Walter tells us *something*," she said to Rosamond. " And when I do write I do not know how to address the letter. Gladdie is sure she was to be married a very few days after they left, but she cannot remember the name of the gentleman, whom she has only seen once or twice, as he lived at a distance, and had made Miss Susan's acquaintance away from her home."

" Address to her maiden name — it would be sent after her," suggested Rosamond.

" But Gladdie is not sure what that is," replied Auntie, half laughing. " She doesn't know if it is

' Lacy ' or if she had a different name from her aunt. She is such a baby in some ways. I am sure she has not the slightest idea what *our* surnames are. You are ' Rosamond ' and I am ' Auntie.' "

" Or ' Madame ' when she speaks of you to the servants. She is getting on so nicely with her French, Auntie. That reminds me Louis has been to the Rue Verte, and has brought back word that Madame Nestor is much better, and would be so delighted to see the children any day we can send them."

" Or take them," said Auntie. " I would not like them to go without us the first time, for fear they should feel at all frightened. And yet it is right for them to go. They must always be grateful to Madame Nestor, who did her very best for them."

" Gladys confided to me she would be a little afraid of going back, though she knows that Anna is no longer there. But she says she will feel as if they were going back to *stay* there, and as if *this* would turn out to be only a beautiful dream."

" Poor little dear," said Auntie.

" And she's going to take her new doll — both to show her off, and that she may feel *she* isn't a dream! She has such funny ideas sometimes. Auntie — "

" What, dear ? "

" If Walter can't find the father — I suppose I should say if he is dead — what is to be done ? "

" We must find out all we can — through that Miss Susan, I suppose — as to who are the children's guardians, and what money they have, and all about it."

"I wish we could adopt them," said Rosamond. "We're rich enough."

"Yes; but that is not the only question. You are almost sure to marry."

"I don't know that," said Rosamond, but her face flushed a little.

"And Walter, too, some day."

"Oh, Auntie! Walter! Why he's only eighteen."

"Well, all the same, time goes on, and adopting children often causes complications. Besides, it is not likely that they have *no* relations."

"Well, we shall see what the next letter says," said Rosamond.

It was not a letter after all, but a telegram, and this was what it said: —

"Found Bertram. Will explain all. Returning to-morrow."

The aunt and niece looked at each other.

"He might have said a little more," said the latter. "This is only enough to rouse our curiosity."

"We must say nothing to the children yet," decided Auntie.

"I do hope, as he is alive," said Rosamond, "that he's a nice good sort of man. If he weren't, that would be worse than anything — having to give up the children to him," and she looked quite unhappy.

"Don't let your imagination run away with you so, my dear child," said Auntie. "It's very unlikely that he's not nice in every way. Remember what

Gladys says of his kind letters, and how fond Mrs.
Lacy was of him, and how she always taught them
to look forward to his return. No; *my* fears are
about his health, poor fellow."

The children went the next morning with Rosamond and her maid to see Madame Nestor, and
Rosamond brought back with her to show her aunt
a letter Madame Nestor had just received, which
threw a little light on one part of the subject. It
was from Léonie telling of Mr. and Mrs. Marton's
arrival at their destination, and alluding to the children as if she had no doubt that they had only been
left two or three days at the Rue Verte. "Monsieur," meaning Mr. Marton, "was so glad," she
wrote, "to find at Marseilles that the children's Papa
was going on to Paris almost at once. He had left
a letter for Captain Bertram at the hotel, as he had
gone to Nice for a day or two; and Madame had only
just had time to write to the ladies in England to
tell how it had all been. And she was writing by
this mail to ask for news of the "dear little things,"
as she called Gladys and Roger. "They had thought
of them all the way, and Madame thanked Madame
Nestor so much for her kindness. She — Léonie —
hoped very much she would see them again some
day. Then she presented her compliments to her
cousin Adolphe, and promised to write again soon —
and that was all."

"It is still mysterious enough," said Auntie;
"but it shows the Martons were not to blame. As
Mr. Marton has written to England again, we shall

probably be hearing something from 'Miss Susan' before long. It *is* strange she has not written before, as she has had the Rue Verte address all this time, I suppose."

And here, perhaps, as "Miss Susan" is not, to my mind nor to yours either, children, I feel sure, by any means the most interesting person in this little story, though, on the other hand, she was far from without good qualities, it may be as well to explain how it had come to pass that nothing had been heard of her.

Mrs. Lacy grew rapidly worse after the children left, but with her gentle unselfishness she would not allow her niece's marriage to be put off, but begged her on the contrary to hasten it, which was done. Two days after it had taken place, Susan, who had gone away for a very short honeymoon, was recalled. She never left Mrs. Lacy again till she died. I think the saddest part of dying for the dear old lady was over when she had said good-bye to her little favourites. For some time Susan felt no anxiety about the children, for, from Marseilles, she had heard from young Mrs. Marton of Captain Bertram's not having met them in Paris, and of the arrangement they had been obliged to make. But, that arrived at Marseilles, they had found he had gone two days before to Nice, to look for a house for his children, the landlord said, whom he was going to Paris to fetch. He had left all his luggage there, and had intended to be back this day or the day before, the landlord was not sure which, and to go on to Paris. No doubt he would be returning that same evening, only, unfortunately, his newly-arrived friends Mr. and Mrs. Marton would have gone, but he faithfully promised to deliver to him at once the letter Mr. Marton wrote and left for him.

"It seems the only thing to do," added young Mrs. Marton, "and I do hope it will be all right. Captain Bertram must have mistaken a day. Anyway he will know where to find the children. I enclose their address to you too — at least I will get it from Léonie before I shut this letter, for I do not remember it, so that in case you do not hear soon from Captain Bertram you can write there."

But in her hurry — for just as she was finishing the letter, her husband called to her that they must be off — the young lady forgot to enclose the address! So there was nowhere for Susan to write to, when, as the days went on and no letter came from Captain Bertram, she did begin to grow uneasy, not exactly about the children's safety, but about their father having gone for them.

"Still," she said to her husband, "if he had *not* got them with him, he would have written to ask where they were. He was never a very good correspondent. But I wonder he hasn't written to ask how my aunt is. I hope there is nothing the matter. I *hope* I did not do wrong in letting them go without actually knowing of his being in Paris."

Of course her husband assured her she had not. But her conscience was not at rest, for Susan had grown gentler now that she was happily married, and she was softened too by the thought of her kind aunt's state. All through the last sad days the children kept coming into her mind, and though Mrs. Lacy was too weak even to ask about them, Susan felt almost guilty when she finally tried to thank *her* for her goodness.

" I don't deserve it," she thought, " I was not kind to the two human beings she loved best," and she wrote over and over again to Captain Bertram at the Marseilles hotel, begging him to send her news of the children, and when Mrs. Marton's letter came from India repeating that she had before written from Marseilles, but with of course no further news, and no mention of the Paris address, poor Susan became so unhappy that her husband promised to take her over to make inquiries in person if no answer came to another letter he sent to Marseilles to the landlord of the hotel, begging him to tell all he knew of Captain Bertram's movements. This letter brought a reply, as you will hear, from Captain Bertram himself.

It was evening before Walter arrived. Gladys and Roger were in bed and asleep. Auntie and Rosamond were waiting for him with the greatest anxiety to hear his news. He looked bright and cheery as he came into the room, still enveloped in his wraps, which he began to pull off.

" It's nice and warm in here," he said; " but, oh, it's so cold outside. And it was so mild and sunny down there; I would have liked to stay a day or two longer. It was to please *him* I hurried back so quickly — poor man, he is in *such* a state about the children !"

"But, Walter, what is the meaning of it all? Why has he not come himself?"

"Do you like him?" put in Rosamond.

"Awfully," said Walter boyishly. "He's just what you would expect their father to be. But I'm forgetting — I haven't told you. He's been dreadfully ill — he can only just crawl a step or two. And all this time he's not had the slightest misgiving about the children, except the fear of not living to see them again of course. He's not had the least doubt of their being safe in England; and only just lately, as he began to get well enough to think consecutively, he has wondered why he got no letters. He was just going to try to write to that place — Market-Lilford — when I got there. So he was mystified too! But we got to the bottom of it. This was how it was. He was feeling ill at Marseilles — he had put off too long in India — and he thought it was the air of the place, and as he had some days to pass before he was due in Paris, he went on to Nice, thinking he'd get all right there and be able to look about for a house if he liked it. But instead of getting all right he broke down completely. He wrote out a telegram to tell Miss Susan that he was ill, and that she must not start the children. It would have been in plenty of time to stop them, had she got it, but she never did."

"Never got it," repeated both ladies.

"No; the waiter told him it was all right, but it

wasn't. His writing was so bad that at the office they couldn't read the address, and the message was returned from London the next day; and by that time he was so ill that the doctor wouldn't allow them to ask him a thing, and he probably wouldn't have understood them if they had. This, you see, he's only found out since I got there. The doctor was meaning to tell him, but he took his time about it, and he did not know how important it was. So, in a way, nobody was to blame except that Miss Susan. That's what Bertram says himself; but while I was there he telegraphed to Marseilles for his letters. There were several from her, and the last so frantic that he's writing to say it's all right; especially as she's been very cut up about the poor old lady's death. But she shouldn't have started the children till he telegraphed *from Paris*. Besides, he had told her to send a maid with them for the journey. It wasn't the Martons' fault; they did their best."

"Was he distressed at hearing of Mrs. Lacy's death?" asked Auntie.

"*Very*," said Walter; "it put him back, the doctor said; but he'll be all right when he sees the children. If you had seen him when I told him about their finding their way to us, not even knowing our names, all over Paris! He didn't know whether to laugh or cry. He's weak still, you know. And then he's so *dreadfully* grateful to us! I was glad to get away."

"And when does he want them?" said Rosamond dolefully.

"As soon as possible. He can't come north this

winter. And he's not rich I can see. So I was thinking — "

" What, my boy ? "

" It *is* so cold here," repeated Walter; "it really feels terrible to come back to. Supposing we all go down there for a couple of months or so, to escape the cold? We could keep the children till Bertram is strong again and able to make his plans. I think we'd feel quite queer without them now. Besides, I promised him to bring them back to him."

" What do you say, Rosamond ? " said Auntie.

" I should like it very much. It would be so nice not to part with them just yet."

So it was decided. You can imagine how much had to be told to the children the next day. Mingled sadness and happiness — warp and woof of the web of life !

But when they found themselves once more on the railway, with the kind friends they had learnt to know so well, really on the way to " Papa," I think the happiness was uppermost.

He proved to be the dearest of Papas; not the very least like what they had imagined him. "Of course not," Gladys said; "people and things are never like what one fancies they will be." But though he was older and grayer, and perhaps at first sight a little *sadder* than she had expected, he grew merry enough in the great happiness of having them with him, and as he gradually got strong and well again he seemed, too, to become younger.

" Anyway," said Gladys, a few weeks after their

arrival at Nice, "he *couldn't* be nicer, could he, Roger?" in which opinion Roger solemnly agreed.

"And now he's getting better," she added; "it's not a bad thing he's been ill, for it's made the doctor say he must never go back to India again."

* * * * *

Is that all there is to tell about the "two little waifs?" I think I must lift the curtain for an instant "ten years later," to show you little Roger a tall strong schoolboy, rather solemn still, but bidding fair to be all his father could wish him, and very devoted to a tiny girl of about the age at which we first saw Gladys, and who, as her mother is pretty Rosamond, he persists in calling his "niece," and with some show of reason, for her *real* uncle, "Walter," is now the husband of his sister Gladys!

And long before this, by the bye, another marriage had come to pass which it may amuse you to hear of. There is a new Madame Nestor in the Rue Verte, as well as the cheery old lady who still hobbles about briskly, though with a crutch. And the second Madame Nestor's first name is "Léonie." She is, I think, quite as clever as Mademoiselle Anna, and certainly *very* much better tempered.

And whenever any of the people you have heard of in this little book come to Paris, you may be sure they pay a visit to the little old shop, which is as full as ever of sofas and chairs, and where they always receive the heartiest welcome from the Nestor family.

I wish, for my part, the histories of all "little waifs" ended as happily!

A NEW UNIFORM EDITION

OF

MRS. MOLESWORTH'S

STORIES FOR CHILDREN

WITH

ILLUSTRATIONS BY WALTER CRANE AND LESLIE BROOKE.

In Ten Volumes. 12mo. Cloth. One Dollar a Volume.

Tell Me a Story, and Herr Baby.

"Carrots," and A Christmas Child.

Grandmother Dear, and Two Little Waifs.

The Cuckoo Clock, and The Tapestry Room.

Christmas-Tree Land, and A Christmas Posy.

The Children of the Castle, and Four Winds Farm.

Little Miss Peggy, and Nurse Heatherdale's Story.

"Us," and The Rectory Children.

Rosy, and The Girls and I.

Mary.

THE SET, TEN VOLUMES, IN BOX, $10.00.

" It seems to me not at all easier to draw a lifelike child than to draw a lifelike man or woman; Shakespeare and Webster were the only two men of their age who could do it with perfect delicacy and success; at least, if there was another who could, I must crave pardon of his happy memory for my forgetfulness or ignorance of his name. Our own age is more fortunate, on this single score at least, having a larger and far nobler proportion of female writers; among whom, since the death of George Eliot, there is none left whose touch is so exquisite and masterly, whose love is so thoroughly according to knowledge, whose bright and sweet invention is so fruitful, so truthful, or so delightful as Mrs. Molesworth's. Any chapter of *The Cuckoo Clock* or the enchanting *Adventures of Herr Baby* is worth a shoal of the very best novels dealing with the characters and fortunes of mere adults."—MRS. A. C. SWINBURNE, *in The Nineteenth Century.*

MACMILLAN & CO.,

66 FIFTH AVENUE, NEW YORK.

I

2

TELL ME A STORY, and HERR BABY.

"CARROTS"; Just a Little Boy.

A CHRISTMAS CHILD; A Sketch of a Boy's Life.

MACMILLAN & CO.,

66 FIFTH AVENUE, NEW YORK.

THE CUCKOO CLOCK.

GRANDMOTHER DEAR.

TWO LITTLE WAIFS.

MACMILLAN & CO.,

66 FIFTH AVENUE, NEW YORK.

4

THE TAPESTRY ROOM.

"Mrs. Molesworth is the queen of children's fairy-land. She knows how to make use of the vague, fresh, wondering instincts of childhood, and to invest familiar things with fairy glamour." — *Athenæum.*

"The story told is a charming one of what may be called the neo-fairy sort. . . . There has been nothing better of its kind done anywhere for children, whether we consider its capacity to awake interest or its wholesomeness." — *Evening Post.*

"Among the books for young people we have seen nothing more unique than *The Tapestry Room.* Like all of Mrs. Molesworth's stories it will please young readers by the very attractive and charming style in which it is written." — *Presbyterian Journal.*

"Mrs. Molesworth will be remembered as a writer of very pleasing stories for children. A new book from her pen will be sure of a welcome from all the young people. The new story bears the name of *The Tapestry Room* and is a child's romance. . . . The child who comes into possession of the story will count himself fortunate. It is a bright, wholesome story, in which the interest is maintained to the end. The author has the faculty of adapting herself to the tastes and ideas of her readers in an unusual way." — *New Haven Paladium.*

CHRISTMAS-TREE LAND.

"It is conceived after a happy fancy, as it relates the supposititious journey of a party of little ones through that part of fairy-land where Christmas-trees are supposed to most abound. There is just enough of the old-fashioned fancy about fairies mingled with the 'modern improvements' to incite and stimulate the youthful imagination to healthful action. The pictures by Walter Crane are, of course, not only well executed in themselves, but in charming consonance with the spirit of the tale." — *Troy Times.*

"*Christmas-Tree Land*, by Mrs. Molesworth, is a book to make younger readers open their eyes wide with delight. A little boy and a little girl domiciled in a great white castle, wander on their holidays through the surrounding fir-forests, and meet with the most delightful pleasures. There is a fascinating, mysterious character in their adventures and enough of the fairy-like and wonderful to puzzle and enchant all the little ones." — *Boston Home Journal.*

A CHRISTMAS POSY.

"This is a collection of eight of those inimitable stories for children which none could write better than Mrs. Molesworth. Her books are prime favorites with children of all ages and they are as good and wholesome as they are interesting and popular. This makes a very handsome book, and its illustrations are excellent." — *Christian at Work.*

"*A Christmas Posy* is one of those charming stories for girls which Mrs Molesworth excels in writing." — *Philadelphia Press.*

"Here is a group of bright, wholesome stories, such as are dear to children, and nicely tuned to the harmonies of Christmas-tide. Mr. Crane has found good situations for his spirited sketches." — *Churchman.*

"*A Christmas Posy*, by Mrs. Molesworth, is lovely and fragrant. Mrs. Molesworth succeeds by right to the place occupied with so much honor by the late Mrs. Ewing, as a writer of charming stories for children. The present volume is a cluster of delightful short stories. Mr. Crane's illustrations are in harmony with the text." — *Christian Intelligencer.*

MACMILLAN & CO.,

66 FIFTH AVENUE, NEW YORK.

5

THE CHILDREN OF THE CASTLE.

FOUR WINDS FARM.

MACMILLAN & CO.,

66 FIFTH AVENUE, NEW YORK.

NURSE HEATHERDALE'S STORY.

"*Nurse Heatherdale's Story* is all about a small boy, who was good enough, yet was always getting into some trouble through complications in which he was not to blame. The same sort of things happens to men and women. He is an orphan, though he is cared for in a way by relations, who are not so very rich, yet are looked on as well fixed. After many youthful trials and disappointments he falls into a big stroke of good luck, which lifts him and goes to make others happy. Those who want a child's book will find nothing to harm and something to interest in this simple story." — *Commercial Advertiser.*

"US."

"Mrs. Molesworth's *Us, an Old-Fashioned Story*, is very charming. A dear little six-year-old 'bruvver' and sister constitute the 'us,' whose adventures with gypsies form the theme of the story. Mrs. Molesworth's style is graceful, and she pictures the little ones with brightness and tenderness." — *Evening Post.*

"A pretty and wholesome story." — *Literary World.*

"*Us, an Old-Fashioned Story*, is a sweet and quaint story of two little children who lived long ago, in an old-fashioned way, with their grandparents. The story is delightfully told." — *Philadelphia News.*

"*Us* is one of Mrs. Molesworth's charming little stories for young children. The narrative . . . is full of interest for its real grace and delicacy, and the exquisiteness and purity of the English in which it is written." — *Boston Advertiser.*

"Mrs. Molesworth's last story, *Us*, will please the readers of that lady's works by its pleasant domestic atmosphere and healthful moral tone. The narrative moves forward with sufficient interest to hold the reader's attention; and there are useful lessons for young people to be drawn from it." — *Independent.*

". . . Mrs. Molesworth's story . . . is very simple, refined, bright, and full of the real flavor of childhood." — *Literary World.*

THE RECTORY CHILDREN.

"It is a book written for children in just the way that is best adapted to please them." — *Morning Post.*

"In *The Rectory Children* Mrs. Molesworth has written one of those delightful volumes which we always look for at Christmas time." — *Athenæum.*

"A delightful Christmas book for children; a racy, charming home story, full of good impulses and bright suggestions." — *Boston Traveller.*

"Quiet, sunny, interesting, and thoroughly winning and wholesome." — *Boston Journal.*

"There is no writer of children's books more worthy of their admiration and love than Mrs. Molesworth. Her bright and sweet invention is so truthful, her characters so faithfully drawn, and the teaching of her stories so tender and noble, that while they please and charm they insensibly distil into the youthful mind the most valuable lessons. In *The Rectory Children* we have a fresh, bright story, that will be sure to please all her young admirers." — *Christian at Work.*

"*The Rectory Children*, by Mrs. Molesworth, is a very pretty story of English life. Mrs. Molesworth is one of the most popular and charming of English story-writers for children. Her child characters are true to life, always natural and attractive, and her stories are wholesome and interesting." — *Indianapolis Journal.*

MACMILLAN & CO.,

66 FIFTH AVENUE, NEW YORK.

www.ingramcontent.com/pod-product-compliance
Lightning Source LLC
Chambersburg PA
CBHW031101110726
47900CB00003B/1011